The shining splendor of the Zebra Lovegram logo on the cover of this book reflects the glittering excellence of the story inside. Look for the Zebra Lovegram whenever you buy a historical romance. It's a trademark that guarantees the very best in quality and reading entertainment.

THE WILD PLEASURE OF A COWBOY'S KISS

At Rory's coaxing, Norah went down on her back with him straddling her, kissing her wildly, wonderfully, then sitting back before she'd had enough. He grinned and resisted the impatient hands that would pull him back to her.

"Now, Norah-honey, you gonna try an' tell me you're not liking this?"

She couldn't resist his smile or the silliness of his suggestion. Not like it? She was loving it! And he knew it. Hang him for his arrogance! She laughed softly, unable to maintain her annoyance.

"God, I love lookin' at you," he said suddenly, enthusiastically. "And seeing you smile like that, and hearing you laugh out loud. And the way you smell like violets. And the way you taste like . . ." He bent and kissed her hard. "Like woman," he concluded gruffly. "Damn, I like that." So he kissed her again, feeding off her lips like a man starving, drinking from their sweetness like a man thirsting. Moaning like a man half out of his mind with wanting.

DANA RANSOM'S RED-HOT HEARTFIRES!

ALEXANDRA'S ECSTASY   (2773, $3.75)

Alexandra had known Tucker for all her seventeen years, but all at once she realized her childhood friend was the man capable of tempting her to leave innocence behind!

LIAR'S PROMISE   (2881, $4.25)

Kathryn Mallory's sincere questions about her father's ship to the disreputable Captain Brady Rogan were met with mocking indifference. Then he noticed her trim waist, angelic face and Kathryn won the wrong kind of attention!

LOVE'S GLORIOUS GAMBLE   (2497, $3.75)

Nothing could match the true thrill that coursed through Gloria Daniels when she first spotted the gambler, Sterling Caulder. Experiencing his embrace, feeling his lips against hers would be a risk, but she was willing to chance it all!

WILD, SAVAGE LOVE   (3055, $4.25)

Evangeline, set free from Indians, discovered liberty had its price to pay when her uncle sold her into marriage to Royce Tanner. Dreaming of her return to the people she loved, she vowed never to submit to her husband's caress.

WILD WYOMING LOVE   (3427, $4.25)

Lucille Blessing had no time for the new marshal Sam Zachary. His mocking and arrogant manner grated her nerves, yet she longed to ease the tension she knew he held inside. She knew that if he wanted her, she could never say no!

DANA RANSOM

DAKOTA DESTINY

ZEBRA BOOKS
KENSINGTON PUBLISHING CORP.

For Kathe Robin
who told me
"Give us characters
we can care about!"

and

For Kathryn and Carol
at Romantic Times
for all their enthusiasm.

ZEBRA BOOKS

are published by

Kensington Publishing Corp.
475 Park Avenue South
New York, NY 10016

First Printing: February, 1993

Printed in the United States of America

Chapter One

It took Rory Prescott all of fifteen minutes to find the woman he wanted to marry. And all of one glance to believe himself in love.

It wasn't as though he'd come to Deadwood to find a woman. At least not the kind a man married. Spending the precious handful of days—not to mention nights—in his first big city with a nice girl wasn't even in the back recesses of his mind. With his pocket full of gold bits, he planned to put a quick cinch to the business end that brought him off the grassland range of his grandfather's cattle empire. Then he meant to see if what the ranch hands told him was true. That from the Mansard House on Wall Street down the entire block on the west side of Main in the city's notorious badlands, a man could walk the length of the district's whorehouses on the second floor. Not every one of the twenty-two bars left from the city's original seventy-five had prostitutes but every house of prostitution had a bar. He was looking forward to carrying tales back to the Bar K of just how far his coin would take him and hoped he wouldn't be bringing back anything of a more permanent and unpleasant nature.

Like any green-as-grass newcomer, Rory spent his first minutes in Deadwood gawking. Never had he seen so many folks in one place without a holiday attached to it. They all seemed in a hurry to get somewhere, crowding the walks, not letting the sloppy condition of the streets slow their conveyances. It was truly a sight to behold and for several awed moments, he was content to just stand idle at the edge of the boardwalk soaking in the excitement of it. And damn, it was exciting. Having lived his life in the company of cows on the wide open Dakota range, all he had to compare it to was the little drink-water town of Crowe Creek. And there was no comparison. This was civilization the likes of which he'd never imagined, even in his dreams.

Having just stepped off the train and knowing he had an hour in which to find the Deadwood Business Club, Rory lingered with his single bag at his feet, drinking in the air of sophistication and prosperity. It was intoxicating. As much so as the badlands liquor he meant to get his fill of as soon as he saw to the purpose of his trip. Business first. He wouldn't let the Major down for the world, not even to cut the travel dust from his throat. Being trusted with these negotiations meant too much to him. Anyone could bully a batch of cows on the range. Bullying a businessman into seeing reason was a whole other animal. He'd sat in on many of Garth Kincaid's dealings, had even put in his two bits on occasion. But this was different. This was the kind of responsibility he'd yearned for and now that his pestering had paid off, he was nervous as a calf with a norther brewing. He thought longingly of that bracing shot of tanglefoot. He could taste the smooth, courage-building bite of it rolling across his tongue, easing down to where his belly twitched like a yearling's hide at branding time. Just one. His gaze strayed to that side of town where the saloons and gambling hells were visible and beckoning. There was time.

Then something hard slammed into the backs of his knees. The sudden bump upset his musings and his balance. For a brief, time-suspended moment, Rory tottered on the high Cuban heels of his new boots, desperately pinwheeling his arms before pitching off the high edge of the porch boards. Then, what filled his mouth was the taste of thick Dakota mud.

Spring thaws had turned the streets of Deadwood to the consistency of batter some eight inches deep. For a panicked second, Rory floundered like a man drowning until he managed to find hands and knees to hoist himself up out of the muck. Spitting mud and obscenities, he rolled and skidded about to face the one responsible for his dignity-bruising plunge. There'd be lead to pay for it. He could feel the ooze seeping down the insides of his custom-made fifty-dollar boots. With a fierce oath, he cleared his vision with the swipe of his now filthy shirt sleeve to glare up from his ignoble position in the bog of Deadwood's street.

And stared.

He wasn't aware of settling abruptly on his rump or of consciously halting the spew of cuss words. He sat, jaw unhinged, like a pole-axed steer, struck dumb by a pair of beautiful gray eyes. That's all he could see of her from beneath a wide brimmed hat and above the gloved hands that had risen in horror to cover the lower half of her face. But what eyes they were. Heavily fringed and as clear and cool as the dawn. Immediately, he clamored for his hat rather than his brace of Colts and was at a loss with his bare head. His fine new black Stetson was floating in the mire several feet away.

Slowly, her hands came down and Rory found himself wondering if he'd drowned in the muck of Deadwood and awakened in heaven. Not that they'd be apt to welcome him in after all the epithets he'd just finished. But danged if she wasn't a vision unlike any he'd expected to see this side of the Pearly Gates. Sable-colored tendrils framed a heart-shaped face blessed with those mesmerizing eyes, high cheekbones and a wide, full-lipped mouth. His mama's best Haviland had nothing on the porcelain quality of her skin. From the tip of her buttoned shoes, up the knife-edged pleats of her fluttery skirt, to the wide belt encircling a narrow hour glass waist, along the tucks and frills of her filmy white blouse right up to the silly hat atop all that glorious dark hair, she was a lady. A real lady. He only knew one woman who could claim that distinctive title; Gena, his brother's wife, and here in all her ethereal loveliness was another. And he was simply awestruck.

"Are you all right? I'm so sorry." She glanced helplessly at the bandboxes in her hand that had dealt him the crippling damage. Hers wasn't the voice of an angel. Those heavenly creations would speak in pure, sweet tones. Her voice was low and throaty, like the silky fire from that first sip of whiskey. The sound of it made him suck a quick, cooling breath as heat raced the length of him in response.

When he continued to gaze up in an entranced silence, the vision came closer to the porch edge. Her fair brow crowded with worry.

"Are you all right?" she repeated in that husky, thought-stopping ripple. "I didn't hurt you, did I?"

Senses finally returning, Rory flashed her a wide white smile. "No, ma'am. Lessen you consider my pride. That do ache some. Name's Rory Prescott."

She'd just begun to answer with a smile of her own, one that held the promise of warm spring sunlight, when the man beside her gripped her arm and urged her to follow him down the walk. She glanced back over her shoulder once and said again, "I am sorry," before turning her attention to her older companion.

Oblivious to the fact that he was sitting hip deep in mud and grinning like a fool possum, Rory stared after her in a daze, hypnotized by the sultry sway of her skirt. Lordamercy, what a woman! The kind that made a man's heart jump up to choke him. The kind that turned his brain to batter and started it sizzling from the fires down below.

The kind a man took home to his mama.

And he didn't know her name.

Galvanized into action, Rory slipped and slid and scrambled out of the sucking mud but by the time he'd gained purchase on the boardwalk, she was gone. He let out a rapturous sigh and frowned in disappointment. He had two days to find her and to court her and to taste those red lips. A man used to accomplishing what he set his mind to, Rory smiled determinedly.

Yes, ma'am. You and me are going to get acquainted.

Gingerly, he stepped one foot back into the quagmired street to fish out his hat. Slapping it against his mud-caked thigh, he glanced about to find several city folks standing around taking their amusement at his expense. And that went against his grain.

"Something strike you as funny?" he growled with enough menace to send them scattering like settler's hens to go about their business. Then, he positioned his hat upon his head, picked up his bag and ambled toward his hotel, leaving clods of dirt in his wake.

Within the hour, he was washed, changed, groomed and waiting at the exclusive men's club. A quick dunking, a good brushing and stern shaping left his black Stetson good as new and now he was mangling it in nervous hands. He greeted Darv Potter with a firm handshake and a disarming smile and offered to buy him the best dinner in the house. Over slabs of thick

Dakota beef, they talked rail rates. Rory did a lot of nodding, a lot of innocuous smiling, letting the dapper gent play him along like the bumpkin he appeared to be. Then, when the shipper was relaxed, sipping brandy and drawing on a fat cigar, Rory turned the tables in his favor. Finally, they were shaking hands on a reduced rail fee for Kincaid beef and the befuddled packager had no idea how he'd lost control of the situation.

"Danged if there isn't a lot of your granddaddy in you, son," he marveled begrudgingly. "I had no intention of letting you get away with a deal that good. And I'm still wondering just how you managed it."

"Why I thank you for that," Rory beamed with a swell of confidence. Yessir. Like Garth Kincaid. Pride puffed him up and carried him all the way back to his hotel on a cloud of satisfaction. Where he was greeted at the desk by the call of his name.

"Mr. Prescott. A young lady left this for you."

Rory took the bottle and curiously examined the label. Champagne. A grin split his features. A classy way to beg forgiveness if he ever saw one. With a nod and a hefty tip to the desk clerk, he carried the bottle and its accompanying card up to his room. There, he used the tip of his knife blade to draw the cork. Without turning up the room's gas lamps, he crossed to the window and drank directly from the bottle while looking down on the lights of the city. Only after the second effervescent swallow did he examine the card. A single line of block letters. Miss Norah Denby.

Norah. He whispered her name softly and savored the image that appeared. His thumb ran in a slow caress over that line of type. Miss Norah Denby.

He grinned and took another long drink. The lady had a name. The lady was unattached. She'd taken the trouble to find him and now he'd be more than happy to return the favor. In the morning, real polite and civilized, he would look her up and go a-calling, the way a lady was meant to be greeted. Tonight, his time was his own and his palms were restless, itching for the feel of a good deck of cards and a stack of gold winnings. It didn't occur to him to wonder why the appetite for wild women was suddenly sated. Dropping two bits for a romp with a prostitute had lost its appeal. Not when his mind was spinning with the memory of Miss Norah Denby's smile.

The night was cool, a refreshing change from the stale scents of hair oil, brandy, strong cologne and cigars. Cole was working the room, as usual and that left her adrift to mingle and smile in ready invitation. Only tonight, she didn't feel much like flirting with the eager older men Cole would have her cultivate. She was suddenly very tired of it all. Oh, it was a different town, a different state but after so long, all the faces got to looking the same. Sly, hopeful, leering. And she'd had enough for one evening.

Gathering her shawl about her shoulders, Norah Denby looked down the wide street. Deadwood. It was the first time she'd been here but she'd been in dozens of towns like it, on both sides of the Missouri, on both seacoasts. Sleek and sophisticated on the surface. Bawdy and unsavory underneath. Like her, Cole was always quick to compare.

Though the sounds of delicate strings plucked a soothing melody behind her, the tinny bang of saloon pianos rose up from the seamy side of town as if in flaunting challenge. Pounding out songs she knew well. She could imagine the laughter and raucous voices

11

raised hell-bent for fun while inside the Bullock Hotel lobby cultured voices murmured genteel dissertations on politics and progress. Tonight, she walked an unhappy line between those two worlds and was at odds with her own melancholy. She wasn't one to look back, not when everything she wanted lay up ahead. Her plans were right on track so why was she feeling ripe for a change? After the next stop in Wyoming, maybe she could convince Cole to go East for a time. There, she could lose herself in museums and theaters and shake off the uneasy fit of blue-devils by buying clothes. Maybe Europe. Cole talked about that sometimes when he was feeling full of himself. Maybe Europe where she wouldn't fear meeting herself around every corner. Maybe if she could get enough money ahead, she could go on her own. That's what she'd been working toward, wasn't it? The chance to be totally independent.

But there always seemed to be another town up ahead. Cole always managed to talk her into getting on one more stage, on one more train. It was habit and she'd had no reason to break from it. Until now. Maybe it was time she found one.

She would never have believed fate could answer in the form of one reeling drunk cowboy stumbling along the walk. She'd seen more than enough of them in her time, too. Enough to know they could be a dangerous and cantankerous lot of whom she'd best steer clear. Irritated to think she would be forced back inside from the cool solitude of the walk, Norah scowled at the man as he made a wildly irregular approach. Then, she paused. There was something vaguely familiar about this one. The black hat. The broad, broad shoulders. Of course, she'd only seen him once, covered in Dakota mud.

12

Just then, his knees gave away, dropping him to the porch boards on all fours, where he swayed like an old hound. His hat fell off and did a lazy circle on its brim. He had red hair, a bright beacon even against the twilight. A low moan rattled up from him.

Norah hesitated. Strict common sense told her to leave him be. It wasn't her affair. Even if she'd helped him to this disgraceful position with her gift of champagne. A rough-edge cowhand like Rory Prescott had probably never tasted it before and had guzzled it down like cheap beer. While she could sympathize, it didn't make him her problem. The smart thing would be to walk away, to leave him to his own devices. And if he spent the night in jail recovering from his excess, it was none of her concern.

Another gusty groan disputed her claim.

And Norah had the unfortunately clear recall of a wide roguish smile gleaming from out of a dirty face.

Chiding herself for being a fool, Norah knelt down and put a hand atop his head. His hair was surprisingly soft, like liquid flame.

"Have a bit too much to drink, Mr. Prescott?"

The low, melodious tones woke something in Rory's fogged mind. He struggled for a moment to bring memory and fact together. Not an easy feat, considering. When the pieces finally fit, he doubted what they told him. And hoped they were wrong. The last place he wanted to meet up with Norah Denby was on all fours, reeking with the scent of the Desperado.

"No, ma'am," he mumbled hoarsely. "I mean, yes, ma'am, but I can hold my liquor."

"So it would seem," came her kindly caustic reply. "Well, you can't stay here. The sheriff will be by to find you new accommodations for the night. Do you think you can stand?"

13

" 'Course I can," he muttered but made no attempt to move.

"Now would probably be a good time to try. I'll help you."

"Why thank you, ma'am." He reached reflexively for his hat only to be puzzled again by its absence. Smiling tolerantly, Norah clapped it down atop the fiery thatch of hair.

"Come on, cowboy. On your feet."

She straightened as he dropped back on his heels. And rocked precariously, sucking for air. Something about his sweat-slicked features and glassy dark eyes wasn't right.

"Mr. Prescott, are you all right?"

Clutching at his middle, he bent forward to groan with all sincerity, "I'm gonna be sick."

Norah swept her skirts back with a curt, "Oh, no you are not!"

Rory clenched his roiling stomach muscles. No. That would be too awful. And no way to impress a lady. Bad enough he was next to prostrate on the porch and fogging the tip of her shoes with his uneven breaths.

"I think I'm gonna die," he amended, weakly.

The alarm went out of her posture and her chuckle was warm. "Not from a little too much good champagne and bad whiskey. Though you probably deserve to for mixing them together in the same stomach."

He muttered what sounded like, "Something in my drink."

"What was that?" She leaned closer.

"At the saloon. Put something in my drink. Laid me out like a wedge. Woke up in the back alley with 'em going through my pockets."

It was then she noticed the slight split of skin at the corner of his left eye and the abrasions across his big

14

knuckles. Whoever had picked Rory Prescott for an easy mark had obviously been mistaken. "Slipped you a Mickey, did they? No wonder you feel so badly." A touch of chloral hydrate could surely put the miseries to a man.

"Like I swallowed a hive a bees and they're madder than hell inside me. Beggin' your pardon, ma'am. Think I'm jus' gonna lie down for a minute." He started to pitch forward, his big body sagging bonelessly. Norah caught him by the shoulders, propping him up. If he went down now, there'd be no moving him. She didn't stop to consider why it should matter to her.

"Not here. Come on, Mr. Prescott. Help me get you on your feet. We're right outside the hotel. Where's your room?"

"Third floor. Never make it."

Norah believed him. And there was no way she could drag him through a room full of elegant people in the lobby and up those three flights. Cole would murder her if she caused him that kind of embarrassment. The answer came quickly and she acted upon it without undo thought. Or she never would have considered such craziness. It must have been his smile, so boyishly amiable in its charm, that scrambled her usually-level thinking.

"My room's on the first floor. I seem to recall a side door. If we can get you on your feet, do you think you could walk with me that far?"

"Lay here," he mumbled groggily.

"No, no, no. Up. On your feet. Come on, Rory." The coaxing use of his first name seemed to stir him so she tried it again. "Get up, Rory. I'm taking you to bed."

"Sounds good to me," he slurred, giving her a sloppy grin.

Norah sighed in exasperation and stood. "Up!"

With a colossal groan, he shifted forward, climbing her like a cottonwood. His big hands reached, groping for purchase, catching on a trim ankle, a slender thigh, narrow waist, plump breast and rigid shoulder as he hauled himself upward. Norah gasped beneath the clumsy fumbling and had to remind herself that he wasn't in full grasp of his senses. But then maybe he wasn't so far gone, after all, for he grinned at her smugly as he muttered, " 'Scuse me."

"Come on, Mr. Prescott. You're not dead—yet," she grumbled as she wound his arm about her shoulders.

Oh, he was heavy. And uncooperative. When she turned left, he veered right, nearly pulling her into the street. Swinging him around was like circling a freight wagon with a full load. He clung to her with both arms curled about her neck, his weight dragging down on her shoulders at the frequent buckle of his knees. And the most frustrating of all was the way his face nuzzled into her hair. His breath blew warm against her ear, followed by a low, appreciative male murmur of contentment. Breathless and struggling, that was about the last straw for Norah. Sorely tempted to dump him on the side walkway, she grumbled, "You might try helping yourself a bit more, Mr. Prescott."

"Yes, ma'am," he muttered obligingly and set his heels, snapping her up against the suddenly very solid brace of his chest. Before she knew what he was about, he was kissing her.

It wasn't the wet, slobbering kiss she expected from a drunken cowboy. It was firm and masterful, coercing her response with a devastating ease. His mouth persuaded hers to yield with a simply will-sapping finesse, provoking rather than demanding, shifting with just the right degree of temptation, tongue stroking with a tantalizing, bone-melting brevity. And Norah found herself clutching at him, fingers clenching helplessly at the back of his shirt while her head bent back over his arm. Where betwixt heaven and hell had he learned to kiss like that? she wondered in a mindless daze.

It took a moment for her senses to return enough for her to realize that he was staring down at her. There was a calm candor in his dark gaze intense enough to make her tremble. And then he spoke to her with a heart-stopping sincerity.

"I love you."

Norah gulped in a panicky confusion. And part of her wanted wildly, crazily to believe him. Of course it was the liquor and his loins talking and she knew better than to listen. But still . . .

Then he began to blink, slowly at first, then more rapidly as his gaze lost all focus. Released from the surprising spell he'd managed to catch her in, Norah was quick to supply support. He wobbled and started to collapse.

"Sure you do, cowboy," she muttered . . . with what? Regret? No. It couldn't be. She was too jaded to be moved by a cowhand's drunken devotion. A sentiment that would last about as long as his hangover. She forced a wry edge into her voice as she urged, "Come on, lover. Let's get you bedded down for the night."

His eyes had closed and his bright head rolled forward, bumping hers lightly. She stood for a moment, absorbing the feel of his dependent embrace, recognizing his strength and now more than a little cautious with his virility. A real man. Not one of those soft, aging, balding businessmen that usually occupied her time. And he felt — good.

Norah shook herself from the silly, digressing thoughts. *Stop dreaming, Norah. There's no point in it.* With an almost angry determination, she yanked and half-

17

dragged the semiconscious cowboy into the dim back hall of the hotel. By the time she reached her door, she was nearly doubled over beneath the sag of his unresponsive weight. Her key scraped in the lock and at last, she was able to maneuver him inside. He stumbled awkwardly beside her then sprawled out, with a heartfelt moan, across her coverlet on his belly.

Norah stood watching him for a long moment. What on earth had she been thinking to bring him here? To her room. He looked so big, so — male stretched out on her counterpane. Disturbing little flutters of unrecognizable emotion quivered through her. All right, she chided herself sternly. He was young and handsome and undeniably appealing. But that was no reason to go all giddy just because he happened to have the most nerve-rattling kiss. And an endearing smile. And those penetrating dark eyes. She cut the list short and laughed softly at herself. She was being foolish, getting all stirred up over some potently masculine ranch hand who probably made all of twenty-five dollars a month and spent it on cheap rye and easy women. Her mouth tightened at that thought. She wanted to scrub the feel of his off it. But didn't.

Well, since he was here for the night, she'd make him comfortable. Norah reached for one of his boots and was surprised by the expensive quality of the hand-tooled and stitched leather. She sighed. Just like a cowboy. Grubbing from month to month for a few precious coins then throwing it all away on fancy foot gear. She gripped heel and toe and jerked hard. And was again surprised by the flutter of paper money that scattered about the bedspread. She let the boot fall and began picking up the greenbacks. Lots of them. Lots and lots of them. With an impressive stack in her hand, she looked up at the motionless figure and frowned. What

18

was a working man doing with so much ready cash? Unless he'd been lucky at the tables. Very lucky. Was that why his fellow players had drugged him and dragged him out back? She glanced at the sizable sum in her palm. More than enough to get killed over in a place like the badlands. The man was either incredibly stupid or very sure of himself. She deposited the small fortune on the night table and turned her attention to the other boot.

After wiggling his toes, the cowboy muttered insensibly and rolled onto his back. Norah reached up gingerly and unfastened his gun belt, careful because some men were testy about being relieved of their sidearms. It was a fine rig, double holstered, guns well-made. She was glad to see it wasn't cut for a fast draw but rather made for show. With considerable tugging and pushing, she wrestled it out from under him and slung it over the back of a nearby chair. His black Stetson joined it there. By then, she was sitting on the edge of the bed beside him. She studied his unmoving form, trying to decide if there was anything else she should do to ease his situation. And unbidden, her hand found its way atop one denim-clad thigh.

Almost unaware of what she was doing, Norah moved her palm up and down, testing the rock-hard curve of muscle, toned from endless hours of riding in the saddle by day. Her gaze lifted to his relaxed face. And how many hours of riding by night, she mused. He was a fine-looking fellow with that playful shock of red hair over strong, ruggedly handsome features. She imagined he fired up his share of palpitations with that lazy grin and inviting gaze. And even as she thought of it, her own pulse altered into a hurried little fever of anticipation. And the tip of her tongue came out to taste the luxury of his kiss left on her lips. Realizing

19

where her mind was straying, Norah sighed in aggravation. She was getting ready to stand, when his dark eyes
flickered and finally opened. And he stared at her as if
doubting the truth of his vision.

An unsteady hand rose up until his rough fingertips
brushed her cheek in a wondering caress. It was a light
touch. It sent a stir of unsettling emotion through her.
And when his fingers splayed wide, Norah found herself leaning into his callused palm, allowing him to
draw her down without a trace of resistance toward the
enticing promise of his mouth. Her eyes began to drift
shut in a sort of sensual daze.

And then the seducing touch was gone. His hand
thumped loosely atop the covers.

Norah's eyes snapped open to find Rory Prescott out
colder than a stone. While she was wound up tight and
trembling with the expectation of his kiss. She straightened and scowled down at his reposed features. Hang
him! No man had the right to suck a woman's soul from
her with just one kiss. In a nervous agitation, she shot
off the bed and began to pace, casting occasional
glowers his way. And with each step, she tried to reject
the crazy way he had her heart jerking. And the tin-
gling urgency swelling through the breast his hand had
covered in an innocent squeeze. Or was it so innocent?
Innocent was not a word she would apply lightly to
Rory Prescott.

Because there seemed to be a purpose to the way he
turned her settled life upside down. And Norah Denby
vowed she would not be coaxed to discover just what
that purpose was.

Chapter Two

Silky softness.

Rory moved his fingers slightly until they picked up the recognizable contour of a woman's breast. Strange, he couldn't remember bringing a whore back to his room at the hotel. But he obviously had for a shapely figure was tucked suggestively against him. And they were both dressed. That meant nothing worth remembering had happened between them. Which was a relief. He wanted to concentrate all his energies on one particular lady, not scatter them indiscriminately.

For that reason, he didn't open his eyes. That and the fact that he was sure the dazzling brightness of morning would sear his eyeballs. He didn't want the sight of a coarse, unfamiliar face to cloud the luxury of his dreams. Dreams of porcelain skin and a clear crystal gaze. Of tempting lips and untouchable beauty. His Miss Norah. A woman like that you didn't take to wallow in bed for a brief sporting moment. A woman like that a man treated gently, with respect, with an eye toward the future. He smiled to himself when he thought of the look on his mama's face when he came back to their valley with Norah Denby on his arm. He'd never brought a woman to the Lone Star. The fiery Aurora Kincaid Prescott would have met one of his painted harlots at the porch with a scatter gun. She never put out an opinion on what he did with his nights or who he spent them with in the upstairs rooms of Crowe Creek but that charity didn't extend to her door. What would she think of Norah? Wouldn't she be surprised? She'd expected Scott to come home with a fine lady but had no such illusions where her younger son was concerned. Right then, he settled it in his mind. He'd be bringing Norah Denby home to his father's Lone Star Ranch. Maybe not tomorrow. But someday. He'd just have to bide his time. Which wasn't going to be easy after the impatient chafe of his dreams.

He'd dreamed of Norah Denby. Of the feel of her stockings. Silk not cotton. Of the enticing curve of her waist fitted to his palm. Of the fullness of her breast within the span of his fingers. Of her lips. Sweet and willing. Sensations so real they had him aching. Just then the harlot at his side decided to wiggle her rounded little bottom against him and roll her head on his outstretched arm. He caught the tantalizing scent of violets. Odd, because ladies of pleasure usually preferred a muskier, more exotic perfume. He burrowed his face against the woman's slender throat to breathe it in and his body responded to the teasing fragrance. And to the shifting of the woman's lush figure that called for his attention. He moved his lips lightly down her neck, surprised that she should taste so good and clean. As good as she smelled. Not cheap and stale and used. But fresh. Nice, he thought as he nuzzled her ear. Well, since she was here and obviously paid for . . . Eyes still closed, he eased his weight over so that his thigh rode the flare of her hips

22

and his fingers began to blindly ply the small pearl buttons of her bodice. Interesting. He'd never been with a woman who wore quite so many clothes.

With determination, he worked his way from neck to waist and nudged the fabric aside to find — more clothes. And these more hostile than those hundreds of tiny buttons. He figured it was some sort of corset from the stiff feel of it beneath his palm. And it fastened down the back. He was going to need her cooperation to manage this piece of female wrapping. But in the meantime, her bosom pushed nicely above the shaping form. He let his thumb drift over the pleasing swells then bent down to trace the same path with his lips. It was then he felt her start of surprise.

" 'Morning, sweet thing," he drawled softly. "Sorry I couldn't do much in the way of impressing you last night but I mean to make up for it now."

Lord, she smelled nice. The delicate aroma made him think of Norah Denby and he wasn't sure why. Until she spoke. And the husky quality of her voice made his eyes pop open.

"I don't think so, Mr. Prescott."

She caught his transgressing thumb to still his hand and bent it back until it — hurt! But she didn't need force to render him harmless. Shock stopped him as cold as a 230-grain bullet between the eyes the instant he looked upon her face.

"Ohmagod," he moaned with a distress so acute it was almost comical. He not only ceased his attentions, he scuttled as far from her as the width of the mattress would allow. And stared, all glassy-eyed in disbelief.

Norah sat up and turned away from him to rebutton her bodice. Her hands were shaking and that

23

made her almost as angry as the feelings coursing through her. Feelings that had gone from lazy pleasure to outrage. When she'd laid down beside him the night before, she never figured Rory Prescott for an immediate threat. She'd only planned to close her eyes for a moment. Surely there was no harm. He was dead to the world and his guns were in easy reach of her fingertips. Falsely secure, she'd fallen deeply asleep only to wake in the middle of his seduction. As she lingered on the edge of awareness, hot, dizzying sensations flirted through her. They were teasing, tormenting, and all too tempting. Just like his lips. She didn't think to react in modest shock. He was too good at what he was doing. Slow and sweet. There was no sense of danger, no urgent alarm. But there should have been. There would have been if she'd found herself in a similar position with anyone else. Rory Prescott was different and it was that difference that should have warned her. Remembering his kiss held her pliant as he woke her body beneath his coaxing touch. And then he spoke. It was his words, not his deeds that sparked fury inside her. Because after tantalizing her with his wickedly clever mouth, he spoke to her as if she was a whore. And all the warmth she felt toward him fled.

Securing the final button, she spoke without looking his way. Her tone was cool and aloof, as if he hadn't been touching her flesh with knowing fingers. "Good morning. How are you feeling?"

"I don't rightly know," he stammered. "I thought I was awake."

She smiled wryly, recalling the unmistakable feel of him against her skirts. "Oh, I think you are quite awake. You don't remember how you got here?"

24

His dark eyes did a quick survey of the room and came back to her confused. "I don't know where I am."

"My room at the hotel."

"Oh God." With that groan he fell upon his back, eyes squeezed shut. Now *that* was something worth remembering but his mind returned with a frustrating blank. How much of his dream was real? He was afraid to ask. What on earth had he done last night? And this morning!

Sympathy for his agonized plight beginning to replace her sense of umbrage, Norah explained simply, "Some rather unscrupulous fellows slipped something in your drink with plans to rob you. I rescued you on the front walk and brought you here to sleep it off."

He bolted upright with a soft oath, taking stock of his missing boots and what that meant.

"It's all right here."

His gaze darted to the night table, to the tidy stack of bills. And he gave a gusty sigh of relief.

"Do you always carry such sums in your boots, Mr. Prescott?"

"Always figured if someone got 'em off me I'd be past caring about the money."

Norah smiled slightly. "I guess you were wrong."

"Guess so," he muttered awkwardly. Finding the sight of her as uncomfortable as it was delectable, Rory swung his legs off the opposite side of the bed and let his head dangle between his knees. *Let me remember something. Anything that would prove I didn't act the total fool in front of her,* he prayed in earnest. First night in a big city and what did he have to go and do? Let himself be taken by a couple of card slicks like the country rube he was and then disgrace himself completely before the woman of his dreams. But then, he guessed they might not be dreams at all. Had he really kissed her? The memory was there, tauntingly out of reach, held in a vacuum along with her response to it. She must not have been too displeased. After all, she'd brought him here, to her room, to her bed. Where he'd continued to make an utter ass of himself by groping her like a prostitute. Oh Lord, how could things get worse?

The sudden loud knock on the door snapped him upright.

"Norah, honey, you ready for breakfast?"

In answer to Rory's questioning gaze, Norah whispered, "My father."

Her daddy! And him sitting there on her bed in his socks! With a silent oath, he snatched for his boots and began to wrestle them on.

"Norah?"

Smiling at the sight of the cowboy's panic, Norah called easily, "I'll meet you in the dining room."

There was a moment's pause. "Everything all right?"

"Fine. Just slept a bit late, is all. I'll be there in a minute."

By then, Rory had come around to her side of the bed and was buckling on his gun belt with unsteady hands. The crisp greenbacks were stuffed hastily into the pockets of his snug Levi's. He grabbed up his hat then looked to her for the first time. And couldn't look away. Something about her, perched on the edge of the bed, her sable hair sleep rumpled, her clothing mussed and the softest sketch of a smile upon her lips set his heart to hammering fiercely. And an indescribable warmth began to seep up from his toes.

"Ma'am, I'm right grateful you took me in like you did. I hope my being here didn't compromise you none." He glanced down at his boots and missed the quirk of her lips. "I don't recall what happened last night but if I did or said anything to—offend you, I'm purely sorry."

I love you.

The words came back to her with a sultry whisper of insincerity. "You didn't, Mr. Prescott," she assured him somewhat tersely.

He shuffled his feet in a second of shy boyishness then looked up. There was nothing the least bit youthful in the heated intensity of that gaze. "I'm leaving for home tomorrow morning and I'd really like to see you again, Miss Norah. I don't much like leaving you with a bad impression of me."

A bad impression? Oh, the impressions she had were far from bad; the strength of his arms, the devastating thoroughness of his kiss, his light, sensuous touch, the thick evidence of his manhood. She steeled herself against the seditious thrill of remembering and said with a noncommittal reserve, "We'll see."

There wasn't a trace of guile in Rory Prescott. His features fell with disappointment. In a small voice, he murmured, "Yes, ma'am."

Abruptly, Norah was moved by his despondency to ask, "And where's home?"

He brightened in an instant. "The Bar K Ranch up Belle Fourche way. I'm the foreman." Pride fairly glowed from him, making her hold back her remark about him being awfully young for the job. No, perhaps not, she reconsidered, taking in the height and breadth of him and the sudden surety of manner. Rory Prescott looked altogether capable. A touch of

27

that admiration must have shown in her gaze for his attitude of confidence redoubled into a swaggering arrogance.

" 'Bout that dinner, Miss Norah?" he pressed.

Smiling, she repeated, "We'll see."

"Yes, ma'am. We will."

And he gave her a long, searing look she supposed would have brought most women right up into his arms. She had to fight the pull but she did so with a dignified aplomb. "You'd better go, Mr. Prescott." There was no sign of her inward agitation in that cool dismissal.

Hat in hand, he let that compelling stare linger just a moment longer, long enough to have her quivering in response. Then, he merely nodded and left her to shakily unwind from the tense exchange.

What was it about this one Dakota cowboy that so completely undid her common sense?

Cole Denby looked up from his cup of coffee and a copy of the *Deadwood Daily Pioneer Times* to see her settle into the chair opposite.

"Good morning, my dear. You're looking a bit flushed."

Norah regarded him unemotionally then turned her attention to the eager waiter to order up a light meal. She was more than a little annoyed to find her companion smirking smugly when she looked back to him.

"Whom did you have in your room with you this morning, dear Norah?"

She didn't respond to the baiting question with the shock of dismay registering inside. Damn him for being so observant. "I beg your pardon."

"Oh, please don't. Cut the coy games. Who was it?"

"No one of any importance," she claimed with a bored drawl. "No one who would interest you."

"But I am interested. Very. Not doing a little business on your own, are you?"

"Oh, Cole, don't be crude," she snapped and he grinned at his ability to get a rise of temper from her. "He's just a cowboy who got himself into more trouble than he could handle."

Cole's brows lifted in amazement. "And you, sweet Norah, played the good Samaritan? Please don't tell me you wasted your considerable charm and talent on some empty-pocketed, ignorant cow nurse."

Norah's gray eyes chilled to brittle ice beneath his wry contempt. "Hardly empty-pocketed. He was carrying enough cash to—" She bit that back but not quick enough to avoid the snare of Cole's interest.

"Oh? I am intrigued. Tell me more about your lover."

"He's not my—" She sighed angrily in the face of his knowing amusement and concluded curtly, "He's the foreman at the Bar K."

"Garth Kincaid's Bar K?" The laziness left his pose as Cole Denby sat upright with a glitter of shrewd business in his pale eyes.

"I guess so."

"And did this Mr . . ."

"Prescott," she supplied sullenly.

"Did this Mr. Prescott express an interest in continuing your—friendship?"

"He wants to take me to dinner tonight."

Cole leaned back in his chair, tenting his fingers thoughtfully. "Perhaps we should join him then."

"Cole, no."

The small tug of reluctance in her voice made him frown. Norah, his cool, cold-hearted Norah, wanting to protect a lowly cowboy she claimed was not her lover, from him?

"Yes, Norah. I find I am quite anxious to meet your Mr. Prescott."

Schooling her expression in careful lines, Norah accepted a cup of coffee from the waiter. And while she sipped it, she wondered wildly, *what have I done?*

What should have concerned her was, why should she care?

Rory Prescott arrived right on time looking fresh and handsome and so painfully young that her conscience twisted. She ignored Cole's glance that said plainly, *this — this boy is the one who has you so het up?* She gave the cowboy her most charming smile and watched the redhead reel as if she'd struck him. Oh, why did he have to look so inexperienced, so infatuated. Wanting desperately to call the whole thing off, she stiffened beneath the sudden hard clamp of Cole's fingers upon her arm.

"Introduce me, dear daughter," he urged with a silky insistence.

"Rory Prescott, my father, Cole Denby."

The two men exchanged a firm handshake before Rory took a chair at the table. The summons to supper in the hotel's private dining room in the presence of her daddy had him in a nervous quake. But one look at Norah settled all his misgivings. She was stunningly dressed in emerald taffeta and her smile was warm enough to melt him right down into his boots like a pat of butter left in the sun. He could endure just about anything for the privilege of her company. Even the cool assessment of her father.

"Norah speaks quite highly of you, young man."

Rory received that news with surprise and undisguised pleasure. "I'm right honored to hear that, sir." He tore his gaze from beauteous daughter to dapper father and studied him with interest. Cole Denby was in a word, elegant. His manner of dress spoke of sophisticated taste. His silvered hair was immaculately groomed and oiled and so was his smile. It would have been hard to guess his age. His handsome face was unlined despite the distinguished color of his hair. His eyes were equally steely as they touched on Norah with a possessive fondness.

"She tells me you're the foreman of the Bar K. You must be something indeed for Garth Kincaid to place his trust in you."

Rory sat straighter beneath the compliment and murmured humbly, "I do my best not to let the major down."

"I'm sure you do," Cole drawled smoothly. "And with such trust comes a great degree of responsibility."

"Yessir," the young cowboy boasted quietly.

"I know all about that kind of responsibility. You see, I'm a livestock broker. Did Norah tell you?"

"Nossir." He glanced her way to find her sitting prettily with a fixed smile upon her face.

"Have to know the market to get ahead in these times. The glory days are behind us, sad to say." He waited for the ranch hand to nod his agreement. "That's why I do some investing on the side. Keeps me in capital, if you know what I mean."

Just then, Norah's knee brushed his thigh, the

31

briefest whisper of meeting, but it was enough to jar his thinking. Cole Denby could have been talking about how many banks he planned to rob and Rory would have still smiled and nodded. Norah had that effect. That attention-stealing, soul-absorbing loveliness that scrambled a man's brain. What he wouldn't have given to appear important in her clear gray eyes.

"As a matter of fact," Cole was saying with a furtive confidence, "I've been putting together a little deal that could amount to a considerable return of funds. A smart man could better himself if he got in on it now. Couldn't he, Norah?"

Wishing she could just sit silent and not be a part of Cole's scheme, Norah managed a strained smile. Playing on Rory Prescott's emotions made her writhe inside. If the accidental nudge of her knee could catapult him off the deep end of devotion, she hated to think how vulnerable he'd be to her practiced charms. But at Cole's stern look, she added, "That's quite true. Cole is a genius when it comes to money."

Bemused by the fact that she called her daddy by his first name, Rory missed the sarcasm in her words. Just as he missed the meaningful nonverbal sparring between father and daughter. He was too busy feeling a dry-mouthed fascination with the way her slender fingers stroked the damp sides of her wine glass.

"Now if a fellow like you was to want to invest, say, a couple of hundred dollars." Cole let that suggestion dangle then scowled at the way the cowboy seemed inattentive and lost to Norah's lure. His tone sharpened in annoyance. "But then I don't imagine you have access to that kind of money as a simple ranch foreman."

Without acknowledging the slur or taking his eyes

32

off Norah, Rory said nonchalantly, "How 'bout five hundred?"

And Cole began to smile, his good humor restored.

"So how long you planning to stay in Deadwood?"

They'd been walking along Williams Street of the prestigious Iron Hill Row in silence. From where that elite section of impressive houses clung precariously to the northwest side of the valley, they could look down on Main Street all the way to its end in the badlands. From where they stood, the air was cool and fresh, scented by the pines growing thick in the surrounding gulches. And laced with it was the delicate touch of violets.

"Until Cole finishes his business. A few more days, at least."

"Then where will you be headed? Home?"

Her laugh was soft and faintly cynical. "No such place for the two of us. Our home's been on trains and stages for as long as I can remember. We'll be going to Cheyenne for a while. And from there, I can't say I know."

"Do you like it? All the traveling, I mean."

"Sometimes. It can be real exciting. But lonely, too." Why she said that, she didn't know. It wasn't to exact any sympathy from him, though it did. His arm slipped lightly about her shoulders, resting there to instill a surprising sense of permanence. So strong it startled her, so comforting it scared her. "I don't mind it, though," she put in quickly, hoping to discourage him. But it didn't. He left his arm where it was, in the easy, disturbing loop.

"Don't you ever get to missing roots? You know, belonging somewhere?"

"I've never had any so I guess you could say I don't know what I'm missing. How about you?" she asked to distract him from his questions. She didn't really want to hear about him. She didn't want to know any more about his life, to feel a closer involvement with him. It was simpler to maintain a distance, an objectivity. But that was hard when his fingers moved in a gentle caress upon her shoulder.

"I got roots that go back to the founding of the Dakotas. My daddy was one of the first to settle when they opened the Black Hills. This is the first time I've ever been out of our valley." He admitted that with an embarrassed smile. And a wistfulness that touched to the heart of her.

"You sound like a man who can't wait to get back home." That observation wasn't teasing. It was almost envious.

"There's no place on earth I'd rather be." Then he glanced at her with a sudden hot, bone-melting candor. He was smiling to himself when he looked to the stretch of dim walk ahead. "Well, almost."

Norah swallowed down the choking lump of panic in her throat. She could almost believe him. She almost wanted to believe him. Miserably, she reminded herself that tomorrow he'd be gone from her life and she'd continue on, untouched by his passing. Or would she? She canted a look at his pleasing profile then fiercely shook off the tender swell of longing. It was crazy. And she knew it. But the drape of his arm felt good. Just as his kiss had felt good. And waking beside him had felt good. For a moment, her thoughts stretched beyond that to dwell on more heated intimacies.

34

What would it be like to have him in her bed, awake?

It was no good thinking along those lines. It would bring up equally impossible ideas like what would it be like having a place to call home, having children of her own and a man who loved her?

I love you.

Crazy thoughts. Impossible thoughts. Casually, she shrugged off the uncomfortable closeness of his arm. She let her anger rise unchecked, anger toward a simple man like Rory Prescott who had no idea of what life was all about. Anger toward herself for wanting, just for a little while, to see things through his unjaded eyes. Better she stick to the old men who had few illusions than to break the eager heart of this younger one. And possibly her own in the bargain.

They had reached the hotel and Rory saw her inside. She started toward her room and he followed with reluctance. She could tell he was looking for a way to prolong their time together.

"Would you like to get something to drink or see a show or something?"

She stopped outside her door, turning to look up at him. He seemed so much taller, broader in the narrow hallway. And awkward. She was sure his evenings with a woman usually didn't end in the hall but rather on a horizontal plane. And it was tempting.

"I don't think so. Better we say good night. And goodbye."

He hid his disappointment better this time. "All right. I got to get an early start tomorrow anyway." Still, he lingered, wondering desperately what a gentleman did with a lady at such a time? Did he kiss her? He wanted to. Badly. He surely couldn't invite

35

himself in. Though he wanted to. Just as badly. He couldn't just stand there forever feeling stupid and graceless. What would Scotty do with all that Eastern polish?

"It's been a real pleasure, Miss Norah," he told her softly. They seemed to be the right words for she extended her hand and let it disappear inside his far bigger one. He shook it companionably for a second then at her puzzled smile, realized that wasn't what she was waiting for at all. Keeping it snug within his fingers, he used the gentle grasp to draw her up to him, then, oh so lightly, brushed his lips against her temple. He heard her quiet sigh and was almost shaken from his resolve. But he leaned back and he let her go.

"Good night, Miss Norah."

He was about to turn away when she reached up, her fingertips grazing along the contour of his cheek to hold him there a moment longer. Her clear gaze had suddenly grown cloudy.

"Goodbye, Rory," she whispered in a husky tone.

Her hand slipped around to the nape of his neck, curling there, coaxing him down to where her lips were parted and waiting. The first touch was tentative and tender. The second scorching. The third heaven.

How long they stood in the hall experimenting, exploring, exciting one another with their kisses, neither of them knew. Forever, it seemed. Not long enough. Time and place had no meaning. Norah drifted in the luxurious lapse of reality, letting Rory Prescott charm the emotions from her with the leisurely movements of his mouth over hers. It was just kissing. He didn't try anything else. He didn't have to. His big hands rested at her waist, not holding her, not clutching at her, not compelling her. Just resting easy. Just thoroughly destroying her control with their lack of demands. She felt like wriggling with impatience. She wanted to place them up higher where her bosom pressed against his crisp shirtfront. Or lower where he'd created a restless fire. But she couldn't move. It was all she could do to respond to his kiss and not swoon from the sheer delight of it.

With an anguished moan, she tore her mouth away and panted wildly into the cove of his shoulder. What was wrong with her? She was a rational, intelligent woman. She knew it was folly to desire a man—especially *this* man—to the extreme of madness. He had nothing to offer her. No future. No security. Just the same kind of desolation she'd already known and refused to return to. Why couldn't she just take his money and walk away without looking back? The way she always did. Without remorse. Without regret.

Her knees were weak. With one arm, she clung to him about the middle. The other hand roamed helplessly through the thick thatch of red hair. She felt his cheek rub against the top of her carefully coiffed sable curls. And his lips tease tenderly along her brow. Recklessly, rebelliously, she put back her head so he could kiss her again into that senseless, sensual oblivion. And when she'd begun to think she had no recourse but to invite him in or lose all dignity in the public hall, he stepped back and broke the spell of temptation.

He was smiling a dangerously confident smile and somehow that irritated her to no end. How could he be so rock steady when her world was whirling? Hang the man anyway! The no-account, good-for-nothing-but-cows ranch hand who didn't even have

the decency to look shattered by what had passed between them. His arrogance infuriated her.

Chin angling up in defiance of her own careening
emotions, she said stiffly, "Goodbye, Mr. Prescott,"
and closed the door of her room to his smug features.

Rory placed his palms on either side of the door
and sagged for a long moment, letting the crippling
waves of urgency ride him to a standstill. Finally the
breathless, helplessly needy sensations eased and he
was able to straighten.

"I'll be a-seeing you, Miss Norah," he promised
softly.

Chapter Three

"You can kiss your five hundred goodbye, Rory. You've been taken but good."

There was no one in the world Rory considered smarter than his lawyer brother, no one else whose word he would take without question if he was to say it was broad daylight in the middle of the night. But at those words, Rory scowled across his parents' dinner table and growled, "You don't know what you're talking about, Scotty."

Scott Prescott shook his head and explained with a kind exasperation, "Rory, if you'd bothered to check with any of the financial papers before blindly handing over your cash, you'd know that Royale-Standard closed its door two weeks ago. Whoever's got your money is long gone. I wouldn't be holding my breath for a return if I were you."

"Well I ain't you," the younger Prescott snapped as he sullenly digested the information. "Don't you go blabbing none of this, you hear?"

Scott spread his hands wide in a blameless manner and glanced toward the kitchen where his mother and stepfather had gone. "Won't hear of it from me. I'm sorry about the money. Next time you want to put some funds into something, talk to me first. I could fix you up in—"

"Indian blankets and reservation land, no doubt. No thank you, Scotty. I think I'll pass on it." He shoved back from the table and stalked to the front door, letting it bang behind him.

"That son of a—"

"Scott."

Scott caught hold of his temper and deferred to his wife's gentle caution. Still he seethed at the unfair and unexpected cut of his half brother's words. "I was only trying to help," he grumbled.

"I know," Gena Prescott soothed. Her fair hand rubbed over her husband's much darker one. "I'm sure he didn't mean it."

"The hell he didn't." He fell silent for a moment, nursing his hurt and anger. It was a rare time when he and his younger brother could get together without the bite of words flying. Not that there was any true ill-feeling between them, just the strain of one strong outside shadow. Their grandfather, Garth Kincaid. The man poisoned everything he touched. If only Rory would see it. He sighed in frustration. "Ah, Gena, it's getting so I can't hardly talk to him anymore. He's such a dadblamed stubborn, thickheaded fool."

"Takes after the rest of the men in his family, you might say," she chided mildly. At Scott's glowering glance, she reprimanded, "You were rather hard on him, Scott."

"It's because I care about the pig-headed mule. Aww, hang it, I'll go make it right with him."

"No, I'll go."

Gena waddled with the gracelessness of a woman over seven months gone with child out onto the porch where she found Rory as she expected, sulk-

40

ing at the rail. She came up behind him to place a light hand upon the stiff rack of his shoulders. He gave a start of surprise then smiled when he saw who it was.

"Come to make the peace offering, Sis?" he asked with a sheepish smile. His arm lifted to easily enfold her cumbersome figure beneath it and his other hand spread wide over the ripe curve of her belly. Only Rory would dare such an intimate touch without quickening her modest blushes. Rory, the affectionate scapegrace, whom she loved without the shyness of her natural reserve. He bent low over her protruding stomach as if to speak to the life within. "How's my favorite nephew tonight? Thinking his daddy and his uncle are a pair of jackasses?"

"No more than usual," its mother replied tartly.

Rory straightened and bussed her forehead with a repentant kiss. "I'm sorry, Gena. It's just that Scotty's being such a—"

"Dadblamed stubborn, thick-headed fool?" she supplied with a smile.

He grinned back. "Yep, that about says it." Then he was unusually serious. "Shoot, Gena, I don't like the way things are getting to be between us. I'll go on in and apologize if you think it'd do any good. He knows I didn't mean anything by it. I think the world of him."

"I know," she said with a quiet strength. "I wish there was something I could do. I hate seeing the two of you snapping at each other."

"I don't have no answers, Gena. Scotty, he's just pushing, pushing all the time. He's making things hard. He's got me in a corner and I can't like it. It's bad enough with all the settlers crowding in and

41

choking the range but we've got him in there making a big noise on behalf of the Sioux. He's made some powerful enemies in the Stock Grower's Association."

"Like your grandfather."

Rory's evasion was answer enough. "I'm scared half out of my mind that somebody's gonna up and put a bullet in him to keep from stirring things up the way he's been doing. If he's not the death of us ranchers first."

He stopped suddenly, aware of the fragile woman's pallor. She was staring up at him through huge, haunted eyes. He was quick to draw her close to his chest in a protective hug.

"Damn my big mouth. I shouldn't have said that, Gena. I'm sorry. I don't want you fretting none with the little one on the way and all. You know I'd never let anything happen to Scotty. Not ever."

After a time, she hugged him back and whispered in a thin little voice, "You're not saying anything I didn't know. And I'm scared, too. So is Scott but he tries hard not to let me see it. You will keep him safe, won't you, Rory? Promise me."

"With my life," he vowed.

She patted his back firmly and stepped away. "Let's talk about something else," she commanded, pushing the worries down into the dark corner where they crouched ready to terrorize her with dread every time her husband was a few minutes late coming home. She forced a smile. "Let's talk about her."

"Who?" He looked genuinely confused.

Gena pursed her lips knowingly. "Her, the one

whose had you spinning in circles since you got home."

His face fused a deep crimson as he muttered, "Oh, her."

"I was right," Gena cried gleefully. "I knew it! I told Scott it had to be a woman."

"You told Scott!" he yelped in dismay. "He's gonna ride me to the grave with this one."

"Don't worry. He didn't believe it. So," she coaxed conspiratorially, "who is she? Tell me everything. Is she pretty?"

He rolled his dark eyes heavenward. "Oh, Gena, she's a beauty. Smart and a real lady, like you. Every time I think of her, my insides get all crazy." He paused, coloring up like a boy but there was no hint of uncertainty in his tone when he concluded, "I want to marry her, Gena."

"Oh! Oh, Rory, that's wonderful!" Gena squeezed his large hands as she looked up through happily misting eyes. "When? When do we get to meet her?"

He scuffed the toes of his boots awkwardly and mumbled, "I ain't exactly got that far yet. Don't rightly know if she'll have me."

"She'd be crazy not to." Her palm pressed to his rough cheek. "They don't come any better than a Prescott. I'd be happy to tell her so myself."

He gave her a shy little smile that managed to look both endearingly youthful and poignantly somber at the same time. "I don't know what I'm doing when I'm around her. I ain't sure how to deal proper with a lady. I can't think of what to say. Hell, the only kind of female I know ain't too interested in conversation. If you know what I mean."

43

Gena blushed. She did.

"This one's special, Sis. I don't want to let her get away. I—I love her."

That claim charmed her completely. Rory, who was quick to flirt and skitter away from involvement like a frisky colt, talking of love and marriage. She wanted so much to hear more of this mysterious lady who'd snagged his roguish heart, to offer up the best advice she could, to assure him that he was taking a wonderful step forward but the door bumped shut behind them and the big cowboy quickly cut the ties of their conversation loose as his brother eased up to the rail on the opposite side of his wife.

Rory slid a look at Scott. He was sober-faced, having put on that impassive Indian front he used when stronger emotions were struggling underneath. That half-Sioux heritage he earned from his father, Far Winds of the Lakotas, made him impossible to read so Rory did what he always did where his half brother was concerned. He relied on feelings and he knew Scott was chewing on the same chunk of misery that clogged his own throat.

Gena made the first move to push them together. She reached up a hand to Rory, drawing his bright head down so she could kiss his cheek. Then she turned to her husband and did the same, only he met her kiss full on the mouth and let it linger there with a savoring sweetness. The mask of stoicism fell away when he looked into her beloved face and she could see everything she might want to know etched upon his golden features, shining within in his golden eyes.

Rory watched the silent interplay. He'd seen it

44

hundreds, probably thousands of times before but this time was the first time he saw with his eyes open. It was the first time he'd ever had a clue as to the depth of emotion linking his brother to the fragile Eastern woman he'd wed. And it made him feel all strange inside with an achy sort of anticipation and restlessness. With an impatient insight into how things would be between him and Norah Denby. And what he saw, he wanted for himself.

"You two talk nice," Gena warned with mock severity. Then she put a small hand on either man's arm for a slight squeeze and left them alone on the dark porch.

Scott and Rory exchanged a long, wary look. Finally, the younger Prescott broke down to mutter, "I'm right sorry, Scotty. I had no call to say what I did."

"Forget it," Scott said, with an easy shrug.

But Rory wasn't willing to let it go. "Can you? Can you really?"

Scott didn't answer. Instead he turned partway and stared out over the endless acres of Prescott grass, toward the barren plot of land his father's people were forced to call home. And bitterness twisted in his belly. Toward those who would suppress them. Toward those who would cheat them from what little dignity they were allowed. And he didn't want to think his brother was a part of that enemy. A part of Garth Kincaid, who had paid for his enviable Harvard education then had cut him to the quick because he'd wanted to use what he'd learned to aid the Lakota. He was the one who stood between the two brothers, shadowing the love

45

they'd known as boys, threatening the closeness they enjoyed as men.

"What are we gonna do, Scotty? Go on like this until I end up beating the hell outta you?"

"As if you could," came the laconic challenge. Golden gaze locked to brown and for a moment both were measuring the other as a possible rival. And neither of them wanted to believe it would ever come down to a test. But the grim possibility was there and they couldn't ignore it. Neither of them would have believed things could deteriorate as far as they already had.

"I don't like it, Scotty. It ain't right putting Gena and our folks in the middle."

On that, they were agreed. "I've tried to keep you out of it, Rory."

"It's kinda hard to kill the body and still keep the head alive."

"Is that what I'm doing?" The tension welled between them. Scott's voice was taut with it, Rory's posture tight with it. "What do you want from me, Rory? Do you want me to just up and stop? To just step back and say it's all right to go on robbing and raping and killing the spirit of the Sioux? Well, I can't do that. I won't do that. Not even for you." That last was said very softly, almost apologetically.

"I know, Scotty." That was said just as soft.

"Then what? What the hell do you want me to do?"

"Stay alive."

As Scott blinked, off balance and surprised by the fervor of his brother's request, Rory gripped him by either side of his dark head and shook him. Hard.

"You be careful. You think of Gena and your

46

baby. You think of Mama. And me. Dang you, Scotty, don't get yourself killed over this." His voice broke painfully.

Scott took hold of his brother's forearms and pressed. Hard. "I don't plan to."

"I'm gonna need you to hold me up at my wedding."

"Well, hell, that means I'm going to have to wait around another fifty years or so while you test out every woman in the state of South Dakota."

Rory's big hands dropped to his brother's shoulders, kneading there restlessly in a reluctance to let go. "Maybe not so long as that. You just be there for me."

"Wouldn't miss it."

The moment played out between them and finally, Rory pushed back. He seemed to hesitate then spoke his mind. "There is something, Scotty. There is something you could do for me."

Scott was instantly alert and guarded. And he hated that he was. "What's that?" The caution must have crept into his tone because Rory stiffened slightly and wouldn't look at him.

"Help push the land lease bill through." When there was silence, Rory turned to face his impassive brother. "You can do that, Scotty. There ain't no one who knows the law better than you. You know the Bar K don't own much more than the plot of land the house sits on. All the rest is public domain and we're losing it acre by acre. Help us dig in our heels. You can finagle it so it's registered all legal-like as accustomed range."

"No." That word was slapped down all flat and final.

Rory wasn't surprised. What he was, was desperate. "Do you want me to pay you? Do you want me to beg you? What's it gonna take, Scotty? I'm asking for your help, not your first born."

"What you're asking for is my soul and I won't give it."

Rory drew himself up to his formidable height and glared down at his older brother. "Well forgive me all to hell for asking you to compromise a grain of that stiff Lakota pride. I just hope I'm left with a big enough plot a dirt for you to bury me."

He started to spin away only to have Scott catch him by the upper arm and jerk him to a standstill. "Did he send you?" he demanded in a hard, suspicious voice.

Rory tore away, wildly angry. "No. You know better than that. He wouldn't want your help. I'm the one asking. I'm the only one dumb enough to think you'd give it."

"For you," Scott said so softly Rory thought at first he might have mistaken the words.

"What?"

"I'll do it for you. Not him. For you." His forefinger tapped Rory's chest.

"Fair enough."

And because the mood was still too strained to offer up any kind of thanks, Rory simply inclined his head before striding off to fetch his horse. Scott looked after him for a minute then directed his molten gaze toward the far grassland empire of his grandfather. And he said with quiet feeling into that darkness, "You son of a bitch."

"Oww!"

Rory slapped at the muzzle of his brown and white paint stallion and rubbed the back of his calf.

"Chance, you sorry bit of wolf bait, what call you got to go snapping at me?"

The horse nickered softly and butted him in the belly with its wide head. Apologizing. It was then Rory realized that while he stood deep in thought, he'd been brushing the same spot on the animal's withers until the hide was almost bare.

"Sorry 'bout that, son. Next time you want to go getting my attention, be a little more gentle about it." He pushed the broad head away and resumed the smooth grooming strokes. The horse went back to its contented snoozing, blowing the chafe up from its feed with its regular breaths. And Rory went back to his troubled musings.

He loved Norah Denby. He'd told Gena as much but the idea of it purely terrified him. Besides his mother and Gena, the only women he knew outside a handful of plain, giggly prairie mudhens who worked their folks' farms, were the bawdy girls of Crowe Creek. They were easily accessible, frisky, willing to drink and cavort for the flash of a coin and a smile. He'd never treated a one of them as if they weren't worthy of respect or less than decent females fallen on hard times. They didn't complain if a man came to them smelling of horse after long, hard, lonely hours in the saddle, nor did they expect more than a curt civility from him when he was bone-weary.

But a virtuous woman — that was something altogether different. From observing the way his brother fancy-footed it around Gena, he wasn't quite convinced that having a wife was all that practical or convenient. A wife would expect things like frequent bathing, regular comings and goings, church on Sunday, language that wasn't a liberal one-third profanity. It'd be worse than moving back in with his mama! And there'd be no more trips to Crowe Creek. Ever. He'd seen Scotty go through hell when Gena suspected him of stepping out. And that was before they were hitched! Women were funny like that.

When he considered the sacrifices and stacked them up beside the image of Norah Denby, there was surprisingly little conflict in his heart and mind. The whores were out. No problem. He had an uncomfortably detailed recall of how the sablehaired beauty fit so snug and sweet against him. And of the way she came up on tiptoe to greet his kisses. Nope, he couldn't imagine wanting to wander from her bed for the rest of his natural years as long as she was waiting with a ready welcome. Hell, he'd even bathe and give up swearing! Just for the pleasure of coming home every night to look at her, to feel the clever snap of her wit, to lose himself in the luxury of her silken flesh and to wake stretched out beside her. What more could a man ask for?

With a sigh, Rory leaned his forearms on Chance's back and made himself entertain the possibility that Norah Denby wouldn't want him. Maybe she wouldn't find him dandified enough to suit her. Not smart enough. Not rich enough. Not good enough. He was flustered when he thought of talking to her though he'd never had any problems with Gena. And women didn't come any more decent than his brother's wife. She thought he was worth

50

something. And when he mulled it over, he was sure she was right. He was passably good to look at. He didn't have any real offensive habits like spitting tobacco, gambling to the point of losing his boots or consistent drunkenness — though he did them all on occasion. He would never — ever lay a mean hand on a woman. He didn't track mud and manure into the house, when he thought of it; one of the first things his mama had taught him. He was normally polite and only mildly truculent and not too awful fast to use his fists. He had the inheritance of the Bar K awaiting him and with it would go all the wealth and power a woman could want. And she'd made it powerfully clear that she enjoyed all the intimacies they'd shared so far. Why wouldn't she want him? All he had to do was work up the gumption to ask.

Then there was the five hundred dollars.

Losing the money didn't mean half as much as the consequences of the deal. Had Cole Denby known about Royale-Standard before selling him on the investment? Had Norah? Damn, he didn't want to believe that. Which was what made him such an easy mark. Why hadn't he paid closer attention to what Denby was saying instead of making calf-eyes at his daughter? Thank the Lord it was his money gone after bad and not his grandfather's. It was a minor relief. What if she were in some kind of trouble? Her daddy had invested heavily in Royale-Standard. Did that threaten the comfort of her lifestyle? He frowned hard. He didn't like thinking of Norah struggling. For anything. A woman like that should never have to struggle or worry or want for nothing. And he would see to it. He would fetch her to the Bar K and care for her with all the considerable love he had to give. And he'd dedicate the rest of his days to making her happy.

"You planning on wearing the hair off that basket tail or putting him away some time tonight?"

Rory straightened from his woolgathering and gave his grandfather a sheepish smile. "Just finishing up here. Was you waiting on me for something, Major?"

The "Major" was an honorary title recalled to Garth Kincaid's heroics during the skirmish with the Mexicans. No one would think to call him Mister Kincaid. And Rory never called him anything else. He spoke the title with the utmost respect. The stocky, barrel-chested man didn't answer right away in his big, booming voice, a voice that shivered glass in the frame and sent his underlings to quaking. Instead, he leaned a shoulder against the stall post and watched his grandson put the final spit and polish to his mount. Like everything that had to do with the ranch, Rory took the extra second to make the job perfect. It was that extended measure of care that endeared the boy to him. There was so much of his son, Seth, in him. Had he survived the bloody battle between North and South, Garth could well imagine the two of them standing together in such companionable silence. Rory Prescott was all he had left of his once proud family. Two sons he'd lost to the War Between the States. And his daughter, Aurora, he'd lost to the Sioux and Ethan Prescott. He wouldn't give up Rory, his heir, his hope for the future. He hadn't had to push the boy toward the big step into his shoes. Rory was more than eager and willing. He shared the older man's passion for the land and the four-legged wonders who grazed atop it. And he would fight to preserve it. But just how far he would go, Garth wasn't sure. And he wanted to be sure. Loyalty was something he insisted upon. Blind, steadfast loyalty.

"He's stirring things up again."

Rory didn't need to ask who 'he' was. When the major used that tone, he meant Scott Prescott. He made every effort not to show anything beyond a neutral face. "What can he do? Rile up a few reservation squatters? Push back a few fences? Since that business with ole Sal Garrick was buried with him, there ain't much he can toss up in our direction. Is there?" He paused, dark gaze lifting, quietly demanding a reassurance.

Kincaid smiled tightly. "And if there was?"

Rory went back to his currying. "I ain't sure I want to know about it." His eyes dropped before his grandfather's shrewd study. They betrayed too much of the terrible rift of emotions he was feeling inside, that pull between love and loyalty. To ease it, he murmured, "Scotty's going to help push the land lease issue."

"Is he?" Kincaid knew a moment of surprise. The enmity between he and his daughter's half-breed bastard wasn't the sort that could lend to good deeds. It was Rory, of course, who'd coaxed it from him. The major felt a tug of regret. He'd held high hopes for Scott Prescott. His mind was razor-sharp, his instincts honed, his talent for serving the law powerful. If only he could have been bent to serve the Bar K. But no. He was too noble, too self-sacrificing, more concerned about a passel of blanket Indians than the survival of his family. Good

53

riddance. But Rory, too, had those same qualities, raw, untapped because of his youth. And he would shape them to the Bar K mold. Or he would break them. Garth Kincaid didn't like having other hands tampering with his creation. Especially not those of a Prescott. "You believe him?"

Rory glanced up, the comb pausing in mid-stroke. His reply was simple. "Yes."

"After all he's done to grind us under his heel, you think he'll prop us up in this?"

"He said so. An' that's enough for me." He went back to the firm ply of brush strokes through his horse's thick mane.

Kincaid saw the edge of testiness in the boy's stance. Ethan and Scott Prescott put it there and he cursed them silently. Aloud, he said, "You know, don't you, Rory, that your daddy and I have had our share of bad blood between us but we settled that a long time ago. Just like I want to get over this business with your brother. If he's willing to come halfway, I'll step in the other."

Rory's dark gaze flashed up, brimming with a grateful relief. It was his one frustrated wish to bring the people he loved and respected together. Dividing himself equally between them all was ripping away at the seams of his heart. "I'm right pleased to hear you say that, Major. I'm sure Scotty can be made to come around." Even if he had to beat him into it! If their grandfather was willing to put the ugliness of the past behind, he'd shove his brother forward to take his hand in truce.

"A lot of years ago, I had a dream," Kincaid began. "A dream of green grass high enough to shine a man's boots when he was atop the back of a

54

good-sized horse. Of cattle as far as the eye can see. It's a dream I want to pass down to you, if you want a share in it."

There was no hesitation. "You know I do."

"The Bar K is a part of the destiny of the Dakotas. It will live on far beyond small-sighted men like your father and bleeding hearts like your brother. Because there's strength in the land. But it takes strength to rule it. I'd hoped you had that kind of strength. Do you, Rory?"

"Yessir."

"The kind of strength that doesn't look right or left or make judgments of right or wrong?" He saw hesitation then—plenty of it. He held to his patience, taking his time to sew a good, tight, binding seam. "I've done things I'm not particularly proud of to keep this ranch running. I've made decisions that ripped my conscience raw and pulled my family apart. But I made them for the best interest of the Bar K. Your brother's efforts are a mere annoyance, like a black fly biting at the heels of something too big to bring down. What is going to cripple us, isn't men like him. What's killing us, is the lack of capital and the loss of range control. I've always been proud to take sole claim for keeping the Bar K running. And I'm proud of what you've put into it, boy. But to have staying power, to hold out for top market prices, we need access to capital. We need to take in an investor."

Rory stood still and silent. He was stunned by what he was hearing. The idea galled inside him, just as he knew it did inside his grandfather.

"I know I've always stood fast against letting go the reins but, Rory, a man does what he has to."

"Things that bad?" the younger man asked softly.

"Could be. And I'll take my humility down a notch before I'll surrender up one blade of Kincaid grass. Are you with me, boy?"

Rory chewed on his lip a second then, because there was no other answer he could give, he muttered, "Yessir."

"We'll have to go to Cheyenne and latch onto one of those damned aristocrats. They're always quick with cash. And when we have it in our hands and they're back all cozy in their castles, nothing will have changed."

Cheyenne. Rory heard the name and his insides tightened and twanged like a guitar string. Cheyenne, where Norah would be.

"I'll go," he was quick to offer.

Kincaid looked at him long and expressionlessly. "That brings me up to another hard decision I had to make today. I'm getting myself a new foreman for the Bar K."

Rory's jaw dropped. "What?"

The blanking devastation on the young man's face was all the answer he needed. He had no further question of where the boy's loyalties lay.

"Because I'm taking you on as full partner in the Bar K. Grab your gear and move on up into the big house. If you think you're ready. If you want it."

Rory sucked in a shuddering breath. "Sonuva . . . You mean it, Major? Hell yes, I want it!"

Garth Kincaid smiled. "To the future of the Bar K. Long may she rule the range and heaven help anyone who gets in her way." He put out his hand.

And Rory Prescott took it.

Chapter Four

The Mansard House, like its predecessor, the Cheyenne Club, sat proudly on the rough Wyoming prairie, a grand dame holding court. Its membership boasted the elite of the elite, the Who's Who of the livestock industry. It had weathered the Big Die Ups to the industry that shook the Cheyenne Club to its foundations because it was quicker to include upon its impressive roster the pseudo-Westerners; the new barons of the plains from titled English families and blooded Eastern stock. In order to overcome the humiliation of opening its ranks to foreigners, the Mansard clung tenaciously to its policy of snobbery where the true sons of the range were concerned. Its applicants were sponsored by members of long standing and their backgrounds thoroughly screened. An air of gentility was preserved in the richly paneled rooms by a strict code of behavior prohibiting wagering, smoking in the dining room, drunkenness to an offensive degree, profanity, boisterous noise, and ungentlemanly conduct. Nonmembers residing over fifty miles away could visit for seven days, not more than four times a year. And a small discreet proviso authorized members to take "persons" to their rooms when so disposed. All very proper and civilized.

Rory Prescott didn't care a hoot about the proper as he stood at the double doors leading to the Mansard's elegant social rooms. His gaze was anxiously roving the guests crowded into the vaulted parlors, searching for one single shining jewel set in the glittery crown of society. His heart was pounding. His palms were damp. And scurrying around inside his head was the panicked fear that maybe once he saw Miss Norah Denby again, the same magic wouldn't be there. What if she wasn't at all what he remembered in the hot nighttime thoughts that had kept him awake since Deadwood?

What if she wasn't happy to see him?

What if she didn't remember him!

"Good evening, sir."

Rory shot a quick, impatient glance toward the gentleman possessed of the desert-dry tones. " 'Evening."

"Might I be of some assistance, Mister—?"

"Prescott. I'm looking to find a Miss Norah Denby. She and her daddy are in there with the other folks. I was just fixing to join 'em." He took a step forward only to find an immaculate hand making a tentative barrier against his shirtfront.

"I am sorry, sir but I cannot allow that."

Rory could have easily moved the little fellow out of his way but he decided to be obliging. "I'm sorry, Mister—?"

"Cedric, sir."

"Mr. Cedric. Guess you didn't realize that I'm a-staying here for the week."

"Just Cedric, sir. And you must not be aware that our guests are required to maintain proper dress for the evenings."

Rory blushed. His features heated to match the

58

flaming color of his hair. And he stammered with the utmost mortification, "Well, Mr. — ah, Cedric, I means to tell you, t'weren't my intention to shuck anything off. I just want to talk to the lady."

To his credit, a genuine smile quirked the corners of the majordomo's dourly set mouth. "What I meant to say, sir, is that we require our guests to assume correct clothing while in the social function areas."

"Oh." He sounded vastly relieved by that news. He cast an assessing glance downward. His shirt was new, a gleaming white against his sun-swarthy skin where it lay opened at the neck. His dark coat had been borrowed from his father. He and Ethan were alike enough in size for the fit to be close along his broad shoulders and tailored down to hug at narrow hips. His denims weren't new but they were freshly laundered. And no one could fault his boots. Upon looking down, his face was reflected up in their glossy shine. Even the Stetson crunched in one hand was brushed to soft perfection. "Somethin' wrong with what I got on?"

Then he looked closer at the other male guests within the parlor and he frowned with an unpleasant understanding.

"You mean to say if I want to go in, I have to gussy myself up in one of them white broad fronted shirts and silly suits and parade around like a fatted Hereford?"

Cedric's smile cracked wider but he clung to the dignity of his reply. "I'm afraid that's exactly what I'm saying."

"Well, I ain't gonna do it!"

"Then I ain't going to let you go in," the stuffy little man drawled.

"And you the feller what's gonna stop me?"

59

Cedric Beaumont looked up, way up, at the sturdy cowboy and swallowed hard. His voice was faint but unfaltering. "Yes, sir, Mr. Prescott. I am." Then he sucked a quick breath and held it, waiting to be pummeled flat by one of the young man's massive fists.

But Rory grinned at the little man's desperate bravado. "Well, hell, if you have to, you have to. It ain't your fault that this place's rules were made for prissy idiots."

Cedric's breath rattled from him. "No, sir. Thank you, sir."

Just then, Rory saw her. What a fool he'd been to doubt the power of his memory. He stood, fixed to the spot with a wondrous sort of fascination and nearly strangled on his awe.

"Is that the lady in question?"

Rory managed a nod. Speech was impossible with his heart crowding his throat and beating there with a choking thunder.

"Might I say she is very lovely, sir," Cedric murmured softly. Now he could understand the brash cowboy's eagerness as he stood towering over him, humbled by the blatant emotion melting in his gaze. The comely Miss Denby would do the same to any man with eyes to see.

"You might," Rory agreed hoarsely.

As he watched from the doorway, barred from her side, Norah was approached by a dapperly clad gentleman with a cap of golden curls and a silky smile. He said something that made her turn his way. She smiled, took his arm and laughed in response.

And a freight train of jealous fury tore through Rory's chest.

Supportive of unrequited love, Cedric was moved by the younger man's despair. Enough to offer,

60

"Might I suggest you send the lady a token to let her know you've arrived. I would be more than happy to take it to her."

"Would you? That'd be right nice of you, Cedric. A token?" His brow crowded with uncertainty.

"Your card, perhaps?"

"I don't got one of those." He thought frantically for a moment, eyes tortured by the sight of his Miss Norah being squired by the preening polecat. Most likely the Mansard House would consider his putting a bullet in the man as ungentlemanly behavior. Then he saw the potted palms flanking the door.

"Here. Give her this."

Cedric looked down at his hand and pursed his lips with displeasure. "Dirt, sir?"

Rory snatched a goblet from a passing tray and wet the potting soil. "Mud," he corrected.

"Very good, sir," the very proper servant muttered, not attempting to make sense of it.

Charles Monthaven wasn't bad company. He was handsome. He was wealthy. He had the impressive stiffening of generations of English lords and ladies behind him to add starch to his unbending carriage. Perhaps it was the thinness of that royal blue blood that had Norah ready to scream with boredom.

Charles had been consistent in his court since their meeting two nights prior. And Cole couldn't have been happier. The Englishman, it seemed, was enamored of the West and was looking to buy into a piece of it for his own amusement. And Cole Denby was more than eager to be of service. He'd fairly flung Norah at him and ordered her to stick tight. Hardly difficult since the sultry-eyed lord seemed disinclined to let her wander far enough from his side to draw a decent breath. So far, he'd been the perfect gentleman. She couldn't complain of his behavior. Nor could she truly find fault with him in any area. Quite simply, he was the catch most women would die for. So why was she simply dying to escape?

For hours, she'd been holding to the practiced smile and nodding to anecdotes of Queen and country while pretending not to notice the increasing intimacy in the way Monthaven's fingers caressed her arm. She pretended not to care that the proper gentleman angled himself slightly behind her so he might have an unrestricted view down the shadowed valley of her bosom. Impatient with his well-bred ogling and squirming beneath Cole's encouraging stare, there seemed no way to flee the situation gracefully.

It was during a thankful respite as Monthaven was fetching her a glass of champagne that Norah was approached by a somber-faced servant.

"Excuse me, madam. A gentleman bade me to convey his regards."

Norah almost sighed her aggravation aloud. Another gentleman. Heaven save her from another pedigreed pursuer. But she forced an attitude of mild interest. "Does the gentleman have a name?"

"He instructed me to give you *this*."

Norah stared down at the lump of damp soil in the man's hand. For a moment, she frowned in bewilderment. Then a delightful rush of significance arose. In a breathless little voice, she demanded, "Was this gentleman—Was he—" How to describe Rory Prescott with tactful diplomacy? But the droll messenger needed no adjectives.

"Yes, madame, he was. Very."

Norah's head jerked up. Bright eyes scanned the

crowd of unimportant faces. "Where is he?"

"I believe he intended to wait for a reply out in the foyer. And what would the lady like me to tell him?"

"I'll tell him myself."

The stuffy little man cleared his throat. "And what would you like me to do with this?" He deferred to the mud in his hand with a distasteful cant of his eyes.

The beautiful young woman surprised him with a quick, flashing grin. "I'll take it." She scooped it from his palm and clutched it tight in one dainty hand. Almost as an annoyed afterthought, she asked, "Would you mind telling the gentleman I was with that I had to—" Norah groped for an excuse.

"Powder your nose?" Cedric suggested helpfully.

"Yes."

"It would be my extreme pleasure, madame." Then he allowed himself an undignified grin as the lady hurried toward the hall.

Realizing that she was almost running through the tightly pressed gathering, Norah made herself slow to a restrained walk. It was hard. Especially when her heart was racing all out of control. Rory Prescott. The last person she'd expected to ever see again. And the swell of anticipation inside her was frighteningly intense. Just like his kisses. But was it the kisses that brought him to Wyoming?

Or was it the five hundred dollars?

Her fist clenched about the earth she held. Why had Rory Prescott come to see her? For a reunion? Or for restitution? She struggled to check her eagerness with a degree of caution. Five hundred dollars to a ranch hand was a fortune, a life's savings. Guilt, the same guilt that had been torturing her with merciless regularity since she'd allowed Cole to bilk the cash from his pockets, seized tight within her breast. How could she face him now that he knew? How could she stand to see the warm admiration in his gaze harden to a cold suspicion? Logic told her to seek Cole's guidance. He'd taken care of hundreds like Rory Prescott. He would know what to do. But that meant surrendering up the unexpected pleasure of seeing him herself.

She was moving forward again, hardly aware of making a conscious decision. When she searched the elegant lobby and found it empty, her disappointment was a palpable pain. Then, through one of the side windows, framed against the dimming sky, she saw the silhouette of wide shoulders and Stetson hat. And the beat of her heart ran rampant all over again.

Whether he heard her quiet approach or smelled her delicate scent on the cool night air, he knew she was there and slowly turned. Norah stopped where she was, stunned by the strength of her emotions. She couldn't remember the last time she was ever glad to see anyone. But having Rory Prescott greet her with a half-shy, half-sly, simmering smile pumped a surge of elation through her second to none. Like finding friend, family and lover all in one when he had no real claim to any of them.

For a time, they stood in silence, taking the measure of one another by slow, appreciative degrees. Even scrubbed and laundered, Rory Prescott looked fresh off the range. It was the raw, rugged ease in his stance. Norah couldn't help comparing it to the pallid poseurs from inside. There was nothing pretentious about the young cowboy. Everything he was was right there for her inspection. Big, tanned, weather-roughened, crudely educated, dangerous and vulnerable all in one handsome package. Not what she'd look for in

64

a suitor but everything she dreamed of in a man. If she stepped closer, she knew she wouldn't be assaulted by the odor of cloying spice or floral or fruit. He would smell faintly of leather and gun oil and horse. Manly and potently virile. And a shiver of excitement weakened her grip on her composure. As his smile leisurely stretched wide and white in unabashed welcome, it would have been a simple and natural thing to move into his arms in hopes of one of those scorching kisses. But she held herself back, waiting, wary and unexpectedly ashamed.

"Howdy, Miss Norah." With that low, husky greeting, he swept off his hat.

"Hello, Mr. Prescott."

He stood, smiling, smoldering, looking at her through hungry eyes. For some reason that honest evidence of want was not as offensive as Charles Monthaven's subtle leering. She felt the stirrings of response tongue through her with scalding little laps of desire. She had to say something before she gave in to the tremendous pull of need.

She opened her hand, palm up, to display the drying clumps of dirt. "Quite a calling card."

Rory's smile flirted through his dark eyes. "I was hoping it would be memorable."

Memorable? Norah detailed the curve of his mouth with her gaze. Oh, yes.

"Was I intruding on something?" he asked politely when what he wanted to demand was, *Who was that feller and what's he to you?*

"No." She couldn't get any plainer than that. "Just socializing while my father conducts his business."

Norah was aware of how those words hung between them. Now he would bring up the five hundred dollars and she would have to think of something to tell him. What could she say? The truth? *Cole got me to dazzle you to the point where you didn't know he was stealing from you. I didn't mean for it to happen that way when we met because I really liked you. I'm sorry you're out the money but there's nothing I can do about it now?* Or a silky lie? She was better at those and there was a chance he would believe her. Or she could go to Cole with the threat of Rory Prescott and he would make the young cowboy mysteriously disappear. None of these options settled the need inside her to make right the wrong she'd done him. She was crazy to meet him alone like this where if he chose to, he could exact his retribution most forcibly. But oddly, she wasn't afraid. Her anxiousness had nothing to do with the fear of personal harm. She cringed beneath the thought of his contempt.

But it wasn't there.

And neither did he bring up the subject of the money.

"I'm here on business, too," he told her with the awkward scuff of his boot toes on porch boards. He seemed intent on studying the swagged hem of her pale blue evening gown. "I'll be staying on for a week and I was . . . What I was wondering was . . . I'd really like to spend some time with you. If you'd be of a mind to, that is. Maybe dinner tomorrow night." He looked up hopefully. She was engaged by the way he could appear both boyishly uncertain and full of searingly male confidence. What she felt at the receiving end of his easy smile warmed her. What she saw in his steeping stare sent a shuddering shock wave through her.

"I'm sorry," she began with genuine regret. "I have plans for dinner."

"With that there fancy feller?" The tartness of his

tone was unexpected. And surprisingly sweet.

"Yes. And my father. They're concluding some business together."

"Oh." His big shoulders slumped and he looked at a loss.

"But I have nothing planned for the morning," she offered up.

Rory's brows soared. "Morning? I thought . . . I thought ladies weren't much inclined to be up and about before noon."

"Not this lady, Mr. Prescott. Is eight too early for you?"

He grinned. "No, ma'am."

"What did you have in mind?"

Taken off guard by the question, he blushed hot. "Beg your pardon?" he stammered. Norah had a very good idea of what thoughts caused him to go so red. And she wasn't in the least bit insulted.

"What would you like to do tomorrow morning?" she restated.

"Oh. I—I don't know. We could go for a drive or something. If you're partial to the outdoors, that is." He considered her buttermilk soft complexion and wondered if that was such a good idea.

"Mr. Prescott, I spend the better part of my waking hours in stuffy, cigar-scented parlors listening to men wheel and deal. If I didn't look out a window occasionally, I might forget the sun still shone. I would like nothing more than to breathe clean air and soak up a little unclouded sky." With you.

"I'll have a buggy waiting."

Norah smiled suddenly. "No. I have a better idea. I'll take care of it." She looked reluctantly toward the inside of the exclusive cattle club and gave a soft sigh. "I'd better get back."

Before he could stop himself, Rory took a quick step forward, closing the distance between them. The proximity made Norah snap to rigid attention. Not out of objection. Rather out of want. He was too close, too easily in reach. And she wanted to touch him, to feel the hard cording of his arms, to taste the wild, sweet passion in his kiss. The temptation was so great, she trembled. She wouldn't have resisted. He knew it. But he chose not to act on it.

Very gently, Rory lifted her hand in the warm curl of his fingers and carried it to his lips for just the briefest brush. And then, he strode away, fast. As if trying to outrun the urge to abandon all control. He was still shaking with it when he encountered Cedric in the lobby.

"Did your lady find you, sir?" the little man inquired knowingly.

"Yessir, she surely did."

And then he followed Cedric's look to where the lady whispered in from their outside rendezvous. She paused at the sight of him and from across the length of the room the heat of longing flared hot. Then, she seemed to shake it off, donning her air of cool reserve the way she would a lacy shawl before continuing into the parlor. Where her fancy beau waited. Excluded from her company, Rory gave a frustrated sigh.

"If you would like to join her, sir, I could always look the other way."

"That's right kind of you to offer, Cedric but I wouldn't want you to go getting into no trouble."

He was about to claim it was no trouble at all when the cowboy shook his head.

"I don't fit in with that fat, grain-fed herd. I'd stick out like a rangy ole longhorn." He turned away from the open double doors and the temptation from within. "Cedric, you got something around this place to wet a man's whistle?"

"We have an excellent wine vault, sir." He paused, making note of the cowboy's puckered response, and then he offered, "Or I could procure a Scotch you'd find smooth as a baby's behind."

"Now that sounds right inviting. You join me in tipping a few?"

"I'm sorry, sir. I'm on duty."

The redhead nodded glumly. Drinking alone held no great charm. And here in this fine building, with the cream of Western society under its slated roof, he felt very alone. Give him a group of rowdy cowhands and easy laughter over the stiff formality of the Mansard's parlor any day.

"Another time, Mr. Prescott?" the small majordomo suggested, feeling the other's unhappy isolation.

"Sure, Cedric."

In the solitude of his grand walnut and marble furnished room, Rory opened the bottle. After a moment of marveling over the electric lights by switching them on and off, astounded time and again by the even glow, he ambled toward the private bath. Turning the brass spigots on high, he set the bottle on the floor and stripped down to the skin. He folded up each piece of clothing with uncharacteristic care, quirking a smile at his own naïveté. Maintain proper dress, indeed. To hell with that, he snorted.

With a long, shaky draw of breath, he eased his big frame into the hot water. Then sighed. It wasn't so bad, this taking a bath on a weekday. Felt right nice, actually. Hat tipped down over his eyes, he picked up the bottle of whiskey and settled in for a leisurely soak and heated thoughts of Norah Denby.

* * *

"Where have you been?"

Cole's voice was low and sharp, like the snap of a leather strap against the unprotected back of the leg. Norah flinched. Then she turned a chill glance upon him.

"Out taking some air. Do you mind?"

Ignoring her icy drawl, Cole nodded across the room. "I don't, but he might."

Norah followed his gesture to Charles Monthaven who was pacing the length of the hors d'oeuvre table with a restless but very proper lack of patience. And suddenly, Norah lost hers.

"You entertain him then. I'm going to bed."

The pinch of his fingers on her arm held her fast at his side. Her gray eyes grew glacial as they stared at his offending hand.

"Unless you would like me to make a scene, I suggest you let me go. Right now." The grip slackened and she eased away. "Thank you. Don't forget. You don't own me, Cole. I come and go as I please and it pleases me to go."

Cole scowled, then arranged his suave features into composed lines for the sake of those who might be watching. "Don't play with me, Norah. I don't like it."

"I wouldn't play with you, Cole. We both know how unconstructive that is." His pale eyes glimmered dangerously, forcing her to wisely relent. She sighed in resignation. "I'm tired, Cole. As you can see, I'm not fit company. You wouldn't want me to ruin things with a careless word, now would you?"

He gauged her closely, with cautious eyes. She did look wan and her tongue was honed to cutting sharpness. No, that wouldn't do. "Go to bed, Norah. I'll tantalize his lordship with what he can expect tomorrow once our business is concluded."

70

"Just don't let him expect more than I'll deliver."

Cole chuckled and squeezed her chin gently. "You are in fine form this evening, my dear. Why, I wonder?"

A bland smile masked her alarm. "Good night, Father. Give my regrets to his lordship." With that, she was quick to leave the too all-seeing presence of Cole Denby.

It was a two block walk to their own hotel. Norah was in no hurry. The night felt good, calming, and she needed that calm. Rory Prescott had shaken her from it.

Why had he come back?

I love you.

No. That wasn't the reason. She didn't want it to be the reason. Emotions like that created complications she couldn't afford. The last thing she wanted was for the young cowboy to love her.

So why was she encouraging him?

It was dangerous. It was reckless. It was totally unlike her. She could be courting disaster along with that wide, wicked smile. And she didn't care. That was the most frightening fact of all. When caution should have served her, she found she was all too willing to cast it aside. For what? A fling with a virile ranch hand? Sex. Was that what it was all about? No. That was too simple. And what she was feeling inside was far from simple. If it was simple lust, she would have gone upstairs with him and flushed it from her system. No, the physical attraction was just a part of it. A very exciting, very enticing part. But not the whole truth.

She liked him.

She just plain liked Rory Prescott. And the genuine warmth of that emotion had staggered her. He stirred

71

up a host of conflicting feelings when he was near. A wistful want to be what he saw through those dark, dreamy eyes. A need to laugh, to experience joy inside where a chill anger had dwelt for far too long. A deep, desperate desire to feel loved. That was his appeal. He made her want to reach out for what she'd banished from her life, to touch another honestly, caringly. He brought a freshness back into her. Rory Prescott was a teasing spring breeze after barren years of winter and she wanted to let down her hair to capture the sensation of him blowing warm and wonderfully free against her.

Norah drew up her shawl as the first cool patters of rain began to fall but didn't increase her stride.

She wanted him to kiss her again.

For that, she was willing to consider the unthinkable. And the more she thought, the more she liked the idea. Later, she would probably see it as madness. Cole would never understand why it was so important. She wasn't sure she understood it, either. But it felt right. It felt good. And she found herself smiling with anticipation.

First thing in the morning, she would draw five hundred dollars from her own account and give it back to Rory Prescott.

Chapter Five

The twentieth century!

Rory had succumbed to its fascination since his arrival at the Mansard House. Electric lights ablaze with a touch. The strange contraption called the telephone that carried a voice across the wires with the ease of the telegraph. But his amazement with those things could no way compare with his stunned discovery of how Norah Denby planned to take their ride in the country.

He came down off the porch in a daze of excitement to where it perched with a regal air, its fragile pneumatic tires caked with last night's mud. Slowly, as if it was some ill-tempered beast that would charge without warning, Rory circled, putting out his hand to touch the smooth metal. His breath gushed out in awe. He'd read about them, seen pictures and shared a good laugh with the bunkhouse boys over those who said this spindly bucket of gears and bolts would replace the horse. But face to face with the brand new motorcar, he lost a goodly degree of his mocking humor. Staring at it through wide eyes, he saw the future. And he liked it. Both the motorized buggy and the woman at its helm.

Norah sat comfortably in the driver's spot on the

right side of the high seat, her fashionable attire amended by a wide sash securing her straw hat beneath her chin in a big yellow bow. She enjoyed every moment of Rory's childlike wonder, feeling it quicken within her own breast in response. She beamed at him when he finally tore his gaze from the oil sidelamps to regard her with a grin.

"Ready for that ride?"

"Hot damn! You bet. What do you have to do to get it started?"

"Grab that crank down there in front and start turning until the motor catches."

That sounded easier than it proved to be. Rory's enthusiasm gave way to an earnest sweat as he heaved mightily on the lever. Finally, when his grin had become a grimace, the engine gave a series of spluttering gasps and chugged powerfully. He leaped back out of the way as if expecting it to lunge at him. Then he grinned all over again.

"Ain't that something! Now what?"

"Climb on up. Let's go for that ride."

As cautious as if he was mounting a bronc, Rory eased up into the hard seat at Norah's side. He licked his lips in a nervous anticipation, eyes glowing bright.

"Hang on tight. She tends to kick like a mule at first."

He'd barely time to comply when Norah finished tinkering with the levers to adjust idling speed and kicked out the clutch. A spine-shattering vibration rattled through the metal components as she pushed the gear lever into low, released the clutch and sent them bounding away in a series of jackrabbit jerks up the muddy streets of Cheyenne.

Fortunately, the early hour meant few rivals for the

road. What horses were out on the street bawled and balked in white-eyed terror as the horseless carriage puttered by with Norah at the steering tiller. Rory sat braced and white-knuckled at her side. He clutched at his hat as they bumped along at a gusty twenty miles per hour until the buildings grew sparse and finally the countryside spread out before them. By then, he'd determined that he wasn't going to be thrown and let the tension ebb from his limbs to enjoy the filtering breeze on his face and the lovely woman at his side.

It was warm. The sun was just beginning to dry patches of the road to a baked surface, making the air steamy. Norah felt flushed. Her high, choking satin collar was already wilting and her bodice and long tight sleeves stuck unpleasantly to her skin. But it wasn't the atmosphere making her overly warm. It was the company. The way his Levi Strauss's rubbed her thigh to the rhythm of the road. The way his arm circled behind her on the seat so that her back was constantly brushed by his thumb. The way his low, drawling voice gabbed on and on about things she could hardly focus upon as the feeling inside her continued to swell. She had to do something before the sensations burst.

"Do you want to drive?"

"What?" Rory's eyes grew round and glassy.

She slowed the vehicle into a rocking idle and turned to the suddenly stricken cowboy. "It's not hard. I can show you. Afraid of trading one horse in for five?"

Her light teasing brought the cocky bravado back into his manner. "Honey, there ain't nothing this here contraption can do with five horses that I can't do better on one."

The challenge was unbearable. And so was his handsome arrogance. It provoked her beyond what was cautious and proper. To what she'd been thinking of since she'd seen the mud in the stuffy majordomo's hand. Impulsively, she acted, unable to let another second go by with the terrible tension quavering between them.

"I can think of one thing," she told him in a daring invitation.

"What's that?" he was quick to enjoin.

Because he didn't suspect a thing, he was leaning close, a smile of friendly smugness upon his face. It was a simple matter to shift on the seat, to bring her lips up to press upon his. His mouth immediately slackened with surprise but to his credit, he agilely overcame it to engage hers in a skillful interplay. The hand resting idle behind her moved up to splay wide on the small of her back, not to impel her forward but to offer a firm support. His other rose to curve around the softness of her cheek, caressing, guiding the angle of her head to compliment the slant of his own. She kept her hands like leadened weights in her lap, afraid that if she touched him, her fingers would be drawn irrevocably to his shirt buttons. And things couldn't be allowed to go so far. Just a kiss. That's all it could be.

It was a hellish delight for Rory. He struggled to relay all the tenderness filling his chest without indulging the desire crowding his jeans. The unexpected kiss was a test of his resolve to act the gentleman with her. But how could he tempt her with the mating flickers of his tongue without wanting, wildly, desperately, to do the same with his ever-thickening body between the silken spread of her legs? He was dying to be inside her. The need was a prodding

76

ache. And she would let him. He knew it, instinctively from the way she encouraged—no, pursued him. But not here. Not yet. He wanted more from her first. More . . . he wasn't sure what. Having taken all the sweet torment he could from her luscious lips, he pulled away.

And because he did, something tremendous moved within Norah's heart. It was as if he knew she was weak and was depending upon him to be stronger. And he didn't fail her, even though he wanted to. For the second time, he could have pressed the advantage he held over her unwise passions. And for the second time, he stood firm against it. My God, what special manner of a man was Rory Prescott? And in that instant, she almost wished he would have pushed beyond the proper just so she could safely relegate him with the pawing others who'd sought her favor. But his restraint made him dangerous, more dangerous than she'd ever imagined. Because it made her like him that much more.

Rory licked his lips, savoring the taste of her upon them, before murmuring with a will-shattering huskiness, "Sweet darlin', someday I'm going to show you exactly what I can do in the saddle." With that sultry double meaning hanging between them, he vaulted from the motorcar and walked around to the driver's side.

Norah sat paralyzed with hot longing. Would he? Would he someday do exactly that? No. It was impossible. And knowing that made some of the joy within her crumple. Wordlessly, without looking at him, she scooted over, feeling him settle heavy and solidly male beside her. A simple kiss. How very foolish of her to think so. Not from Rory Prescott.

"All right," he announced with an edgy excitement.

"I got the reins. I reckon there's more to it than a 'giddyap'."

He was waiting, patiently pretending the kiss hadn't happened. So she would, too. Smiling narrowly, she positioned his feet and hands, instructing as she did, the steps necessary to coax the metal beast into motion.

"You need a delicate touch to shift without grinding and clashing the teeth off the gears. Real easy. Real gentle now, the way you'd treat a woman."

What a thing to say to him! If her hands over his hadn't forced her into nearly intimate proximity, she would have withdrawn in embarrassment. Until his dark eyes turned to hers, steeped in promise.

"I will be."

And a frantic shudder shook through her.

Taking a deep breath to restore her composure, Norah looked down at their hands; his so big and brown beneath her small slender fingers. Would those hands be gentle? Yes. She knew they would be. In a strained little whisper, she urged, "All right, Rory. Let out the clutch and shift into low gear."

The vehicle spouted strange staccato noises, then trembled into a jerky forward motion. Rory gave a delighted laugh then a loud, "Whooee." Charmed by his boyish pleasure, Norah was able to relax her tense posture and have fun. Fun! Lord, how long it had been since she'd had fun. And laughter. Ridiculous, side-clutching laughter. It felt wonderful, freeing. And she could have kissed him gratefully for reanimating her spirit. Instead, she just watched him, soaking up the playful shifts of his expression with a lighthearted wonder. Her arm found its way along the back of the seat and the wisps of red hair straying over his collar were too tempting to ignore. Soft as she remembered it to be, she marveled, combing it lightly with her fingers beneath the shading tip of his hat brim.

It was a slight, fleeting touch but more than enough to distract Rory from the road. Their gazes locked for a long, seeking moment. The pull was strong and vital. Passions throbbed in time to the pulsing motor. Norah's fingers stilled then curved around the back of Rory's neck, urging him to lean toward her and she—

"Rory, look out!"

The tree loomed up in front of them. In his inexperience, Rory did all the wrong things too quickly for Norah to correct them. Skinny tires skidded in the muddy furrows on the edge of the road. The back end fishtailed. The front popped up onto the grassy shoulder and hit with abrupt stopping power against the trunk of the small sapling.

Rory's first move was to see to Norah's safety. His arms were stalwart supports about her. "Are you all right?"

Straightening her bonnet, she answered, "I think so. You?"

"Shook my liver loose. That would never have happened with a horse."

"Oh no," Norah wailed as she beheld the steaming front of the car. "Cole's going to kill me!"

"This your daddy's motorcar? I hope he knew you were fixing to take it." Her stricken gaze made him frown. "Well, let's see if we can get it straightened up some."

He hopped down to examine the front end. When he looked up at her, it wasn't with an optimistic view. "The thingamajig you turn is busted clean off. Will it start back up without it?"

79

Norah shook her head glumly.

"I'm plumb sorry about this. I ain't used to the things I'm riding on running me square into trees. I'll pay for whatever ails it. You jus' make yourself comfortable there and I'll walk on back to town to get some help. A wagon and team'll have it towed out in a jiffy."

Norah sighed. There was no help for it. What was done, was done. Cole would be furious enough to find she'd taken his precious, attention-getting toy, let alone to discover it had been demolished at the hands of her cowboy friend. But that was back in Cheyenne and she had no intention of forfeiting the rest of the morning in apprehensive terror. Not alone, anyway.

"I'm coming with you."

His heavy brows arced up in the center. "Miss Norah, it's better than a ten mile walk back into town."

"I can walk as well or better than you can drive. Besides, someone's bound to pass us along the way." She extended her hands to him, waiting imperiously until he came around to assist her from the high seat. Then, with her narrow shoes set on hard-packed ground, she looked resolutely toward town. She could feel her feet aching but would rely upon her pride to carry her the distance. When she lifted her beaded bag from the seat, its bulkiness reminded her of its contents.

"Before we start out, I have something for you."

Rory looked down at the wad of currency she pressed upon him. "What's this?" There was a whole lot of money. It looked to be about . . . five hundred dollars? His dark gaze came up to hers in question.

"Your investment," she explained. "Father never

80

had a chance to put it into Royale-Standard. It seems they went out of business rather suddenly."

"I know."

That quiet claim threw her for a long minute. Then she asked, "Why didn't you say something last night?"

"I was waiting for you to bring it up."

Norah studied his features. Before she'd thought them ruggedly handsome yet quite innocent. Now she could discern a deeper layer. Of doubt and suspicion? She didn't think so. More like a shrewd patience. He was waiting to see if she'd tell him the truth. Or at least a believable version of it. That disturbed her more than if he'd come straight out with a demand, that image of him laying in wait like a cougar on a branch, watching for her to make a wrong move before springing with lethal consequence.

Rory Prescott wasn't stupid and she wouldn't be able to fool him forever.

"He didn't want to reinvest it in something else until he had the chance to speak to you. He was going to telegraph before we left Cheyenne."

"That so." It wasn't exactly a question. Nor was it a challenge. Just a calm observation that made her uncomfortably aware that she couldn't read him as easily as she'd first suspected.

"Yes," she concluded rather tersely. Her chin angled up combatantly.

"Thank you," was all he said as he stuffed the money into his pant's pocket. "I'll use it to take my brother out to dinner. See if they can serve up some fillet of boot sole for him to chew on." He grinned to himself, then offered his arm. "Miss Norah, shall we?"

She took it in a testy humor and they began to walk. After about a half mile, his hand slid downward until his fingers laced through hers. She didn't pull away. There was something strong and satisfying in the clasp of his warm, rough hand. Hers tightened imperceptibly.

About a mile later, one of the heels of her fine Eastern leather shoes broke away. She tried gamely to hobble then exclaimed in disgust at her hopeless situation. Finally, she spied a boulder and dropped upon it to begin unhooking both shoes. Rory got a good look at her slender calves and at the fabric hugging them. Silk. Pure, glimmering silk. His mouth went dry.

Damaged footgear tossed unceremoniously away, Norah firmed her lips and looked once more in the direction of Cheyenne.

"I could carry you," Rory suggested suddenly. "Heck, you wouldn't weigh no more than a calf. Wouldn't be no problem."

Norah sniffed at that as she stood in stocking feet. Not that she didn't think he could do it. He was a big, obviously brawny man. It was the idea of being coddled close to his all too inviting chest with the feel of his arms curled tight about her that had her rebelling against the offer.

"Mr. Prescott, if I desire to be swept off my feet and carried away by a man, it will not be on some muddy road to Cheyenne."

Grinning softly, he reached out to tuck up a loose strand of hair that had escaped its careful pinning. His hand lingered there, thumb sketching the whorl of her ear, fingertips testing the flustered pulsebeats along her warm neck. His dark stare simmered invitingly.

"Where's it gonna be, Norah?"

A chill of inevitability prickled along her soul. As if she had no choice in the matter. Rory Prescott was going to calmly, determinedly, burrow under the walls of reserve that had survived the battering of countless others. It was an attack she had no defense against. And suddenly she saw what a terrible mistake she'd made by thinking herself safe with him. She'd been protecting the wrong thing. It wasn't her virtue that was in danger. It was her heart.

The approach of a lumbering farmer's wagon spared her from making a response. Rory snatched off his hat and waved the fellow down, giving her a momentary reprieve from his attention. After hearing their plight, the farmer was willing to take them into Cheyenne. Rory hoisted Norah up onto the seat beside the burly homesteader. His hand lingered a bit longer than proper upon the smooth silk of one shapely calf. It felt as good as he remembered in that long ago hazy dream. Then, when she snapped her skirt down, he merely grinned and ambled around to the back to ride on the tail gate with the man's slobbery dog and stacks of fresh produce.

She was so preoccupied by the knowledge of Rory Prescott seated behind her down that bumpy road into town, Norah completely forgot about Cole Denby and his treasured motorcar. Until they rolled down the main street and she saw him standing, arms akimbo, on the porch of their hotel. His features were inscrutable. That told her nothing. He wouldn't display it upon his face if he was ready to come after her with a scatter gun. She glanced back over her shoulder to see him following the progress of their wagon along the sidewalk to where it stopped before the large mercantile. She was quick to leap down

83

from the box unaided and came around to where Rory sat with his lap full of shaggy, smelly dog.

"I've got to go explain things to my father," she told him tonelessly.

Rory looked beyond her to where Cole Denby was bearing down fast. Then he searched her lovely face for signs of worry. "I'll talk to him."

"No!" At his frown, she softened her tone and smiled. "Better it come from me."

He shoved the dog over and stood, towering above her in a way that made her want more than anything to trust him with her troubles. But that was quite impossible. No man was as strong as all that.

"You sure you'll be all right?"

"Fine. Father will be angry but he'll get over it. He always does."

"Then you talk to him and I'll go down to the livery and make arrangements for someone to go fetch his buggy back. Don't let him go a-blaming you too much now, you hear?"

"I've got to go." Then, impulsively, she put her hand to one warm cheek and gently kissed the other. She came down from her toes smiling. "And thank you, Rory, for the best time I can ever remember, unscheduled stop and all."

Then she was hurrying across the street, her hem held up out of the mud and her silk stockings black with it.

"Where the hell have you been?" Cole started in on her in a low, chill voice. Her first thought was that he didn't know about the car. "And what were you doing with him?" He jerked an impatient nod toward the redheaded cowboy.

"Out for a morning ride. Why? Did you miss me?" Norah started into the hotel, her regal bearing besmirched by the dirty track of her feet on the tiled floor.

"Not me. His lordship. Apparently you forgot all about an arrangement you made with him to share champagne for breakfast. He was not at all amused to find you gone. Nor was I."

Norah cursed silently. She had forgotten. Rory Prescott had a way of sucking things right out of her thoughts and supplanting them with his own image. "I'm sorry. I'll make it up to him tonight."

"Damned right you will. We need to have a talk, Norah. Now."

She was on her way up the wide stairs, leaving her own mark upon the brightly patterned carpet. "Not now, Cole. I'm hot, I'm dirty and my clothes are ruined."

"From a lustful rendezvous with your cowboy lover?" he sneered in a careful sotto voce. It wasn't something he'd want another to overhear.

"If you want to believe so," she returned. She didn't honor him with a glance, hurrying now. However, he kept pace.

"What's he doing here anyway? Come to whine about getting his precious pennies back?"

"I repaid him the five hundred. He thinks it's due to your munificence so don't forget to crow humbly."

"Repaid him." That notion stunned him so badly he came to a complete halt, then had to jog to catch up to her again as she rounded the second landing. "You gave it back?" His outrage echoed through the stairwell.

"It was my money, not yours so you don't need to go on so about it." She slipped the key into her door and despite her best effort to keep him out, Cole pushed his way in to pace and fume.

"What is wrong with you? Norah, I don't understand this at all. What could you possibly see in him, beyond the obvious? If you need a man that badly . . ." He reached out to run long, sensitive fingers beneath one ripe breast. "I haven't forgotten how good things once were between us."

"They were never all that good," she snapped, placing herself quickly out of his range. "What I do is my business. Who I do it with is my business. I thought we settled this a long time ago."

"Yes, but back then you weren't beset by this particular insanity. Lusting after a range hand with the intelligence of a half-green squash. And it isn't your business, not when it interferes with ours. I want it stopped, Norah. Right now. You're wasting precious time and endangering a valuable investment. You have work to do where there's a profit to be made. If you have an insatiable itch between your legs, scratch it where there's the greatest return."

Norah stood silent, white with fury while he continued on with merciless fervor.

"Monthaven wants you. He's taken a fancy to the way you twitch your skirts and bat your eyes. If you want to play games, play the best percentage. We've worked weeks to reel in someone like him. Don't you dare jeopardize it now. If he sees you with that no-account and discovers what a cheap little trollop you really are, do you think there's a chance we'll ever see a dime of his fortune? No. Not one thin dime. You're playing with my profits. And you are not going to play fast and loose. Is that understood?"

She said nothing. Her eyes glittered frostily as each of his words hit and hit hard. And she knew he was right. Damn him, he was right.

"Where's my motorcar?"

The change of subject came so quickly Norah had no chance to reach for a more palpable lie. "He—I hit a tree. A very little tree. There's not much damage. Rory's having it towed back so—"

Cole went very pale. He had waited months for delivery of that car and pampered it like a spoiled child. In his mind, it was the ultimate image of success; the one he wanted to portray, the one he wanted to claim. And now she'd dented that symbol. She and her cowboy.

"You'll make it up to me, Norah," he said with a soft menace. "Both to me and to his lordship. This deal will go through. And you will do everything in your power to guarantee it. Everything. Whatever Monthaven wants, he gets. Understand?"

Norah knew him well enough to fear his mood of deadly quiet, but she wouldn't let him know she was intimidated. She wouldn't cower, not before any man. No man would ever have that power over her. Rebellion sparked in her gaze and thinned her lips as she boldly stood her ground. "I will not—"

Her words gave to a painful yelp as Cole seized the back of her neck. "You careless little fool! Don't you realize that whores like you are thick for the taking? You ever, ever cross me again and I'll see you're on your back in the foulest, meanest crib I can find. And you'll be begging me for just a few of the fine things I've gotten for you. And what will your cowboy think then? When he can have you for two bits whenever he wants? Him and anyone else with the price."

A terrible screech tore from her lips, a sound so wounded, so fierce it would have horrified any other man. Norah came at him with fingers bent into claws but he'd anticipated her attack and easily caught her wrists.

87

"You bastard! I'm no whore! Don't you ever call me that!" The words spat from her as she writhed within his grip.

"You are whatever I tell you to be. Don't forget that again, Norah. Don't you forget it."

And he reminded her. Once. Hard. With the flat of his hand.

Chapter Six

Rory knocked, then waited for what seemed forever. Finally, the door gave a cautious few inches.

"Howdy, Miss Norah. It's me, Rory Prescott."

He'd expected that to open the way but the crack in the door shrank even farther until all he could see of her was one wary gray eye.

"What do you want?" Her voice was strangely muffled and thick sounding. And not at all welcoming.

"I come to tell you about the motorcar." He waited some more, hopefully, but there was no encouragement in her reply.

"Well? What about it?"

"I got it towed back to the livery. The feller there said he could fix the whatsit in front and bang out the dents so it'll be good as new. Said it'd take a week or so and that . . . Norah?"

As he spoke, she'd slackened her defense and the door crept open. Far enough for him to see the trails of wetness down her one pale cheek. That sight opened up a whole deep well of unbearable tenderness inside him.

"Norah-honey, what's wrong?"

89

He acted quickly, wedging his hand between door and jamb as she tried to slam it closed between them. The crunch of pain made him yell out and utter a vigorous oath.

"Norah, open up. You're breakin' my hand!"

The sound of his distress won out over her want of privacy. The pressure gone, Rory tucked his aching hand beneath his other arm with the tight whisper of several colorful curses. Then he pushed open the door with the toe of his boot and stepped inside. Norah had retreated to the center of the room and stood with a rigid back presented to him. Something was wrong. Uneasiness wriggled in his belly as her shoulders gave a slight hitch.

"Norah?"

She turned toward him then, her chin angled high, proudly, defiantly. The first thing he saw was the ugly welt marring her beauty. And he'd been in enough fights to know the mark of a hand when he saw one. The thought of someone — anyone — taking a hand to Norah Denby kindled a fury in him that rose up so quick and dark he was stunned by the violence of it.

Norah pressed her fingertips to the tender swelling beneath her left eye and smiled wryly. "He didn't take the news about the car as well as I'd hoped." She tried to make light of it but the slight quiver of her lower lip snapped Rory's stupor of surprise. He swooped down on her like an avenging angel. His big hands cradled her face between them as he examined the mark through angry, anguished eyes.

"That sonuva — Your daddy did this to you?" When his thumb brushed over the discoloration, she winced. And that was all it took to fracture his control. His expression grew frighteningly calm as he announced casually, "I'm gonna kill him."

He meant it. Wildly, Norah realized that he meant it. Rory was willing and able to crush out Cole Denby's life because he had hurt her. The magnitude of it shocked her to the soul. Feeling the hurt and humiliations at Cole's hands all over again, for a minute, just a minute, she thought yes, do it! However, that madness wasn't lasting. There was Rory to think of, too. She almost didn't react quick enough when he dropped his hands and began to stalk toward the door.

"Rory, no. Wait!"

She ran and frantically grabbed his arm, dragging on it as if trying to wrestle down a stubborn steer. She put herself between him and the door, desperate to halt the dangerous power of his wrath.

"Rory, stop. Please. It's my fault. My fault. I goaded him into it. Please."

That shocked him to a standstill. He looked down at her through dark eyes glazed with the shiny dampness of impotent rage. Again, he fingered the bruise, cautiously this time.

"Your fault?" he echoed in a gruff voice. "How could it be your fault? There's no reason good enough to justify this. None at all." His hands began to shake with the tremendous rips of emotion inside him. "He hurt you and I can't just stand by and do nothing. I can't."

She let him draw her into the comforting fold of his arms, up to the safe bastion of his broad chest. There, Norah closed her eyes and rode the pull and ebb of the breaths chugging from him with a harsh, jerky violence. She laid her achy cheek over the hard

91

hammering of his heart, taking strength from its aggressive beats.

"Rory, promise me you won't do anything foolish," she whispered into the crisp front of his shirt. "Forget it happened. I have. It looks much worse than it is and it hardly hurts at all."

A low sound vibrated through him, one of personal pain and fierce protectiveness. It quickened a panicked pleasure as she felt it rumble beneath her cheek. Never, ever, had anyone wanted to protect her from harm. Well, maybe Cole, at first. But never like this. Norah was overwhelmed by the tenderness of his care, by the powerful brunt of his anger. Gathered in his arms, tight to the thunder of his heart, she felt cherished.

She felt loved.

"Ain't nobody gonna hurt you again, Norah. Nobody," he growled with rough certainty and the wetness on her cheeks had nothing to do with pain.

His hands had been moving with a tender restlessness along the gentle curve of her back. It occurred to Rory all at once that the silky fabric was sighing over nothing but bare skin. Norah was wrapped in a slippery dressing gown that snagged on the roughness of his palms and slid against her like liquid gold. He could feel the ridge of her spine, the flare of her hips, the taunting cleft of her buttocks. And his breathing altered from gusts of anger to pants of pure ardor.

Norah felt the change in him; the low throaty breaths, the roving impatience of his hands, the increasing pressure of his hips against her belly. And his desire felt as good as his devotion. Right. Honest. Inevitable. There was no use struggling against

92

it so she put back her head to accept his heated kiss.

After a long moment of tasting and teasing with temperatures rising, Rory leaned away. His dark eyes searched her flushed features. The look was ravening, hot but oddly restrained. He was gasping for breath, grasping for the control he'd lost the first time he saw her on the porch in Deadwood.

"I gotta go, Miss Norah," he groaned huskily. "If I stay, I'm gonna have to make love to you all afternoon right on that there big bed."

She reached up, catching the brim of his Stetson. A toss sent it whirling across the room.

"Stay."

She couldn't state her willingness any plainer, yet still, Rory was uncertain. She was a lady and he was used to the jaded company of whores. The last thing he wanted to do was frighten her or hurt her or offend her. Innocent ladies were known not to appreciate indelicate handling of a personal nature. And damn, he was dying to get personal! His hands were suddenly clumsy in their placement as his body's demands grew more urgent and evident. She was a lady. He shouldn't be here, doing this, wanting this so badly he couldn't garner the will to walk away. He had the utmost respect for virtuous female kind and if he was to rob Norah Denby of hers in a hotel room in broad daylight, he'd have no choice except . . . to do the honorable thing.

"Rory? What is it?"

He looked down then up then everywhere except into the gray of her questioning gaze.

"Rory?"

The light stroke of her hand on his cheek brought him to face her. Where was the dashing, roguish cowboy of seconds before? He looked so suddenly shy, it bemused her. And scared, too, she realized. What on earth?

Then, he caught her hand and pressed it tight to his chest. His voice was low and husky with feeling. "Are you sure about this, Miss Norah? I'm not gonna . . . I mean, I aim to be real careful with you." The words became a throb of tenderness, pounded out from his anxious heart. "Norah-honey, you know I wouldn't for the world cause you any hurt. But if I should, if I do, I promise to make it as quick and easy as I can. And I'll make it good for you."

"Oh," she murmured as understanding overtook her. Then, more softly, "Oh . . ." Tears came flooding to her eyes and she couldn't help hugging him, to the great big, strapping cowboy who was trembling in his boots at the thought of taking her virginity. Of hurting her in the act of love. Had any of the others ever shown her a trace of that concern or care? Even one? Had any man ever considered her when his pleasures were at stake? None but this one. None but Rory Prescott.

Upon feeling her quivering in his embrace, Rory's chest seized up something fierce. He'd never have believed he would be brought to this point of poignant panic in the name of love. Stopping was out of the question. There was no way he could leave her room without completing what they'd started. Even if he wanted to, she wasn't inclined to let him. The not so innocent kneading of her hands upon the taut seat of his jeans spoke that plain. There seemed no help for it, so he swallowed hard and whispered thickly, "Just don't be afraid of me,

Norah. I'll be real gentle, just like I promised this morning."

She made a sound that was strangely half sob, half laugh as she leaned back to look up at him. She was smiling and that confused him. When he started to speak again, her fingertips pressed over his lips to silence them.

"Don't go fretting, Rory Prescott. There's no need. We've both done this before and I know it's going to be good." Then she stretched up to kiss him on surprise-slackened lips.

Not a virgin. His mind was slow to take that in. She'd been with another man, his sweet, pretty Norah. He didn't think ladies were supposed to be experienced and it gave him pause, not sure he liked the idea. Until she began tugging and nibbling on his lower lip.

"Have I disappointed you?"

Norah whispered that quietly against his mouth. Never would she let him know how hard it was to ask, how hard it was to wait for his answer. For a moment, she was simply terrified that she had. To ease her agony, she licked along the sweep of his upper lip, tracing its sensual line until his arms convulsed tight about her.

"No," he growled low in his throat and crushed his mouth over hers. How could he object when she was doing things to him that drove him crazy with want? Things no maiden-lady would ever conceive of. At that instant, while her tongue was mating fiercely with his own, he didn't care if she had six husbands, all at the same time and waiting at home for supper.

"Let 'em wait," he rumbled deep within his chest.

"What?" she panted into the next urgent kiss.

95

"Nothin'."

Breathless, Norah rolled away from his hungry mouth and let her forehead rest upon his shoulder. She was panting. Her knees were quaking. The second of respite she'd hoped for, evolved into another kind of seducing torture. Rory's kisses scorched across her temple where threads of sable hair tempted him down to the sensitive nape of her neck. She arched, moaning softly, undulating her slender body so that it conformed enticingly to his. Things simmering for so long took on an agitated boil. And there was no going back.

"Rory, think you can sweep me up and carry me away, here and now?"

"Yes, ma'am," he murmured into the curve of her throat. To prove it, he lifted her up with one arm tucked beneath her bottom and the other about her waist and walked with her as if she weighed a little more than nothing to the edge of the smooth satin comforter. He held her suspended for several long, torrid minutes while he stoked her passion to a frenzy with knowing thrusts of his tongue, inviting her to imagine what he'd soon be doing inside her. Her arms twined about his neck, fingers digging deep and twisting in the thick thatch of red hair. Slowly, he let her slide down the length of his hard body. She moaned his name in a mindless whimper as he laid her down upon the cool spread. He sat beside her. Sat and simply stared for the longest time. Then, he reached up and loosened her hair strand at a time, arranging each soft twist upon the ice blue satin to suit him until it framed her lovely features like a dark halo.

From the fever-pitch of his desire, she'd expected

him to make short, vigorous work of their union. And she wouldn't have minded. Her own feelings were strained to a fine tension, just trembling for release. Yet suddenly, Rory seemed in no hurry and that had her shifting restlessly beneath his leisurely gaze. Finally, he moved one big palm up to cup her silk covered breast. She closed her eyes. Her breathing came in quick, jerky gasps of anticipation. He squeezed gently, testing the firmness of her flesh, teasing it into an eager nub. Then, he performed the same slow torment upon the other.

He said her name softly, bringing her desire-glazed eyes open. Then he gave her that slow, wide, confident-of-being-satisfied male smile. "I sure as hell hope you ain't got nothing planned for the next few hours."

His thumbs hooked into the neckline of her dressing robe and slowly parted it, drawing it away from the glorious white breasts so he could feast, first with his hot dark stare, then with his hot, hungry mouth. By the time he shifted his attention to the sash of her gown, Norah was shaking with impatience. When he fumbled with the slippery knot, she pushed his big hands aside to untie it. He stilled her trembling fingers before they could pull the gown open and settled them atop the coverlet on either side of her. Then, he made a slow, teasing game of loosening the sash and easing the edges of silk away from the pearlescent splendor of her naked form. His breath suddenly shuddered. Norah Denby was the most beautiful thing he'd ever seen. When his callused hand stroked down the length of her, Norah sighed, a slave to the sensation.

It was harder then for Rory to pretend he was in

no hurry. Not when her exquisite flesh slid so warm and tantalizing beneath his touch. Not when her thighs opened the way to her private places and she moaned so sweetly as he explored them. His breathing quickened apace with hers, growing just as raw, just as ragged in expectation until, abruptly, she pulled his hand away.

"No," she panted. "I want it to be with you."

He grinned that slow, sensuous grin. "Oh, sweet darlin', it will be. We got plenty of time for that. Right now, I want to watch you. I want to see how much pleasure I'm giving you."

It was an incredibly arrogant thing to say. An incredibly erotic image to suggest. Norah's eyes closed helplessly, envisioning his smoldering gaze upon her as she shook with impatient need. He returned his hand to the slick folds of female flesh, moving it in a knowing rhythm, tempting her, tormenting her. He watched her reach for the ultimate reward with greedy thrusts of her hips and saw the first tiny shocks of fulfillment ripple up her glorious long legs. And then she cried out as the ripples grew to mighty waves. He rode them to their completion, marveling at her response, excited by her passion, thrilled by her loveliness. And swelling him up with a proud sense of accomplishment when her sultry eyes finally opened and she smiled lazily up at him. She dozed happily for a moment, appearing drained and dazed by the strength of her release. She made a little purring sound of contentment as he stroked her flush body and it nearly drove him crazy.

Finally, she sat up, slipping her arms over his shoulders and kissing him with considerable gratitude. As she tempted him into a panting urgency with provoking flickers of her tongue, her fingers moved down the buttons of his shirt, opening it, pushing it from the broad range of his shoulders. Her palms adored the sleek, hard swell of muscle and teased through the light furring on his chest. Then, she broke away from his demanding mouth and slipped off the bed to kneel, naked, at his feet.

"Mind if I relieve you of your boots?" she asked. And desperate for any kind of relief, Rory shook his head jerkily. What a torture to the senses, having her bending over him, giving him an unrestricted view of her smooth white back and shapely buttocks, having her thick sable hair fall in a glossy curtain over his knees. His hands knotted helplessly in the coverlet as she tugged his boots free and reached for his gun belt. His breath sucked in as she flicked the end out then pulled briefly to release the buckle's hold. She leaned close to unwind it from around his hips, her bare breasts brushing his lap and increasing the fiery ache pounding inches away from that succulent bounty.

With a gentle tug, she coaxed him to his feet and began to unbutton his Levi's. But not before she used her palm to sample the hard ridge of his desire through the taut gloving of denim fabric. Determinedly, she wrestled the jeans down, followed by the second skin of pinkish long underwear. And then she made a small sound of anticipation.

Rory Prescott was built like a young stallion.

The fingertips that brushed over him were sure and admiring. Rory's jaw ground in agonizing enjoyment. Norah Denby knew exactly what she was doing. And he might have been disturbed by that fact. Except that he was totally devastated by it.

Norah's icy-hot stare rose to his in challenge. Her words were husky, thick with desire. "You were boasting about how well you ride. Time to show me, cowboy."

"Yes, ma'am," he rumbled with a trace of that wicked grin. "But I was raised to believe it's ladies first."

With that, his big hands cupped her bottom and lifted her up off her feet. Alarmed, she frantically grabbed for his shoulders. But she had nothing to fear. He was in complete control. Instead of turning her toward the bed, he parted her legs and dropped her down on top of him. She gasped in response to his impaling fullness. And then she sighed in wonder. He delighted in that sound.

"You want to drive, Miss Norah, or do you trust me to do it for you?"

Goaded by his growling taunt, she wrapped her legs about his lean hips and began a thorough experimentation by rocking and lifting within the firm support of his hands. It was a hot, wild rhythm and making the ride much shorter than she'd believed possible considering the magnitude of her first climax. All too soon, a trembly weakness spread through her legs. She clutched at Rory, moaning his name, begging him to help her finish. His hands took over, moving her upon him at a rough, demanding pace until her fingers clenched in his hair, until her body jerked and spasmed around his.

Patience, be damned. Rory fell with her upon the rumpled comforter. His thrusts were deep, hard, reaching for the very soul of her as his hands tipped her hips to receive him more fully. Norah clung to him, feeling torn asunder and marvelously burned by the heat of his passion. At last, he gave an expansive groan and sent his seed scalding up inside her.

As he stayed shaking and panting above her, he grinned and said with an impossible immodesty, "I ride better than I drive."

And Norah laughed in breathless agreement.

"Yes you do, Rory Prescott. Yes, you do."

There was something deliciously decadent about lying with a naked man in the middle of the day. Especially one as undeniably voracious as her red-headed lover. It took him a remarkably short time to recover his randy energies and already, she could feel him stirring against her thigh as his thumb lazily flicked her budded breast. He was smiling and smug and she could have sworn he'd be purring in lusty satisfaction if he was able. And she couldn't argue that it had been spectacular between them. Rory Prescott made love as well as he kissed.

There was nothing she would have liked better than to spend the remaining hours of the day and night in a salacious union with Rory Prescott. But even as she tried to hold it at bay, reality began to intrude on their steamy idyll. Nothing had changed. And that was a cruel truth.

"You'd better get dressed, Rory."

The quiet request escaped him completely the first time. "Ummm," he mumbled, moving his mouth over to taste the taut pucker aroused by his clever fingers.

"Rory, you have to go."

"What? Whatcha talking about? I am very disinclined toward moving right now."

101

Norah pushed at his head, forcing him to take her seriously. He lifted up, questioning her with eyes dark and deep with quickening desire. "I've got to get ready for dinner soon."

"And my appetite's jus' started to come back." He grinned and she frowned back in frustration. He wasn't going to make it easy for her. When she started to rise up, he slid over the top of her, pinning her to the bed with the applied pressure of his weight. The hot, manly length of him was already prodding impatiently between her thighs.

"Rory, stop it. Get off. We can't—"

"Shore we can," he objected. And proved it by surging upward to skillfully penetrate her silken defenses. Slowly, with meaningful provocation, he rotated his hips over hers, letting her feel the strength and power of him inside her. "What was that you was saying there, Norah-honey?"

"Oh damn you, Rory," she breathed heavily against the swelling thrust of him. Then she moaned in sighing resignation and accepted his determined kiss.

There was nothing unhurried about the way they greedily rushed toward mutual satisfaction. They moved together, showing with hands, with tongues, with incoherent sound, what worked best. Having decided on a hard, lusty tempo, they refined upon it until they found completion within shattering heartbeats of one another. Then sagged, spent and satisfied, in one another's arms.

A lump of bittersweet emotion lodged within Norah's breast. Absently, her fingers threaded through the strands of damp red hair and over the glistening contour of Rory's shoulders. How easy it

102

would be to love a man like this if she was anything other than what she was. How had this big, handsome and thoroughly unsuitable cowboy managed to stir her guarded heart into such a palpitating frenzy? It would almost be worth giving everything up to linger in his brawny embrace. Almost. And it was that damning almost that brought a sheen of tears to her eyes.

Rory shifted gradually onto his side and propped his head up on his hand so he could look down upon the beautiful Norah. The shimmer of tears was unexpected. He touched them with tender fingertips and whispered, "What's wrong, Norah-honey?"

She gave a quavering sigh and looked away from the dark sincerity of his gaze. "I'm finding it too darned easy to care about you," she replied with quiet candor.

"So? What's so wrong in that? We're good together, Norah, jus' like I told you we would be."

She drew a miserable breath. "Because it makes it so hard to say goodbye. I hate goodbyes. It seems I'm forever saying them. I'm going to miss you, Rory."

He was silent for a long minute. When his fingers stroked along her cheek, trying to coax her to look at him, she fought against it. Finally, he stopped and settled for feathering light kisses along her brow and temple and cheek. "I ain't going anywheres long enough for you to miss me."

He sounded so sure, so set that she turned to him with the beginnings of a frown. And found her lips quietly conquered by the warm, insistent press of his. It was so sinfully simple to melt beneath that pliant persuasion, so easy to long for the perma-

103

nence of his arms around her, his body beside her, his heat inside her. Too easy. Too simple. Too damn tempting. She tore away from it, panting, fighting, frightened.

And then Rory told her with all the confidence in the world, "You ain't gonna say goodbye, Norah, 'cause I ain't gonna be gone. When I go home to the Dakotas, you're coming with me."

Chapter Seven

For a long tortured heartbeat, Norah stared at him. Then, without a word, she grabbed up the discarded robe and whipped it about her suddenly chilled form as she strode to the hotel window. She stood there with her back to the bed, trembling fitfully, looking out at nothing beyond the shadowed ugliness of her own thoughts.

"Norah?"

"No."

That came out flat and final. She heard the mattress groan as the big cowboy came up off it. By the time he reached her, he found her shoulders braced and her body stiff. She shuddered slightly when his warm hands rubbed along the arms she'd crossed defensively over her bosom. His cheek nuzzled against the soft spill of her hair and his words brushed warm in her ear.

"Norah, I'll take such good care of you. And it will be like this, every day, every night."

The potential of that low, seducing promise made her tremble. She wanted it, she wanted him with a fearful desperation. She struggled for resolve. There was no choice. It was hurt him now . . . or destroy him later. There was no easy way.

"I'm sorry, Rory but it's not possible."

The chill of her tone gave him a dreadful moment of pause. "Why?" he whispered. "Why not?"

"I'm sorry," she repeated in a necessarily brittle voice. "I thought you understood. I wasn't looking for any kind of involvement with you."

She could hear him suck a pain-filled breath and closed her eyes tight to combat the tears.

"Well, I don't understand. I thought we had something going between us." His tone was strengthened by steely threads of anger. "I didn't come all this way jus' to throw you down on a bed and walk away. I want you, Norah. I want us to be together. Come with me back to the Bar K."

"I can't," she sobbed, then she restated firmly, "I won't."

"Why, dammit?" He grabbed her by the upper arms, bringing her flush against him. It was hard to cling to her will when pressed to Rory Prescott in all his naked splendor. "You said you cared."

"I do. I mean, I can't. Rory, I'm sorry. I should have known better. It's just that you were so persistent, so sweet, so alive, so darned good at kissing. You made me want to think, for just a little while, that it was possible. But it isn't. Rory, you can't give me what I need."

There it was.

"There it is," she whispered in an agony of regret.

"What do you need, Norah?" That was said in a tight, controlled voice.

"More than you have. I've gone without before and I don't like it. I've scratched, I've struggled and I won't do it again. I won't, Rory and if you cared for me, you wouldn't ask."

106

He stared at her through oddly opaque eyes that no longer displayed a mirror of his thoughts. He released her arms and took a step back, rubbing his palms distractedly upon the hard swell of his thighs. "Money, Norah? Is that what it's about?"

"Lots of money," she corrected in a cold little voice. Using it tore the heart from her just as she knew it was ripping his. "Lots and lots of money so I can have things, nice things. That's what I want, Rory. That's what I have to have. Now please, get dressed and go. I really think it's best we don't see each other again. There's really no point in it after all, is there?"

She made herself walk away from him, over to her fancy dressing table where she sank down upon its stool. She couldn't bear the sight of her own reflection so she concentrated upon the bruise high on her cheekbone. Slowly, with practice, she began to apply a whitish paste to conceal the mark and restore her flawless complexion.

She hadn't meant to watch him quite so hungrily. But she couldn't take her eyes from the image of him in the mirror; the smooth pull of muscle across his browned back, the taut flex of his flanks as he shinnied into his jeans, the strength in his arms as he tugged on his boots. Rory Prescott was the most arousing man she'd ever seen. He made even the simplest movements into virile poetry. When he turned toward her, she averted her stare and sat waiting tensely as his boot heels clacked across the floor. She wasn't sure what to expect from him; temper or tantrum, but certainly not the gentle caress of his hand beneath her chin.

Rory tipped her head back and leaned down to

107

kiss her one last time, a long, lingering mix of sultry sweetness and sassy tongue action. Then, when she began to respond with a helpless urgency, he straightened, leaving his palm against her cheek.

"That was to thank you for amusing yourself at my expense."

"Rory—"

His fingertips sealed her lips in silence. It was a light touch, almost reverent. Unlike the slashing candor of his words. "I thought the world of you, lady. Guess I'm just a dumb son of a bitch. I'll stick with what I know from now on. At least whores is honest with you. And with themselves."

She sat frozen, tears burning against the fierce fight not to shed them. Her expression was painfully impassive. Even when he pulled out the front of her silk robe and stuffed a one hundred dollar note between her creamy breasts.

"There now, Norah-honey. Now you can't say I didn't do my part toward making you rich."

And he was gone.

Somehow, Norah managed to look cool and pretty when she joined Cole and Monthaven in the lobby of the Mansard House. It was an artful mask over an empty shell. She was numb with confusion inside, part of her still throbbing from Rory Prescott's enthusiastic loving, part of her still aching from the cut of his last words. She stood immobile while Cole brushed a fond kiss upon her cheek.

"There's my girl," he said for Monthaven's benefit. And to her, in a low undervoice, he murmured, "Are you all right, Norah? I am sorry about this

108

morning. I just got carried away. You know how much this means to us. Can I count on you, my dear?"

"I won't disappoint you, Cole," she murmured back in a lackluster tone that he couldn't miss in spite of his eagerness to pin down the Monthaven deal. No, she wouldn't disappoint him. In her entire life, Cole Denby was the only constant, the only one who was there for her on a regular basis. And in his own selfish way he cared. That kind of caring was better, safer. They knew each other too well for games, or lies, or regrets. And he'd been right, after all. Monthaven was the prize. He was the one she should concentrate upon. There was the future, the detached, profitable future she should never have let escape her focus. He was the one she could walk away from without feeling as if the walls of her chest were about to cave in upon her heart.

Summoning her most fetching smile, Norah laced her arm through the golden-haired lord's. She could see the admiration, the interest, spark in his gaze and she fought down the cold feeling of disgust. Disgust at him for his shallow lusting; at herself for her selfish ploy.

It was then she happened to glance around. It was then she saw Rory Prescott on the far side of the lobby. His handsome features were compacted into sharp, somber lines. He was staring at her—through her. And he started toward them in long, determined strides.

Oh, no Rory, not now, please!

"My lord, shall we go to dinner?" she suggested with a coquettish flicker of her lashes. "Then, I understand you and Father have much to talk about."

She began towing the staid Englishman with an inarguable strength toward the private dining room Cole had arranged for the evening. She didn't look back. Her pulse was fluttering wildly. And she prayed. *Please, Rory. Don't do this. Let it go. Can't you just let it go?* Her breaths came in tiny little gulps of panic and upset burned behind her eyes. She couldn't confront him, not now when her emotions were so raw, so turmoiled. Not when Cole was on the edge of the deal of a lifetime and smelling gold in his pockets.

"See we're not disturbed," Cole murmured to the uniformed servant outside the dining room door. He squired Norah and their fatted guest inside and at last, Norah released the tension aching inside her.

Cedric Beaumont looked up to see the tall red-headed cowboy striding purposefully in the direction of the dining rooms. He was clad in his inappropriate range wear and had six guns flapping at his lean hips. Totally unacceptable for the Mansard's private rooms. He stepped forward to intercept him and was cut cold by a dangerous glare.

"Get outta my way, Cedric," came the gravelly command.

"Yes sir, Mr. Prescott," he stammered and jumped aside, for the big cowboy showed no sign of shortening his step.

Rory shoved open the door to the dining alcove. The look of utter despair on Norah Denby's face should have gratified him. But it didn't.

"Excuse me, folks. Miss Norah and I needs to exchange a few words. I'll bring her right back." He said that with a quiet, lethal power, offering no point of compromise.

110

"See here," Cole began in chilling outrage. He started up out of his chair. It was then that Norah acted.

"It's all right, Father. Let me see what Mr. Prescott deems as so important. I shan't be but a moment. Please order for me." Her fingertips touched Monthaven's shoulder in an encouraging caress. "Please excuse me, Charles. I'll be right back."

Then she turned to Rory and her stare could have severed stone. She swept past him and past an apologetic Cedric into the wide open lobby. It was her plan to face him where there was no chance of intimate conversation. Surely he wouldn't air the sordid details of their relationship in public.

But she didn't know Rory Prescott.

"You grooming that there pretty foreigner to take my place in your bed tonight?"

Norah blanched and cast a quick, mortified look about the cavernous room. Cedric cleared his throat discreetly. Several heads turned at the sound and content of his booming statement.

"Shall we take this somewhere a little less conspicuous, Mr. Prescott?" With that cold snap of words, she marched toward a sheltered niche beneath the wide, winding staircase. She didn't need to listen for the clatter of Rory's boot heels. She could feel him like a hot gust of wind at her back. The moment they were out of eavesdropping distance from the other guests, she whirled upon him in a fury. Much of that rage was fed by fear, a deep, desperate fear. Of Rory Prescott and his ability to snatch control from her. And she couldn't lose that control. Not now.

"How dare you!" she threw up at him. They were

111

standing toe to toe. The irate heave of her gorgeous bosom was nearly brushing his shirtfront. Rory assumed a posture of deceiving ease, only his dark gaze challenging hers with any degree of aggression. And it was that dark, dangerous stare that flamed her attack. That he should look so sure, so confident, so smug, so indignant!

"You are interrupting a very important dinner. Speak your peace and let me get back to my life. I can't imagine that there's anything we left unsaid. Make it brief, if you please."

His brevity was commendable.

"I love you."

Norah gasped. An incredible terror surged inside her. No. She wouldn't listen. She wouldn't believe him. Even though she'd heard him speak those words before, they struck her with a devastating force. Like a shotgun blast. Tearing, shredding, damaging, crippling mercilessly upon impact. His aim was unerring. Right for the heart. For a moment, she was too stunned to move, then she struck him back in a fierce defending volley. Like a cornered animal caught in a painful trap.

"The feeling is not returned, Mr. Prescott. Now please will you leave me alone!"

He was amazingly quick for a big man. His hands flashed up, securing either side of her head, holding her immobile while he bent to claim her lips. It was a searing, mind-numbing kiss, the kind he did so well. It wrung a plaintive moan from her just as it wrung her heart and soul. Unbidden, her hands fluttered up, touching, stroking his rough cheeks, his silky hair, trembling as they clutched at the front of his chambray shirt. Then abruptly, angrily, she was

112

pushing at him. He didn't have to, but he let her jerk away. Then he smiled.

"That felt pretty returned to me."

"It doesn't prove anything!" she shouted at him. It took a conscious effort to calm her tone but she couldn't quiet the fierce tremors quaking inside her. "It proves I like kissing. So what? You're not the first man I've kissed and you won't be the last."

"Yes, I will be." He said that with such conviction, she wanted to scream. She wanted to hit him.

She wanted to believe him.

"You simple, arrogant fool. What makes you think you have any right to dictate to me? Because we made love? Surely, you know you weren't the first there, either."

She fought dirty, brandishing her well chosen words like a stiletto blade, striking with swift, mortal jabs into vital, vulnerable regions. Not to wound but to kill. Rory had seen that kind of fighting before. It was the way the Sioux had taught his brother.

"I know that, Norah," he responded quietly, as if she hadn't severed a major artery of emotion. "But I'm the only one of them who wants to marry you.

Marry him. Oh, God. *I love you.* Norah reeled in a moment of intense confusion. Marry him. A home. Children. Rory Prescott in bed beside her. Loving her. It was too much. It was torture.

"No," she rasped out. "No. I won't marry you. I won't be tied to a man like you. I can't marry a man who lives from month to month out of a saddle. I want nice things, I want to go exciting places, not to be stuck in the daily drudgery of a prairie wife. I don't want to look fifty when I'm twenty-five. I don't want to breed babies and not know how I'm

113

going to feed them. I won't, Rory." Desolate tears streaked her face. "I can't."

There was nothing clean or neat about the way that truth cut through him. His eyes were dulled with pain. His stance was stiff and braced to bear the hurt. She almost faltered. She almost, at the sight of his anguish, gave in to what beat in her heart. She almost succumbed to the temptation of his embrace, of his love. Almost. But that would be the greater cruelty. No, there could be no backing down. She was doing the right thing for both of them. Now, she had to withdraw, to give him time to lick and wrap his wounds with what little dignity she'd left him.

Norah drew upon her considerable talent of role playing. She shifted her shoulders back. She blinked away the weakness of her tears. And she spoke in an emotionless voice.

"I have to get back to my dinner. My father and Lord Monthaven are waiting. We have business to attend, so if you'll excuse me."

His hand caught her wrist.

"I'm rich, Norah."

She stopped cold.

"I'm rich. I have land and cattle and money, all you could ever want. I don't work the Bar K, I'm half owner."

Norah swallowed convulsively and stared up at him in voiceless shock.

"There wouldn't be no living out of line shacks, no patching faded dresses. I could afford to send you to San Francisco, to New Orleans, to Boston, to New York every year for a new wardrobe. Is that what you needed to hear? Is that what makes

114

the difference to you, Norah?"

She stood there, stunned, speechless but the sudden glitter in her pale silvery eyes spoke plain. Yes. Yes, it made all the difference in the world.

And he wished like hell it didn't.

"Everything all right here, Norah?"

Rory looked from Norah's still features to Cole Denby's confrontational glare. And he smiled tightly. "Miss Norah and I were just finishing up a personal discussion. But seeing as how you're here, how 'bout we make some business talk. I hear tell that English feller is burdened with too much cash. Well, I'm suffering from a surplus of land and cows. Could be we could help each other out. My grandfather, Garth Kincaid, has empowered me as part owner in the Bar K to do some negotiating. You want to get in on it, Denby?"

Grandfather, power, cash, business. The magic words to turn Cole Denby's affections. He beamed at the redheaded cowboy cum rancher. "Why, Mr. Prescott, could be I got the answer to both your problems. I'm an investment broker, as I said. My job, my joy, is getting men wasting opportunities together. Right now, Lord Monthaven is paying me a sizable retainer to find him a piece of the West to invest in. Perhaps I can play matchmaker. Why don't you join Norah and me for dinner?"

"I ain't exactly dressed proper," was the wry reply.

"Why, Mr. Prescott, don't be modest. You own a goodly chunk of South Dakota. Who's going to object?"

And it was then Rory Prescott learned the power of the Kincaid name. It gave him a rush of importance. But he wasn't sure he liked it. Because just

115

like Norah's interest, it had nothing to do with him.

"Let's make some talk."

And they did. Over the china and crystal, over viands of caviar, pickled eels, French peas and Roquefort cheese, over the best wine in the house, they talked cattle, Kincaid cattle and the capital needed to sustain them. As he listened, as he spoke, the humble cowboy manner fell from Rory Prescott. In its place was a smooth, hard veneer. Norah watched the transformation with a disconcertion akin to horror. She didn't know the man who talked about cattle as if they were mangy gods on the hoof. She'd never seen the cold, clear light that had come into Rory's eyes. She'd never heard him speak with concise, curt self-interest. She hadn't known he could be so shrewd, so controlling.

But then, she'd never met Garth Kincaid.

When the plates were cleared away and the men got down to some serious cigars and liquor, Norah quietly excused herself from their company. She had to get away. She had to get a hold of the confusion beating in her brow. She had to escape the suddenly speculative glint in Rory Prescott's eyes. The way his dark stare turned all black and unreadable when he looked at her. She was afraid she would go quite mad if she had to spend another minute watching the cool stranger manipulate the body that had loved her so well. My God, what had she done to Rory Prescott?

And when the knock came on her door later that same evening, she was stricken with an uncertain panic. What would she say to the man she'd scorned over his empty pockets now that they proved to be plump? Would he come to carry her back into the

116

bed they'd shared so wonderfully that afternoon? Could she resist him if he did? Or had he come to taunt her for the harsh words that lost her the very thing she sought to gain — wealth. He had every reason to hate her for cutting him cold with her calculated cruelty. She had every reason now to play upon his desire for her. He would never believe any of the sentiments she held within her jaded heart were genuine. And she couldn't say she blamed him.

Why hadn't he told her earlier?

Would it have made a difference? Money was only a part of the reason she'd said no.

Though she wanted desperately to ignore the knock when it came again, Norah advanced to turn the knob. Cole Denby was outside her door, not Rory Prescott. Her relief — and her disappointment, was staggering.

Cole swept her up in an enthusiastic hug. "Norah, my darling, you are a gem, a genius, a wonder!" He set her down at last, grinning ear to ear in smug, unabashed greed. "How did you know there was such a jewel beneath that rough surface? I never would have guessed. He sure had me fooled."

"I didn't know," she said flatly.

Cole gave a great whoop of laughter. "All the better. It proves how lucky you are, how lucky we are. Two fat pigeons; Monthaven and Kincaid, both falling into our lap at once. Can you believe it! Talk about your good fortune smiling."

Norah said nothing and her quiet finally penetrated his jubilance.

"Now, Norah, don't tell me you're still stewing over that little bump I gave you. You know I didn't mean it. I'll get you the best spa treatment money

117

can buy. Why that'll patch up that old bruise and your pride faster than you can say dollar bill. A week in Eureka Springs. How does that sound to you? As soon as we're done in South Dakota."

"South Dakota?" Her tone echoed with dread.

"Why sure, Norah. You think I'm going to let those money bags get out of reach? Pack up. We're heading out in the morning. Can you believe the luck! Things are finally going our way, Norah. We'll finally get the things we want, the things we've worked for, the things we deserve. And Monthaven and Prescott are going to give them to us on a silver platter. Think of it."

She couldn't help but think of it. Of the trip to South Dakota with Rory Prescott. Of his bland dark eyes skewering her soul and making her writhe with guilt and longing. "I'm not going, Cole."

His jaw dropped perceptibly. "Not going?" He gave a short, disbelieving laugh. "I won't hear that kind of crazy talk. Of course, you're going."

"You don't need me anymore. You've got them thinking with their heads not their loins. I've done my part. I'm through. I need to get away for a while."

"Sure, darling. Get away to the Dakotas. To the Bar K Ranch. You've done your job, a great job, now rest on your laurels, girl. Think, Norah. Think of the future. Think of what he could give you, not just for the moment but for a lifetime."

A lifetime. A home. Children. Rory Prescott in bed beside her every night. In a fine, comfortable house. Her insides shivered. A stroke of fortune too good to be believed. She was afraid to believe it.

"Yessir, old Lord Monthaven is mighty taken with

you. I bet it wouldn't take more than a couple of your kisses to convince him to take you back to England with him."

"Monthaven?" She was confused, her heart and mind tumbling over images of Rory Prescott making love to her in their own big elegant bed.

"Why, sure. Norah, dear, get your thinking straight. There's the future. You could live like a queen. Go for it while you've still got your considerable looks. You could be the next Lady Monthaven."

Lady Monthaven? That meant nothing to her. She brushed off the idea like the veriest gnat. Charles Monthaven would not be sharing her bed, her love or her children. Charles Monthaven was strictly business. Rory Prescott was all pleasure. So why was she so afraid of him now that she knew he could give her what she wanted?

Because she was so inexplicably vulnerable where the rugged redhead was concerned.

I will not fall in love with you, Rory Prescott.

She had nothing to worry about, she told herself sternly. She wouldn't fall in love with him. She was much too sensible. She was much too selfish. She was much too cautious. Hadn't she learned a long time ago that there was no such thing as an honorable man?

No, she would not love him.

Tell that to her wayward heart. The heart that leaped at the sight of him the next morning over breakfast. The heart that had ached all night in his absence. Why hadn't he come to see her, to be with her? Thank God, he hadn't. It was hard enough to maintain a semblance of normalcy with what already lay between them. Did he make it easier or worse by

119

not favoring her with his ready smile or warming glances? In fact, he was the perfect gentleman, charming, polite, aloof as they discussed the trip to the Bar K, the four of them. Had she hurt him that badly? Did he hate her that much? His courtesy grated on her fragile nerves. As if they were merely business acquaintances. Instead of lovers. But then, that had been her choice. She had pushed him away, no, thrown him away. And now it did no good to whine over the loss. If she had truly lost him. The occasional hot fire flickering behind that opaque glaze gave her hope. Why was she wishing for that which she wanted to avoid? It would be better for all concerned if things continued as they were going. She should be thankful for his restraint instead of chafing.

Did he still want to marry her?

She looked at the big, stoic figure across the table. He was dressed in Western fine; starched shirt, silky bandana, open coat, Levi's, gunbelt and boots. And of course, the inevitable Stetson hung upon the back of his chair as he ate. The same in appearance but so different in perception. This Rory Prescott was somehow unreachable, untouchable. She couldn't imagine him grinning up from a muddy street, being distracted enough by her charms to plow a motorcar into a tree, holding her suspended in his arms while his magnificent body plunged upward inside her. She didn't see that man this morning and she mourned the loss. It was as if her rejection had severed a part of him, a part she valued above all she saw now. It was as if she'd stolen the joy from him. And she didn't know how to restore it.

Oh, Rory, I'm so sorry. Please forgive me.

120

But how to forgive herself?

As their bags were being loaded upon the train that would carry them to the Dakotas, Rory drew Cole Denby aside. He smiled amiably and put a friendly arm about the older man's shoulders. Cole was relaxed and pleased with life in general so the soft drawling threat came as a stunning surprise.

"Just between us, Denby, just so we know, if you ever, ever lay so much as a finger on Norah again, I'm gonna tear your damn arm off." He grinned and tightened his fingers until they sank deep bruises into the other man's flesh. And then he sauntered off with a rattle of silver spurs to get on the train, leaving Cole Denby feeling a cold powerlessness.

It wasn't a feeling he liked. Or one he would tolerate.

Chapter Eight

The Bar K. Norah sat stunned as their carriage carried them over miles and miles of it. An endless sea of lush green short grass and fat beef cattle. Her own memory of the prairie was in dire shades of brown, not this verdant splendor. She remembered dust and drought where the sun, wind, hard soap and cold water burned tender skin until hands were swollen, black and hurt as if scalded with boiling water. And a four-walled sod house made of prairie grass papered over with old newspapers; dark, dirty and infested with mice and vermin. Not a grand Victorian home with turrets and stained glass and wraparound porches. She recalled the terrible loneliness, the sound of emptiness, the echo of hopelessness but here she saw bustling industry in the corrals and outbuildings, the hurrahing of cowboys who recognized their rowdy young boss, the noisy clamor of life. This was not the same kind of life she'd left, she realized with a shiver of relief. The Bar K may have been on the edge of civilization but it was far from a prairie tomb.

Beside her, Cole was covetously counting cattle and tallying the price per pound in his eager mathematician's brain. When he noticed her scrutiny, he smiled with ill-restrained excitement and squeezed her hand.

She got no such encouragement when her gaze touched upon Rory's. He was as he had been since that night in Cheyenne — inscrutable. He responded politely if she addressed him but made no advances of his own. He watched her. She could feel his stare, dark, brooding, unreadable. She hadn't figured Rory Prescott for the moody type but on the long hot trip into South Dakota, he'd been silent as the hills and twice as foreboding. Cole seemed to have a new respect for him and she wondered at that. It wasn't anything he cared to discuss when she'd brought it up in passing conversation. Rory had done something to put his back up and Cole Denby was mean as a stick-teased grizzly when provoked. At one time, she would have worried over a confrontation between the two men. Now, she reckoned the young redhead could more than hold his own. In any given situation. Hadn't he been bearing up much better than she herself was? She was glad their forced travel closeness was almost at an end as composure became more strained by the mile and minute.

It was good to be on solid ground again. Norah stood at the front steps, grateful that the earth beneath her didn't move or sway. The thought of a night's sleep in a real bed was deliciously anticipated. Beneath the same roof as Rory Prescott. In his home. The home he'd tried to give her. She glanced up at the fine structure, seeing in it a permanence, a comfortable stability, just like Rory. Then Cole gripped her arm to compel her up the stairs, breaking her mood of speculation.

What would it be like to live here with Rory Prescott, as his wife?

Rory lost his stiff manner upon mounting the steps to the Bar K. He didn't climb them, he leaped up to

123

the porch and advanced toward the sturdy figure waiting there, a broad grin on his face.

"Howdy, Major. Brung home some company. This here's Lord Monthaven from over there in England and he fancies himself as a cowboy." A second of silent contempt passed between the two men, unseen by the others. "And this is Cole Denby. He makes things happen and wants to marry the Bar K off to his lordship, providing you gots no objections. Think it might be just what you had in mind." He paused to let the men shake hands. "And this here is Cole's daughter, Norah."

Their host wasn't big in stature but he was enormous in the powerful aura he exuded. Norah took his hand as they were introduced, letting her small fingers be swallowed in the beefy palm. This was Rory's grandfather. She summed him up in a glance. This was the part of Rory she'd seen as he negotiated for the Bar K; the hard, unbending strength, the shrewd caution, the controlling force. And he left a cold, engulfing impression. Garth Kincaid was not a man she'd trust. Yet, curiously, she could see the surging respect and adoration in Rory's gaze as he stood proudly in the aging patriarch's shadow. Either there was more to Kincaid than he allowed outsiders to see, or Rory wasn't quite what she had come to . . . To what? Not love. She didn't love him. What then described what raced in hurried little beats along her veins when he looked at her and offered for the first time in a long while that small, sly smile? Then he turned away and the pulse of excitement faded in resigned misery. *Get a hold of yourself, Norah! You're setting yourself up for a fool, yearning for his attention like you are. Let it go! Let it alone. It won't work. He'll hurt you. He'll disappoint you. There's no such thing as an honorable man.*

The self chastisement starched her resolve, making it easier for her walk by Rory Prescott, close enough for her skirts to brush over his boots, without leaning into him for the pure salacious thrill of feeling his hard body against hers.

"Shall we talk some business?" Garth Kincaid suggested. Only his grandson would note the urgency in his tone. And he held to his frown.

"Can it wait until morning, Major?" Rory hung back on the porch, drawing Kincaid's glance. "I gots me some things to attend."

Like your damned family?

Kincaid would never say that to the boy so he chose, instead, less confrontational words. "Like that ugly broomtail of yours? Been kicking the hell out of everything in range since you left. Lucky he hasn't been turned into a meal for the dogs."

Rory grinned. "Heck, ole Chance just been a-missing me. Best go give him a stretch of his legs while some of the barn's still standing."

"You do that, boy," the major concluded softly. He fought the impulse to hold his grandson back. Let him go, his cunning instincts whispered. Let him get it out of his system. Then he'll be back. Like always. Because this is where he belongs. To me. Not them.

He stood watching the young cowboy stride in that loose, ambling gait across the yard, seeing with pride the way the other men greeted him. With fondness. With respect.

Like a Kincaid.

Rory's painted stallion was quick to welcome its master. By biting him. It was a hard pinch to the upper arm. Then, while several of the wranglers gath-

125

ered around to grin and poke one another in amusement, the cantankerous animal sent their boss spinning with an abrupt shift of its hind quarters. When a saddle blanket was placed on its back, it reacted by flicking it off and stomping it beneath angry hoofs. Undaunted, Rory reached down under the animal's girth to retrieve the blanket while the men held their breath. None of them would get within shooting distance of the mean-tempered animal and here Rory was sticking his head in the lion's mouth without a trace of concern. The blanket settled a second time and was again, sent flying, this time with a punctuating kick that set the stall boards shivering.

"Rory, that horse's gonna kill you some day," one of the ranch hands cautioned. "Heck, he nearly broke Johnson's leg the other morning when he was mucking stalls."

"Ole Chance don't like nobody but me taking care of him," Rory murmured fondly as he went after the blanket again. And again, one of the viciously flung hoofs just missed nicking him.

"Doan look like he has much use for you, either. That animal is just plain cussed mean."

"Why, hell, ole Chance loves me, don't you, son?" Rory moved up by the stallion's head and reached for its hackamore. Huge yellow teeth were quickly bared and snapped together an inch from Rory's face. The men jumped nervously as one but Rory never flinched.

"Had a woman love me like that once," one of the wranglers muttered. "Damn near kilt me with kindness." There was a ripple of uneasy laughter. They marveled at their young boss's bravery. And would be sad to bury him.

Rory stood his ground at the animal's tossing head.

126

When one of the movements caught his shoulder hard enough to knock him against the side of the stall, he scowled and told the stallion crossly, "If you're gonna be that way, you ornery ole cuss, I'll just saddle me up one of these other fine Kincaid horses to take for a ride. See if I don't."

And as he started to move, the paint stretched out its thick neck to block his retreat. And its velvety soft lips plucked loverlike at Rory's shirtfront. As if it knew it had gone just a tad too far.

"Had a woman do that to me, too. Almost married her!"

Rory grinned and rubbed the spotted hide affectionately. The animal stood still as stone while he slapped on a saddle and took the bit in its mouth as if accepting candy from his palm. Then Rory walked from the stall with a soft, "Come on, Chance. Let's shake off the dust." The stallion immediately backed out and turned, sending the loafing cowhands scattering to a mindful distance, to follow its master as meek and mannerly as a pup. Once in the yard, Rory took up the trailing reins and hopped up into the saddle. Chance sidled and danced in its eagerness to run, feeling the restlessness of its rider telegraphed to the bit. Just the slightest signal sent the animal exploding forward in a series of half lunges. Then the strides lengthened to a ground-gulping gallop.

"Danged fool," one of the men muttered admiringly.

"Got more guts than me to get on that keg o'dynamite."

The others nodded in agreement and as the dust sworls settled in the distance, they went back to work.

* * *

Aurora Prescott had just finished dressing the table when she heard the thunder of hoofbeats race right up under the eaves outside. Smiling softly and shaking her head, she called out, "Gena, fetch another plate."

And sure enough, in another second, a voice behind her hollered, "Got enough left for me?"

She shook her head. Gaslight gleamed all gold and red fire against the coil of her hair. "I have never known you not to show up in time for a free meal. You have an uncanny knack of knowing when the platter hits the table. Grab a seat."

Grinning, Rory whipped another chair up to the table and dropped into it as his gaze swept the fare spread out before him in anticipation. "Looks good, Mama."

"Hard tack looks good to you," she grumbled but the compliment pleased her. She finally came around to the back of her son's chair and leaned down to kiss his temple. "Welcome home, honey."

Rory caught the hand she brushed along his bright hair, pressed a quick kiss on its tough palm and cradled it to his cheek. He gave a long, expressive sigh. And his mother frowned slightly.

"Everything all right, Rory?"

He was silent for a second, eyes closed, soaking up the feel of her embrace. Then he said softly, "Just tired, Mama. Tired and happy to be home."

She didn't believe him. Not for a second. Rory Prescott was never tired. He was bubbling from dawn to dark and hours beyond, like a hot mineral spring. Only tonight, the effervescence was missing. His mood was quiet, as flat as champagne left open too long. And she wondered. But she didn't ask.

"Let go or you'll be starving, too."

128

"Yes, ma'am." He released her with reluctance and that provoked her curiosity even more. Her big, strapping son never let anything get between him and a full plate.

"Hello, Rory. When did you get back?"

The dark eyes brightened as they fell upon the mammoth swell of his sister-in-law's belly. "Good God, Sis. Ain't you dropped that baby yet? Hell, he's gonna be born ready to ride and rope."

"Or sew and cook," his mother added. With two strong, rowdy sons, she made no bones about her preference for a granddaughter.

Gena set the plate before Rory and bent awkwardly to hug him. Aurora noted that he clung to her with the same needy grasp. When Gena lumbered on to her own seat, Rory asked, "Where's Daddy?"

"He's taken some horses over to the Lawsons. If I know Ben Lawson, he's probably drawn a cork and the two of them are drunker than skunks. Your daddy knows how to find his way home." She started dishing up the thick, savory stew. Almost as a casual aside, she asked, "How's the major?"

"Fine. Why don't you come over an' see for yourself?"

"Your grandfather knows where I live, too," she replied shortly. Then, seeing her son's unhappy expression, she amended, "Maybe I will stop by. For a little while."

Rory smiled his thanks and the poignant gesture went straight to her heart. She knew it was hardest on him, this split in their family but she knew of no way to bring her husband and older son together with her father. She didn't know if she wanted to try. The potential was too combustible.

"We got us some guests at the Bar K. If you're up

to it, Gena, you might want to ride on over, too." He fiddled with his fork for a moment, then asked, "Scotty home? I got to make some talk with him tonight."

Gena's pallor was unmistakable but it was Aurora who answered. "He's gone in to Crowe Creek. He might be pretty late getting back."

"Mind if I bunk over then?" His worried gaze went between the two women. "Lessen you've turned my room into a nursery already. Don't rightly know if I could get a decent night's sleep with a passel of fuzzy little ducks and things a-looking down on me."

That brought a pair of faint smiles and Rory wondered in a stir of panic, *Scotty, what you gone and gotten yourself into now?* That tension made for a mostly silent meal and as soon as she could, Gena escaped to the shadowed porch. When he came up behind her to wrap his arms around her, Rory felt the shiver of her weeping.

"Scott?" he asked softly.

Gena shuddered. "He should have been home hours ago. I can't help it, Rory. I keep seeing him all broken and bleeding like that time before. Or stretched out cold in some alley. He's changed. He's so angry all the time. Ever since those men who — who raped Morning Song and hurt me disappeared before the trial. Scott feels responsible. He said he should have taken care of it when he had the chance."

Rory said nothing. He shouldn't have kept his brother from slitting the throat of the varmint who shot Gena when she came upon him and three others violating the Indian woman who'd been his lifelong friend. He understood Scott's guilt and fury. They'd done things the right way, the lawful way, and justice had escaped them. How that must gall a man like

130

Scott Prescott who was torn between a mind that knew what was legal and a heart that beat with the vengeance of the Sioux.

But his own guilt went a layer deeper. Because he'd seen the vile Jake Spencer at the Bar K the day before he and the others disappeared. Had seen Garth Kincaid give him money. And had said nothing.

"I'm sorry, Gena," he murmured, the words thick with feeling. He shut his eyes tight, trying to shut out the sight of his brother after Garth Kincaid's men delivered their message with their fists. And worse. Oh, he was sure the major hadn't named any specifics, just that Scott Prescott needed to be taught a lesson. And it was a rough school. He had to keep that from happening again. He had to keep the situation defused, because like dry tinder, the tiniest spark would set their whole family up in flames. Which was why he hadn't then and wouldn't now tell what he'd seen the day Jake Spencer left town.

"Things will get better, Gena. I'm doing my best. I'll talk to Scotty, get him to back down."

"I don't think he'll listen."

"I'll make him listen."

Gena gripped his forearms frantically. "Please, Rory. Don't push too hard. He's on the edge now. It wouldn't take much. He works all the time. He doesn't sleep. He has these dreams, nightmares he won't talk to me about. He feels helpless and when a man feels helpless, he does crazy things. Dangerous things. Where is he?" She jerked from his embrace and paced to the edge of the porch. Her slender shoulders shook with a new flood of tears. She struck them away impatiently. "I promised him I'd be strong. I wish I could be."

"Gena-honey, you're the strongest woman I know.

131

Mama must be rubbing off on you."

"Thank you for the compliment." She looked to him with a small smile and his heart nearly broke in two. She shouldn't have to feel such pain. Not Gena, who was sweet and kind and innocent of the troubles stemming back a generation.

Then she looked back out over the Prescott grasses and gave a little gasp.

"Oh thank God."

There on the far horizon, just a skimming shadow, moved horse and rider. Scott. No one else rode like that. Like a wild Indian. Rory stepped up quick to catch Gena as she reeled and almost collapsed.

"Gena? Gena? You all right? Is it the baby? Shall I get Mama?"

She was breathing in quick pants of breath, shaking all over but she shook her head firmly. "No. I'm fine. Just hang on to me for a minute."

"Shore. Shore thing." And he hung on tight. Right up until they could make out the sleek gleam of Scott's black hair awash with moonlight. Then she pulled away.

"I can't let him see me like this. Rory, keep him outside for a minute while I pull myself together." She was wiping at the dampness on her cheeks, trying to control the haunted look darkening her gaze. And Rory was suddenly very angry.

"Maybe he should see it. Maybe he should see what he's doing to you."

"No," she stated resolutely. "No. He doesn't need that. He needs me strong and I will be. Remember, you were the one who told me not to fold up under him."

"Damn my big mouth."

"I love him, Rory."

132

"So do I. I love the both of you. He'd better be worth all the trouble."

Gena looked him square in the eye and smiled with absolute certainty. "He is. Every second of it." She kissed him then, just a quick peck on the cheek and fled into the house.

Rory waited for his brother in the concealing darkness. He watched him roll down off the winded animal and pull up short. He stood in the yard, senses alert and quivering like a wary wild thing. Lone Wolf, son of Far Winds, son of Yellow Bear. And Rory wondered why he spent so much time worrying. Scott had instincts honed for survival. Like all his father's people. Like Aurora Prescott.

Rory eased out of the shadows and he could feel his brother's tension ebb away.

"When did you get back?"

"A bit ago. Where you been?"

Scott hesitated. Just a thread of a second. "Working."

Dang you, Scott. He'd never in his whole life wanted to punch someone in the face so bad. Until he got a look at that face. "Scotty, you look like hell."

A brief smile quirked the haggard features. "Thanks so much." He came up the steps to the porch, moving slow, like he could have easily staggered beneath the weight he bore. "Gena inside?"

Rory nodded then added with a deliberate drawl, "Cryin'."

Scott's face stiffened. "The baby?"

"The husband."

Scott scrubbed his hands over his face. "Don't lecture me, Rory."

"Don't plan to. You look like a man who knows he's being a selfish bastard."

133

"Thanks for sparing me the lecture."

" 'Welcome."

Scott glanced toward the house, his stoic face revealing a hint of his remorse. "She real upset?"

"Depends on how you define upset. I'd say, you bet. She's just about wore out with worry. Why don't you take her somewheres till the baby comes? Someplace safe."

"She's safe here. I moved her off the reservation so she'd have Mama to look after her."

"I ain't talking about Gena and you know it. She wants you to look after her. Why ain't you? Hell if she was my wife, thick with my baby—"

"She isn't." That was snarled with a possessive fury and Scott was immediately ashamed of himself. He drew a deep thought cleansing breath. "I can't leave right now, Rory. 'Sides, Daddy said it wasn't good for her to do much traveling this far along."

"Why don't you give her a little less cause for worry then? Start by getting a good night's sleep. When was the last time you had one?"

Since the dream. Or vision. The kind visited on his grandfather, Yellow Bear, speaking of what was to come. A vision so disturbing, he couldn't face it anymore. Of his brother's betrayal. Of Rory bringing his motionless body home to their mother. Of a truth revealed by terrifying bits and pieces until he couldn't close his eyes for fear of learning all. He looked up into the care-darkened brown eyes of his brother, searching them for some reason to believe or disbelieve. What could he do? Ask Rory if he planned to stand by while Garth Kincaid had him killed?

"Rory," he began somberly, "if something should happen to me, I want you to see to Gena and the baby."

Rory made a small sound of objection. It strangled in his throat. He swallowed hard and tried again. The result was a hoarse whisper. "Nothing's gonna happen to you, Scotty."

"Your word, Rory. There's no one I can trust with something so important except you. Take care of them. See they want for nothing."

"Count on it," came the raspy reply.

Scott sighed his relief. "Now maybe I can get that sleep." He'd started for the house when Rory's call came softly.

"Scotty, would you come over to the house with me tomorrow?"

His half brother was instantly on guard. "Why?"

"The Bar K is taking on an investor. I'd like you there to hear out the terms."

"The Bar K's none of my concern."

"But it's mine. And I want to make sure I'm not making a mistake."

"Like the five hundred?" Scott couldn't resist the gentle jibe.

"Got that back."

Scott waited for him to crow about it but Rory stayed oddly silent. His intuition prickled. "All right, Rory. I'll sit in on it with you."

Rory was nearly felled by his surprise. He expected a long, heated battle, not this quick concession. "You will? Why?"

" 'Cause you asked. 'Cause it's a smart move on your part and I don't want to see you hanging out to dry."

Just then the door banged softly and both men turned toward Gena.

"You're late, Scott." She said that with a smile, as if she'd been suffering from no more than a mild annoyance over it. Her kiss was light upon his cheek.

"I didn't mean for you to worry."

"Me, worry?" She chuckled. "I've got better things to think on than your sorry self."

Scott smiled and relaxed. Rory watched all the strain shrug off his shoulders at that soft supportive lie. It wasn't so much that he believed the unconvincing claim, rather that he needed to. Gena put her arms around him and in that loving embrace, she healed his brother's soul right before his eyes. Rory had never seen anything like it and he was awed.

With her delicate chin in the vee of his brown hand, Scott kissed his wife with an indecent amount of passion, considering her condition. "God, I love you, Gena." She simmered in response. "I promised Rory I'd ride on over to the Bar K in the morning but while I'm gone, why don't you pack up a basket and we'll have lunch together down by the creek." He caressed her cheek and smiled tightly. "And I hope for my sake that the water's good and cold." He hitched his arm around her burgeoning middle. "Come on, *mitawicu*. To bed. I'm tired."

Over her husband's shoulder, Gena mouthed a *thank you* to his brother.

After they went inside, Rory sat on one of the rockers his father had made and idly let his thoughts wander as darkness thickened and hours thinned. Try as he would to steer them away, they tended to always head in the same direction.

Norah.

He'd come to his family's home on purpose, to hide himself in their loving embrace in hopes that troubles couldn't find him. Only here, there were more waiting. Only the nature of them changed. His parents, Scott and Gena. There was so much love in this house. For the first time, he felt on the outside look-ing in. Not even when he moved to the Bar K had he felt estranged from the rest of the Prescotts. Why now, he pondered unhappily.

Because of Norah.

Damn her! Why couldn't she love him back?

Watching Gena sacrifice her peace of mind for the sake of his brother's made him ache with emptiness. He wanted to see that melting look of satisfaction in a woman's eyes, to have her stand beside him with feet set like a good roping horse. Who was he fooling? Not any woman—just Norah.

Just Norah.

Over his heavy sigh, he heard the approach of a horse and smiled to himself at the sight of the tall Texan weaving in the saddle. When the an-imal stopped at the porch, it was a long minute before Ethan Prescott muttered an unnecessary, "Whoa there." He spilled out of the saddle onto wobbly legs and started in an irregular path up the steps.

"Howdy, Daddy."

Clutching at one of the posts, Ethan murmured a gladsome, "Well, 'evening, Rory. Got a chair saved for me?"

"Need some help finding it?"

"Don't get lippy with me, boy. I hate that in a man."

"Yessir." His grin flashed white as his father plopped down beside him. "Mama's already gone to bed," he told him meaningfully.

Ethan sighed. "Well, guess I'd might as well make myself comfortable right here. Here. Try this on for size."

Rory took the earthen jug and tipped it obligingly.

And gasped. "Whooeee! That's awful! What is it? Horse liniment?"

"Ben Lawson's home brew." He took another swallow.

Rory made a gagging sound. "Sure that won't eat right on through to the soles of my boots?"

Ethan glanced down at the bottom of his foot gear. "Not yet."

"Then let me have another taste."

They sat and drank companionably for a long quiet while, then Ethan began to study his son. There was something different there. Something beyond the pleasant blurring effects of Lawson's Own. Something strange and sobering. As if Rory had gone to Wyoming a happy-go-lucky boy and had returned—older. Far older than the few days he was gone. Something in Wyoming had jaded his thinking and made him inexplicably harder. A man could feel that about his only son. He was guessing at best where Scott was concerned. But Rory read like a sign printed in bold, bright red letters. Until tonight. Only three things he knew acted on a man so fast: money problems, killing a man and loving a woman. And he wondered which had hit his son so hard.

"Go on an' talk, boy. Ain't never knowed you to be shy for words."

"Nothin' much on my mind, Daddy."

He might have believed that. A week ago. "You fixing all right for pocket change?"

"Can't complain."

"Handle yourself all right in Cheyenne, did you?"

"Mama'd be pleased to hear I never even had time to visit anyplace unsavory."

Two down. And that left . . .

A woman?

Rory?

He gave a lazy grin. Poor boy. No wonder he looked so wrung-through-the-wringer miserable.

"Scotty's coming over to the Bar K in the morning to tend some legal stuff for me."

Ethan had been in the middle of another swallow and nearly choked in his surprise. After struggling for breath, he wheezed, "Scott? Ain't that like shoving a half-starved wolf in a cage with a gut shot grizzly? You know what you're doing? Does the old man know what you're doing?"

"I'm doing what I can to mend the tear in this family. Nobody else seems to want to do a damned thing about it."

Ethan heard the pain and frustration in his son's voice. And it shocked him. Because he'd never worried about Rory. Scott was the volatile one, the one who ripped things open, the one who made his wife of almost twenty-three years weep at late hours in the night. Scott was the one who needed special handling, who caused the Prescotts and Kincaids to divide. No that wasn't quite true. He'd had his hand in it, too. His feud with Garth Kincaid went back to a time before Aurora, a time he could hardly remember. His wife, his children, his ranch were his life now and what came before was forgotten. Even Aurora had put aside many of her hostilities toward her father; the manipulative old bastard! As a family, they'd rallied behind Scott, involving themselves to the extent of overlooking the fact that Rory, too, was wedged in the middle. Because Rory didn't draw notice the way Scott did. He managed in his easy-going manner to convey the message that everything was fine with him. Obviously, things weren't fine, hadn't been fine for a long time. If only he'd paid attention.

He and Aurora had made their hard decisions early on. Scott, she'd tried to shelter from his heritage to no avail. Rory, they'd let run wild. And when he started spending all his time at the Bar K, they hadn't called him back. Maybe they should have.

"Son, I don't rightly know if there's anything anyone can do. It'd take baling wire to stitch the edges up and that's not a job I'd want to take on."

"I do."

"Then you be careful, boy. You keep an eye on the old man. He can be a pretty slippery customer and he don't always play fair. A pasture's a nice place to be but you got to watch where you're putting your feet or you'll step in something nasty. Watch where you walk, Rory. That's all I'm saying. You make your own choices. Then you sleep with 'em. It's always easier to sleep with a clean conscience. Do what you think's right, the way your mama and I raised you."

Rory said nothing. He was seeing Jake Spencer take money from Garth Kincaid. He was hearing Scotty's moans from having his ribs kicked in.

And he knew he wasn't going to sleep well at all.

Chapter Nine

A half-starved wolf and a gut-shot grizzly.

Had Norah heard that summation, she would have agreed. From the moment Scott Prescott stepped inside the Bar K, they were in the calm eye of the tornado. She wasn't sure what it was that whirled with such deadly violence around the gathering in Garth Kincaid's study but the atmosphere was thick and tense with it.

Scott Prescott was a strikingly handsome man with jet black hair and sculpted features against deep golden skin. And his eyes, they were gold, too. Intense, penetrating eyes that touched on her for an instant and saw all. He hadn't Rory's height or breadth but there was a subtle strength to him. Perhaps it was the fluid ease of movement or that piercing gaze. Scott Prescott made her uncomfortably aware that he could strike without warning. There was something disturbingly different about him but she couldn't quite pinpoint what it was.

Rory's brother. The two of them together made a contrast of day and night. Rory was warm, bold sunlight, Scott cool, mysterious dusk. She could picture Rory on the range, working cattle, mending fence, flicking rope with the other cowboys. But Scott, no. He was no cowboy. He was . . . what? Her curious gaze ran down the cut of his obviously expensive coat worn over a crisp white shirt and unfaded denims to his feet.

Where a pair of moccasins protruded.

Indian moccasins.

My God, that's what Scott Prescott was. He was part Indian.

And he was also less than welcome at the Bar K.

"What's he doing here?"

Garth Kincaid's demand cracked in lieu of greeting.

"I asked him to sit in," Rory answered mildly. But the hand he placed on his brother's shoulder made a solid statement.

"As legal counsel," Scott concluded for him. He drawled that out softly in words edged with steel. Just like the stare he leveled upon his grandfather.

"Is that really necessary?" Cole protested. He'd summed Scott Prescott up in a word — smart. Too damned smart not to be dangerous.

Surprisingly, it was Garth Kincaid who settled it. "It's not a bad idea considering how much we all have in the balance. And Mr. Prescott is an excellent lawyer. Harvard trained." His inscrutable gaze locked with his grandson's for a long moment, then Scott nodded in acceptance of the compliment. "I'll defer to Rory's judgment as to what's in the best interest of the Bar K." And Scott was the best his money could buy, if he would be bought. In this instance, he had been, not by loyalty to the name Kincaid or by coin but by his deep love for his brother. While he didn't care if his grandfather and every blade of his grass went to hell in a hurry, he wouldn't let Rory go with them. So he could be trusted in this case to use his considerable legal mind on the side of the Bar K.

Rory gave a gusty sigh of relief and clapped his hand against his brother's back. "Corral a seat there, Scotty."

Scott smiled thinly at his grandfather and replied, "I'd rather keep my feet under me."

Rory followed the direction of his cautious glare and

142

shrugged. He took a chair by the big desk enthroning his grandfather. Then, as if for the first time, reacted to the knowledge of Norah Denby sitting across from him. He stiffened.

Norah wasn't pleased by his reception. No smile, no warming of his dark eyes. Just a wary bracing of body. And suddenly she could see the resemblance to his brother. They were both wolf-cautious.

Where had he been? Norah had prowled the windows of her big room all night wondering, watching. Where had he gone when he rode out in a hurry after depositing them into the hands of the Bar K's housekeeper? To a woman? Was there a special one waiting? Or many? She wanted to believe it was the strange new surroundings that kept her restless until the pink of dawn. But it wasn't. It was the image of Rory Prescott rolling pleasurably with someone else.

"Let's get on with it," Cole declared. "Lord Monthaven has engaged me as his agent to find a good investment for his capital. And I must say, from what we've seen, we are very favorably impressed with the Bar K."

Norah listened to him talk. He was good at it, at painting a pretty picture with words, of building confidences with his smile. He presented the terms of the business union as if introducing the blushing bride to her stalwart groom. He talked of capital gains as if wooing a fat dowry. He played his part of promoter and genteel pawnbroker to the hilt with his suave looks and good presence. But he wasn't playing to a room of country hicks. Kincaid and Scott Prescott were a hard sell. But on one point, Cole had the advantage. They needed what he offered to survive. It was just a matter of finding out how badly.

The Bar K housekeeper, Ruth, slipped in silently with an urn of coffee and some yeasty smelling rolls.

143

She drew up short at the sight of Scott, her expression confused then delighted. After serving the guests, she crossed behind him where he stood close to the big bay windows and put her arms around him for a quick hug. For the first time, Norah saw a crack in his stoic facade. His expression gentled in a way she wouldn't have believed. And she saw the vulnerability of a caring heart.

"Now what we're proposing," Cole summarized at the end of his skillfully spun oration, "is a partnership situation whereas his lordship will assume title to the land."

"No."

The pale eyes cut to Scott Prescott in annoyance. "No? What exactly is your objection?"

"The land stays as a family holding. That is not negotiable."

Cole smiled smoothly to reveal bared teeth. "But you must agree that his lordship have some guarantee before funds are exchanged."

"No partnership. We're talking a capital investment, not ownership, otherwise there's no point in continuing this conversation."

Cole looked to Kincaid, hoping the fear of losing his backer would lead to an override. But Kincaid was in impassive agreement. Cole was forced to relent and rethink. "All right. Keep the title in the family. We'll talk long term loan. Say at ten percent interest with assurance of capital gains."

"The bank will credit at two percent just by word of mouth."

Damn, he was good. Cole held his smile. "Then why aren't you going through them?"

"Gentlemen, that isn't the issue," Kincaid interrupted. "I agree that ten percent is too high. We'd be hamstrung from making any improvements. Then, no one profits."

"Shall we consider eight percent?" Monthaven suggested. He was thoroughly charmed by the entire affair, by the romance and excitement of it. He could afford to be generous. He wanted the Bar K.

"We might consider that but five percent would be more motivating," Scott offered.

"Seven," Cole said.

"Done."

"With provisions."

"Being?"

"Seven percent on the loan. His lordship will provide the financing and Mr. Kincaid will furnish the foundation herd. He will serve as manager at a salary with full operating expenses. The investment plus interest will be repaid in full at the end of five years or a portion of the residual property will revert in ownership to him. At best, you will be financially secure for the rest of your lives. At worst, you will have a new partner."

"Damn," Rory muttered softly.

Seeing the ranchers squirm beneath those terms, Cole bestowed his most congenial attitude. "You may think on it, discuss it amongst yourselves. And if you can find a better arrangement elsewhere, please feel free to do so."

Rory looked to his brother. The golden gaze signaled toward the door. With a brief mutter of excuse, the two of them went out onto the porch. Rory leaned against the rail, staring out over the vast rolling acres of Kincaid ground. Scott stood at his shoulder, watching the house.

"What do you think?" Rory asked.

"I think you're going down a hole there's not much chance of climbing out." He heard his brother's expansive sigh. "How bad do you need this?"

"Bad."

"The terms are brutal."

"It's either let Monthaven in or lose it all piece by

145

piece anyway. I don't see that we've got much choice."

"I'll draw up the papers for you. Then I want out of it. I don't want to be tied to the Bar K and I don't trust Denby."

"He's the one who gave me back my five hundred."

"That so." Scott narrowed his gaze thoughtfully. "Watch him, Rory. I got a bad feeling."

"Going Injun-queer on me, Scotty? I thought this was business."

They exchanged smiles and brief glances.

"It's what makes me good at what I do," Scott confided with a measure of pride.

"Pretty soon you'll be telling me you saw it all in one of ole Yellow Bear's dreams."

Rory's teasing comment wiped the humor from his brother's expression. There was a cold caution in his words. "Just be careful."

Puzzled by the abrupt change, Rory said simply, "I appreciate it, Scotty." To which his brother merely gave a distracted nod. He was seeing remembered dreams.

The company looked up as one when they returned to the room. At Rory's slight nod, Cole beamed.

"It's settled then."

Monthaven was beside himself with satisfaction. A piece of the West. Splendid. "I would like Mr. Denby to stay on as my personal representative. He will be responsible for the administration of my funds and for issuing reports on a timely basis."

Scott tensed. His sharp stare cut to Rory, full of meaning.

"I don't know," Rory began but his grandfather overruled him.

"Fair enough. Scott will begin the proper paperwork. Rory, why don't you show his lordship around while Mr. Denby and I see to a few matters between us?"

It wasn't a suggestion. It was a command. As much

as Rory wanted to balk, he knew the futility of it. Garth Kincaid had the deciding vote and he'd cast it in Denby's favor. He shrugged slightly in Scott's direction and the golden gaze said plainly, *Watch him.*

"Come, Mr. Prescott," Monthaven announced energetically. "I am most anxious to see all there is to see."

Rory muttered an apt expletive under his breath.

When they were alone, Garth Kincaid studied Cole Denby and his lovely daughter from across the top of his massive desk. He knew Denby. He'd recognized him from the start. Oh, not personally. He had no knowledge of the man but he knew him. And what he knew was to his advantage.

"A cigar, Mr. Denby?"

"It's Cole and yes, thank you." He made a show of selecting from the box of imported Cuban smokes and took his first draw from it with relish.

"Cole, what exactly is Monthaven paying you?"

Denby smiled. He knew Garth Kincaid, too. Kindred spirits connected quickly. "He paid an initial $1,250 plus expenses and then there'll be an additional $2,500 in common stock when the deal goes through in his favor."

"An indirect bribe, you might say."

"You might," Cole agreed amiably.

Kincaid glanced at the pretty young woman sitting in silent witness. "Would your daughter like to freshen up?"

Norah bridled up at the smooth dismissal but Cole claimed easily, "I have no secrets from Norah. She is, you might say, one of my greatest business assets. Please speak freely."

Kincaid scrutinized her for a moment, gauging the tempered steel of her gaze, then he nodded and turned back to business. "Cole, how would you like to double whatever salary Monthaven levies as his manager."

"I'm listening."

"As Monthaven's manager, you'll be handling the purchase of herd additions and providing him with a book count. He will rely on the accuracy of that tally to release expense funds. Now if an ambitious agent were to paint an optimistic picture, his dividends could amount to, oh, shall we say, twenty-five percent."

"We could say that. Figures have been known to inflate quite by accident."

Kincaid smiled at the man's quick understanding. "You could be a great asset to me, Cole. I need a man like you. Have you ever done this kind of work before?"

"What kind of work did you have in mind?"

Kincaid's lip curled back. "We've got nesters popping up like cottonwood seedlings. They need to be plucked out by the roots to keep them from spreading. Used to be they'd scare like a flock of band-tailed pigeons at the crack of a gun but not anymore. When one stands, they all stand. I employ good men who'll run an iron on a maverick for an extra two dollars a head but they can't be counted on for range protection. They're cowboys, not killers."

"I can see the problem. It's been a while but I still have some useful connections. What about your boy?"

"Rory's a good man and I've got a lot of faith in him. But for now, I'd just as soon keep this between us. I'll bring him in when the time comes."

"I meant the other one."

Kincaid frowned darkly. "Scott?" He spat out the name as if it fouled his mouth in the speaking. "Yes, he could be a serious liability."

"Should he get to be a problem, I can have things taken care of. When do you want me to start hiring on men?"

"Just a few should be enough for now. The rest can

148

wait until Monthaven is gone. Have we an agreement, then?"

And Norah watched stoically as the two men shook hands.

"I don't like it, Gena."

Gena Prescott saw a savage sigh lift and drop her husband's shoulders. She was picking up the remnants of their feast while he stood pitching pebbles into the clear creek running behind the Lone Star. The shift of mood was all too evident. The pleasant, relaxed companion of moments ago was gone, leaving this tense, all too familiar figure.

"What's wrong, Scott?"

"Nothing solid. Nothing I could get Rory to go along with. It's just a gut feeling, the kind he doesn't believe in. He laughed at me, Gena." He paused and she could feel his hurt. "I just hope he has enough sense to be careful."

"Is it Monthaven?"

"No. He's all right. It's his man, Denby. He's—not honest. He's too slick. He smiles too much. I don't know. I just don't like it. Then, I don't like anything that has to do with Kincaid. It makes me feel like I need to wash my hands." His posture grew rigid with whatever was gnawing at the inside of him. Gena waited unhappily for whatever it was to work its way to the surface like a bothersome sliver. "Maybe I'm wrong to get worried over Rory. Maybe he's just fine. Maybe . . ." His voice trailed off with a pensive restlessness.

"Maybe what?"

"Maybe he knows exactly what's going on and it doesn't matter to him one bit. He is Kincaid's man, after all. Maybe I'm watching out for the wrong feller."

"Scott! He's your brother."

Scott turned toward her. An uncertain anguish etched his features into sharply defined angles. His eyes glowed a pure hot gold. "Gena, he was a brother I remember from ten years ago. We were kids together. He was only ten years old when I went away to school. A boy. A boy who grew into a man I don't know. A man who lives in our grandfather's house. Am I supposed to believe that none of the ugly things that go on at the Bar K have touched him?"

"Not his heart, Scott. That hasn't changed." She held up a hand to him. "Come here."

He did so, reluctantly, his agitation making him balk at the summons. But when her gentle hand closed around his and she tugged, he gave in and settled on his knees facing her. She reached out to put her palm against his cheek, stroking his face to rub away the lines of anxiety. But she couldn't chase the shadows from his eyes.

"Don't, Scott. Don't turn from those who love you. Rory would never stand against you. All you have to do is look to your own heart to know that's true."

He let her draw his head down to rest upon her soft bosom. There, he closed his eyes. Because he didn't want her to see the panic that beat in his heart, the panic of an unrealized truth revealed to him in dreams. He closed his eyes to the vision but couldn't shut out the sound. Of Garth Kincaid's voice commanding, *Shoot him!* The thunderous report of a handgun. The feel of a bullet tearing into his body.

He opened his eyes then, seeing through the mists of his vision the smoke dribbling up from the barrel of his brother's pistol.

And that was the truth that tormented his days. A truth not of *if* but *when*.

* * *

150

Danged fool foreigner!

Rory looked down from his perch upon Chance's back to where Lord Monthaven strode leisurely through Kincaid grass. No Western man in his right mind would choose to go afoot when he had a horse at his disposal. It just wasn't right. It just wasn't done. And it wasn't practical. It would take him weeks to walk the boundaries of the Bar K but his lordship seemed in no particular hurry. He simply strolled along swinging his umbrella as a cane with enough energy to send Chance sidestepping nervously.

"It's all very grand, isn't it?"

"What's that?" Rory mumbled disinterestedly.

"This land of yours. All the vast silent spaces, the lonely rivers and plains. How lucky you are to be a part of it."

Rory grunted noncommittally.

"It has always been my dream, your American West. My family thought me quite mad to suggest it, the financial and physical risks, don't you know. But then at Eton and Harrow, I was trained to be a doer not a shop-keeper."

Rory slid him a sidelong glance. Though he was contemptuous of what the man represented and would pretend to ignore him, he couldn't help being curious. What kind of man would come halfway around the globe to pretend he was a part of a world that didn't want anything to do with him? Who would spend a fortune to buy himself a piece of someone else's life? He may have lacked for common sense but not for courage. He was a young man, maybe a couple of years older than Scott. To a man like Rory, who saw going to a neighboring state as a monumental journey, to venture so far from home was not the act of a cowardly spirit. And as much as he wanted to dislike Monthaven, he was forced into a grudging respect. But that didn't make him any less strange. Imagine, striding along in Sunday best out in a cow field as if it was a park promenade. Toting a gentleman's manners like that ridiculous umbrella. What kind of man acted like that?

The kind of man Norah Denby might marry?

Rory scowled and stared ahead darkly.

"We need shade."

The comment startled Rory. He glanced about the rolling hills. They were as treeless as the palm of a roper's hand. "If you're feeling faint, your lordship, flick up that there umbrella."

"Not me, the land. We need to buy trees and to plant crops for feed and to dig ditches to irrigate."

Rory gave a hoot of laughter. "You aiming to put the Bar K hands into ankling? We ain't running no goddam granger outfit. No self-respecting man would work a-foot even if jobs was as scarce as prairie hens in a hailstorm."

"I never fail to marvel at the arrogance of you people," Monthaven drawled inoffensively. Even so, Rory's eyes narrowed in anticipation of further insult. Not perceiving the danger, the Englishman continued his observation. "T'would seem that a man who turns a lot of cattle out onto a barren plain without making provisions for feeding them will not only suffer a financial loss but the respect of his fellow man, as well."

"What the Sam Hill you think you're walking in? The best God-given feed on earth, that's what. We hay our stock in the winter. Have since back in '87. We don't starve no beef here on the Bar K."

"Oh, I say. I wasn't suggesting . . ."

" 'Course not. Only a crazy man looking for a taste of lead poisoning would think to tell a cow man how to run his range."

Rory Prescott said that easily, almost with good-humor but there was no trace of amusement in his cool, dark gaze. And Charles Monthaven had taken about enough of his cocky cowboy snobbery.

"Mr. Prescott, I have made it my business to study the best techniques in animal husbandry. It is my plan to improve your range stock with imported Angus beef. I have followed their bloodlines as carefully as those of the peerage. And if I fail here, it will not be through lack of background but rather from the failure of others to aid me in my inexperience. If you wish to see this venture fail and your ranch along with it, please feel free to continue this childish petulance. Are you afraid you might learn something? Or has this to do with Miss Denby?"

"Miss Norah ain't got nothing to do with it," Rory growled.

"No? Only a blind man could mistake your interest in the lady. And she is a lady, sir, one who could not help but be offended by such crude pursuit. Really, I cannot see why you would think yourself of a class to pose a serious threat to my intentions where the fair Miss Denby is concerned."

Rory stared at him, red-faced and speechless. Of all the pompous, high-minded, low-handed, snotty-sounding . . . Rory's teeth ground on the want to sneer, *I was good enough for her to invite to her bed. Can you say the same?*

But then, maybe he could.

Icy fury spreading through his belly, the young rancher forced an amiable smile and drawled, "Why I wouldn't even presume to compete for Miss Norah's affection on your level. That is, if she prefers a pretty feller like yourself aground to having a man astride."

Monthaven glowered up at the redhead sitting confident in the saddle with his arms crossed over the horn in a pose of indolence. He refused to lower himself into giving a response. Instead, he lifted his umbrella and flicked it open.

And Chance blew up like a Dakota thunderhead.

Caught unaware, Rory had no opportunity to grab for solid purchase as his mount lunged violently from the unknown threat. The first hard jolt sent him flying out of the saddle to land smack on his pride, much to his lordship's entertainment. Feeling as though a mule had slammed both hoofs into his rump, Rory clamored gingerly to his feet. He refused to give the smirking Englishman the satisfaction of watching him rub his bruised posterior.

"Gawdammit, Chance," he bawled after the bucking animal. "Get back here!" He let loose a piercing whistle but the horse continued its terrified gallop toward the Kincaid barn, its hoofs slashing backward in rebellious disregard. "Hang you, you skiddish ole broomtail. I'm gonna skin you out and make a coat outta your ugly hide!"

"It appears we are both aground, Mr. Prescott," Monthaven observed with a droll chuckle.

Rory whirled on him in a considerable temper and gritted out, "Ain't you got a lick a sense? Spooking a good horse thata way."

"T'would seem if it were that good a mount, you would not be standing humbly instead of riding."

Rory huffed in outrage. "What do you know from horseflesh, Mr. Fancy Pants? Why that there horse is God's gift to a working cowboy. He can turn on a dime and give two bits change. He can set his feet against a four-year-old steer and bust 'em end over end against a rope. He's got more brains and more heart and more speed than anything on four legs."

Monthaven arched an imperious brow, doubt written clearly on every aristocratic line of his handsome face. "Really? It would happen, Mr. Prescott, that I have a fair knowledge of equestrian pedigree. I have raised

154

and run thoroughbreds for the glory of my shire for ten years. In fact, one of my horses is being run in the East and is making me a tidy sum of capital. So if I were you, I would not be so quick to boast the questionable qualities of your mangy little mustang to me."

Mangy? He could call his horse any number of foul things but to hear another man spout them was like taking an insult on the virtue of his mama. Rory Prescott drew himself up to every imposing inch of his six foot plus frame and ground out in seething offense, "You bring that horse out here and you'll eat my dust."

"Is that a fact?"

"You're damn right!"

"Are you proposing a wager?"

"Name the stakes. I mean to best you, on horseback and everywhere else that counts."

And with that declaration of vinegary pride, Rory set off walking toward the Bar K. He set a fast pace, not caring if he left the Englishman behind. In fact, it would give him great joy to come across his bleached out bones in weeks to come. But even if his stubbornness would hold out, his footgear wouldn't. The high Cuban-heeled boots were made to nestle stirrup iron, not to tramp in manly fury on hard-packed earth. By the time he reached the fenced boundaries of the Bar K compound, he was limping and more than a little riled.

"Your horse come in a while back, Rory," one of the men called out. "We was about to head out a-looking for you."

"Just thought I'd take a stroll. You got a problem with that, Abel?"

Abel Collier wouldn't dare grin in the face of that majestic fury. Instead, he shook his head with an innocent lift of his brows and did his grinning after his boss hobbled by. "By the way," he yelled at the retreating figure. "Chance is in the barn. Ain't none of us fool

155

enough to take his gear and rub him down."

"Let him stand wet," Rory snarled as he continued to stalk toward the house. "The sonuvabitch."

Abel slipped off to the barn to warn the other wranglers that Rory Prescott was no one to be messing with today.

The final insult was to find Norah Denby sitting cool and pretty on the porch swing. The indelicate toss from his horse and five mile walk had him nearly crippled and running with sweat. He was in no mood to act the proper beau. Not like Monthaven would when he arrived, probably still starched and smelling sweet.

Norah stood as he stomped up the steps. She tried not to betray the concern that had twisted inside her since his paint had returned with an empty saddle but she could see he was obviously lamed. Her lovely brow puckered and she was about to speak when he cut her dead with a glance.

Because all the hurtful bruising he'd taken, the worst wasn't to his pride. It was to his heart.

What if Charles Monthaven could boast a similar knowledge of his Miss Norah beneath the sheets?

Wordlessly, he stormed past her and let the door bang shut with the force of a slap in his wake.

Chapter Ten

As the days passed all cool, green and lazy, Norah wasn't sure whose suit was more persistent and more entertaining to observe. Cole's, in his avarice for the Kincaid money or Monthaven's, in his claim upon her attention. Both, so sure they were being too suave to be obvious, provided her endless hours of empty amusement. There was little else to do at the Bar K. She was relegated to guest status, which meant she was an outsider. She had no patience for needlework, no talent for music or art and though she enjoyed reading, the library selections were slanted toward masculine interests. All in all, there was little for her to do other than rock on the porch, make polite conversation at dinner and hunger after the sight of Rory Prescott in his tight Levi's jeans.

He had all but ignored her since her arrival. Was it because she'd rejected his proposal or because she'd hurt his pride? Or, most disturbing of all, was it because she had proven herself shallow in his eyes? She hadn't thought he'd be a harsh judge of character. Perhaps she was wrong, for he had no use for her. And that left her chafing miserably, wondering through the long, dark nights who he'd found use for.

Because a man like Rory Prescott hadn't learned those devastating kisses by practicing on Bar K fence posts.

The morning was crisp and filled with the blue Dakota sky. Norah sat on the porch swing watching Rory and several other hands work a group of wild horses in the big corral. While Charles Monthaven sat beside her reading aloud from a book of dry verse, her heart was pumping madly within her breast as the mustang Rory clenched between his knees shimmied like a sunfishing chunk of fury. All the shy awkwardness she remembered about him while he was tottering atop his high-heeled boots disappeared when he sat a saddle. There, he was all confidence and control, like a powerful centaur. He moved with a swinging undulating motion as the animal tried its best to unseat him. She sat with breath suspended, muscles taut, pulse racing until the wild creature finally admitted mastery and let Rory ride him. And what a ride. The animal surged around the perimeter of the corral while Rory showed off to the delight of his ranch hand friends. Norah found herself smiling with them. Heaven above, he was some kind of man, with his broad grin, and free-spirited manner, part mounted cavalier, part flashy showman, all fun, all excitement. He'd earned the right to swagger and brag amongst his fellow hands. Because there was nothing he wouldn't try, no horse he wouldn't ride, no job he'd send a man to do that he wouldn't uncomplainingly do himself.

Norah watched with achy little palpatations, as he swung off the newly broken horse and accepted the rowdy congratulations of his peers. He moved through them easily to hop up astride the gate, while another bronc was readied. He whipped off his hat to mop an untanned brow, then used the Stetson to shade his eyes as he squinted in the distance. Then, with a loud whoop of welcome, he came off the fence rails with the smooth, easy grace of a tiger, as if his muscles flowed beneath the skin. It was hard to tear her gaze from him to see who was approaching.

The rider was bareback and bareheaded. She could see the gleaming ebony hair and flash of white teeth against a bronzed face. Scott Prescott. Rory strode out to meet him, gripping the reins in one hand and his brother's knee in an easy show of affection. As the two men talked, she watched Rory gesture toward the house and Scott stiffly shake his head. Then the horseman passed down a roll of papers and Rory sent him off with a slap to the horse's withers and a wave of his hand. When Rory turned toward the house, Norah was quick to pretend an interest in Charles's recitation. She glanced up only when she heard the rattle of his spurs upon the porch steps. Then she managed a remote smile.

Rory looked right by her to the Englishman. With a quick show of the papers in his hand, he said, "All drawn up and ready for signing. If you can take a minute out from quoting that there book of fluff."

"This is poetry, my good fellow. Hardly fluff. As you would know . . . if you could read."

Rory sucked in a harsh breath and expelled it with a growl of, "I can read."

"Oh, good for you. But this is probably beyond your limited frontier learning."

Aware of Norah's gaze upon him, Rory simmered and said quietly, "I can read as well as you."

"Can you? Then perhaps you'd care to recite a line or two." He was smiling a particular smug smile that should have warned Rory had he been less preoccupied with proving himself to the lady between them. The book was snatched from Monthaven's hands. For a long moment, Rory studied the pages, his features still, his

159

breathing shallow. Then he flung the volume down upon the porch boards and strode inside to the sound of Monthaven's mocking chuckles.

"I shall return in a moment to finish our soliloquy," his lordship promised in an intimate aside. When he was gone, Norah picked up the book, turned it over in her hand and looked at the small print.

It was Latin.

It took them less than a half hour to go over the papers Scott had prepared and affix their names to the bottom. That done, Rory declined a toast to their combined success. Nothing could make him lift a glass with Charles Monthaven. Instead, he stormed out of the house, past the woman on the swing with his spurs jingling like a rattlesnake's warning and marched down to the corral. Norah watched him go, feeling her heart crowd in her throat. Such a prideful man. And the Englishman had stripped him right down to the skin in front of her. She sat, with the open book across her knees, absorbed by the sight of him practicing his roping. He made it look so easy, so graceful. She never saw his arm lift or move as he held his rope low by his leg, snaked it out full length and sent it twirling to fall true about one of the corral posts. It was lonely business, that solitary repetition. She wondered what in his expression warned the friends he'd been sharing rawhide good humor with moments ago away from him now.

The book was taken off her lap, giving Norah a start of surprise. Her concentration on the tall cowboy had been complete. In that instant of broken focus, she noticed Monthaven's hands. Smooth, long-fingered hands, lily-white and unblemished. Hands meant for holding books and arranging the folds of a silky ascot to perfection. Not like Rory's. His were working hands; dry, rough, split like the parched Dakota ground and capable of creating a wonderful friction upon her

160

soft skin. What would Monthaven's touch awaken?

She looked up at him through dispassionate eyes. He was handsome and wealthy and spoiled. Throughout the week, he'd made it plain that any woman lucky enough to have him would have her every desire. He'd spoken of his country estates in England, of his grand townhouse in London, of his holdings abroad. And of how he would treat his wife like a queen. He was exactly what she'd been looking for. Security without involvement. Nothing about Charles Monthaven even remotely touched upon her emotions. It would be the perfect business arrangement. She would have all the money and freedom to do whatever she wanted. He'd made that very clear. She'd be living a life of luxurious plenty. And be barren inside. A month ago, that would have been a fair trade, her personal fulfillment in exchange for capital gain. In fact, a marvelous trade.

Until she'd tasted the wild pleasure of a cowboy's kiss.

How could she casually shut the door on those chafing passions? How could she pretend that living the life of external comfort could compare to the hot promise of Rory Prescott's kiss? Knowing she'd be better of with one didn't make her want the other less.

"Shall we continue, Miss Denby?" Charles drawled as he positioned himself at her side with a possessing confidence.

"I think not, my lord. I seem to have lost my taste for verse."

"Oh? Is it that Prescott fellow? He should be taught some manners."

"By you, my lord? I think not."

Charles Monthaven's fair brows rose to an apex of disbelief. "Surely you are not suggesting . . ."

"No. I am not suggesting. I'm telling you outright. What you did was an incredibly cruel and insensitive

161

act and I find myself quite disappointed in that character flaw."

Flaw? Monthaven was aghast. "But Miss Denby, surely you must agree that the strutting bumpkin needed to be shown his place."

"Not by you, sir. Now, if you will excuse me, I believe some fresh air is in order."

She could feel him gaping at her back and somehow that was a very satisfying feeling.

Rory sent the length of Manila soaring and cinched quick to snag the post. It was a reflexive act, one practiced so often it could be executed in his sleep. A good thing because his thoughts were far away from the destination of his loop.

Damn them! Sitting cool and smug, laughing at his expense. He didn't look but he could see them plainly and the image riled him something fierce. While he was down here working up an honest sweat, the fancy lord, who would rather die than permit himself such a lowly function as perspiration, was up there sweet talking Norah Denby. And she was agreeable to the listening. Well, he was welcomed to her. They suited each other just fine. She was looking for a man with money and Monthaven was reeking with it. She was looking for a man who would take her to exotic places and read to her from books all filled with funny-looking words. Fine, she had found him. He hoped she was very happy.

"You make that look very easy."

Surprise made the rope drop from its spin into a limp coil upon the ground. Rory reeled it in brusquely. "It is when you practice enough."

"Umm. May I watch?"

"Suit yourself."

He worked out another loop and silently cursed the sudden shakiness of his hands. Dang if his insides weren't jerking around like a Mexican bean on a hot skillet. She was standing too close. It was the smell of violets. That delicate scent clashed with those of leather and hemp and horse. It went straight up his nose to numb his brain. He gave his head a conscious shake and sidestepped a few paces, using the diameter of the loop to hold her at bay.

She was so pretty. Like a wild prairie flower abloom on its graceful stem. Smelling good, fluttering with layer upon layer of lace upon a soft lavender ground. Inviting him in like a bee to heady pollen. Wondering why she'd come down to the dusty realm of the cowboy from her shaded throne, he remained carefully stoic. If it was some kind of game, he didn't appreciate the teasing.

She was watching the twirling circle. "That's not like any rope I've ever seen."

The topic seemed safe enough. "I'ts a roper's lariat. It has to be stiff to get the job done."

"Umm, I see where that would be a definite plus."

Hell's afire, if the woman didn't shift cool gray eyes to draw a low, right personal bead on his Levi's with her calm gaze. It was a struggle not to rise to her expectant stare. The circle increased and spun faster. "We're talking about roping, right, Miss Norah?"

"Of course," she responded with a mild smile. "What else?" Then her steely eyes took on a sheen of sultry humor, daring him not to laugh. And he tried. He tried until his face muscles ached then reluctantly let loose with a wide, helpless grin. To Norah, who'd been suffering from his guarded chill, it was like the warming heat of summer sun breaking across an overcast sky. And she soaked it up greedily. He relaxed enough to do some showing off for her, moving the flat loop in front of him so he could step in and out of its coil without entangling his feet.

"You do that very well," she said, duly impressed.

"I do a lot of things very well," was his immodest reply. His dark stare engaged hers with sudden directness, daring her this time to deny it. She didn't.

"Yes," Norah agreed in a husky ripple of bone-shaking sound.

Just when Rory was ready to cave in completely, the stubborn lines returned to his face. He looked away. "Including reading. My mama taught me. I can't tangle with them fat books Scotty totes around and I didn't get no fancy college edge-u-cation, but I ain't ignorant either. And I don't much like folks treating me like I'm some kind of dumb grub-line rider."

"Ignorance measures more than what a person learns in books."

Rory canted a glance in her direction to find Norah staring up toward the porch with a surprising degree of vehemence. A smile worked the corners of his mouth but he clamped down on it when she looked his way again.

"Show me how you do that," she asked abruptly, watching the undulations of the rope with a fascination. "Is it difficult?"

"Naw. Kinda hard on the hands though. This little eyelet at the head of the lariat is called a honda. You take your main line and your loop in your throwing hand, feed the honda 'bout a quarter of the way down for balance. Hold your coil in the other hand, letting out extra line with the thumb and first finger. Your last two fingers are for holding your reins. You want to have a good grade of Manila so that when you send a loop flying it'll stay flat and open." He did so and the circle dropped with lazy accuracy over one of the posts. "Then you tie off your rope around the horn with a few quick dallies and a half hitch or a hard and fast figure-eight knot. Nothing to it."

He sauntered over to jerk loose the knot and began to recoil his lariat. Norah was mesmerized by the way he performed that simple chore. Her awareness of him as a man was heightened to an excruciating level. When he came close enough, she reached out to stroke her fingers over a hard row of knuckles. He immediately went still, as if her touch represented the threat of something very lethal to his system.

"You have beautiful hands," she said. It was a strange comment to make and certainly not true as she must have known. Contrarily, she turned one of them over within her palm and rubbed the callused spurs with her thumb. An unsettling roil of sensation radiated up his arm, then settled low to stoke already simmering fires. He gave an uneasy laugh and pulled away, chafing his palms together with a shy kind of nervousness.

"No they ain't. They're all the time rough and dirty and about as beat up as a pair of old work gloves."

"But they're warm and they're gentle. Like you."

That throaty observation made Rory's heart drop to his feet. It took him a minute to remember to breathe, then the breath he sucked in was ragged. Absently, he picked up his rope and started it whirling again, the quick snaps it made an echo of his agitation.

"Why are you coming on to me like this, Norah? Trying to get a rise outta your fancy feller? I don't want no part of that."

"It has nothing to do with Charles."

"Charles, eh?"

Frustrated by his stubbornness and provoked by her own desperate straits, Norah said bluntly, "What would you do if I came right out and asked you to kiss me, right here, right now?"

165

Rory kept the lariat spinning. He didn't look at her. "Depends. Are you askin'?"

"Yes. I'm asking."

With the effortless movement of his wrist, he sent the loop spiraling up, then down, then up again. And with another twist, brought it gliding over her head where it settled and was cinched up lightly about her arms and torso. One big hand slid down to the honda while the other took up slack. When he took a step toward her, he saw the way her eyes darkened and the way the deepening movement of her chest put a tugging tension on the rope. And he couldn't trust the passion in her widened eyes any more than he could control the way it burned inside him.

"And I'm saying no."

With a slight jerk from him, the lariat fell limp to the ground. As limp as her hopes at that moment.

"You decide what it is you want, Norah-honey, then you ask again. Now step on outta there. I gotta get into town."

"Could I go with you?" That was said breathlessly, impulsively, as she sidestepped out of the loop.

"I don't much care," he drawled easily. From over her shoulder, he watched Charles Monthaven's approach. It was a study in displeasure. "Bring your boyfriend along, too. Give him a taste of a real frontier town."

Before Norah could protest that Charles Monthaven's company was about as desirable as diphtheria, she heard his lordship chime in behind her, "Oh, I say. That sounds like a splendid idea. Let me get my umbrella."

"Splendid," Norah echoed sourly.

The trip to Crowe Creek was a miserable experience. Rory found them a driver, and while she sat helplessly listening to mile after mile of Charles Monthaven's dissertations, the redhead rode alongside on his vinegary little stallion. Halfway there, they came upon a buckboard driven by a horribly plain woman and her budding daughter. Rory chose, to Norah's extreme aggravation, to keep pace with them. He rode easy in the saddle, leaning his weight lazily in the stirrups and his crossed forearms on the horn. Both weatherworn females responded to his broad grin and amiable attention with giggles of delight. Norah would have enjoyed strangling the lot of them but only the fierce narrowing of her eyes betrayed her seething temper.

In Crowe Creek, things got worse by the second. As soon as Rory climbed out of the saddle, a woman of obvious professional lines shrieked his name and launched herself into his arms. With her elbows holding his head immobile and her fishnetted legs hooked about the backs of his sturdy thighs, the female engaged him in an impossibly long, open-mouthed, tongue-thrusting kiss. And he didn't show any signs of objecting.

"Well, howdy there, Sally Jean," he grinned cheerfully when she let him have his breath back. "You been behaving yourself?"

"Like always," she simpered. "I been a-saving myself for you, Rory Prescott."

With that unlikely claim, she wiggled herself suggestively against him like a kitten in heat. Rory gave a big, resounding laugh and squeezed her saucily beruffled bottom. "Sure, darlin'. I believes you. Ain't I worth waitin' for?"

Norah's fingers whitened on the handle of her parasol. The memory of him holding her like that, of his big body driving up inside her kept her up nights panting for release. And here he stood, playfully imitating that same searingly sensual act with a common prostitute right in front of her, right in the middle of the sidewalk.

As if he didn't care. As if she didn't matter. As if it was just the natural course of things for all women to want to wrap themselves around a big stud horse like Rory Prescott. The arrogance of him to flaunt his virility and prowess before anyone with eyes to see! Never had she wanted to geld a man so badly. Except that it would be denying herself the same that she begrudged the others.

Seeing the direction of her glare, Monthaven remarked in huffy tones, "The man hasn't a speck of decency to carry on in such a fashion with a lady present. Look away, my dear. You shouldn't be witness to such a carnal display."

Turn away? As if she could. Norah's attention was riveted. Jealousy roared through her. Along with a curious sense of loss. She knew whose sheets he'd be tangling in tonight and it was not a gratifying knowledge.

Just then, Rory whispered something to the woman and she laughed with delight. Her arms and legs uncurled to allow him to set her on her feet. It was then Norah noticed to her horror that the woman was obviously pregnant. Though not very far along, there was a definite swell beneath the tight stretch of satin. A fact Rory was aware of because he put his hand right over it in a light caress before handing the expectant woman a tolerable amount of cash. She clutched it for a moment, her big kohled eyes welling with tears.

"Oh, Rory, I just love you all to pieces," she cried and attached herself for another wet kiss.

"Go on with you, Sally Jean. Now you take care of yourself, hear? And don't spend that on no whiskey. It ain't good for you, considering."

"See you later?" The hope in the woman's voice was heartrendingly sincere. And Rory's reply broke Norah's in two.

"You betcha."

He smiled after her for a long moment then turned

his attention casually back to the couple in the buggy. "Y'all gonna sit up there all day?"

Norah was glad for Charles's aid. Her knees were trembling too much to support her. She felt flushed as if with fever but her face was quite pale. And her eyes glittered like a knife edge when they fixed on Rory Prescott. Purposefully, she wound her arm through the English lord's and made a show of batting her lashes up at him. As if he, Charles Monthaven was the only man in the world worth her attention.

Ain't I worth waitin' for?

Her jaw hurt from the force it took to smile.

Apparently, Rory wasn't the kind of man who waited for long.

"Well," he drawled out leisurely as his dark, inscrutable gaze assessed Norah's response. Or the lack of it. "I guess I'll be leaving you two to enjoy the sights whilst I attend my business." He glanced along the shabby row of false fronted buildings and grinned wryly. "Have fun."

And as she watched, her fingers biting into the fine imported cloth of Lord Monthaven's coat, Rory swaggered away down the walk. And into the nearest saloon.

Damn you, Rory Prescott! Norah thought fiercely. *If you were my man, I'd follow that sassy behind right through those bat wing doors. I'd grab you up by the nape of the neck, drag you out into the street and beat you within an inch of your miserable life!*

But he wasn't her man.

She'd had her chance. He'd offered her all that considerable potent, fun-loving charm. And she'd said no. And she would still say no were he to ask again. But for different reasons than the ones he believed. He thought it was the money she craved and that he wasn't good enough to accept without full pockets. Silly man. Sweet, silly man. If he only knew it was just the opposite. She was the one not good enough for him.

But that didn't stop her from wanting him. That didn't keep her from longing for his touch, for his company, for just the basking heat of his smile. If only it were possible. If only she could take the name and security of a man like Charles Monthaven, a man who meant nothing to her, and still enjoy what she felt for the redheaded cowboy. Then she could be free to . . . to what? Love him? No. Never that. To have fun. To indulge in the fiery promise of that first afternoon together. To laugh and talk and smile. If only it was possible to have those things and not break both their hearts.

You decide what you want, Norah-honey . . .

If only she knew exactly what that was.

"Come along, Charles," she announced with an air of proper boredom. "Shall we see what this quaint little town has to offer?"

And she walked right by the half doors to the saloon. She refused to glance inside to see Rory Prescott's black Stetson up at the bar. Because she was afraid she'd find him there with his breeding whore, Sally Jean, in his arms.

Much to her surprise, Lord Monthaven fell in love with the town of Crowe Creek. He adored its raw vitality. He was excited by its crude ruggedness. He was enthralled by the townspeople. Because it all spoke to him so clearly of the West. And to him, that was the ultimate adventure.

They strolled the warped sidewalks for over two hours, poking into every dingy shop, every noisy hotel. He glanced at the saloons with longing but was too much of a gentleman to leave Norah unescorted to indulge his curiosity. It was beyond her to understand why a man of impeccable lineage, who had toured the finest cities of Europe could be charmed by a mud hole

170

like Crowe Creek. However, the excitement did lend a bit of animation to his otherwise stuffy converse and the time passed more pleasantly than on the ride in. She was just beginning to relax and smile when they came out of a mercantile to come face to face with Rory in the arms of yet another female. This one was no common tart. Her clothing was casual but well-fitted and of good material. She was burrowed into his shoulder, hugging him with an obvious affection. And he was smiling serenely down into the soft cluster of her pale blonde curls. It wasn't a look of lusty appreciation. It was one of love. It was almost the way he had once looked at her, Norah realized in an agony of truth.

Then Rory spotted them and turned the woman toward them. Norah's jaw dropped. The woman was enormous with child. Good God, was the man trying to seed the entire Dakota prairie in a single season?

Norah held her ground as Rory squired the awkward female across the street. His solicitous attitude made her want to scream. Finally, the two of them stepped up onto the porch and stood, he with his arm easily about her delicate shoulders and her with hers snug about his waist. They looked incredibly cozy. Norah's teeth ground.

"Gena, I'd like you to meet Miss Norah Denby and Lord Charles Monthaven. And this dainty little beauty," he paused while she laughed and poked his ribs, "is Gena Prescott, my brother Scotty's wife."

Did she look as foolish as she felt? Scott's wife. Rory's sister-in-law. She took the other woman's small hand and nearly crushed it in her gratitude.

"Mrs. Prescott, I am pleased to meet you." Was she gushing? Norah couldn't help it.

"It's Gena, please."

Then the fragile woman lifted her soft gaze to Rory's and she raised her brows in silent question. He looked

171

down at his boots rather quickly and for all his deep tan, his cheeks seemed to glow with a tinge of pink. Apparently satisfied with what that conveyed, Gena Prescott beamed up at Norah then heaved an exaggerated sigh.

"Oh, I swear if I don't sit down soon you're going to have to carry me home in the back of the buckboard."

"You drove out here by yourself? Where's Scotty? I'm gonna whup him good. What's he a-thinking letting you go off traipsing around alone?"

"Firstly, Scott doesn't know and second I wouldn't listen even if he did tell me to stay home. I'm with child, I'm not disabled. Heavens, your father tells me I'm healthy as a horse and getting to look more like one every day. Now, quit your fussing, Rory Prescott. You're worse than your mother. What I'd like, if Miss Denby is willing, is a nice cup of tea at the hotel. Why don't you boys run along and let us get to know each other."

Gena, for all her dainty manners, gave her brother-in-law a look that brooked no nonsense.

"Yessum," he mumbled with a grin. "Come on, Charlie. I'll stand you to a taste of tanglefoot."

Monthaven balked at the familiar use of his name but was too eager to explore the insides of a saloon to protest. With her arm looped through Norah's, Gena steered her in the opposite direction and soon, they were seated at a lace covered table, sipping tea.

"Don't you just love him?"

Norah glanced up at the warm statement. "Whom?"

"Rory. He's such a sweetheart. When Scott brought me from Boston, I thought I'd fallen off the edge of civilization. Rory was my first friend. He's as dear to my heart as any brother could be."

Norah remained wisely noncommittal. She wasn't sure what the lovely Gena Prescott was after. Was she

172

trying to lure her in or warn her off? While she was trying to decide, Gena threw her off with a genuine smile.

"But then you know all about Rory, don't you?" And immediately, she began talking of other things, feminine things that she'd missed discussing with a friend close to her age.

Gena was a puzzle. This frail flower of a woman couldn't possibly be wed to Scott Prescott. Scott was all cold, sharp edges and intense fire. He would consume the delicate Gena who was as obviously of fine Eastern blood as he was combination of white and Indian. Intrigued, she would have pressed for more details, however at that moment, Charles and Rory came in search of them. Gena studied Norah's features as she looked upon her brother-in-law. Then before the two men were close enough to overhear, she told the woman in a friendly sort of way, "Norah, please don't take offense at this. Rory is very special to me. He has a wonderful, big heart. If it were to be broken, I might be provoked into taking up my husband's scalping knife."

Then, smiling warmly at the two men, Gena struggled out of her chair while Norah gaped at her in abashed surprise and put an unsteady hand to the hair coiled at her nape.

Chapter Eleven

He was going to her.

Norah paced her room, restless and aching.

Telling herself it was foolish, telling herself it was self-torture, telling herself it was for nothing didn't stop the swell of anguish. Knowing she was crazy for doing it, didn't stop her from waiting at the windows for him to ride out. *Go to bed, Norah. This is no good. Let him go. What does it matter?* But it did matter. And there was no use pretending otherwise.

Throughout dinner, she hadn't been able to swallow down a bite of her meal. Agitation had completely dammed her throat. While Charles rambled on about how he would like to be a part of a real life Western celebration before returning to England in two weeks time, she wasn't thinking about how to endear herself to him in those scant days ahead. She wasn't thinking about him at all. She couldn't tear her thoughts from Rory Prescott and the woman twined about him. The way she would be twined about him in the darkness of that very night.

Norah watched the barn. Any minute, he would head for it then ride out on his frisky paint stallion. To the town of Crowe Creek. To the woman Sally Jean. The woman thick with his child. Her palms pressed to the flat slide of silk over her midriff. What would it be like to feel his child move inside her? The sudden yearning twisted tight and hard. She thought of Gena Prescott, so glowing and happy, full of another life, proud of the fruit of her husband's love. How glorious that must feel.

Norah, the man has made you crazy! she chided herself harshly. She didn't want to be fat with any man's child. She had what she wanted. She had her independence, her freedom, control over her life. Why would she surrender that to tend a whiny babe? What kind of mother would she make, anyway? One like her own? No sir, she didn't want that. A sacred responsibility that she could only fail. *No, not me. Let his whores have his children.* A sob snagged in her throat.

Then she saw him, a bright beacon of red crossing the yard below.

"Rory." It was a hoarse whisper, thick with emotion. Her palms pressed to the windowpanes. If she yelled out, he'd hear her and he'd stop. And what then? What reason could she give? What could she tell him? That the thought of him spending the night with another woman was tearing the heart from her?

She stood silent at the window, her panted breaths fogging the glass as she fought not to cry. The more she told herself it was better to let him go, the more she wanted to grab him and hold on tight. He was supposed to love her, after all.

If he loved her so damn much, why was he riding off to meet with someone else?

Resolutely, she knocked the insistent dampness from her cheeks. Her lips thinned and struggled not to quiver. *So much for your devotion, Rory Prescott. I should have expected as much.* Good, she decided with grim relief. Now she could put aside the fantasy and get back to what she should be doing.

Then he came out of the barn. Not astride but afoot. And he headed not toward the gates but back to the

175

house. As if he had no intention of going anywhere.

Norah hesitated for a long moment. Then, with her thin silk wrapper tangling about her legs, she raced to the door and eased it open. And waited. But there was no sound of him coming inside.

So where was he?

The aggravating man! Well, she wasn't about to spend another second of her time pacing and fretting over what Rory Prescott might or might not be doing. She'd just go and see for herself.

The porch was as dark and quiet as the yard and out-buildings beyond. She stepped out, her feet chilling against the bare planks. She was tempted to call out but then he'd know she'd come looking for him. And wouldn't that please him to no end. Determined, she began to walk along the rail, squinting casually into the dimness, her frown deepening with every step. Where the hell . . .

" 'Evening."

Norah jerked a good few inches up off the boards as his voice rumbled from the shadows. Her hand went to the neckline of her robe as if trying to catch back a cry of alarm. She could make out his outline where he sat slowly rocking in the porch swing and there was no mistaking the white flash of his grin.

"You nearly scared the life out of me," she scolded fiercely.

"Think you were out here all alone, did you?"

"Yes, of course." She clutched her dressing gown modestly. That was quite ridiculous. He'd seen her without it.

"It's mighty late to be out for a stroll."

"It's not all that late."

He leaned forward to peer up at the sky. "Well, the Big Dipper is past nine o'clock to the North Star so it must be after midnight."

"I had no idea. It was too hot to sleep."

176

"I thought it was right comfortable."

"Are you determined to argue with me about everything?" she snapped peevishly.

"That what I'm doing?" he challenged in mild amusement. "Miss Norah, if you were looking for me, just come out and say so."

"I wasn't," she was too quick to reply. She moved in sharp, angry strides to the rail, unaware of what an enticing silhouette she made against the backdrop of the moon and stars. "I didn't expect you to be here at all."

"Oh? And where would I be?"

"I was under the impression that you had business in town." Oh, Lord, how that sounded. Like she was some nagging wife, harping mercilessly for attention. She squeezed her eyes shut, praying he would read anything into the taut tremors of her voice.

But he knew how to read just fine.

"Now, Norah-honey, what would I be going into Crowe Creek for? It's after midnight."

"Don't patronize me, Rory. I saw you give that whore money."

His low chuckle set her back up as rigid as a cottonwood post. "Is that what this is about? Sally Jean? Hell, she's just a friend. We get together sometimes and share a few laughs."

"Oh please. Friends don't suck your lips off right in the middle of town then take money for it."

"That what you think?"

"That's what I know."

Rory's voice lowered a notch, growling slightly with displeasure. "Sally Jean is a nice girl fallen on bad times. Her folks used to live just north of here till they got caught out in a blue norther and froze to death. Sally Jean moved into town and got the only work she could. She's a sweet, decent, loving girl and you got no cause to be bad mouthing her to me."

177

"Is that your child?"

The directness of her question took him back. "What?"

"Is that your baby she's carrying?"

"Don't think so. Guess it could be mine as much as anybody's."

The calm way he confessed that shook Norah's posture of indifference. "Is that why you're giving her money? Because you feel guilty?"

"Guilty? I don't feel guilty 'bout nothing. Sally Jean's a working girl. That baby could belong to any one of a hundred or so fellers. She could take up a collection from most men within a week's riding distance. I told you, she's my friend. She's trying to set some money aside for when she won't be able to work no more. I was just helping her out, that's all. Friend to friend."

Norah said nothing but her stiff posture conveyed her disbelief.

"Why should it matter to you one way or another?"

"It doesn't," she declared hotly.

"Then you wouldn't care none if I was to head on into Crowe Creek right now to find me some pretty little thing to curl up with for the night? It wouldn't bother you a'tall athinkin' of me and some filly getting naked and—"

"No!" She gulped a quick breath and calmed her tone. "No. Why should it?"

" 'Cause if it was you doing them things, I'd be plumb outta my mind crazy."

A shudder shook her slender form from head to toe.

"Norah-honey, look at me." When she stiffened in rebellion, his voice pitched to a husky persuasion. "Norah, turn around now and hear me good." She did so with the utmost reluctance. He could just make out silvery trails of wetness down both sides of her face. "I ain't going into Crowe Creek, not tonight, not any night. I'm gonna be right here. Waiting for you." He heard her draw a raw breath and expel it shakily. He continued in a slow, se-

178

ducing drawl. "Figured you'd come find me when you made up your mind that you wanted me."

There was a long moment of silence with only the creak of the swing to punctuate it. Then Norah answered with unfaltering clarity.

"I want you."

The swing stopped.

"Then you come on over here and you show me."

After a moment's hesitation, she came gliding across the width of the porch in a glimmer of pale silk. Rory was seated square in the middle of the swing and made no move to provide her room beside him. Undaunted, Norah stepped her knees up over the spraddle of his thighs, settling astride his lap with her forearms resting on his broad shoulders. Her thumbs rode the strong angles of his cheeks as her fingers stretched back for the soft feel of his red hair between them.

"I want you, Rory Prescott," she repeated, then came down for a long, reacquainting kiss. She moaned against his mouth as his big hands made a slow inventory of her body. The silky night clothes were hiked nearly to her waist. She wore nothing beneath them. His touch centered where he found her wet and welcoming and began to stroke and rub and thrust and tease. She moved with it, swaying the swing gently then making it bang loudly against the side of the house with the sudden strong burst of her pleasure.

"Shhh," he cautioned in her ear with a chuckle of smug male mastery. "Easy, darlin'. You want to wake everybody up inside?" He couldn't help sounding pleased. He'd been dying to bring her to that particular heaven again. She was so sweet, so responsive. And he was certain that he hadn't been alone in his urgent need of her. For a moment, she rested against him, her head on his shoulder, her light pants for breath caressing his throat. He could have held her there all night without complaint. Until she began to circle her hips in a tempting motion against the swollen crotch of his jeans. Then thoughts of just holding her were quick to extinguish in the blaze of want. He started shifting to that seductive tempo.

"Let's take this inside for a proper finish," he suggested huskily.

Norah sat back, rocking on his lap, enjoying the hot excitement in his uplifted gaze. "How about right here, right now?"

His answer was a low growl of impatience. "Oooh, honey, sounds fine to me."

Deftly, she tackled the buttons, freeing him from the taut strain of denim an inch at a time. Then she lifted up over him and settled just far enough to begin a flirtatious pulse of motion. But Rory wasn't in the mood for teasing. After several titillating seconds, he gripped her shoulders and with a lusty groan, jerked her down.

Norah gasped, feeling as though he was crowding all the way up under her ribs. She tried to ease up but his fingers tightened, crunching the bones of her shoulders.

"Norah-honey, don't move just yet," he panted fiercely. Tension shook through him for a long minute then he relaxed cautiously and gave her a wide smile. "There now. Figured you'd be wanting more than an eight-second ride."

"Much more," she agreed with a sultry smile. And then she proceeded to put him through his paces. A slow, scorching rhythm meant to answer all the lonely hours she'd been without him. A languorous movement that let her savor the sense of fullness and strength. A purposeful beat giving her complete control of the desire in his dark eyes and the rush of his breathing from lazy to labored.

Rory was sprawled back comfortably, his arms draped along the back of the swing, his heels on the porch boards to move them in a rocking motion, carrying her weight easily. He was bemused by her self-satisfied expression and said finally out of curiosity, "Whatcha grinning at?"

She was grinning. She was smiling all over. "You. I want to watch you this time."

An incredible complexity of emotion swept over his features. Abruptly, so quick it took them both by surprise, his breathing altered. His fingers clenched the back of the swing and his eyes rolled back white. Norah squeezed her knees tight to ride out the plunging buck of his hips that sent the swing pitching wildly beneath them. When his gusty moan started to climb to a wailing velocity, she clamped her mouth down over his to seal it in, kissing him hungrily, encouragingly until the last of the shuddering spasms eased. The swing resumed its gentle rocking.

"Easy, darlin'," she whispered playfully, "you want to wake the whole house?"

His head rolled weakly against the back of the swing. "Oh, God, I'm past carin'. I'm sorry, Norah-honey," he murmured in a breathless ramble of words. "I didn't mean to go without you. I just — you just — Damn, woman, you shook me right outta my boots." Then he grinned up at her with a weary contentment and enfolded her into a tight embrace. His heartbeats shifted from the hard thrust of passion to more powerful surges of feeling until his chest filled to the point of bursting.

"Rory," she complained mildly. "Rory-honey, you're squishing me."

"Sorry," he muttered happily. "I just love you so much."

He hadn't meant to speak that out loud. Immediately, he felt the tension gather along her limbs. Damn, he'd ruined it. Leaning away, he put his fingertips over her soberly shaped lips and urged almost frantically, "Don't say nothin', Norah."

That soft, pleading note moved as cruelly on her heart as his involuntary admission. Both brought her more

181

misery than she could stand. She clamored for her resistance, saying, "I've got to go . . ."

"No. No, not yet. Not now. Norah, stay with me. Just a minute or two."

His arms locked about her waist. His cheek rubbed against her tousled hair with endearing tenderness. His lips moved upon the soft curve of her neck. And inside her, he began to stir to life.

"No!" There was nothing remotely coy about the way she spoke that word. She pushed against his chest and wiggled off his lap.

"Norah . . ."

She stood posed and trembling against the glimmer of moonlight for a long second, fighting the attraction, struggling against the pull of logic. Then she fled soundlessly into the house.

"Damn," Rory sighed, slumping down in defeat. "Damn, damn, damn."

When they met at the breakfast table, no one would have guessed that neither had gotten a lick of sleep after shaking out the chains of the porch swing the night before. Neither would look the other in the eye, Rory in fear of what he'd see, Norah in fear of what she'd give away.

Charles Monthaven provided a bridge to the silence. He was going on enthusiastically about his idea of a Western gala complete with music and dancing. And horse racing. He caught Rory's attention with that last, announcing casually that he was bringing his thoroughbred from the East to put down all comers.

Rory recognized the slur and the challenge, responding to both with a lazy smile. "Why Charlie, I don't think you gots any idea what racing is out here in these parts. If you're planning to have a real Dakota blow out, you got to top it off with a real Dakota race."

Monthaven's eyes narrowed at the bastardization of his name that the young cowboy was growing so fond of. "Why of course, I realize you have no standardized track or anything that could pass for it."

Garth Kincaid leaned back, amused by the testiness flaring between the two men. He understood and shared Rory's chagrin and took his direction with a great deal of pleasure. "You see, your lordship, a Dakota race isn't on a track. It stretches out across the plains, over the hills, down in the gullies, wherever man and horse can manage fifty miles out and fifty back."

"One hundred miles?"

"The man can add as well as he can read," Rory drawled. "You don't think your fancy bale-burner could go the distance against our best broomtails?"

Cole Denby's eyes lit up bright. "Just think of the wagering; West versus East. Everyone would want to get their two bits down."

Rory tipped back in his chair, eyes goading, smile daring. "Whatcha say there, Charlie? You game for it? Hell, you been dying to plant us cowboys in our place. Last chance. We'll give you a real taste of Western hospitality, too. Whatcha say, Major? Ain't kicked up our heels here on the Bar K for a while. Shall we start digging some barbecue pits, ordering up some kegs of whiskey and rounding up some broncs?"

Kincaid waved a hand. "Do what you like, Rory. Open up the doors. They're your doors, after all."

"Guess I best go rustle up some help." He shoved back his seat. "Come on, Miss Norah. Take a ride with me. Show you some of the countryside you won't see from a buggy. You ride, don't you?"

Her chin angled up a notch. She met his wicked gaze without the trace of a smile. "Very well, Mr. Prescott. I'll go up and change."

Cole looked between the two of them with a niggling

183

suspicion. "Norah, dear, I could use your help this morning in drafting some correspondences."

Norah stood and placed a brief kiss on his brow. "I'd be happy to, Father. First thing this afternoon." And then she hurried from the room.

Rory waited restlessly in the yard. How long did it take a woman to get out of all her geegaws when she wasn't properly motivated? He'd saddled her a dependable bay gelding, not quite certain if her claim to being a good rider was bluff or truth and held Chance's reins in the other hand. Sensing its master's mood, the little paint danced at the end of its leads, prodded him in the back and nipped playfully at his pockets.

"Stop it, Chance," Rory growled, shoving its nose away. "You're as bothersome as an ole tick. You'd best act right nice with Miss Norah along or I'll stuff a parlor sofa with you."

Just then, Norah came out of the house. If Chance had chosen to nudge him then, Rory would have gone over like a tipped log. The reins fell from slack fingers the same way his mouth dropped open from a slack jaw.

It was worth the wait.

He'd never seen a woman other than his mama in man's britches. And this was altogether different. The tan Levi's skimmed along her long, fine legs from turned up cuffs to narrow belted waist, curving and tucking in places no man's ever did. She wore boots and a pintucked shirtwaist stuffed into the waistband of her trousers. The heavy locks of sable hair had been neatly woven into a braid. The overall effect was drop-dead staggering. If pure sensuality could be carved into the shape of a woman, he was looking at it. And totally lost in the looking.

"Is something wrong?" Norah asked tartly as she pulled on her thin leather gloves. The way his dark eyes

184

had gone all over glassy made her queasy inside, as if he'd just put his big warm hands on her bared body. If he was going to continue to stare like that, she was going right back into the house. Or she'd be undressing for him right there on the porch.

"What?" Rory muttered at last.

"I asked if something was wrong."

His smile came slow and sassy. "Oh, no, ma'am, Miss Norah. Nothin' wrong a'tall."

He came toward her with that languid, spur-jangling amble that reminded her so much of a big lazy cat. She almost retreated. He was sly and dangerous and she couldn't let herself forget that no matter how gosh-golly awkward he might pretend to be. She held her ground as he came up to the edge of the steps. It put them at eye level. She liked staring at him straight on. It made her feel less intimidated. It was a false security.

Rory took off his hat and settled it atop Norah's head. "There. Wear that so's your face won't end up the same color as my hair. I'll go fetch me another. Be just a second."

Rory was halfway into the house when one of the men stopped him with a blood-chilling call.

"Rory!"

He turned and the spit dried in his mouth. Norah had picked up Chance's reins and was looping them over his head. The temperamental stallion was eyeballing her, ears rotating in an agitated manner, spotted hide quivering tensely.

"Oh my God," Rory moaned hoarsely. Chance was going to kill her, sure as the day was long. He forced a bit more volume and said with what he hoped was calm, "Norah, you get on away from him, you hear. Honey, don't go arguing with me. Just do what I said, real slow and easy. Norah!" *Sweet Jesus!*

Norah reached up a hand to adjust the split-ear bridle.

Chance's eyes were showing wild and white. Rory was afraid a sudden move from him would set the skittish animal off so he edged slowly down the steps.

"Hey there, you handsome fellow," Norah was crooning softly. "We're going to get along just fine, aren't we?"

The horse's ears twitched forward. Its nose lifted to nudge Rory's hat, blowing warm air out and breathing in Rory's scent.

"I'll bet you're Rory's big baby, aren't you?"

Chance nickered softly and stood calm while Norah went around to notch the stirrups up. By then, Rory stood at the horse's head, hands firm on either side of the bit. His voice wavered. "Norah, Chance don't let nobody but me on him."

"Oh, nonsense. Chance and I understand each other just fine. I'm going to ride him or you'll turn him into tonight's dinner." She fit her foot into the stirrup and swung lithely up into the saddle. Rory held his breath, waiting for the volatile little horse to explode. Nothing happened. Norah gathered up the reins and smiled down at him as though he was silly to have worried. What he was, was sweating buckets.

"Are we ready?"

"Guess so."

Rory let go of the bridle, muttering a soft warning under his breath. "You act up, son, and Ruth'll be spooning gravy over you."

As they rode out of the yard, a line of gawking cowboys hung on the corral rail.

"What the hell are y'all staring at?" Rory hollered at them. "Get back to work." Then to Norah, in a carefully modulated tone, he advised, "You just let him go real easy there, Norah and — Dang it, woman!"

Her heels flashed back, startling Chance into a forward hop and a full out gallop. Rory had no option but to set his mount on their heels. Eating her dust.

Dang, the woman could ride!

Ethan Prescott shaded his eyes. He let his chair roll down from the edge of its rockers and called into the house, "Rory's coming in."

"It's not even dinnertime," came his wife's wry reply.

"Got someone with him. Looks to be a woman."

Aurora showed no undue interest. "Must be that Denby woman from the Bar K. Scotty told me the new manager had a daughter."

"You might want to come look at this, Ora."

She scowled, wiping a blotch of flour off her nose. "I'm right in the middle of these biscuits. What's so important it can't wait until they get to the house."

"She's riding Chance."

Flour scattered every which way as the sifter fell to the tabletop.

Aurora joined her husband on the porch, dusting the remnants of her baking off her skirt and tucking in wisps of her hair. The fact that the strange female could ride Rory's feisty horse was nearly as stunning as the notion that he would let her. This was one woman Aurora was curious to meet.

"Gena. Scott. We've got company," she called back into the house. And soon the porch was crowded with Prescotts.

The minute they crested the final hill, Norah was taken by the neat spread, from its log house to its tidy corrals and big barn. A fine cavvy of horses were in evidence, both in the paddocks and in the far fields of green Dakota grass. Rory hadn't said anything as to their destination. He was still pouting and fuming over the way she'd outrun him. She admired his choice of horseflesh. The little paint was a firebrand, quick, smart and responsive to the slightest touch. She'd expected him to put up a fuss when she swung astraddle but not the intensity of his objection. For the first few miles, he looked as though he'd swallowed one of his boots. Then he was just plain simmering mad. She knew the first rule of the range was never to borrow another man's horse without permission, and that permission was rarely granted. But a quirk of vinegary spirit had provoked her to take Rory's mount. To show him she could ride. To earn a new level of respect in his dark eyes. But first, he'd have to get over being irked.

"What a beautiful place."

"It's the Lone Star," he told her with a hush of pride and a small smile of pleasure.

Norah didn't have long to puzzle over those things. They were close enough to make out the figures on the porch. She recognized Scott and Gena Prescott right away. And she had only to glance at the older woman's fiery hair and the tall man's rugged features to know them, as well.

Rory had brought her home to meet the family.

Chapter Twelve

Gena was the first to advance upon their guests. She smiled with genuine pleasure and exclaimed, "Hello, Norah, Rory."

Rory jumped off his yet moving animal to be at Chance's head when Norah dismounted. He needn't have gone through the trouble. The little horse pushed its head at the woman in an affectionate gesture usually reserved for him. At his astounded expression, Norah laughed and chided softly, "I told you I could ride."

Rory's grin was sudden and dazzling. "Yes, ma'am, you did at that."

And there it was, that hot, admiring look she'd wanted. Only instead of giving her a sense of satisfaction, it filled her with a clutching panic. Because it reminded her of the way the two of them had rocked a porch swing. Because he had brought her to his home to meet his parents. And suddenly all the playful challenge of the morning ride became something altogether different. Something she didn't want at all. She balked when he reached out to secure a possessive circle about her waist.

"Come on over here, Norah. I want you to meet my folks."

She moved beside him with a stiff reluctance, growing angrier and more alarmed by the second. Again, he had jumped to all the wrong conclusions. They'd made love and he was assuming way too much from it. Like it implied her consent for his cosetting attitude. Like it gave him call to adopt the prideful stance beside her as if he'd brought home a coveted trophy for his family's inspection. Then, she hadn't hindered that illusion. She was snugged up next to him after coming in on his horse and was wearing his hat as boldly as he was wearing his grin. What else would they think? It couldn't be clearer if he'd smacked a brand on her hindquarters. She was Rory Prescott's woman. It was an illusion she couldn't allow any of them to believe. Especially Rory. Especially herself.

Norah stepped away from him, coming up the porch steps on her own with hand extended. "Mrs. Prescott. Mr. Prescott. It's a pleasure to meet you. I'm Norah Denby. My father is the new manager at the Bar K. I guess that makes us neighbors."

Rory hung back, a bit bewildered by her sudden desertion, then he took the steps in a single bound and swept his arms around Gena. His rumbling, "Howdy, Sis," was followed by a gentle bussing of her cheek. Gena held to his hand fondly and Norah was taken all at once by the image of the rounded, delicate Gena Prescott coming after her hair with her husband's big blade. It wasn't a comforting thought. Nor was the feeling of being swallowed up whole by the Prescott clan.

For all their warmth of Western welcome, Norah felt the honed edge of curiosity. Though gracious with her smile, Aurora Prescott was candid in her study. She summed Norah up after only a few minutes of conversation; beautiful, intelligent, a hard-edged survivor in the soft guise of a lady. The golden gaze said plainly, *What do you want with my son?* Ethan had the same lazy charm that Rory used to wind himself about her heart. She wasn't sure what worked behind his steady, dark stare. Interest, mostly. Scott regarded her warily, a sentiment she readily returned. Only Gena seemed to have no questions. She was beaming at the other woman with unabashed acceptance.

"How good to see you again, Norah. I'm glad Rory brought you out to visit. We don't get a lot of guests and I'm not in any condition to do a lot of calling."

Again, Norah puzzled over the fragile Boston flower set in amongst all the deep-rooted Dakota gamma. She wouldn't have thought the fair Gena strong enough to flourish let alone multiply. With Scott Prescott? She couldn't imagine a less likely nurturer than the cold-eyed, self-contained, half-Indian man. What would make a delicate woman of obvious genteel breeding want to stay in such a lonesome place with such a remote husband?

Then Gena reached out her other hand to him. Scott instantly engulfed it within his own dark one and drew it up to rest over his heart. The gesture was unconscious and incredibly intimate, a bonding of two souls. And Norah looked away, embarrassed and acutely aware of how little she knew of the nature of love.

"What brings you home before my biscuits are even in the oven?"

Rory grinned at his mother and went to put his arms around her capable shoulders. He looked down into her suspicious gaze, his own melting with an endearing degree of helplessness. "I come to ask a favor, Mama. We're fixing to have a big shindig over at the Bar K and ain't nobody can whip one of them together as good as you. And with Daddy there to cook up some of his famous Texas sauce, why hell, nobody in the next ten counties would stay away." He slid a glance toward his glowering father but knew if Aurora gave the go ahead, the big Texan would relent. "What do you say, Mama? You promised me you'd come a-calling and I ain't seen you yet. Ruth can't take care of everything on her lonesome. And me, I gots the grace of a goat."

"What about your grandfather?"

"The major gave me leave to do whatever I wanted. And I want my family with me. About time, don't you think?" Some of the more obvious cajolery faded to a more candid plea.

"I think it sounds wonderful," Gena spoke up enthusiastically. "I've been dying for something to do. I won't be much good at setting up tables but I can handle my share of the planning."

Rory grinned at her gratefully, then his hopeful gaze shifted to Scott. Who immediately went rigid.

"Scotty?"

"If Gena wants to go, I won't stop her," he said tonelessly. "But don't expect me to go make nice where I don't belong."

Rory drew a deep, disappointed breath. "Two days, Scotty. Just some dancing and horse breaking. No politicking. Just a bunch a folks having a good time."

"No."

"Can't you put aside your crusade for the Sioux Nation and your damned Kincaid pride and just be my brother for two lousy days?"

When Scott's expression didn't alter, Rory muttered a soft oath and jumped down off the porch. He stalked across the yard in long, angry strides, kicking at clods of dirt to send the dust flying.

Gena pulled her hand from her husband's and crossed her arms over her bosom.

"What?"

"You know what, Scott."

"Gena, I'm not going. None of those folks want me there."

"Rory does."

"Rory wants too much."

"It's just a party, Scott," Aurora put in gently.

"What? You, too?" He turned in exasperation to his stepfather.

Ethan shrugged eloquently. "Grin and bear it, pard. If I can spend two whole days with the ole bas—bandit without burying anything in him, so can you. Better'n spending a week sleeping on the porch and eatin' cold grits."

"There'll be trouble," Scott predicted somberly.

Ethan grinned wide. "Hope so. Trouble makes going to parties tolerable."

Scott looked out toward his brother's broad back, wishing fervently he had something to twist in it. "Oh, hell," he grumbled in surly resignation. "What's two days?"

He scuffled across the yard, every inch sullen, to where Rory stood. "Don't expect miracles, Rory," he cautioned softly.

Rory turned and scooped him up in a rib-crunching hug. "Already got one, big brother," he vowed happily, rumpling the short black hair with one affectionate hand. He let Scott's feet find ground again and told him with heart-bruising sincerity, "Thank you, Scotty. It means a heck of a lot to me having you there." He swallowed hard, once, then was all confident smiles, as if he had no doubt that his stubborn brother would come around. "Betwix you and me on horseback, I figure we can rake in enough in bets to winter easy." His arm draped casually along the line of the smaller man's shoulders as he continued to rattle on in easy camaraderie. Scott's hand rose to rest a bit awkwardly in the center of Rory's back, then gave it a hearty thump with his palm.

"Daddy, you got a good horse I can borrow long enough to ride Rory's baskettail into the ground?" Scott called back over his shoulder. Grinning, the big Texan ambled out to join them by the corral.

How much more was happening than a mild family dissension, Norah wondered as she watched Gena's soft gaze fill with moisture. The currents were deep and murky with suppressed emotion. She was chillingly recalled to the conversation between Garth Kincaid and Cole. Scott Prescott was a liability to the Bar K. Did Rory know? If not, what would he think of the subtle plotting against his brother by the man he both loved and admired?

"Well, I'd better get those biscuits baking," Aurora announced. "Please excuse me for a moment, Miss Denby."

"I'll keep her entertained, Aurora," Gena volunteered cheerfully.

When the two women stood alone on the porch, Norah's bemusement got the best of her. "Tell me about Scott."

Gena warmed instantly to the topic. "What would you like to know?"

"He's part Indian, isn't he?" There was no condemnation in her tone, only curiosity.

"His father was a Lakota warrior. He's very proud of that. So am I." Norah had to admire the firm way she said that. When Norah glanced into the house, frowning slightly, Gena understood her confusion. "Scott was conceived while Aurora was a captive of the Sioux. His father was killed up in the hills and Ethan found her, frozen and on the verge of delivery. It's very romantic, really, but sad, too. Major Kincaid refused to accept a half-breed child into his family. He insisted that Aurora give Scott up. She wouldn't, of course. She married Ethan instead, and he raised Scott like his own. Unfortunately, the major's bitterness hasn't eased with time. A lot of the area ranchers are of the same mind. Especially with Scott defending the land rights of his father's people."

"So how did you and Scott . . ."

194

Gena smiled with remembrance. "We met while he was a student at Harvard. I'd never seen a man like him. He took my breath away." She looked toward the corral. "He still does. I'd have no life without him."

"But working for the Indians, I can see where it is quite noble but it can't be very profitable."

"It has its rewards. And," she added more quietly, "its drawbacks." She was silent then, but the cloudy look in her eyes spoke volumes. How, Norah wondered, had she ever thought Gena Prescott wasn't strong?

"Do you love Rory?"

Norah was taken aback by the sudden question.

"I hope you do," Gena went on optimistically. "He needs a good woman to love and I could sure use a good friend."

"I can be your friend without being related."

Gena chuckled at her evasive response. "You didn't answer."

"Rory . . ." Norah sighed and thought hard. How to explain Rory Prescott. She looked down toward the corral, letting her eyes take their fill of the big, redheaded cowboy. "Rory, takes my breath away," she said at last with a small accompanying smile. "He's maddening and sweet and impossible and funny. He deserves the love of a good woman." Then her smile faded, becoming a thin line of regret. "But that woman isn't me."

"Are you sure?" Gena challenged gently.

"Very sure. When our business is finished here, we'll be moving on to the East or maybe even Europe. Rory's not a part of my plans." She took a great risk by admitting, "I wish he could be."

"Things change, Norah."

"Not the past," she stated flatly.

Gena put a caring hand upon her arm and squeezed. "Sometimes it can. And sometimes, it just doesn't matter. Rory's a lot like Chance. He's part Kincaid pure-bred, part Prescott mustang, steady and dependable and still prone to kicking up heels. And he's stubborn, like all of them. If he's decided that he loves you, nothing's going to stand in his way. He'll stick like a saddle burr until he's worn you down. Just a friendly word of warning. If Rory loves you, you can't help but love him back."

And Norah was deathly afraid that she was right.

"Heya, Sis, you gonna have that baby in time to go a couple of reels with me?"

Gena beamed up at her brother-in-law as he bounded up onto the porch. "No promises. If not, I'm sure I can manage something a little more sedate. If you can reach around me, that is."

"If not over the front of you, then like this." He stepped up behind her, lifting one hand in his and placing the other over the swell of her abdomen. He leaned his cheek against her pale blonde hair and closed his eyes, humming "There'll Be a Hot Time in the Old Town Tonight" in a pleasing baritone. Norah was aware of a funny little stir of envy, so unworthy because she knew they were family. Still, she couldn't help the prick of resentment at seeing Rory's tender devotion to his brother's wife.

Then his dark eyes opened and fixed upon hers. Something hot sparked between them. And he smiled, that slow, sly smile.

"How 'bout you, Norah-honey?" he drawled sweetly. "You gonna save me some dances?"

He gave Gena an easy twirl, having to step back fast to avoid the bump of her belly. Then he reached for Norah's hand. She wasn't quick enough to resist and found herself up flush against him. His free hand cupped the seat of her Levi's, urging her into an intimate contact between the straddle of his thighs.

"A waltz or two? Something slow and long and lazy so's I can hold you tight and maybe steal a kiss or two?"

He started to lean down as if he planned to begin the

sampling right on his family's porch. From the corner of her eye, Norah saw Aurora at the door. Determinedly, she ducked her head from the tempting nearness of Rory's parted lips and she pushed hard against his chest.

"Rory, stop. Your family will get the wrong idea."

"Oh, I don't think so."

His hand scooped under her chin and his mouth settled snugly over hers. She didn't fight the kiss but her rigid stance stated clearly it was without her consent. Rory leaned back to regard her through hot, glittery eyes and found her stare flaming just as bright. With fury. The short, hard jab of her fist caught him neatly under the ribs. He gasped, more in surprise than hurt. The moment his grip lessened, Norah was off the porch, striding in a beguiling twitch of britches to step up onto the bay.

"It was nice meeting you, Mrs. Prescott," she called as she wheeled the animal about and applied her heels.

Rubbing his middle, Rory was all grins. "Ain't she something, Mama?" he gushed with a wondering admiration. Then he hop-rumped it into Chance's saddle and set out after her. His black Stetson blew back off Norah's head and without breaking his mount's stride, Rory swung down to snatch it up off the ground with a loud, "Whooee!" And the two of them were out of sight.

"I like her," Gena announced unconditionally.

"For Rory?" Aurora sounded doubtful. "She's not the sort I figured would interest him."

"What sort is that?" Scott asked as he and Ethan joined the ladies on the porch.

"I'm not sure. A little too cool, a little too classy, a little too clever. Something."

"Got a nice seat, though," Ethan allowed. Then he grinned at his wife's severing glare. "In the saddle, I meant. Probably one of the things Rory likes about her."

"I'm sure," Aurora muttered. She frowned in the direction they'd gone. "What does a sophisticated woman like

197

that want with our son? She doesn't seem the type to settle on a ranch and raise a passel of babies and Kincaid calves."

"I've seen stranger matches work out just fine." Gena moved up beside Scott and slipped her arm about his taut middle. He kissed her temple absently. He was frowning, too.

"Maybe it's just a fancy," he thought out loud. "You know how fickle Rory is."

Gena smiled knowingly. "Not about this. Not about her. Depending on when this baby decides to make an appearance, you might have just met the next member of the family."

Scott's consternation deepened. "Guess I better make it my business to find out everything there is to know about my future sister-in-law and her father, then."

"Norah, wait up!"

Contrarily, she bent lower over the gelding's neck, urging it to greater speed.

"Fool woman," Rory muttered. But he was smiling into the snap of Chance's mane. An exciting woman, too. Dang but she led a good chase. He coaxed the paint to notch out a longer stride and within minutes, they were pulling up abreast of her. In an easy show of strength and skill, he reached out to snag her around the waist, hoisting her up in front of him. And immediately, he realized his mistake.

She was a wildcat. Spitting, writhing, clawing. A prime roping horse, Chance set all four feet, jerking them to a stop. A squirming, angry Norah Denby was more than Rory could handle atop his horse. With one arm pinning her close, he swung his leg over the pommel and lightly jumped down. Norah hit the ground fighting.

"You son of a skunk! You polecat! You cur, you side-winding snake, you arrogant pig!" She punctuated each new title with a well-aimed punch. Rory dodged and ducked and laughed which made her all the more angry. Until he saw that she was crying. That brought him up short. And gave her time to land a jarring right to the jaw. "I hate you! I wish I'd never laid eyes on you!"

Enough was enough. Rory didn't mind the sting of her puny whollops but those words cut clean to the core. He chased and finally caught her flailing hands then held her close and harmless against his chest.

"Norah stop. Honey, what's wrong? What'd I do to get you so riled?"

She was jerking with hard sobs of fury. Hands that had sought to hurt him now clutched and clung. "You rotten son of a bitch," she cried out in depthless anguish. "How dare you!"

"What? Norah-honey, what?"

She was weeping almost too hard to get the words out. "How could you do that to me? How could you treat me like that in front of your family? Like I was something you owned. How could you maul me like that, without a trace of respect for my feelings? They must think I'm some kind of cheap skirt you've been chasing, like I was your casual whore!"

He went stone cold with shock. Then his embrace gentled into one of tender coddling. "No. Oh, Norah, I didn't mean that a'tall. They won't think bad of you. You're the first woman I ever brung home. And as for mauling you—I'm always a-hugging and a-kissing on my mama and Gena. 'Cause I love 'em. The way I love you. I can't help but show it. I want 'em all to know how I feel about you."

He couldn't have chosen any words less likely to calm her. With a fierce screech, she twisted in his grip. "No! Don't say that. Don't say that. I don't want to hear it!"

His heel hooked behind her ankles and he bulldogged

199

her down onto the thick Dakota grass. She wriggled and bucked beneath him, refusing to relent to his greater weight and strength.

"Norah, I love you. I'm gonna marry you."

"No!"

He grappled with her thrashing legs and arms and finally succeeded in spread-eagling her to the ground. She was panting wildly, her breath coming in raw pulls timed to the thrusting of her bosom. Her eyes shook him to the soul. They were brimming with anguish and fright. Why? What was so awful about the idea of him loving her?

Abruptly, she just gave up and lay limp upon the sharp-scented crushed grass. She looked up at him through those large, glistening eyes and said, "Rory, please don't do this. Please don't make me hurt you."

"I love you, Norah."

Her eyes squeezed shut and she shuddered. "I don't love you. I won't love you. Ever. Don't you understand? I can't love you back."

Now he was breathing faster, tasting the panic and the chill of fear. She couldn't mean that. She couldn't.

"What about last night? What do you call that?"

She described it in a word, a very vivid word, one he didn't like to hear spoken by a lady and one he hated to hear used in terms of what they'd shared.

"No, Norah. We made love. And it was beautiful."

"Wanting doesn't mean loving, Rory. I tried to tell you that. I wanted you. I do want you. But that's all. That's all."

His eyes narrowed. His jaw grew lean and tense. "So, you want me to mount you like a stud bull whenever you present yourself. That about it? All quick and — how did you put it — uninvolved? I don't treat women like that, Norah. Not even whores. Even they deserve more respect than that. I love you. I don't want there to be no

200

mistake about that when we're pleasuring each other. You got to feel something more than want, Norah. I know it. And I'm going to prove it to you. Right here, right now. When I'm done with you, I dare you to tell me that we're uninvolved."

Chapter Thirteen

He took his time undressing her. One by one, the small pearl buttons of her shirtwaist gave way. The front hooks of her corset followed. Before he turned the stiff fabric back, he eased up to kiss her but Norah rolled her head away with a stifled sob of objection. Undiscouraged, Rory let his lips trail wet and warm from cheek to throat, from throat to the soft white swells he leisurely bared. He drew on one pouted nipple, suckling lightly, feathering the sensitive tip with his tongue while teasing the other into a hard, needy nub. She held firm against that sensual persuasion, her body stiff, her breath seething harshly. He continued to taunt her to the edge of distraction with the playful nips of his teeth upon the tender underside of her breast and the lolling lath of his tongue. She bit her lip, hard, to shock herself from the want to moan with the delight of it. He returned to the slow massage of his hands over those generous globes. Her back arched, her hands clenched into fists.

"Norah, your heart's a-racing like a runaway team. You sure there ain't the tiniest bit of love for me in there drivin' it thataway?"

She swung at him, cuffing the side of his head before he could imprison her wrists again. He pressed them down to the loamy earth on either side of her tossing mane of hair. Then, she went still, glaring up at him with a damning fury. And he smiled in the face of it.

"God, you're beautiful."

She gave an angry snarl and bucked beneath him. He rode out her twisting wrath as easily as he'd sit a bronc. And his maddening smile never faltered. *He'll wear you down*. Norah could hear Gena's warning. That's what he was doing. He was letting her get all the fight out of her system. Well, she wouldn't play into his hands. She went still and stared up at him icily.

"Take what you want, then. Get it done and over with."

A chuckle rumbled like thunder through his chest. His grin widened. "You don't get it, do you, Norah? This ain't about me and what I want. I know what I want. I already done told you that. I got what I want already." He freed a hand to stroke through her hair, along her cheek and throat. "This is about you."

Her eyes shut and the breath shuddered from her. "Rory, please. Let me go. You don't know what you're doing."

"Yes I do, darlin'. I hope I'm doing it right. Feels right, don't it?"

Yes, she admitted to herself in a daze of panic. Yes, it had always felt right with him. That was the problem. That was what was wrong with enjoying what he was doing. Because he was doing more than pleasuring her. He was asking more than the surrender of her body beneath his. And that more she couldn't allow him.

"I don't want to take from you, Norah. Hell, I can take from anybody. I want to give and I want you to need what I'm givin'. I got so much building up inside me jus' dying to be shared. All I got, it ain't nothing if I'm all alone. Let me share it with you."

"Why me?" she cried in anguish. "There must be others. Other women who'd—"

His mouth cut off the rest of those words as it moved in

203

tender answer upon her lips. "Just you," he whispered huskily. "Only you. I knew it the first minute I saw you. You fill me up, Norah. You make me warm inside. I can't explain it any better. Don't I make you feel any of them things, too? Even just a little?"

She looked away from his searching gaze. She couldn't let him see the answer. His dark eyes showed a terrible vulnerability. She could stop it all with a stern denial. But her silence encouraged him because she couldn't force out that simple word, "No."

"What do I gotta do? What'll make you love me? The ranch? It's yours. My money? It's yours. Take it. Take everything I got an' jus' love me back." He was panting slightly, his big hand moving restlessly in her hair. "Is it gonna take more than that? I'll get you more. I'll get you anything you want." Then he stopped cold and said in a strangled tone, "Is it him? You in love with Monthaven?"

"Oh, Rory, how ridiculous," she half-laughed, half-sobbed and wholeheartedly kissed him. Long, deep, passion-drenched kisses that shook the thought of Charles Monthaven from his mind. And a flood of tears that kept him from feeling too reassured.

"Norah?"

She clung to him around the neck, refusing to let go, forbidding him from seeing the distraught twist of her features, the raw edge of her emotions. "I'm scared, Rory."

He sat back, cross-legged, hauling her into his lap so he could cradle her there like a frightened child against the distressed beat of his heart. "Of me? Oh, honey, don't be. God strike me dead if I ever give you reason to be."

She sniffled hard into the fabric of his shirt collar and shook her head. "Not of you, of loving you. I can't let myself care for you, Rory. Once I let you in, there'll be no stopping things from happening. I won't be able to — to control them. I can't trust you to keep on loving me."

His laugh was low and throaty and full of confidence. "Sweet darlin', that there's the least of your worries.

Norah pulled back far enough to look up into his dark eyes. She could see the tenderness reflecting back, the swelling of his emotions. And she told him softly, truthfully, "That's my only worry."

He didn't know what to say. He didn't know what he could do short of turning himself inside out so she could see the way she occupied every inch of him. It was no game she was playing. He could see the fright, the uncertainty, the fragile need to believe fraying before those weightier truths. Who the hell had hurt her so bad to make her so shy of love? He touched his fingertips to her temples, gently stroking back the spill of her hair. The caress of his words came even softer. "Guess I'll jus' have to convince you of it."

She didn't take comfort from that claim. Her protective barriers went too deep, were too strong to be shaken by one quiet vow. Somberly, she let her fingers learn the distinctive angles of his face and weave through the fiery thatch to lace at his nape. "I don't know if I want you to, Rory," came her cautious reply. But he made it so tempting, how was she to resist?

She couldn't.

His grin broke big and wide.

"Norah-honey, believe you me, you're gonna like every minute of it!"

His mouth took hers in a wet, open-wide kiss that demanded heart and soul. She tried to hold back, to resist being sucked in completely but there was no halfway with Rory Prescott. He was too overpowering. Too damned desirable. He created a stampede of emotions that ran rampant over her without a pause. Her dainty blouse was shucked off her shoulders, avidly pursued by the trail of his lips down the length of each arm. She arched against him, moaning helplessly until his mouth came back up to swallow the sound. A rumble of rough, purring contentment rose up from his chest as he worked his tongue around the inside of her mouth, then he came away smiling and panting lightly.

"What would you say to me kissing you over every inch of your body?" he asked with another flickering tease of his tongue.

The possibilities were intriguing.

"I'd say you've got a lot of ground to cover, cowboy," she returned with a provoking little smile. Her pulse was racing, hopelessly hurried by his suggestion.

"I got the time and I gots me plenty of inclination. Where you want me to start? Here?" He bussed her cheek warmly. "Here?" He sucked long and hard on her throat. "How 'bout here?" He tugged at a puckered nipple and her fingers seized up in his hair. "I been there already," he murmured, nuzzling that throbbing peak. Her hands tightened. "Oh, I guess it's worth another look see." And he did, long and thoroughly until Norah was shaking fitfully.

At his coaxing, she went down on her back with him straddling her, kissing her wildly, wonderfully, then sitting back before she'd had enough. He grinned and resisted the impatient hands that would pull him back to her.

"Now, Norah-honey, you gonna try an' tell me you're not liking this?"

She couldn't resist his smile or the silliness of his suggestion. Not like it? She was loving it! And he knew it. Hang him for his arrogance! She laughed softly, unable to maintain her annoyance with a man who was squeezing her breasts like a pair of overly ripe cantaloupes.

"God, I love lookin' at you," he said suddenly, enthusiastically. "And seeing you smile like that, and hearing you laugh out loud. And the way you smell like violets. And the way you taste like . . ." He bent and kissed her hard. "Like woman," he concluded gruffly. "Damn, I like that." So he kissed her again, feeding off her lips like a man starving, drinking from their sweetness like a man thirsting. Moaning like a man half out of his mind with wanting.

Norah turned her head to the side, gasping. "Rory, stop. I can't catch my breath."

"Good," he proclaimed and kissed her again. "Good. I aim to keep you breathing heavy for as long as it takes. Till you take to trustin' me." Before her eyes could cloud with doubt, he gave her a kiss so achingly tender, she wanted to hug to him forever. But he was full of energy, full of rambunctious passion and nowhere near finished with what he'd started. "Where'd I leave off in my kissing?"

He fastened his mouth to the soft concave of her belly, sucking loudly then blowing out hard to make a rather rude noise that, along with the sudden prod of his fingertips beneath her ribs, had Norah writhing with gales of laughter.

"You're crazy, Rory Prescott. You know that?"

"Yes, ma'am. Crazy 'bout you. Don't you go moving a muscle." He slid off her and reached down to pull at her boots, giving them a reckless toss far out into the grass, startling a threatening snort from Chance. Then his fingers hooked at the waistband of her provoking Levi's and skinned them down and off. He hung on to one of her long, shapely legs, setting her ankle up on his shoulder so he could bend down and lick behind her knee. She jerked in surprise and eyed him warily.

"Rory . . ."

"Ready to say 'Uncle' yet?" he asked, grinning wickedly. His teeth nibbled along the curve of her calf. As he massaged the arch of her foot with his thumbs, he began to suck on her toes. He tightened his grip as she kicked out reflexively but quit the exquisite torture. "You want to tell me now that you ain't involved with me?" His lips stroked back up to her knee, tongue swirling along the jerk and tremble of her limb. "You gonna look me in the eye and tell me you'd let another man touch you like this? That you'd let a man stretch you out stark naked in the middle of green grass and do the kind of things I'm doing if you didn't trust him? And maybe love him just a little."

His big hand rubbed in small circles down the taut flesh of her thigh. He heard her pull a hoarse breath when it came to rest. Then began to move again with the same compelling rhythm. The sound became more ragged and insistent when his lips brushed along that same sleek length of leg.

There was no hope of clinging to her resolve. Rory Prescott had shaken her from it with that first wide, white grin. With that first sanity-rattling kiss. With his first soft claim of, "I love you." She'd lost control and the battle to regain it had grown fierce. But now, listening to his seducing words, quivering beneath his seductive touch, she couldn't remember why she was fighting so hard against what she wanted so desperately.

"Norah-honey, let me in," she heard him whisper roughly as he lightly licked at her.

Norah's head thrashed weakly from side to side. *No. No, I won't. I won't.*

"Let me make you happy. Let me take care of you. Let me love you." His mouth grew more demanding, just like his words.

No. I can't. I can't. You'll hurt me!

"Love me just a little. That's all I need."

Her breaths had quickened toward a gusty crescendo then suddenly, he stopped. Norah panted in bewilderment, dazed and confused. "Rory . . ."

He slid up beside her, resting on his elbow. His dark eyes burned hot but the touch of his hand felt cool upon her fevered cheek. She gripped that hand in one of hers and reached the other up to draw his bright head down. Her kiss was greedy.

"Oh, Rory, I want you," she moaned restlessly into that kiss and reached down in an attempt to release the proof of his desire.

"I know you do, darlin'." Contrarily, he caught her hand and eased it away. "But like I told you, this ain't about wanting." He could see she didn't understand and sought the patience to explain. "It ain't about coupling like a pair of wildcats in the night, then going on our separate ways. Like you said, wantin' and lovin' ain't the same thing. I know the difference. Do you?"

Norah rolled her head to the side, desperately aroused and desperately angry with him for blackmailing her emotions at such a critical time. She shut her eyes and tried to cool the fire raging all out of control inside her. But he had stoked it too hot and fanned it too well.

Rory sighed heavily. "Danged if you ain't the stubbornest woman."

Her gaze flashed back to him, mirroring her fear that he was finished with her. He couldn't leave her all ablaze, not after he'd tended the flames so painstakingly.

"Tell me what you want, Norah. Show me what you need from me."

His hand was resting idle upon her jerking midsection. She gave it a meaningful downward push.

"All right, honey. We'd best be seeing to first things first."

And as he gently coaxed her body into yielding a splendid release beneath the knowing revolutions of his hand, the satisfied cry of his name upon her lips was small reward.

Norah couldn't remember ever feeling quite so drained. Or quite so content. She rested her head against Rory's shoulder with her arm hooked loosely over the other. And she sighed. She knew she shouldn't sound so smugly sated when she'd given nothing back to him in return but she couldn't help herself. He had worn her down to this exquisite lethargy so it was his own fault. She would have gladly allowed him to come to as glorious a conclusion as she herself had reached but he hadn't so much as opened a shirt button. And the more she thought she knew him, the less she understood. She'd never known a man with the kind of control it took to walk away unsatisfied.

Rory hadn't said anything since hoisting her up onto his lap as they doubled back to the Bar K. They hadn't been able to find her boots so the feet that bobbed lightly off to one side with Chance's easy stride were bare and grass stained. And the smile that curved her lips was relaxed. When her fingers toyed with the strands of red hair straying over his collar, he tossed his head like a restless stallion. And when she tasted the saltiness of his throat with a nibbling kiss, his growl was irritable.

"Don't, Norah."

She deserved it, she supposed, but she couldn't keep herself from asking quietly, "Are you still angry with me?"

"Ummm? What? Honey, I ain't mad at you." He lifted her hand and pressed a hot kiss to its palm. "It's just that if you go on acting frisky like that, I'm going to have to take you down in the grass again."

Her fingers kneaded the taut cording at his neck while she nuzzled the other side. His thighs tensed beneath her. "I wouldn't mind."

He gave a low chuckle. "I know you wouldn't but I gots to get you back to the Bar K. You've been out in the sun so long your face is as red as a harlot's toenails."

"Voice of experience," she murmured with a mild degree of testiness. "You must have spent a lot of hours amongst them to have learned so very, very much."

She could feel his broad smile against her hair. "I own

210

it was grueling work but my mama always told me if something was worth doin', it was worth doin' well."

"I guess I should thank your mama then for being so diligent about your seeking higher education." Her fingers moved absently down the buttons of his shirt, lightly stroking the warm incandescence of his skin. "Rory?"

"Ummm?"

"Your mother ever tell you anything else?"

"Yep," he drawled and reined Chance in. "She taught me never to keep a lady waitin'."

And he carried her down with him to the warm Dakota ground.

There was no mischievous play. It was drop and get right to the point of pleasure. And a fine, shattering point it was. In a matter of a few heavy breathing minutes, Rory sat up and was stuffing in his shirt tails.

"Come on, sweet thing. Quit your dallying. We gots to get back."

"Rory?" she called softly.

"What, darlin'?" He was busy with his gun belt.

"I love you."

For a long moment, he didn't move. Then his head dropped down between his uplifted knees and she could hear him gulping noisily.

"Rory?"

"M'alright," he muttered thickly. "Jus' went a little crazy there for a second." He took a long, slow breath then turned and pinned her to the ground beneath him in one easy move. His face was wet and his grin was wide. "Hot damn," he whispered, then he kissed her energetically.

She clutched the back of his head and gave herself over to him completely. It hadn't been so hard to say. The words had been beating in her heart for a long time. Ever since Cheyenne. It felt good to let them go. Maybe it wasn't right but it felt good to tell him. But she wouldn't think about what was right or best, not now. Not when he was kissing all over her face.

"Norah, you jus' made me the happiest man alive," he confessed expansively as he rocked back on his heels. He stared down at her for a long minute, breathing quick, bubbling over with smiles, dark eyes sparkling. "Marry me."

"What!"

"Now, today. Marry me, Norah. Let's ride on back to my folks' and tell 'em. I want to carry you upstairs and love you proper in my own bed, under my own roof."

"Haven't we done enough of that for one day?"

He eased back over her and she could feel him, rock solid against her. "Enough? Sheeoot, we ain't even started. You gonna marry me so we can get back to it, or what?"

"No."

"No, to the lovin'?" His voice softened. "Or to the marryin'?"

"To both for now."

She could see him hauling back hard, reining in his emotions the way he would a full team. "Am I movin' too fast?"

"Like a runaway freight." Her smile was gentle, as was her touch upon his somber features.

"I jus' love you so much I want the whole wide world to know it."

That husky admission woke her to the grim reality of what she'd done. Of what she'd committed herself to. And she wondered in sudden panic if she'd suffered from sun-madness out there on the Dakota plain. What was she going to tell Cole?

Rory watched the plays of caution upon her lovely face and the bottom fell out of his joy. Something was wrong. This wasn't the way things were supposed to be when a man and woman loved each other.

212

"Second thoughts already?" he made himself ask.

"About you?" Norah shook her head. "No. About what I'm going to tell my father, plenty."

"I'll tell him."

"No! I mean, I'd rather do it. Just give me some time to get used to the idea myself. This is all sort of sudden. First things first, remember?" She expected him to smile at that but he was oddly reserved in his response.

"How much time you gonna need?"

"Rory, I'm not going to change my mind about loving you. I'd just like to keep it between the two of us for a little while until I can get some things worked out."

Despite her reassurances, she could feel him pulling farther away behind that opaque stare. When he said, "All right, Norah. If that's the way you want it," there was a tonelessness to his voice that made her hug him hard about the neck.

And when she said passionately, "I do love you, Rory Prescott," his arms finally came up to hold her.

Cautiously.

"How are the details coming?" Garth Kincaid asked of his new ranch manager over a glass of smooth Scotch whiskey.

Cole rolled the glass between his hands, admiring the way the liquor gleamed inside the crystal. "Just fine, Major. The new men should start arriving tomorrow. Which brings me to a small problem. How do you want me to handle things with your boy?"

"You don't. You go through me."

"I have no problem with that but he's bound to have questions."

"Tell him to bring them to me. I'll handle Rory."

Cole sipped his drink and regarded the tough old man over the rim. Maybe he could. Maybe he couldn't. He'd

213

underestimated the redheaded cowboy once too often not to be leery of him. "He might object to the way I mean to take care of certain things. I don't want to be hamstrung by him every time I turn around."

"I'll take care of Rory," Kincaid repeated more firmly. He looked thoughtfully out into the hall. "In fact, I'll do it now. Rory, come on in here for a second."

While Norah hung back out of sight with her tangled hair and bare feet, Rory strode into his grandfather's study. He cast an impassive glance at Denby, then went straight to the big desk. "You want to see me, Major?"

"Pour yourself a drink, boy." He waited until that was done, then he got right to the quick of it. "Remember when we talked about the responsibilities of running a spread like the Bar K, how things don't always sit well in your craw but they have to be done?"

Rory canted another wary glance at Denby and muttered, "Yessir."

"We're hiring on some new men who'll answer to Cole. And to myself. Range detectives to look into the loss of stock we've been suffering lately."

Rory stiffened by slow degrees. He knew what that meant. It was a fancy term for hired killers. Scott's warning struck him full bore and he fought not to reel from the impact. Very quietly, he said, "That absolutely necessary?"

"Wouldn't allow it otherwise. You know that, Rory. This kind of thing don't set good with me, either."

Rory should have believed him. But he didn't. And that troubled him no little bit. "I think we ought to hold off for a while, give Scotty a chance to work on the lease bill. We got us a rancher in Washington now. Old Teddy knows grass is worthless until a cow sticks her nose down in it. We get claim to the land and no homeseeker will be able to set down so much as a post."

"That'll be fine. When it happens. But what about

214

now? We gonna let them settlers cut out our best sections of grazing land and stick up soddies? We gonna let them shoot at any of our beeves that happen to stray on their stolen ground? We need to set up a Protection Account and Cole is going to handle it."

"I don't like it." He spoke his mind plain.

Cole observed him wryly. "No guts for a man's work, boy?"

Rory bristled up and growled, "I got plenty of *guts*."

"Gentlemen, please," Kincaid moderated sternly. "Let me handle this, Cole. Rory, you're being naive if you think the threat of passing a bill in Congress is going to keep those locusts off our range or from stealing our cattle. I appreciate you sharing your feelings on it but I need to know you stand behind my decision. I won't act against you. But I want you to think on it real good. This is your land. You want to give up pieces of it to anyone who holds a stretch of wire? You do that and you might as well move into town because there'll be nothing left of the Bar K. With Monthaven's investment, we've got the opportunity to set ourselves up like kings. I thought you wanted that, Rory. I thought we wanted the same things."

"We do," he said softly. He was thinking, hard. About Norah. About marrying her and providing for her. A rich man, that's what she wanted. Not a grubbing cowboy. With her in bed beside him, would it matter so much if he couldn't sleep?

Kincaid allowed a small, fond smile to escape him. "Good. I want your word that you won't interfere with Cole or his men."

Watch him. Don't trust him.

Sorry, Scotty.

"You got it."

He was a man of responsibilities now. He couldn't afford a conscience.

* * *

215

"I didn't think killing was your style."

Cole smiled, unperturbed by the searing accusation. "Why my dear Norah, these hands have never touched a trigger."

"They just point the direction and let others do the firing."

"You make it sound so cowardly. I call it smart."

Norah paced the parlor. She was more than a little disturbed by the conversation she'd overheard. And more than a little alarmed that Rory would throw in with Cole. She knew Cole, knew what he was capable of. She didn't like thinking Rory was like that.

"What are you up to?"

"Why, Norah, dear, I'm looking out for number one, like always. Which is what you should be doing and aren't. You've always been such a smart girl, too smart to fall for a pair of tight pants and big shoulders. Why that boy hasn't a lick of scruples. His morals are just like his male parts, always swelling up over the wrong things. And you're a wrong thing where he's concerned and you know it."

Norah drew up short and glared at him fiercely. "Damn you, Cole," she hissed.

"Go ahead, but I'm only thinking about what's best for you. Norah, you're making a mistake. That boy's not going to take care of you. He's going to use you up and toss you away."

Her cold stare reflected none of the terror his words awoke inside. No, Rory loved her. He wanted to marry her.

But she'd heard him discard decency just minutes ago. She'd heard him turn his back on family and honor. How could she, having heard those things, believe he'd be loyal to her?

"Don't be stupid, Norah. There's nothing for you here," Cole murmured kindly. He was being sincere in

216

his concern, as sincere as Cole Denby could be. "See to your own interests first. No one else will. If you want a good life, you make one for yourself, you don't hope someone else will give it to you. You know that. Your mother taught you that."

Norah didn't want to listen. She didn't want to hear the truth. Clasping her arms about herself, she paced moodily to the opposite window and stared out over the endless green grass. How desolate it would be if one was all alone. Cole's soothing tones worked on her darkest fears as skillfully as Garth Kincaid had plied his grandson's devotion.

"There's nothing for you here, Norah. A whole lot of nothing and you've had that before. Be smart. Don't be like your mother, trusting every promise she heard. Look what happened to her. You want to end up that way after I showed you how to get out?"

"No," she whispered in quiet horror. Then more strongly, she vowed, "No, I won't."

"Play the percentage like the smart girl you are. Throw in with Monthaven. He'll provide for you, if that's what you want. Just don't be any man's fool."

"I won't." And that was said with cold crystal clarity.

Chapter Fourteen

Gatherings were popular between roundups, fencing and haytime. The men were eager to get together for calf-roping and busting broncs that had never been touched by rope or spur, the women to talk and dance. Four freight wagons of outside food were delivered. Two ten-gallon kegs of whiskey and casks of imported and barrels of wild-grape wine were tapped. Washboilers and tubs were polished up to serve coffee. Fat beeves were butchered and the pits to cook them readied for the match. When the Bar K threw a big blow out, the whole prairie turned out in their Sunday bests.

Garth Kincaid watched them roll in by the droves, feeling pride in the name that drew them from their distant homes. But that couldn't touch on the pride he felt for the big strapping man at his side. Rory finally filled that spot like a Kincaid. Since taking his place at the reins of the Bar K, his grandson had been a constant source of irrefutable dependability. The men went to him with their woes, confident of a solution. No detail was too small to escape his full attention. He put in longer hours than any of the hired-ons and never, ever complained about something that needed doing. He did it or he made sure it was done. He was a mirror of Garth Kincaid at twenty; ambitious, indefatigable, passionate, single-minded. Completely, blindly loyal. Except in one galling spot.

One second they were standing together welcoming guests from the porch. Then Rory was gone, bolting off the steps like an anxious, untrained pup unwilling to take a lead. Kincaid followed with a steely gaze, knowing without seeing his destination. Only one thing would call him to desert his duty to the Bar K. The Prescotts had arrived.

"Well knock me down and put pennies on my eyes if the lot of you don't look pretty!"

Rory scooped his mother up and swung her with a flutter of skirts from the buggy seat. After planting a loud kiss on her cheek, he reached up for Gena.

"Careful there, Sis. You want me to go fetch a block and tackle from the barn?"

"Rory Prescott, you sure know what to say to a lady," the pregnant woman scolded as she surrendered herself into his arms. He lifted her down with gentle deference, holding her long enough to make amends.

"You look plumb eye-popping beautiful."

"Better," she murmured as she accepted his kiss.

Rory surveyed the four of them with bright, brimming eyes. "Dang, I can't tell you how grand it feels to have y'all here. Thanks for coming." He slapped his daddy's arm, then turned and hauled Scott up for a rib-bruising embrace. He kept his arm rock steady about his brother's shoulders. If anyone balked it would be Scott. "Come on up and say howdy."

Ethan scowled but Aurora was quick to prod him forward. At Rory's persuasion, Scott marched stiff-legged to meet the hard-eyed patriarch of the Bar K and the family. If he'd been any more reluctant, his heels would be furrowing grooves like a truculent mule.

"Howdy, Major." Ethan put out a big hand to take the other man's in a brief test of strength. The old goat still had a hell of a grip. "Thanks for the invite."

"That was Rory's doing," Kincaid drawled.

"Figured as much."

It was the longest conversation father- and son-in-law had exchanged in almost a year.

"Hello, Major." Aurora stepped up to embrace her father with guarded fondness. She'd made it clear when she and Ethan married that she would love him to the extent that he didn't interfere with her family. She'd surrendered the Kincaid part of her life to become a Prescott. And did so without apology. That was a wedge to any closeness they'd once shared. That and the fact that her oldest son was part Lakota.

Kincaid dutifully kissed the cheek Gena presented. He held no ill will toward the girl but the child that swelled her belly would never be recognized by him, any more than its father. When Gena stepped back, his gaze touched on the molten glare of Scott Prescott. The two of them nodded stiffly.

"There you go," Rory announced happily. "Hell, that was almost civil. It didn't choke none of you to be polite, now did it?" He surveyed the stony faces hopefully, then sighed. No use pressing his luck. "Come on, Scotty. You got to get a look at that long legged cayuse the Brit's gonna run tomorrow."

As soon as they were away from the house, Scott hissed, "Let me go, Rory. I'm not going to go for my scalping knife."

"That's a good thing to know." His forceful embrace eased to the point where his brother could throw it off if he chose to. But Scott allowed it because his brother's other arm encircled Gena with equal affection. And because Rory was his brother and he was trying hard to do the impossible. A sorry, heartbreaking task. But he had to be respected for it.

Gena leaned close into Rory's side to whisper, "Where

is she?" Then she followed Rory's somber stare to a gathering of well-dressed couples standing in the shade of the side porch. Norah Denby stood arm in arm with Charles Monthaven. "Oh, dear. It's good to know you don't have a scalping knife either."

While the two Prescott men stood looking over Monthaven's lanky thoroughbred, the Englishman couldn't resist the chance to taunt them with the innate superiority of his mount. And tucked close to his side, like another superior prize in his possession, was Miss Denby.

It took Norah a long while to look up from her study of Rory's stitched boots. It had been easy to stay away from him during the bustle leading up to the party. No, not easy, but possible. He'd been out on the range long hours rounding up broncs and she'd been helping Ruth with preparations. And then Charles had been most insistent in claiming her evening hours, often at Cole's instigation. It gave her time to work up her resistance. It gave her time to convince herself that a weakness of the heart needn't lead to weakness in the head. She'd been building on that, hour by hour, day by day, working up the strength to face Rory with the truth. She might love him, she might want him but she could never marry him. Loving was no guarantee of loyalty. She knew that and he'd proved it with his own words to his grandfather. He might love his family but he would stand against them for the sake of the Bar K. And what kind of wife would she make for the heir to that great ranch? It might not bother him now, but someday it would. That someday that he would turn his back on her and leave her with nothing but empty promises.

Those were the truths she used to build her guarded fortress high. Those were the reasons she'd stayed away. But now the avoidance was at an end. Charles towed her down to the corral where Rory stood with his brother and his wife and she could feel the heat of his stare upon her. And the answering warmth rising fast.

Clutching at all the remnants of her renewed resolve, Norah let her gaze lift. She would not fall to pieces. She wouldn't. Up those long sturdy legs she'd wrapped herself around in a hotel room in Wyoming. To where his big, tender-rough hands hung idle, thumbs hooked on his holsters. To the lean hips clad in tight Levi's she'd ridden to ecstasy on a porch swing and the proud masculinity that snug denim couldn't hide. Up his buttoned shirtfront that she'd so enjoyed buttoning down. To the rack of shoulders that gave comfort so easily. Then she stopped, unable to continue with the casual charade. Her gaze jerked up to his and was met by a careful scrutiny. That cautious edge helped her retain her own poise. And at the same time rubbed the salt of guilt into the raw places in her heart. Why had she ever thought it could work? She was hurting him already. Why had she told him she loved him when simple wanting would have gained her everything she needed during the scant moments they would share? And it would have made it so much easier for her to leave. Before he demanded that she go.

Gena watched the interplay of emotions flow unsettlingly between them. Something had definitely happened after they left the Lone Star. And she had to discover what it was. Cheerfully, she took Norah's arm.

"If I know men, they'll be talking horse for hours. Come with me, Norah. I'll introduce you to some of the neighbors."

Glad to escape both Charles's possessiveness and Rory's preoccupation, Norah made her excuses and walked slowly away at the pace of the lumbering mother-to-be.

"When is the baby due?" she inquired politely.

"In about six weeks but I'm ready any time he or she is."

222

She pressed a hand to the small of her back and smiled ruefully. "It's like carrying a load of wet wash day in and day out. But then Scott and Aurora spoil me shamelessly so I can't complain." She glanced slyly back over their shoulders. "He's very handsome."

Norah looked and sighed. "Yes."

"I've always found blond men attractive, though please don't repeat that to my husband."

"Blond men?" Norah shifted her attention from the red hair evident under the tilt of a black Stetson to Charles's cap of gold curls. "Oh, you mean his lordship."

"Whom did you think I meant?" Gena asked innocently and was rewarded with a delightfully telling confusion. "I understand he is returning home in a few days."

"The day after tomorrow."

"Good," Gena murmured with an intensity quite at odds with her sweet smile.

The bronc riding drew a crowd around the Bar K corral. In an effort to outshine one another, cowboys and a few daredevil souls clamored up on the back of an outlaw horse with only a hackamore to keep it from bogging its head between its knees and bucking a man out of his boots. Desperate to rid itself of the spur-heeled creature clinging cougar-like to its back, the volatile animals crashed through more than one corral pole and did their mean best to cripple anyone fool enough to climb aboard.

And because Scott chose to stand behind his wife's chair in the shaded yard, Rory Prescott far outshone the others. Though he couldn't match his brother's magic when it came to soothing the spirit of the beast, Rory knew how to wring a wild thing out to his advantage. Watching him, Norah was aware of a breath-suspending, heart-churning excitement. Half the time she was scared he'd be tossed and trampled and the other half, she was flushed with an unconquerable thrill. Rory was like those fresh-off-the-range horses; an ambiguous mix of wild and controlled, subdued and potentially dangerous. And oh, how he pumped the spice of passion through her. Watching him and watching Scott and Gena Prescott share a silent communication of intimacy through their glances and brief touches, was enough to thrust her back into a swirl of confusion. And when Charles Monthaven came up to claim her elbow in his cool, expectant palm, her first thought was to jerk away. But her calmer instincts made her stand and allow him a small smile. It was time for her to be very, very careful, to think out the consequence of each move. Her whole future was in the balance. Did she want to spend it pinching pockets with Cole Denby? Or waiting in a panic for Rory to discover the truth and throw her out of his heart? Or would she settle for the cold, emotionless security at hand? Indecision rose like the spring waterline inside her, all the more frightening because she couldn't seem to climb out to save herself. Standing serenely at Lord Monthaven's side, none would guess how she was struggling with that terror. None would know her thoughts were flailing out wildly for some kind of salvation. The waters kept rising. It was choose or go under.

Charles Monthaven was determined to be her answer. He stuck to her like Ethan Prescott's hot Texas sauce as they ate supper outside, washing the fire from their throats with cool wine. The wine helped. It took the edge off her panic as the music began to play. Aurora's mother's parlor organ had been hauled out in a hayrack. The tunes picked upon it were accompanied energetically by a fiddle, a guitar, a bull fiddle and a hammered harp, dealing out reels and polkas and square dances to which the cowboys stomped their boot heels and swung their girls to set their colorful skirts whirling. The early evening settled into an enjoyable pattern of eat, dance, play poker and talk race horses. Subtle betting on the next day's race grew as steep as the Dakota Hills while cattle deals were made over quiet pipes and cigars and leisurely whiskeys inside the house.

Charles squired Norah around for the more stately waltzes but while he beamed down at her with an admiring pride, her attention was elsewhere. On a big, redheaded cowboy who snapped an endless parade of partners through the lively steps of the country dances. He moved to the squeal of the fiddles with the same romping confidence that served him on the back of a bucking horse, grinning wide and showing off his fancy two-step to the delight of the ladies. And Norah grew more restless by the moment with a longing to keep time. He worked his way through the procession of eager women, taking a wild turn with a flushed and pretty Aurora Prescott and a gentle do-si-do with Gena until Norah was sure she was the only one he hadn't favored within the circle of his arms. And Charles was determined to keep it that way by dragging her about making enthused conversation with all the guests. She made herself smile and speak politely while inside, she twitched to the tempo of the songs and ached for the feel of a special partner.

It was a crazy thing to desire, she knew. She'd asked Rory to say nothing of the words they'd exchanged and he'd kept his promise. But if he moved her about the yard in the deepening twilight, not a soul present would be unaware of how they felt. She would simply melt at his touch and simmer beneath his gaze. And as the bouncy melodies gave to mournful ballads drawing couples close beneath the blossoming stars, Norah came to realize that she didn't care what they thought, any of them. She was dcspcratc for the feel of his embrace.

Drinking down her glass of wine, she searched the swaying couples for Rory Prescott. And didn't find him. Her anxious gaze flickered up toward the house. Had he gone in for a few hands of cards? Or had he disappeared into the shadows with a warm and willing woman? Her need to know made her voice terse when she excused herself from Monthaven's attentions. She moved away too quickly for him to protest. And she didn't care if his gaze followed her hungrily. Or that Cole observed her flight from where he smoked an expensive cigar upon the Bar K's porch.

She could hear the low murmur of his voice but not the actual words as she stepped into the barn. They were soft, loving whispers and Norah was ready to seek out the nearest loaded six-gun. Until she recognized the rhythmic shush of brush bristles. A single lantern suspended outside Chance's stall gave a soft glow to the area and turned Rory Prescott's bared head to molten flame. A fire just as hot and bright quickened in an instant inside her. For a long moment, she stood in shadow, enjoying the sight of him as he frowned in concentration, stroking the brown and white hide to a glossy sheen. The stallion's welcoming nicker turned his attention toward her. His dark eyes registered his surprise then cooled to an impassive blackness.

"Howdy, Miss Norah."

"Howdy, yourself, Mr. Prescott."

"You oughtn't have come down here. You'll get all horsey smelling." He went back to his currying but she could tell by the increased movement of his shirtfront that he was far from unaffected by her presence.

"I don't mind," she remarked easily. She walked around Chance's hindquarters with a disregard to the danger. The animal stood quietly. It was Rory who was tense and trembling. "You didn't come to collect your dances."

"Looked like you was busy." He squatted down, the bunch of his thigh muscles creating an enticing swell of denim. He lifted Chance's hock onto his knee and began to pick at the hoof. "Jus' like you been busy all week long. Sometimes, I ain't real quick to catch on to things. Sometimes, you gotta hit me over the head with it. That what you been doin'?"

"I don't know what you mean." But of course she did. Rory Prescott wasn't the simpleton he pretended to be. He knew she was purposefully staying out of arms reach. What he didn't know was why. And how could she tell him that?

"For a woman who claims herself in love with a man, you been mighty obliging to ole Charlie."

That casual drawl was anything but. Norah bristled at the accusation. Never mind that it was true. "That's business, Rory. I told you I was being nice to him because my father asked me to be."

"Being nice? That what you call it?" He didn't look up. He didn't have to. His voice was gritty with sarcasm.

"What do you call it, Rory? Maybe I'm the one who's a little slow here. Please. Spell it out for me." She came to stand beside him. When he rose up to his full tree-topping size, she had to bend back or step back. And she wasn't about to retreat so much as an inch. "Well?"

"You been in his bed, Norah?"

Rory waited for her yes or no, gut tensed for the worst. He wasn't prepared for her agile attack.

"What if I have?"

He blinked in angry confusion. "That mean yes?"

"It means what right have you to ask such a thing?"

"You said—"

"I said I love you. That's all. I didn't give you any claim over me. I didn't give you call to act as though I was your private property."

"Love must mean something a hell of a lot different to you then." He saw her outrage gather but before it could blow, he said quietly, simply, "You ashamed of me,

227

Norah?"

"What?" His question vented all the anger steaming up inside her.

"I love you, Norah. I want to tell the world. I want to let them know that the most beautiful woman to ever step foot on Dakota gamma loves me back. But you say no. You want to hide it like some dirty little secret. How am I supposed to feel about that? Norah-honey, you're everything I've been looking toward all my life. I'm jus' a plain as dirt Dakota boy. I ain't never seen nothin' else. I ain't never been nowheres else. I ain't never wanted nothin' else. I didn't know how down deep lonely I was till I saw you. I never, in a hundred years, thought a woman like you, so smart and fine and every inch a lady, could care 'bout an ole bowlegged, horsey-smelling cuss like me. But you said it was so and now I want to stand tall with you beside me. I wanted to two-step with you in my arms so all of 'em could see how proud I am that someone like you'd have me. I wanted to show 'em that ole Rory Prescott's worth more than a good laugh and a free beer. Hell, I wanted my mama to look at me as pridefully as she does Scotty. Like I was somebody. Guess that sounds pretty selfish and silly, don't it?"

"No," she replied softly. Norah took the brush from his hand and brought the callused palm up to fit against her cheek. The dampness he found there surprised him and moved his heart to a tremendous tenderness. "And if anybody should be proud, it's me. Because I don't deserve you. I wish I did. I wish I was the woman you were talking about. I wish I was worthy of the love of a good man."

"What the hell you talkin' about, Norah?" His fingertips began to caress her cheek, stroking lightly, with a cherishing gentleness that shook her to the soul.

Tell him. Tell him now! If you want him, tell him the truth.

228

Trust him to understand.

"Rory, I've never so much as kissed Charles. Or wanted to."

He smiled then, a slow, believing smile. "Guess you got all the right in the world to blow up at me like you did. I ain't used to being with a good and decent woman. I should have knowed better than to class you with the kind of female that don't warrant trusting. When Scotty brought Gena home, I knew that was the kind of lady I wanted for myself and that if I settled for less, I'd be regretting it for the rest of my life. I would have waited forever but I sure am glad I didn't have to."

Norah listened to his adoring words with an ever-deepening dread. How could she look up into his dark, devoted eyes and tell him that what he was seeing was all a lie? That she and Gena Prescott were a world apart in goodness. That if he married her, he'd be cheating himself out of everything he revered. She'd been crazy to think that love would be enough. He wanted more than that. He wanted a woman he could be proud of, one his neighbors would respect, one who would bring distinction and dignity to the Bar K empire. And that woman wasn't Norah Denby.

"Oh, Rory," she whispered miserably, helplessly caught between decency and desire. The decent thing would be to tell him but that would mean losing the warm completing heat in his gaze. That would mean never feeling his arms around her or his strength within her. And she couldn't give that up just yet. Not when he was standing so close, not when his gliding touch was quickening a desperate yearning for more. He bent down and the cushion of his lips upon hers was sweet torture. That searching sensuality broke down her meager resistance. Her mouth opened, encouraging his tongue to sweep inside. Encouraging him to cinch her up in a possessing embrace, because she wanted, needed to belong to him.

229

And if it was the only valuable memory she ever had to hold, she would have this moment of belonging to Rory Prescott heart and soul.

Chance's menacing snort woke Rory from his passionate daze. They weren't alone. Without lessening the hungry pressure of his kiss, he opened his eyes, twisting his head slightly so that he could see over her shoulder into the dim shadows of the barn. Where Scott stood smiling inscrutably. Rory made an impatient shooing gesture and tried to ignore him but he wouldn't go away. Worse, he made a beckoning gesture of his own. Rory's brows lowered in a fierce refusal but Scott waved him over more insistently. Norah was simmering eagerly. His own needs were crowding hard. And Scott showed no sign of leaving. He groaned and made himself release her greedy lips. Lips she immediately fastened at the open vee of his shirt. He swore softly.

"Norah, Norah-honey, something important's come up kinda sudden."

"Oh, yes," came her sultry murmur. Her palm rubbed appreciatively against the bulging front of his jeans. Moaning wretchedly, he pulled her hand away.

"Not that, honey." He broke off, returning a long, urgent kiss. Then, breathlessly, he mumbled, "I gotta go beat the hell outta Scotty then I'll be right back. Think you can remember where we were so we can pick right back up with this here conversation?"

"Rory, you're not leaving, are you?" Her voice was husky with impatient ardor. When her palms moved restlessly over his chest and shoulders, he gave a rumbling sound of resignation. With Norah around him, demanding the full attention of his mouth, he gave his brother a helpless, palms up gesture of, "What's a man to do?"

"Excuse me."

The intrusion of Scott's voice brought Norah jerking

around within the circle of Rory's arms. She was flushed and panting and Scott knew in a glance that he was interrupting more than a little playful groping in a barn. He should have felt guilty but he was recalled to a similar situation a year ago Fourth of July when Rory had hauled him away from an equally promising paradise. He smiled wryly.

"Miss Denby, you mind if I have a word with my brother? I think your daddy was looking for you."

Norah clutched at Rory's arm, looking up at him in distressed indecision.

"You go on, Norah," he urged with matching reluctance.

Mindless of the fact that Scott Prescott was watching, Norah came up against him, her arms tight about his neck, her mouth locking over his for a hard, mind-draining kiss. Then, she whispered raggedly, "I'll wait up for you in my room. We won't have so much company there."

Rory smiled in wicked anticipation. "I won't be long. Jus' long enough to murder him and see him buried proper."

She stroked his face, unwilling to stop touching him and sealed their rendezvous with a quick, wet tangle of their tongues. She stepped away before she was tempted to do more and as she walked by Scott Prescott, she told him, "I hope your wife has her baby soon so you can find something else to occupy your time."

Scott grinned unexpectedly and looked back to Rory, who was sagging limply over Chance's back. When he approached, the paint kicked out at him in warning.

"Rory, you've got the meanest nag I've ever seen."

"You'd best be worrying about me, not Chance. Give me a reason why I oughtn't kick the bejeesus out of you?"

Without a trace of sympathy for his brother's anguish, Scott stated, "Business."

"Business? Well, hell that's something I'd much rather

do than make love to a woman." He grabbed his Stetson off one of the stall posts and stalked irritably out of the barn. Finally, he pulled up and gave Scott his attention, noticing the seriousness of the other's expression. "All right, Scotty. What's so danged important?"

"Someone I want you to talk to." He started off into the darkness and Rory followed. He was picking up a strange tension from his brother and he shouldn't have been surprised that the man waiting for them had the same strong, dark half-Sioux features that Scott shared. "Rory, this is Jason Walters. He is called Two Sparrows by his mother's people."

The farmer — Rory recognized him as one by his mode of dress — frowned and mumbled fiercely, "You said nothing about him, Lone Wolf." Then, he went on in the thick gutturals of the Teton language. Rory waited while the two of them argued back and forth until Scott finally held up his hand.

"Enough. I say trust my brother as you trust me. If you cannot, then go and ask no more of my help."

The man hesitated, looking between the stony-faced defender of their people to the redheaded grandson of Garth Kincaid.

"Tell him what you told me," Scott urged softly.

Two Sparrows sighed. "My mother was Sioux but my father, Thomas Walters owned property to the west of your ranch." Rory nodded. That's why the name sounded so familiar. "The land of my father is now mine. I work its soil alongside my wife and two sons. Never have we had trouble with the men from the Bar K." He paused to look at Scott uneasily.

"Go on, Two Sparrows. Tell him the rest."

"A week ago, men ride up to my house when my woman is there alone. They demand to see the few head of cows we keep. They told her they were looking for sucking calves in our corral, calves stolen from the Bar K herd. We do not steal cattle. We farm the land. We want no trouble. She tells them this and they go away. The next day, men bring cattle and drive them through our crops. We dare not shoot because they will have excuse to shoot back even if they are on our land. So we stand and let the cattle rub down our soddy. I come to Lone Wolf. The land is ours. These men have no right to do these things. We do not wish to fight with men of Bar K Ranch. You are many and we are few. But we will not leave our land. Lone Wolf tells me you are man of good spirit. He tells me you speak true. If you say there will be no fight, I will listen."

Scott's steady stare called for an answer.

"There will be no fight," Rory promised somberly.

"Good." Jason Walters nodded to both brothers. "Now my woman can sleep at night."

When he'd gone, Scott studied his brother impassively. "You'll see to your word?"

"Said I would and I will." Rory jerked off his Stetson and ran his fingers distractedly through his bright hair. But it was a lot more complicated than that. He'd seen the new men, the killers Denby hired. They looked inconspicuous enough, picked for their ability to shade off amongst the regular ranch hands. And he'd given his word to the major that he wouldn't interfere between the gunmen and the encroaching settlers. But the Walters weren't nesters any more than they were rustlers. Their parcel was as old as the Bar K. He had that uncomfortable tightness back within his chest, that squeezing in from both sides that made it impossible to breathe easy. Damn Scotty anyway for bringing him his problems. But then, he owed his brother a favor.

"What are you going to do?" Scott pressed quietly. He wasn't completely satisfied with the restless look on his brother's face.

"I'm gonna go get a drink, then I'm gonna love me my

233

woman." He paused, then sighed almost angrily. "Then after the race tomorrow, I'll have me a talk with Denby."

Scott nodded at that. He didn't envy his brother his position but he had faith in his word once it was given. He watched Rory march back toward the lights and gaiety, wishing there had been some other way. Rory would only go so far to aid the interests outside the Bar K and Scott had the feeling he was rapidly overextending his reach.

Just before he turned, he noticed it again. The scent of a good cigar. The same he'd smelled outside the barn. He held himself perfectly still, waiting, listening but there was nothing unusual in the night sounds. Finally, he shook off his prickle of intuition and followed Rory.

Minutes later, Cole Denby snubbed out his cigar and went inside the ranch house. It took him a moment to find the one he was looking for.

"Major, we got us a little problem."

Chapter Fifteen

"Still a-waiting on that dance?"

Norah looked up from where she stood at Gena's side. Her gaze sizzled. "You asking, cowboy?"

"Yes, ma'am, I surely am. Maybe we'd best wait for something with a little more heel kicking to it. Thataway, I wouldn't be so apt to misbehave."

"And what kind of misbehavior would you be tempted into?"

"Oh, maybe something like this." His big hand slipped around her, settling low to cup her bottom through the layers of fashionable female padding. It was hard to get a hold on a real woman. "I think I like the britches better," he complained with a roguish grin. Then his dark eyes detailed the low scoop of her gown's neckline. "I kinda like this, though." His forefinger hooked in the filmy ruching that formed the draping decolletage and eased it down until the generous curve of her bosom was exposed to his appreciative stare. "Why, Miss Denby," he drawled in mock surprise, "wherever did you get such an immodest amount of sunburn?"

"Rory Prescott, how absolutely unchivalrous of you to ask."

"Oh, darlin', there ain't much I don't dare."

"Really?"

"Really."

His hand cradled her chin, tilting it up to give him easy access to her provokingly pouted lips. He savaged them tenderly, not caring who saw. Norah must not have either, for she was kissing back for all she was worth. Finally, he came to his senses and leaned back.

"What were we talking about?"

"Dancing, I think."

"Oh, yeah. If Miss Gena don't mind us up and leaving her."

Gena waved them off. She couldn't keep her smiles to herself. In that short exchange, she'd seen everything she needed to know they were in love with each other; wildly, passionately, blindly in love. She was finally going to get a sister.

And Cole Denby saw more than enough, too. Beside him, Charles Monthaven stiffened in outrage.

"Is there no end to that man's gall?" the aristocrat exclaimed. "How can you allow the man to make a mockery of your own daughter's integrity?"

Cole almost smiled at that. Instead, he said with a heaving sigh, "There is little I can do, your lordship. The man is technically my employer. My daughter and I are at the mercy of his, shall we say, whims. I'm afraid as long as she's under the same roof with him, she'll not be safe from his attentions. If only there was some relative with whom I could trust the girl. Unfortunately, if this harassment of her innocence continues, I shall have to tender my resignation."

"Oh, dear." Monthaven was truly appalled. He didn't like to think of the lovely Miss Denby suffering the rude bounder's pointed affronts to her femininity any more than he liked the idea of losing a valuable intermediary between himself and Kincaid. There seemed only one alternative. And he rather liked it. But before he discussed it, there was business to attend.

236

"Trust me to take care of your daughter's dilemma, Mr. Denby. In return, I would like to know what my odds are of winning tomorrow's race."

Cole took his time lighting another cigar. As he shook out the match, he looked down over the revelry. "The locals have the advantage of knowing the course. Their animals and riders are used to distance. By far you have the best bit of horseflesh and an experienced jockey."

"Who is my greatest competition? Prescott?"

"Both of them, I would think. From what I hear the half-breed has taken in a fortune in bets from the Sioux. They have placed a great deal of faith in his ability. And those who don't care for the man, himself, are willing to wager on the quality of the horse. Ethan Prescott has a pretty good reputation in these parts."

"And Rory Prescott?" He mouthed the name with unfeigned distaste.

"He's tough but not too smart. I look for him to burn out early along with the rest of the field. I see it as a two-man race, your man and Scott Prescott."

Monthaven thought that over. He didn't like second best. He liked to win, especially if it meant defeating the obnoxious cowboy and his renegade brother. "I should like very much to be victorious in this race. Not that I am interested in the prize money, you understand."

"To strike a blow for Queen and country, so to speak," Cole managed without a trace of cynicism.

"Quite. Now if a man were to assure me of a win tomorrow, I would not hesitate to give that fellow the one thousand dollar purse."

"My lord, I might be able to be of some assistance there."

Nothing like killing two birds with one well-placed shot.

* * *

Moving slowly in time to the fiddles with Norah Denby in his arms had a soothing effect on Rory's soul and a devastating one on his body. With her head nestled upon his chest and her slender fingers curled trusting within his, it was easy to push aside the problem of Scott and Cole Denby. It was easy to forget about the Bar K altogether. His senses spun in an intoxicating bliss. There'd be time to come down to earth later. Right now, heaven was holding the woman he loved, smelling her soft perfume and imagining all the things they would do together when they were alone a few hours from now. Imagining the look on his mama's face when he told her he was getting married. Imagining how his wife would look all round and full of the life he planted inside her. Impatient for all those things, he squeezed her hard and happily.

Norah hugged him back. It was unnerving that a man could feel so good. Could kiss so good. Love so good. And could make her believe in good again. How had it happened? How had he stepped off the Dakota plains and right into her heart? The music and the magic of the night seduced her. But that was part of Rory Prescott's charm, too. He made everything change just by being there. He made everything alive and new and exciting. Even the dance, just a simple waltz, was so disturbingly sensual when he moved her through the steps. She could feel the whole length of his body; hard, strong — hers. If she tipped back her head, she would find his hot, dark eyes ready to devour her gaze. How could she keep saying no when the only answer he would hear was yes? Wasn't it the answer she wanted to give? Would have given if things were somehow different. If she had an iron-clad guarantee that nothing from her past would ever reach them out here on this prairie empire. If she could be sure he would never, ever find out about the woman she really was — or rather the woman she had been before he woke the conscience up inside her. The longer she stayed, the safer she felt. Or was that just a dangerous illusion? Like the one that had her believing she could keep Rory Prescott's love forever.

The music came to an end and Rory led her back to where his family had gathered. His arm lingered around her waist, just a light claim but as binding as his length of Manila. Norah looked from one to the other, at the Prescotts who had Rory's unconditional love. The people who mattered most to him in the whole world. What would they think if they knew what she was? Again, she felt the threat of Scott's impassive stare and the curiosity of his mother's gaze. They wouldn't leave it alone. They knew she was not what she seemed. They weren't looking through Rory's love-glazed eyes. These good, decent people would never accept who she was and she couldn't thrust Rory into another tug of war over his affections. She couldn't make him choose.

She was almost relieved when Cole came up to take her away. She gave Rory a small, secret smile that promised him all the potential he could hope for in the night to come so he would let her go. Making a vague excuse, Cole hurried her through the crowd. Toward Charles Monthaven. As soon as she saw his destination, she began to balk but his grip on her arm didn't relent.

"What are you up to, Cole?" she demanded in suspicion. He was smiling. It was a thin, well-satisfied smile.

"You'll see, my dear. I've a surprise for you."

She didn't like Cole's surprises. And she didn't like the way Lord Monthaven exchanged looks with him as Cole transferred her hand from his own arm to the elegant lord's. From their high vantage spot upon the wraparound porch, Cole waved down the musicians and drew the attention of the crowd, preparing them for Lord Monthaven.

"Most kind ladies and gentlemen," his lordship began

239

in a smooth rolling tone that bespoke his breeding. "You have made a stranger welcome in your midst and I should like to thank you. Tomorrow evening, I bid you return to aid in a celebration. We shall toast my victory in the race," he paused for a moment of good natured laughter at that bold claim, "and my engagement."

Norah had a sudden, sickening insight as to his next words. Frantically, her eyes sought Rory in the crowd. He was standing with his family, a frown beginning to furrow his brow.

Monthaven smiled down at the woman by his side and said proudly, "Tonight, I am the happiest of men. Mr. Cole Denby has given me the hand of his daughter, Norah, to be my lady and my love."

Rory took the words like a double barrel blast to the gut. Shock slammed him back onto his heels as a single, startled breath escaped him. And then, one word, made low and thick with disbelief.

"No."

He tried to think and couldn't. He tried to breathe and couldn't. He tried to gain some kind of understanding from Norah's closed expression but couldn't see through the sudden hazy burn that overcame his vision. He watched Cole Denby place a fond kiss upon his daughter's cheek and warmly clasp Charles Monthaven's hand.

No.

It couldn't be happening! Just minutes ago, she'd been moving sweetly in his arms. Just an hour ago, she'd been wriggling impatiently against him, inviting him to her room. Days ago, she'd been moaning underneath him, crying out his name, claiming, *I love you*. That didn't sound like a woman about to get engaged to another man. There was some mistake and he was going to get to the bottom of it damned quick.

He took an aggressive stride forward and was checked by his father's strong grip upon his forearms. Not many men could have brought him to a standstill but Ethan Prescott was one of them.

"Hold hard there, son. This ain't the time or place for it. Ain't nothing you can do right now in the middle of all these folks."

"But Daddy, you don't understand." With those words and a long draw of breath, his bewilderment shifted to a cold, killing fury. Who the hell did Charles Monthaven think he was? And Norah — Norah —

"Yes, I do. Let it go for now. Rory, let it go."

His breath was seething. His chest was heaving like a boiler about to blow. Let it go! By God! But Ethan's grip was unbreakable so he had no choice but to stand and watch Norah and Charles together on the porch. Watch him bend down to kiss her cheek. To see him smile with proud possession. With a raw, tortured growl, he whirled away from that sight and Ethan let him go. To stalk off into the darkness to hide his pain from those who loved him.

How could she do it? The faster he walked, the more confusion rose to torment him. Had it all been a lie then, a way to bed down with him and take her pleasure while waiting for Monthaven to stake his claim? *I do love you, Rory Prescott.* No, that hadn't been a lie. But he'd known she was holding something back from him and just hadn't guessed it was the fact that she was fixing to marry someone else!

She hadn't said she would marry him. She had never told him they would have a future together. Those were his plans. Hadn't they ever been hers?

He couldn't find any answers wandering about in the night. Those he'd have to hear from Norah. He made a wide loop, circling around the merrymakers who were even now indulging in Monthaven's imported champagne. He didn't see the two of them on the porch. With a silent determination, he entered the big house through a side door. From the hall, he could hear her voice, following it to the front parlor. Where he received his answer.

The announcement stunned her. Norah was barely aware of what followed, of the fact that Cole, then Charles, kissed her. She was swallowed up by the incredulous look upon Rory's face. She saw him start forward and wanted wildly for him to come up and claim her, to take her from this sudden, unexpected madness. But he didn't. Instead, he disappeared into the shadowed fringes of the night. It was then she realized what Cole had done. What Monthaven now expected.

And she was furious.

Angrily, she fled the porch and the toasts to her happiness with the wrong man. Inside, she was taken by the need to break something—preferably Cole Denby's neck. But never Rory Prescott's heart.

"Aren't you going to thank me?"

Norah turned to the smiling Cole and slapped him with all her might. He stumbled back but never lost the smile.

"One might think you weren't grateful."

"How dare you? How dare you do such a thing!"

"Now, Norah, dear, calm yourself. When you think on it, you'll see it's for the best."

"Whose best? What are you getting out of it?"

He grinned with immense pleasure. "Why Norah, I'm getting an embarrassingly large dowry for my lovely daughter."

"You sold me to him?"

"Rather crudely put, but yes."

Words couldn't express her outrage, her indignation.

"Now, Norah, you think for a minute. Isn't this what you wanted? Security and wealth? Weren't you looking for a way out? I found it for you and this is the thanks I get. Sleep on it and you'll find yourself looking at it different tomorrow. Tomorrow you'll thank me. Tomorrow, we'll both be richer for Lord Monthaven's generosity."

She spat a single epithet but Cole just grinned. As he left the room, he passed Charles Monthaven and gave him a firm pat on the shoulder.

"My love, you don't look pleased," Charles observed in some surprise.

Norah regarded him narrowly. "That's because a lady likes to hear of things like her wedding before they are announced to the world."

"It was clumsily done, I must admit, but quite romantic, too. Don't you agree?"

"No. I see nothing vaguely romantic about being placed in such an awkward position. How could you be so sure of my answer without even asking me first?"

Charles blinked as if he'd never considered that inconsequential step. What woman wouldn't want to wed him? A mere formality. But if she was incensed, he would soothe her. "I have read the answer a dozen times within your lovely eyes. I have seen your adoration there and it has touched my heart. I must have you, Norah. You will be my wife."

There was a time to behave like a gentleman and a time to take matters more firmly in hand. Now was the time to be assertive. He took Norah by the rigidly held shoulders and pulled her up to him. Before she could draw a protesting breath, he was kissing her.

She was taken offguard. Her hands rose to clutch at him for balance. It gave him time to move his mouth persuasively and with some experience over hers. It wasn't a bad kiss. But it wasn't Rory Prescott's.

Norah jerked back, breathing hard. And it was then she saw him in the doorway.

"Rory . . ."

Monthaven turned, an incredibly smug smile upon

his aristocratic face. "Well, Prescott, it would seem the best man has won."

Rory answered him with a row of hard knuckles.

The blow lifted Charles off his feet and laid him out atop the sofa in a daze.

Norah took a gulping breath, held in place by the fierce angry passion on Rory's face. She swallowed hard and began to speak but he cut her off brusquely.

"You ain't got nothing to say that I want to hear."

With that, he stormed out of the room, out of the house. Out of her life? Norah raced after him, ignoring Charles's disoriented moans. But when she rushed out onto the porch, Cole snagged her arm and held her fast.

"Let me go!"

"Let him go, Norah. It's for the best and you know it. Let him go."

She watched Rory stride across the yard, down to the barn. In a matter of minutes, Chance burst from the door, goaded by its rider into a reckless gallop. Through the gates of the Bar K. Toward Crowe Creek.

Things wound down a little after midnight. The race was planned for an early morning start and none wanted to miss it. Gradually, the Bar K settled into its routine night sounds. And Norah paced.

Where was he?

But then, she knew, didn't she.

He was in Crowe Creek. Forgetting her.

For the best, Cole said. And it was. She knew that. In her mind, she knew it. But her heart had ideas of its own and it beat hard and fast for the redheaded cowboy. She just couldn't let him go. No matter what logic dictated. No matter how close consequence crowded. If it was for one more night, one more minute, greedily, she wanted it. She wanted him. She wanted to let him wrap her up in his love, to feel it surround her with a warmth she'd never known before. And probably never would again. Because he wasn't coming to spend the night in her bed. He'd found another to hold him.

It was the perfect time to cut losses. She'd learned the importance of timing from Cole. Winning was all in knowing when to quit. There was no such thing as riding a lucky streak forever. Sooner or later, it would turn. And that's what would happen if she stayed on. Charles Monthaven was offering an escape, if not love. She didn't and she wouldn't love him. But she could make a good life for herself. She could be respected in a distant country where no one would recognize her face or know her name. She could be free. Free of everything but Rory. He would hang on her heart forever. The same way the look in his eyes would haunt her conscience until her dying day.

She'd never meant to hurt him.

Then she saw Chance come barreling through the gates with Rory sitting sloppy in the saddle. He rode the horse right into the barn. Norah stood at her window, waiting, planning what she would say, how she would explain the unexplainable to a man whose love she'd shattered. But when he didn't come up to the house, her anxiety grew too great to bear. These feelings aching inside her couldn't wait until morning. She had to speak them now. Whether he'd believe them was another story.

For Rory, it started out like a night in hell. He curled himself around a bottle in the darkest corner he could find and commenced to drinking her off his mind. Maybe when he was blind drunk, he wouldn't be able to see her accepting Charles Monthaven's kiss. Maybe when his brain was numb, he wouldn't be picturing them entwined together in lustful pursuits. He'd believed her

245

when she said she hadn't been with him. He believed her. Stupid. Stupid. Stupid. That kept echoing right down to the bottom of the bottle. But no matter how hard he tried to lose himself in the liquor, hers was the face he found.

He was well into his second bottle and a stupor of self-pity when Sally Jean found him. She took one look at the dull sheen in his eyes and coaxed him upstairs. There, she held him and kissed him and told him she was there for him as a friend. And to his utter dismay, he broke down and started sobbing with drunken, heartsick gusto, spilling his guts in abject misery about the woman whose lies had laid him low. He'd passed out then and Sally Jean let him slumber like the dead for some time. Finally, she shook him gently awake to say she had a paying customer. She was kicking him out.

"Go home, Rory," she told him with a kind, world weary wisdom as she pushed him to the door. "Go home, you big fool, and grab up your gal. Tear off her clothes and love her until she's too weak to walk or talk or think about leaving you for anybody else."

And to the heart-sore cowboy, it seemed sound advice. He crawled up on Chance and rode him hard, mercilessly, the way he planned to ride Norah until she forgot all about Charles Monthaven. By the time they thundered into the Bar K barn, both man and horse were lathered and trembling. Rory reined the stallion in and let it walk into the stall. Guiltily, he realized he'd been abusing his mount as badly as he was abusing himself. His eyes felt gritty and there was an empty hole in his chest as big as one blown by his daddy's old Sharps at point blank range. Norah. He would go to Norah and if Monthaven was with her, he'd blast the woman-stealing sonuvabitch to hell. Smiling at that satisfying image, he tried to climb out of the saddle. And it seemed an endless drop into the cushioning hay.

She'd waited long enough. Determinedly, Norah tied her wrapper on and slipped out of the house, down to the barn where all was quiet. She could see Chance standing in his stall, still sporting tack. But no sign of Rory. Unwilling to give up, she squared her shoulders and marched to the bunkhouse. Perhaps he'd bought solace there amongst his peers. Not thinking how it would look, she a lady in her nightclothes entering a room full of sleeping cowboys, she pushed open the door and was assailed by the most particular odors. Each one was strong and identifiable, combining to a pungent whole; sweaty men, dry cow manure, licorice from the chewing tobacco plugs, old work boots and smoke from the lamps. Rows of stacked bunks reflected a chronic untidiness by men who hung their clothes on the floor so they wouldn't fall down and get lost. A couple of the hands were crouched over a deck of greasy-backed cards intent on their play. One of them glanced up and nearly went apoplectic.

"Ma'am, you shouldn't ought to be in here!"

She ignored the host of startled stares and the quick snatch of blankets to throw on over worn long underwear. Impatiently, she scanned the room. "Is Rory here?"

The men were too disconcerted to vent sly smiles. One of them muttered, "He's in the barn."

"I was just there and he isn't."

"He's sleeping it off in his paint's stall."

"And you're going to leave him there? And his horse standing wet?"

"Hell, ma'am, ain't a one of us'd go within biting range of that demon, beggin' your pardon for puttin' it so blunt."

She scowled at them darkly. "A pack of timid old ladies. And he thought you were his friends."

Angrily, she turned from their shamed faces and stormed back to the barn. Chance snorted nervously at her hurried approach and began to stomp. If Rory was inside the stall, he could be trampled under those sharp hoofs. She slowed her step and began to murmur soothingly.

"Whoa there, Chance. You stand easy now."

She edged up next to the stall until she could see Rory, sprawled and still in the straw up by the restless animal's forefeet. Her heart took a nasty jump. Was he breathing? One misstep would be all it took. Then, she could smell the whiskey from where she stood. He wasn't dead. He was dead drunk.

With a firm hand on the spotted withers, Norah entered the stall. The animal's hide was damp and its sides were heaving. Rory had ridden it almost into the ground.

"Damn fool," she growled down at the motionless man. "Kill yourself if you want, but take care of your horse first."

Gently, slowly, she removed the tack from the winded stallion and began to rub it down. It had been a long time since she'd tended such a domestic chore, and never in her nightclothes. The horse stood quiet and content beneath her knowledgeable hands, occasionally stretching an inquiring nose down to nudge Rory.

"Leave him alone, Chance. He's going to feel like hell when he wakes up."

As she brushed the calm animal down, Norah was aware of a silent audience. A group of pop-eyed ranch hands had come to stand and stare while she exchanged Chance's bridle for a soft hackamore. They gasped as one when she reached for the bit but Chance let it drop in her hand as gentle as a sweet-tempered mare. And to a one, they couldn't believe it. With the horse tended, Norah finally went around to the front of the stall where Rory snored in quiet oblivion. As she bent down, she picked up several distinct scents; that of horse, that of whiskey and that of—damn him!—cheap woman. She straight-

248

ened abruptly, startling a snort of alarm from Chance and quick hops back from the cowboys. Angrily, she strode from the stall.

"You gonna just leave him there?" one of the men asked uneasily.

"You want him, you get him," she stated flatly.

They looked nervously from their prostrate boss to Chance's scuffling hoofs.

At the end of her patience . . . and her charity, Norah picked up a bucket of water and threw its contents. Rory sputtered and sat up floundering.

"There," she said with a grim satisfaction. "Now they've both been put away wet for the night."

Chapter Sixteen

Horse racing was held in high affection by cowboys. Little tracks were scattered all over cow-country wherever pockets carried loose change and man had a want to double it. The minute spring round-up was done, dust was stirred by the fastest horses, covering the sweetness of the sand lilies and blowing the slopes of golden banner away.

A long range race brought horses from across the territory to be grained and hardened on the long dusty route. For the most part, they were a shaggy lot. Anyone with a saddle was willing to set aside a day of hardship and the risk of horseflesh for the chance at winning prizes of $1,000, $500 and $250. Spectators clustered around those riders who would carry their hopes — and bets to the finish line. Amongst those broomtails, Charles Monthaven's thoroughbred stood out as sleek and elegantly as the aristocrat himself. The leggy racehorse drew a crowd of the curious. Caught between Cole and Charles beneath the shade of their buggy top, Norah tried not to look as anxious as she felt amongst that mob of eager horse fanciers. And she tried not to be too blatant in the way she searched for Rory Prescott.

It wasn't hard to find him amongst the other arriving participants. He came in flashy, pushing Chance to a ground-eating canter and doing a few riding tricks from his saddle to win a roar of approval from the other Bar K hands. Looking at them, none would know both man and horse had been at the end of their endurance scant hours ago. Neither of them could have had ample time to recover and Norah wondered why Rory was here to compete in the grueling race when his head was splitting and his horse was winded. Then, he paraded by their buggy, whipping off his hat in a jaunty salute and she knew. He was there to best Charles Monthaven in prideful Prescott fashion. He was smiling with cocky bravado but there was no answering vitality in his dark stare. That look was all angry business. He kicked Chance on to where his mother, father and Gena sat in their buckboard and leaned down from the saddle to kiss both women warmly. Norah felt a queer stirring of pain in the vicinity of her heart. To distract herself from it, and the handsome redhead, she followed the turn of the crowd toward a new arrival.

Scott Prescott knew how to make an entrance, too. He did it with dignity rather than show, astride his stepfather's clean limbed, deep chested, black gelding. He rode bareback, bare headed, barefooted and bare chested, like the entourage of silent Sioux who trailed behind him. He looked nothing like the suave, civilized Harvard lawyer in his shiny Eastern suit of clothes Norah had seen the night before. He was Lone Wolf, son of a Lakota warrior and he carried his people's pride and their heavy bets with him. He, too, rode up to the Prescott wagon, nodding to Ethan, hugging his mother and fixing a long, heated kiss upon his pregnant wife.

Gena clung to him for a timeless minute, inhaling the scent of his bared skin. "Scott, be careful," she whispered worriedly.

251

"I'll look out for him, Sis," Rory offered with a grin. "That is, if he don't fall too far behind."

"Don't break your neck looking over your shoulder for me. Just follow my dust." Scott stuck out his hand as the two horses angled up alongside one another. Rory gripped his brother's hand and used it to haul him almost off his mount for a big, bruising squeeze.

"You boys be careful," Ethan warned fondly. "And you look out for each other."

"Yessir, Daddy," his sons echoed, breaking apart and taking up their reins.

"And we'll have ourselves a victory celebration of our own at the Lone Star when it's over and done," Aurora put in softly. None of them were keen on returning to the Bar K for Norah Denby's engagement party.

"Thank you, Mama," Rory muttered huskily and wheeled Chance away.

Scott circled his horse, coming around for one more kiss from Gena and to whisper, "I love you." She squeezed one of his hands in hers, hanging on tight until forced to release him when Garth Kincaid bellowed loudly, "Line 'em up, gentlemen!"

Forty-three horses broke at the firing of his gun, thundering across the plain in an unbroken line. Aurora reached behind her for her daughter-in-law's hand. She smiled reassuringly and said, "Just think of what you're going to buy for the baby with the prize money."

Gena smiled back shakily. She couldn't share Ethan and Aurora's confidence. Or that of Scott's Lakota brethren. Because she alone knew that her husband had been awake most of the night, sweating and shaking in the throes of his dreams.

By the time the sun was directly overhead, that line

had thinned to a straggling procession across near barren prairie. A dozen riders had already dropped out. Monthaven's thoroughbred held to first place and Rory didn't have to look back for Scott, not anymore. They rode side by side. No one knew horses like his brother. So when he noticed Scott pulling his horse in from a run to a steady lope every fifteen miles or so, he began to wonder why. He kept Chance at a good gallop and he was wearing down fast. And Scott seemed to have no trouble catching up to him with his mount much fresher looking. Finally, he caught on to it. Ethan Prescott had bred the same mustang blood in both animals and held in at a short lope, his horses could go on strong forever. By spelling them at intervals, they had a chance to breathe and give more when it was called for. So when Monthaven's racehorse passed them hard on the return fifty-mile leg, Scott smiled confidently and hollered, "He's not going anywhere." And he was right. Within ten miles, they'd made the turn together and were closing on the laboring thoroughbred, finally streaking past on either side, while the jockey cursed them fiercely.

With twenty-five miles of hilly terrain remaining, Rory was hard pressed to rein in. He knew Monthaven's man was right behind him, a man who thought nothing of killing a good animal for a paltry purse. And damn, he wanted to win. The rest of the riders were spread out in a staggered rush cross country to the finish. Chance was lathered and breathing hard but he was good for it. But he'd promised Scott they'd wait until the last ten-mile stretch, then go full out for the money. He wouldn't mind taking second to his brother, but he'd be hanged if he let Monthaven's man pass him.

Restlessly, he pulled Chance in, shadowing Scott's black with a long, steady stride. If he hadn't taken a

253

swipe across his brow with his Stetson, he might not have seen a sudden glint of warning from a nearby out-cropping of rock. A rifle. Beaded on his brother.

There was no time to yell out. No time to draw his own gun. He had a fraction of a second to react, a heartbeat in which to save Scott's life. He cut hard on the reins and kicked back viciously, breaking Chance's gait. A true, big-hearted roping horse, Chance didn't balk but obeyed without hesitation, lunging forward, veering into Scott's gelding with a solid, crippling smack of muscle and bone. With the loud thud of im-pact came an animal's scream of pain, drowning out any echo of a rifle shot.

Taken by surprise, Scott grabbed a handful of mane and locked his legs around the horse's belly to keep from sliding under the tangle of hoofs. In that moment, he realized the collision was no accident. Rory had tried to cut him off. Scott's expert horsemanship kept him astride and his mount standing while Rory and Chance went down. Cursing and shaken, Scott failed to rein in. Monthaven's thoroughbred flashed past with-out altering stride and his horse responded by follow-ing. Scott looked back in a daze to where Chance was thrashing and Rory spilled off in a roll. Rory had done it on purpose. Scott was numb then furious. Goddamn him, he'd done it on purpose! His own brother. Cheat-ing like an untrustworthy Kincaid. Over a race! Over a few hundred dollars! The son of a bitch! Rory had reck-lessly gambled on the fleetness of his tough little mus-tang and had miscalculated, getting tangled up in his own treachery. Angrily, nearly strangling on his hurt, Scott gathered up control of his horse and urged him on after the leader.

Over a race.

To impress that woman.

Damn him!

Scott crouched over the stinging slap of the animal's mane, making a sleek silhouette. Ahead, he could see the churning hindquarters of his competition. Miles flew by, those final all important miles. With the finish in sight, he played out the ends of the hackamore, using it to whip both sides of the horse's flanks, Indian fashion. He bent low and gave a high, penetrating Sioux war cry into the animal's ear. An answering roar rose up from his father's people. He flailed faster with the reins as they glided by the withers, the girth, the powerful shoulders of the wet and played out thorough-bred. And with another shrill cry, Scott urged his horse ahead, across the finish with a length to spare.

It was with a posture of extreme arrogance that Scott Prescott rode up to collect his winning purse from Garth Kincaid. The man handed it over without a shift of expression until his grandson brandished it over his head like a freshly taken scalp and gave a loud, undu-lating Lakota cry. Then his teeth ground.

After hearing the praise of his father's people, Scott cantered his winded horse to his family's wagon and tossed the gold into what was left of Gena's lap.

"Quite a show," Ethan commented dryly, arching a brow toward the major.

Scott grinned disarmingly wide. "Yessir," he owned up proudly.

"More like what I'd expect from your brother."

Scott was instantly sober. His features were as chis-eled and sharp as badlands buttes. "I'm going home," he announced curtly.

"Scott," Gena called out after him, her gaze scanning the horizon. "Where's Rory? Shouldn't we wait for him?"

"I wouldn't wait. He won't be coming to the Lone

Star tonight." His jaw worked tightly for a moment then he spat, "I hope he's in hell."

Rory hit the ground hard. Having ridden broncs for years, he knew how to roll but for some reason his reflexes were sluggish, only half serving him. The slap of the dirt kicked the wind out of him and for a moment, he lay unmoving, dazed. When he could finally suck air, he attempted to get his knees under him and dropped immediately.

"Oh, God."

He hurt.

"Scotty?" he moaned hoarsely, then waited. Nothing. He forced his eyes to focus, his senses to react to something other than the horrendous pain. He could feel the vibration of horses running through ground beneath him, but it was a far away echo, getting farther. "Scotty!" It took a long minute for understanding to sink deep. Scott was gone. He'd left him. The race. Oh, yes. He remembered now. Scotty had to win the race. Then he'd be back for him. He'd be back. Calmed by that knowledge, he let the red haze of hurt overcome him. Hurry, Scotty.

A nudge to his shoulder stirred consciousness again. Moaning weakly, he managed to smile and murmur, "Sure as hell took your sweet time. I'm feeling mighty poorly." He opened his eyes and was confused. Chance stood over him, trailing reins. There was no sign of his brother. He eased over onto his back and let his waning strength gather. He couldn't wait all day. He was going to have to get up on Chance and get himself home.

If he could.

He took slow, uneasy stock of his situation. The brutal fall had done more than stun him. His left wrist was

256

broken. His fingertips tingled and trembled, his arm ached clear to the shoulder but it was manageable. It wasn't like it was the first bone he'd ever snapped. His head hurt, giving a fuzzy edge to his perception. Must have hit it when he fell. The rest of him was a collection of bruises, bothersome but not incapacitating. Until he tried to stand. A shaft of white-hot agony lanced up his left leg. He fell back, writhing helplessly on the ground until it subsided. He reached down, first with his useless left hand then with his right, feeling gingerly along his leg. He could tell where the swelling started just above his knee, where it burned like something had torn loose inside. He muttered a groaning oath. He'd sure done it this time.

Timing his breathing so it matched the pulsing discomfort, Rory managed to sit up. Everything whirled in great black, dizzying loops. Afraid he was going to pass out again and waste time he wasn't sure he had lying out on the prairie, he gritted his teeth and made himself reach for Chance's stirrup iron. The horse stood for him, still as stone. Slowly, fighting down the excruciating protests, he crawled up into the saddle and lay there across Chance's neck for a timeless minute before picking up the reins. When he straightened, he noticed a bright red splotch on his denims. And another. Then several more, making a vivid pattern. He was bleeding? When he shifted his attention by slow degrees to his right arm, he suffered a second of harsh panic. My God, his sleeve was drenched with it. He moved his hand upward, feeling cautiously along his shoulder, up his neck until his fingers slid. Until he could feel the beat of his life's blood pumping out against his palm.

He'd been shot.

He'd taken Scott's bullet.

He didn't remember being hit. Things had happened

257

too fast. But one thing he was sure of, he was going to bleed to death if he didn't get to help soon. Determinedly, he drew the small sharp-bladed knife he always carried and cut away part of his shirtsleeve. He rolled it one-handed against his thigh then held the wadding to his wound. Grinding his jaw and popping sweat, he used his broken hand to hold it in place, securing it there with an awkwardly knotted bandana. Then he grinned weakly. Not as good a field dressing as his daddy could do but it would keep him from leaking the rest of his years out on the barren prairie.

"Come on, Chance. Let's get a-going." Even in his fog of misery, Rory could feel the irregularity of his stallion's gait. He remembered the animal's scream of pain as they went down. He patted the wet neck with his palm. "Come on, Chance. Let's get to the Lone Star an' Daddy'll patch us both back together."

Rory rode slack in saddle, weaving and rocking to the rhythm of his horse's walk. Scotty. Scotty was all right. He'd seen to his promise. With his life? Maybe, but hell, it was worth it. Scotty had Gena and the baby and the things he was doing for the Sioux. He had . . . nothing, nobody. Scott was the important one, the man with the mission . . . always had been. Him, heck, he was a plain, bowlegged fella without too many brains and a way with cows. A fair trade. A good trade. He wouldn't complain on it. And his mama wouldn't weep over him forever the way she would with Scott. He'd done the right thing and they'd be proud.

Norah. Her image danced before him like a shimmering heat mirage. Would she miss him? Would she mourn him? He created a picture of her in black, weeping at his graveside. And of Charles Monthaven supplying her with one of his monogrammed hankies. Of her leaning on him and him leading her away with his

258

arm about her shaking shoulders.

Looks like the better man has won.

"Not yet, you son of a thieving coyote," he mumbled thickly into Chance's mane. "I ain't buried yet."

But he would be if he didn't get help soon.

In a daze of relief, he recognized the terrain. The finish line would be right up ahead. Slowly, he straightened in the saddle and blinked repeatedly to bring the tipping horizon into focus. In a matter of minutes, he'd be stretched out comfortable in the back of his family's buckboard and Norah would be hovering over him, her cool gray eyes shiny with concern. He was smiling faintly as he looked around. At nothing. No one was there. They'd all gone.

He sat, mind blanked. Where was everyone? His mama. His daddy. Scotty and Gena? The major? The boys from the Bar K? Norah? Norah. They were off celebrating her marriage to Monthaven. And it was going to kill him. Literally. How much time had passed since he and Chance had gone down? Surely not hours. He raised his head toward the sun, trying to gauge its position. It flared hot and bright and consuming. Then there was blue sky, lots of blue Dakota sky. And hard Dakota ground.

Again, it was Chance that brought him around. Pain was alive inside him, beating with heavy hammers in his skull, behind his eyes. Throbbing through his arm. Screaming in the torn and twisted tendons of his knee. And he was bleeding again. He was going to die where he'd fallen because he hadn't the strength to get up. A terrible anxiety settled, shaking through him in panicky waves. He wasn't going to see his family again. He wasn't going to look out over the vast Bar K herd from Chance's back and feel the swell of accomplishment. He wasn't going to taste Norah's sweet kiss or hear her

259

say, *I love you, Rory,* not ever again. Who would watch over Scotty? Who would inherit the Bar K? Who would keep Norah from sailing off to England? Who was going to see to Chance? He was scared and alone and so cold. Why so cold when the ground was warm beneath him?

"Oh God, I don't want to die out here. Don't let me die out here."

The sound of his moaning wail startled Chance into sidestepping nervously.

"Whoa, Chance. Stand. Don't you go running off, you hear."

If he was going to survive, he had to clear his mind of the paralyzing fright. He had to quit thinking about dying and start doing something about living. His body was slipping fast into deep shock. He didn't know what it was called, he only knew he was rapidly losing touch with his surroundings. He dragged himself into a sitting position and whistled softly. Chance eyed him uneasily for a long, tense moment then responded to the call. Rory seized a hold of the saddle leather with his good hand and tried to haul himself up. He stood shakily, panting and faint-headed. And he knew there was no way he could pull himself up onto Chance's back. His arm was numb, his leg on fire. Neither would respond with any kind of movement. He wasn't riding out. Leaning heavily against his horse, murmuring softly and praying that Chance wouldn't shy, he undid the pack rolled behind his saddle and let it fall. He eased down beside it and tore open the lacings. He ignored most of the makings inside in favor of his canvas slicker. It would warm him and the tough fabric would give him some protection. It took him a ridiculous amount of time to put it on and fastened it around him. Carefully, he fed his broken hand through the stirrup

260

iron and bent it up at the elbow. Taking off his gun belt, he tossed the fancy Colts aside and wrapped the length of leather around and around to secure his forearm to the saddle, knowing with a grim certainty that there was no way he'd be able to hang on himself.

Rory sat, sucking air and garnering his courage. Finally, he expelled a forceful breath.

"Take me home, Chance."

He slapped at the horse's hocks to start him moving. The binding on his arm snapped taut and tugged sharply against the fractured bone in his wrist. A bevy of quail shot up from the brush at the sudden sound of his scream.

And Chance began walking, dragging him, blissfully unconscious, toward the Lone Star.

Charles Monthaven didn't let losing the race dampen his spirits. Rory Prescott hadn't beaten him and he had a greater victory to celebrate. Beside him was a woman suitable to adorn the arm of any nobleman. Norah Denby was unquestionably lovely. Her dark hair was swept back elegantly from a center part into heavy waves, forming a high coil and ornamented with twists of pearls. He would see them replaced with jewels. Her gown was deep plum-colored velvet with tight-fitting sleeves and a bodice entirely of white lace over satin. He would see such a design trimmed with bands of sable and the rhinestones of her buckle reset in diamonds. Norah would shine beside him to the envy of the Royals. And he couldn't have been more pleased. Unless she were to smile up at him. She remained woodenly upon his arm, without a show of spirit, without a blush of color upon her cheeks. Thinking about *him*, he supposed with a twinge of jealousy. She had been watching the front gate for over an hour but he could have told her that Rory Prescott wouldn't be coming. He would make her forget all about the rude American cowboy who was too cowardly to put an appearance that would mean recognizing his defeat. Once they had shaken the dust of the Dakotas off their feet, he would see she never had reason to look back.

Where was he? Norah glanced toward the road again and held back a frown. He hadn't finished the race. She'd wanted to wait out there on the plains until all the other riders, anxious for refreshment and shade, wandered toward the ranch. But Cole ordered the buggy onward. As the party gathered momentum, weary riders drifted in one at a time for their share of the free whiskey and to tell their tales of the hard trail. The day's victor was conspicuous in his absence but no one was surprised . . . considering. Rory was probably with him at the Lone Star, sharing the closeness of family, turning his back on his heartache. Leaving her to Charles.

He gave up too easily. It wasn't like the brash redhead to concede so quickly. That wasn't the message she'd read in his challenging stare that morning. She hadn't expected him to win the race but she was surprised that he didn't show. His spotted horse was tough and he was more than a little gutsy. It wasn't like him to give up without a fight. And that preyed upon her thoughts and left her restless.

The party was for her, in honor of her splendid catch. An English lord. Who would have thought? What marvelous irony. Cole was in his glory, accepting toasts, smoking up Garth Kincaid's big cigars while he watched her with a father's pride. She couldn't be angry

262

with him. He thought he was doing what was best for her. And he'd definitely made a tidy profit from it, as well. No, she couldn't blame him. So why was she so angry? Because Rory had admitted defeat? Or because he hadn't trusted her enough to listen to her explanation?

When Kincaid engaged Charles in talk of business, Norah prowled the porch perimeter. Did she really want Rory to rush in and rescue her . . . from what? What she'd always wanted? From security, from success? From an unequalled match? Why hadn't he tried, at least one more time? Her nostrils flared with the remembered scent of cheap perfume. And her temper flared, too. The wretch, she cursed irrationally, not crediting herself for driving him to it. The self-righteous Rory Prescott whose favorite cry was "Trust me," who couldn't find it in his heart to trust a little in return. Why had he believed so quickly, so easily what his eyes showed him? What his ears told him? What about that big, wonderful heart of his? Why had it suddenly decided to stay silent? Was he even now drinking cheerfully at the Lone Star thinking himself well rid of her? A surprisingly sharp pain twisted in her breast. Was he even going to bother seeing her before she left? Tomorrow. She was supposed to leave tomorrow. Without tasting his kiss one last time? Without feeling his strong embrace again? Without experiencing the incredible ecstasy of making love with him so she would never forget what it was like to be with a man among men? Charles Monthaven could give her things of creature comfort but he could never supply her with that same elemental passion. And she knew right then, she couldn't leave without having it one last time. One last soaring moment to sustain her for uninspired years to come. If that made her thoughtlessly greedy, she didn't care. She just wanted to know love once more.

There wasn't time to change. In the barn, she had a startled cowhand saddle a horse for her and boost her into it. With the fullness of her skirt bunched and irreparably crumpled between her legs, she kicked the horse into a run. And from the porch, Cole Denby saw her go and shook his head in resigned disbelief.

Norah Denby wasn't the only one going quietly crazy with agitation over Rory Prescott.

"Son of a bitch," Scott muttered as he paced the porch of the Lone Star. His oath lacked its former fierceness. His resentment was slowly giving before a disturbing sense of worry as his golden eyes scanned the fading brilliants along the hills. He gave a slight start as gentle hands capped his tense shoulders.

"He's not coming, Scotty."

"Mama, why would he do such a thing?" he asked in bitter anguish.

"Hush, now. A man frustrated by his love for a woman can do some pretty awful things." Aurora kneaded the tight muscles and smiled. "Remember?"

Scott gave a reluctant sigh and nodded. His shoulders slumped.

"He'll make it up to you and you'll forgive him. Like always."

"I don't know, Mama. It was a danged fool thing to do. He'd better be ready for some serious down in the dirt groveling if I'm going to accept his apology any time soon."

Aurora stroked a hand through her son's black hair and advised softly, "Don't keep him on his knees too long, Scotty. He's hurting already and I don't know how much more bruising his pride will take."

"It was a danged fool thing to do."

"I know."

"He could have gotten us both killed with a reckless stunt like that."

"But he didn't."

Scott sighed, reluctant to surrender up his anger. He scowled out across the rolling hills. "Well, maybe I'll ride on over to the Bar K and hash it out with him tonight."

Aurora smiled in relief, then squeezed his shoulders. "You might not have to."

Scott followed her gaze to the single rider coming in fast and hard from the direction of the Kincaid ranch. No one else he knew rode with such a careless disregard for life and limb. Except, he realized, it wasn't Rory.

Norah Denby reined up, unmindful of what Rory's mother and brother thought of her shocking appearance. "I need to speak to Rory."

"He isn't here, Miss Denby," Aurora Prescott supplied with a frigid dislike. How dare the woman come so brazenly to their door after her callous treatment of Rory's feelings. "And I think you should leave."

Scott had gone very still. He was staring out across the endless grass. "Isn't Rory at the Bar K?"

"No, he didn't come back after the race. I thought he'd be here."

Scott drew a ragged breath and let it spill out in a shiver. "Oh, God." He closed his eyes, seeing Rory flung down upon the ground, rolling bonelessly. He hadn't seen him get up. He hadn't waited to make sure he was all right. His golden eyes opened, glittery and filled with a frantic sort of calm. "I'm going down to saddle up a couple of horses. Mama tell Daddy to grab up his medicine bag. Miss Norah, you head on back to the Bar K and tell my grandfather that we need some men to search—"

He broke off, mouth working wordlessly. After a long second, a low sound of incredible pain escaped him. For just then, Chance came limping over the last low hill. Dragging his brother's body behind him.

Chapter Seventeen

The sight of Scott Prescott's running approach sent Chance rearing back. Lashing hoofs came down within inches of the motionless figure dangling from the stirrup iron. Scott skidded to a halt as the nervous animal sidestepped and snorted in warning. Scott's gaze went from the still form of his brother to the restless hoofs. He started forward more slowly, speaking a low Sioux chant but the paint's ears laid back and the stomping grew more agitated. And dangerous. One kick could end a life. If Rory was alive.

Scott reached out for the loose reins. He was able to jerk back as teeth snapped viciously. He looked down at Rory and swore softly. He reached again and Chance half-reared up, stiff-legging it to one side.

"C'mere, Chance," he crooned low. He tried to flank the anxious animal but it wheeled in an excited circle, keeping between him and his motionless brother. He hated thinking it. He'd hate doing it. He didn't have any choice. Any minute the unstable mustang could decide to bolt.

"Mama," he called out somberly. "Bring me a gun."

"No!"

That was Norah Denby. She came flying off her horse in a swirl of velvet.

"Stay back," Scott barked at her, afraid the sudden movement would set the lamed horse running.

"No." She slowed her step but kept coming. "He'll let me take the reins. I know he will." She came up beside Scott and got her first close up look at the situation. She clutched at Scott's arm blindly, moaning, "Oh, my God." The empty saddle was saturated with blood. She breathed deeply for several seconds, leaning into Rory's brother. And he held her wordlessly. Chance was pawing up the grass, froth flying with the toss of his head. Norah straightened, forcing a calm. "Scott, don't move. Don't move until I tell you."

She eased away from him and purposefully, fearlessly advanced toward the laboring animal. She refused to look down at Rory.

"Whoa there, Chance. Good boy. You remember me. We're old friends. Good boy. You can trust me with Rory. You brought him here, now let us have him. Steady now." She put her hand out, scarcely daring to breathe as the reins brushed her fingertips. Then, she had them. Chance made a low groaning sound and butted her gently with a sweaty head. Norah caught the bridle on either side and held the horse's head down, using her forearms to block its vision. "All right, Scott. Real slow."

She continued to murmur reassuring words, as Scott moved up beside them warily. Chance stood, not so much as flinching as the cautious man knelt down beside his brother.

"Rory?" Scott settled on his heels, fighting back the tearing rifts of guilt. Very gently, he took a hold of the stirrup iron and drew his knife. A quick jerk of the blade parted the leather and Rory's arm, with its distorted wrist and blue swollen fingers, dropped slackly to the ground.

When Norah released the bridle, Chance sidled away, then continued to paw at the turf, agitated by the thick smell of blood. Staying close but making no aggressive moves toward the two kneeling beside his very still master.

When Scott touched unsteady fingertips to his brother's sound wrist, Rory's dark eyes fluttered open for just a moment. Long enough for him to give a weak, recognizing smile before drifting off again.

Ethan raced up, took a quick look and instructed, "Grab his legs, Scott, and help me get him inside."

Once Rory was stretched out atop his parents' bed, Ethan gave the bulging wrist his attention. "Gena, get me some cool water, some bandages and one of Ora's wooden spoons." While she went to take care of it, he hoisted his son up and had Aurora strip the coat off him. She gave a strangled sound at the sight of the blood-soaked shirt but firmed her lips and peeled it off. By then, Gena returned and Ethan set about splinting the fractured wrist. Because no one had shooed her away, Norah stood silently by the door, pale and shaken. She gratefully clung to Gena when the other woman moved up beside her.

The cool water Aurora sponged over his scraped face brought Rory around. He smiled up at her vaguely and muttered, "Don't go fussing, Mama. It ain't so bad."

"Where you ailing, son?" Ethan asked.

"Tore my knee up and—and I cut my head when I fell." His eyes shut with that disclosure then reopened when his father started cutting up the seam of his Levi's. When the blade touched to boot leather, he tried to hoist up on his elbows but was too worn to give more than a feeble shout of protest. "Dang it all, Daddy, I just paid fifty dollars for them boots. Don't go cut 'em to pieces. Jus' pull it off."

269

Ethan frowned. "You sure?"

"Go on and do it. Jus' got 'em broke in right."

"All right. Here."

Rory glanced down curiously at the spoon his father placed in his hand. But as soon as he began pulling on the boot, he understood. Rory clamped the wooden handle between his teeth and bit down hard until the fancy-stitched leather was wrestled free.

"That worth the fifty dollars?"

Rory removed the spoon with its deeply scored imprints and grinned weakly. "You bet." When his daddy began prodding at the ballooning joint, he flopped back on the mattress, graying with pain.

"Looks to be strained but not torn. Should mend all right. Damn lucky, boy. I'll pack it up tight. She'll be stiff and'll hurt worse than a bad tooth for a while but you should be able to walk on it some." He worked his way along the other limbs and poked ribs until satisfied of nothing worse than black and blues. Then he reached up to untie the blood-drenched bandana. "Let's see what we got here." He tipped Rory's head gently to one side and examined the ugly wound. It angled in a bloody furrow down the side of his skull behind his ear just missing the jaw bone and the jugular to take a goodly slice out of his neck. "Cut when you fell, you say."

"Yessir, Daddy."

After patching up hundreds of men during the War Between the States, Ethan Prescott damned well knew the mark of a bullet when he saw one. He rumpled his boy's bright hair and clamped down hard on the fury rising up like bile in his throat. Rory's dark eyes flickered up, seeing the futility of his lie in the stern set of his father's face and begging silently that he say nothing.

270

"I can slap a patch over it and it'll heal but if you want it to knit up pretty, it's gonna take some stitching."

Rory's eyes slid shut in relief. No questions until he could come up with some answers. He silently blessed his daddy. "Let Mama do the stitching. She makes a neater seam."

Ethan chuckled at the boy's shaky bravado and nodded to his wife. "Go fetch your sewing things, Ora. And Scotty, lift up the foot of the bed and stick something under the legs to keep it raised up. Let's get some blood back up into this empty head of yours."

Rory let himself drift in a blurry haze while Ethan cleaned him up. Then his mama was beside him, stroking his cheek with a loving hand, smiling tenderly, regretfully, because of the hurt she was going to cause him. He glanced around at the other worried faces, more shapes than actual features as his vision faded. "Whatchall looking at? You seen Mama put the stuffin's back in me before. Go on an' get." He didn't want the lot of them standing around watching him twitch. He was too tired to endure the mending stoically and if he started in crying, he surely didn't want anybody but his mother as a witness to it. "An' somebody see to Chance. He saved my life. Grain him good."

"I will."

Danged if that didn't sound like Norah!

His eyelids had grown heavy, dragging down over his eyes. He struggled to force them open one last time, just to see, just on the wild, impossible chance that she really was here. But the effort was too much. He was too weak to fight. However, when his lids closed, he was smiling.

Norah rubbed down Chance for the second time in

as many days, finding to her dismay that she was in tears before the chore was half done. She fought it for a while and then finally gave way, leaning upon the spotted hide to sob.

She'd thought he was dead.

When she'd seen the blood on the saddle and Rory so still on the ground, her system had jerked up like a man's cutting horse with its leg going down in a badger hole. And all she could think was, *How am I going to go on without him?* It was a cold, crippling feeling, one so deep and desolate that even now she trembled to think of it. A life without Rory Prescott's devilish grin and dark, smoldering stare. She couldn't imagine anything so bleak. But he hadn't died. He was up in the house being tended by his family and she really had no right to be in their barn crying over him. She was supposed to be at the Bar K with the man they thought was her fiance. But she didn't really care what the Prescotts thought of her, not really. It was Rory she was worried about. Would he even want her near him? Wasn't he in enough pain without being reminded of still another?

Resolutely, she finished with Chance, hugging the tuckered out animal about the drooping neck.

"You did good today, fella. Real good," she soothed, then headed up to the ranch house through the cool darkness. She hesitated on the porch, taking a minute to strike the dampness from her cheeks and draw herself up proudly. She wouldn't slink into the Prescotts home. But before she could enter, Rory's father stepped out, a troubled look furrowing his brow. He smiled when he saw her.

"Is he going to be all right?" She couldn't keep the betraying tremor from her words.

"Fine. Take him a while to mend but no harm done."

Norah's sigh was all too expressive. To distract herself

from the shaky sensations threatening her composure, she said, "Mr. Prescott, you might want to take a look at Rory's horse. He's lamed up pretty bad."

"I'll see to it." He nodded to her and started for the barn. No comment about why she was still here, or why she'd want to be. It gave her the courage to go inside.

Gena was alone in the main room. She was looking with shiny eyes at the prize money Scott had won that afternoon. Weighing it against the price of Rory's pain. There was no comparison and she didn't think she could accept so much as a cent of it for their baby, feeling the way she did. Like it was blood money, tainted by terrible circumstance. She summoned a wavery smile for Norah, heart lifting because the other woman cared enough to stay.

"I don't think he's awake but you can go in. He'll want to see you there."

Norah nodded, wishing she could be as sure.

The lamp was turned down to a dim glow. In its warm light, the hands holding one of Rory's between them were a dark beautiful bronze. Scott Prescott didn't hear her approach. He sat with defenses down, watching his brother sleep. She was privilege to a rare sight, she was sure because the half-Sioux guarded his emotions the way Cole hoarded his gold. Never had she seen so much naked anguish on a man's face. For a moment, she was tempted to withdraw from the very private interlude but she couldn't stand to think of this man who was a part of Rory in such pain. The instant her fingertips brushed his shoulder, his head jerked up and the wary reserve was slammed into place. But she knew what she'd seen and he was uncomfortable with it.

"Your father says he's going to be fine."

Scott nodded a brief acknowledgment. The only sign

273

of his agitation was in the way he worried Rory's fingers with his own. "But he could have died out there. Would have if he hadn't done some pretty quick thinking. I left him there to die. I never looked back. I never looked back to see that he was all right." His voice might have been inflectionless but not the meaning behind the words.

Norah tried to think of something to say. Nothing came to her that would ease the torment of this remote stranger. It was the stirring of Rory's fingers that broke through the long silence. Dark eyes fluttered open and a slow smile spread.

"Scotty."

"Right here."

The injured man seemed very groggy and slow to gather his thoughts. Was it something Ethan gave him or merely a natural reaction to the blood loss he'd sustained. Norah wasn't sure.

"Did you win?"

Scott's hands tightened convulsively. He nodded.

"Good." Rory let his eyes close and he smiled to himself. "Good. Had money on you."

Scott made a low, thick sound in the back of his throat and came off the chair he was sitting on in a blind stumble. But Rory wouldn't let go of his hand. Not for a long meaningful minute.

"If you'd stopped, you wouldn't have beat that smart alecky Englishman. Then I'd have something to call you on. The rest, it just don't matter. Now get on outta here. I can't sleep with you a-staring at me."

Scott crushed his hand, hard, willing him to feel the tremendous emotion weighting his heart. "Good night, Rory. I'll pray to the gods to make you strong."

Rory grinned faintly. "You do that, Scotty. Jus' don't go dancin' and shakin' anything over me." He closed his

274

eyes and breathed deep, hearing the sound of his brother leaving. But he didn't feel alone. There was the faintest whisper of a scent on the air. Something soft and familiar. He looked up and blinked in disbelief. "Norah?"

She assumed Scott's seat and took up his hand. His fingers clutched at hers.

"What are you doing here?"

She tried to smile. "I'm the only one Chance would give you up to."

"Danged fool horse. Never thought a that." His mouth quirked up and he shifted restlessly beneath the light covering. She wondered if he was in much pain. But as it was he grumbled, "Wish you was under here with me," as if he wasn't half dead and could actually do something about it if she was.

A sob snagged in her throat before she could catch it. "I thought I'd lost you, Rory."

He slipped his hand from hers, reaching up, fumbling slightly and finally finding the curve of her cheek. "You know better than that. You can't drive me off with a stick." He stopped smiling and stroked his thumb under her chin. "I thought I'd lost you. Have I, Norah? You going away with him tomorrow? You gonna leave me?"

Her breathing hitched loudly. "I can't." That confession tore from her in a miserable moan.

"Come on down here, Norah-honey. I think we needs to jus' hold to one another for a while."

Wordlessly, she curled up on top of the covers, burrowing close, clutching carefully so as not to hurt him. And with his good hand, he pet the lovely tousle of her hair.

"I love you, Norah. I'll see you're never sorry you stayed."

She was already sorry, about more things than he would ever know.

It took him all of a minute to fall deeply asleep. Norah closed her eyes, trying to draw a sense of peace from the faint rock of his breath but her thoughts were in a turmoil. It was then she became aware of Aurora Prescott standing at the door. The woman's golden eyes were cold as chips of topaz.

"There's no need for you to stay, Miss Denby," Rory's mother told her crisply. "When you return to the Bar K, please tell my father that Rory's here and safe."

"I'd really like to stay, Mrs. Prescott. If you don't mind."

If you don't mind? The woman wasn't short on gall, that was for certain! Did she mind if the creature who tore her son's heart to shreds was now cuddled up to him on her and her husband's bed pretty as you please? Did she mind?

Rory muttered and started to roll. The movement woke a groan from him and a panicked little cry of, "Norah?"

"Shhshhshh. Right here. It's all right. Go to sleep."

"I thought you'd gone."

"No. I'm right here. Just go back to sleep."

He murmured for a second longer then relaxed back into slumber.

Aurora frowned. She watched the woman quiet her son with a touch; a gentle, familiar touch upon his flushed cheek. She heard the genuine care in the soft-spoken words. Impassively, she took Norah Denby's measure. The coolly elegant lady looked positively haggard. Her hair was askew, her eyes swollen and red from weariness, worry and the traces of weeping that yet lined her face. Her stylish gown was ruined. The crisp white lace was streaked with blood—her son's—

276

and the crushed velvet smelled distinctly of horse. She had left her own engagement party to answer Rory's restless moan of her name and so, Aurora could not hate her completely. But neither did she trust her.

"Wake me or Ethan if he needs anything."

Norah exhaled. "I will."

With a short nod, Aurora left the room. And left the door open.

Finding Norah asleep beside him was the only good thing about waking up in the morning. By looking at the soft serene set of her features, he found the strength to ignore the agony assailing his every other sense. She was turned toward him, resting on his good arm to hold him helpless; none of the rest of him seemed to want to work. Unable to move, all he could do was treasure the sight of her soft, sleep-parted lips and the brush of dark lashes upon her cheeks. She was here in his family's house. He wasn't sure why but she was. And she wasn't going to leave him. At least, that's what she'd said last night. He hoped that was true and not just words to ease the mind of a man in misery.

He closed his eyes and tried to rest but with pain beating through his every extremity, it was impossible. So he lay quietly in his parents' big bed and tried hard not to think about the events of the day before. When a lone gunman had tried to kill his brother. They were dark, uneasy thoughts, making him restless with his inactivity. And then there was the smell of breakfast and the murmur of his family's voices from the other room. He couldn't just lie there like a lump with all those things bothering him.

He flexed his sound arm, bringing Norah up against him but to his frustration, he couldn't bend his head far enough to reach her nestled there on his chest.

"Norah-honey, wake up," he whispered. "I needs a kiss and some coffee real bad."

She stirred and stretched like a kitten but there was nothing soft or kittenish in the curves rubbing against him. Or in the intensity of her gaze when it met his. Both were all woman. She stroked a hand along his morning stubble.

"Which do you need first?"

"I'm a firm believer in a bird in the hand."

She eased up, touching her lips to his gently. A low sound rumbled through him. It had nothing to do with hurting.

"Oh, darlin', you can do better than that. It's the only part of me I can move."

And he proved that was so with a bone-weakening thoroughness.

"You must be feeling better," she murmured happily against the cushion of his mouth.

"I feel like breakfast since I ain't gonna get nothin' else with that there door open. Help me with my boots."

Norah sat back in disbelief until he tossed back the covers and hauled himself upright. She realized he was serious when he stuffed his bulky wrist through the sleeve of his long johns and began fastening them over his chest with an awkward one-handedness. "You're not getting up. Lie back down. I'll bring it to you."

"Hang that. I got things to see to today. You gonna fetch me those boots or am I gonna shuffle out there in my socks?"

"Stubborn cuss," Norah muttered. He smiled good-naturedly as she hunted up his footgear. The right one went on easy but she stood with the left dangling in her hand, looking uncertain.

"Go on, honey. Put it on. It won't grieve me more than the idea of hobbling around unshod."

278

There was no gentle way to tug on a pointed-toed boot that was seventeen inches high. It was like wiggling into a tight corset. She pulled and he tried his best to push.

"Give it a good yank," he ordered in a strained voice that scared her into complying. He chewed on a groan of complaint and fell back, fingers twisting in the sheets. Norah stared hard at the floorboards until she heard his breathing ease. She set her jaw against the quivering of tears. *Come on, Norah, you're tougher than that.* But she wasn't, not with him. Not when she felt his pain so personally.

Rory's good hand groped for her shoulder and he pulled himself up, swinging his stiff leg off the bed. He came up, hopping awkwardly and nearly crumpled at the first hesitant test of the abused joint. His fingers bit hard into Norah's flesh but she made no sound. If he could bear it, so could she.

"Get back to bed," Aurora commanded the minute she saw him limping across the room with Norah tucked crutch-like under his arm. "Ethan, tell him!"

"Reckon the boy knows his limits, Ora. Get him a plate."

Rory gave his father a grateful smile but Ethan didn't return it. His expression was somber and he wouldn't hold his son's gaze. With an uneasiness shifting in his belly, Rory settled awkwardly in a chair. It was the most quiet meal he could ever remember taking under his family's roof. He could see Norah was as puzzled as he was by it. There was a careful evasion of his stare. Were they angry about the race? About what they thought he'd done? Scott was rigid. Gena finally pushed away from the table and almost fled into the kitchen with his mother hurrying after her. He put down his biscuit slowly.

"What?"

"Rory," Ethan began and a terrible panic twisted around his heart. What could be so awful? "Son, I wish I didn't have to set this on your plate so soon but it has to be taken care of. Your horse tore the hell out of its leg. I tried everything I knew but the fever set in overnight."

Rory made a low, desperate sound and blurted, "Oh, God, Daddy, you didn't put Chance down, did you?"

"No, son. Wasn't my decision to make. But I know you'll want to do the right thing."

"No." Rory's head shook back and forth as if he was in a daze. "He'll be all right."

"He won't, Rory. It's not something that'll mend."

He shook his head again, fighting the grimness of truth in his father's gaze. "No. You're wrong. You were wrong before, remember? When he was born with screw worm and you said it weren't worth fifteen cents to save him. Well, I did. I gave him the chance to make it. And he did, Daddy. He grew up damn fine. Best horse a man could want. Daddy, he saved my life!"

"I'll see to it for you, son."

"No." He drew a harsh, shuddering breath. "I'll do it."

"Rory, there's no need . . ."

But he was already pushing back from the table. He put a hand to his empty hip. "I'll need . . ."

"Take my Peacemaker."

With the gun weighting down his arm, Rory hobbled down to the barn. One look told him all his father said was true. Even when Chance put down his head and nudged him fondly, it was obvious the animal was suffering.

"Oh, Chance. God, I'm sorry." He unsnapped the lead and walked out of the stall. After he'd gone twenty feet or so, he whistled tonelessly and tensed his insides

280

when he heard the horse back out and follow him. They were a sad looking pair, both lamed, with heads hanging down, moving slow to a shallow gully behind the barn. There, Rory sank down on the dew slicked bank with his head in his arms. He was hurting and weak and so heartsick he couldn't draw a decent breath. After a long minute, Chance's velvety nose nuzzled his damp cheek. Rory reached up to stroke the speckled hide.

"You been a hell of a good friend to me, Chance. Had none better, 'cepting Scotty. You done all I asked without complaint and I'm right proud of you." He took a noisy breath and the animal nickered softly as if in response. "I didn't aim for things to come to this. Damn, I'm sorry, but I couldn't let it be Scotty I was putting in the ground this morning. I know you don't understand none of that." Chance pushed at him, nibbling the sleeve of his long johns gently. Rory wiped the other across his eyes resolutely. "Hell, best get it done. Help me up, son."

He gripped the hackamore and used the lift of the horse's head to get his feet under him. For a long time, he stood with the broad forehead hugged to his chest, rubbing the lazily flicking ears. Then he sighed and pushed away, bringing the barrel of his daddy's pistol to rest between those trusting dark eyes, trusting him to end his pain. He began to breathe deeply and fast, bracing his shaking hand with the splinted one, loving the animal too much to risk a bad shot. He closed his eyes and with a final moaning cry . . . let the pistol drop.

"Oh, Chance, I can't."

The booming report of a rifle brought Rory jerking around from the fateful thump at his feet. His last sight before his eyes filled completely was of Scott lowering

281

his father's Winchester. He stood, swimming in a daze of grief as his brother approached, dragging a shovel behind him.

"I'll see him covered for you, Rory."

After a while of tottering weakly, eyes closed, heart broken, Rory felt Scott duck under his good arm.

"Lean on me," was all he said. And Rory couldn't have made it back to the house without him.

They were waiting there on the porch for his return, faces glum and etched with sympathy. Rory straightened, pulling away from Scott to walk the rest of the way on his own with a hitching awkwardness.

"I gotta get back to the Bar K. Can I borrow the buggy, Daddy? I gotta carry my tack an' . . ." His voice trailed off vaguely.

"Rory, you ought to rest—" Aurora said.

Ethan waved off his wife's worried words. "I'll bring it around, son. And Rory, we've got some things that need saying when you feel up to it."

"Yessir, Daddy," he murmured, canting a look at Scott. "Got me some figuring to do first."

"Whenever you're ready."

Over his mild protest, Norah took the buggy reins after tying off her horse behind it. He leaned back in the seat and let her do the driving. With every silent mile, he forced his grief farther away from his logic so he could think, clear and cold on who would want his brother dead. It was a frightfully long list but there was no getting around whose name topped it and whose hand was probably behind it. For that reason, his temper was short when Norah pulled in the buggy and turned to take him in her arms.

"I ain't feeling much in the mood for that right now, Norah," he growled threateningly. He felt her flinch at the harshness of tone but she didn't relent. Her embrace circled his shoulders and her fingers threaded gently through his hair, coaxing his head down. He didn't want to give in but a sudden soft sound of vulnerability pressed up from his chest and out before he knew how bad the hurt was swelling.

"I'm so sorry," she whispered.

She held him comfortingly, passionlessly, bussing his temple with her tender kiss. And as he clutched at her, shaking in helpless despair, a part of his thoughts moved with a distant calculation.

Yes, she would be sorry. Very sorry when he made the trip to Crowe Creek to buy another pistol rig. For the purpose of very probably putting a hole or two in her father.

Chapter Eighteen

Charles Monthaven stood on the front steps, a picture of indignation. His sandy brows soared in distaste at the sight the two of them presented; all soiled and battered and irreparably compromised. All his considerable fury channeled to the ragged person of Rory Prescott as he crawled down gingerly from the seat and reached, first out of habit with his left then out of necessity with his right hand to claim his saddle and bridle from the back of the boot.

"Where is your scraggly little cow pony?" Monthaven drawled malevolently. "Toss you a-ground again, eh, Mr. Prescott? I must say I wasn't very impressed with the showing. After all your inflated bragging, I rather expected the animal to sprout wings to fly by the others. Instead of not finishing at all. I say, quite indicative of its master, don't you know? How is it you people put it, all show, no go?"

Rory didn't turn toward him right away. He hefted the saddle then called out to one of the hands, "Baxter, see to my gear for me."

"Yessir, Rory. Shorely will."

When relieved of the tack by the unquestioning cowboy, Rory hobbled to the base of the steps and slowly raised his gaze to the sneering English lord. Monthaven took an unconscious step back. Though pinched with pain, the man's dark eyes held a dangerous charge and the promise of a violent explosion.

"I have put up with all the preening and strutting and posing I intend to," Rory doled out with a lethal evenness to his tone. "You ain't nothin' but a scrawny banty cock scratching and pecking at me and I'm ready to wring your neck. I ain't armed but if you go putting yourself in front of my face afore you leave, I aim to get healed quick and you'll be going home in a box. Now shut your mouth and get the hell outta my way!"

The big, battered redhead hauled himself stiffly up the stairs, gratified when his growl sent Monthaven rapidly scurrying to one side. As he limped toward the door, he heard the aristocrat huff, "Well, I never!"

Norah struggled not to smile wryly as Charles helped her from the buggy with a rigid formality.

"Madame," he began frostily, "I will for the moment not inquire as to where you went last evening or why you returned in such a disheveled state—with him— this morning. I do, however, insist that you make haste in gathering your belongings. We have a train to catch and I find myself quite anxious to escape this barbarous place."

Norah saw Rory halt just shy of the door, pausing, his whole body taut, waiting without turning for her reply.

"Then the train will have to leave without me, sir, because I have no intention of going anywhere with you."

Monthaven drew a startled breath of disbelief and stammered, "Miss Denby, please forgive me. I did not mean to impugn your honor."

"Didn't you?" she argued icily. "You, sir, are no gentleman. Now, please let me pass."

Grinning with a weary satisfaction, Rory held the door open and let her sweep through it under the bridge of his arm. He looked back at the stunned Englishman and drawled, "Roping 'em ain't nothin', Charlie. Ridin' 'em's the trick." Then he let the door bang smartly behind him. He watched the sassy twitch of Norah's skirts as she marched up the stairs, smiling at his own arrogance. And after riding them, came taming them, and that was something he had yet to master.

The sound of voices drew Rory to his grandfather's study. There, he found Garth Kincaid and Cole Denby enjoying whiskeys and cigars. The glowing stub dropped unnoticed from the rancher's fingers and for the first time he could ever remember, Rory saw the man shaken.

"Rory, what in God's name happened to you? Are you all right, son?" His startled eyes took in the tattered appearance with obvious dismay.

"Ask him," Rory fired out point blank at Denby. The dapper fellow never paled or altered his expression from mild surprise. Lord, what an actor—or was he innocent? That he couldn't believe. "Your people can't shoot worth a damn, Denby. Can't even hit the right man."

Cole slid a glance toward the granite features of Garth Kincaid, then he shook his head in feigned confusion. "I really have no idea what—"

"Get out. The major and me need to make talk."

Kincaid nodded to dismiss his man, keeping a concerned and now wary eye on his grandson. When they were alone, he urged, "Sit down, son. Let me send for a doctor."

286

"Already seen one and he ain't pleased 'bout somebody putting a bullet in one of his boys. Lessen you want him over here doing the askin', you'd best come up with some mighty convincing answers."

Kincaid didn't want that. A riled Ethan Prescott was no one he wanted to deal with. And now his boy was worked up with that same hard-edged, self-righteous wrath. The major stopped worrying about Rory and started thinking about his own interests. "Ask your questions," he said flatly.

"You tell him to send a shooter after Scotty?"

Kincaid looked genuinely blank. "Scott? This is about your mother's half-breed bas—" He broke off as his grandson's features went rigid. He took a slow breath and eased back from the situation. Rocking back in his chair, he observed the weak, obviously agonized young man barely able to stand before him— yet doing it with such prideful courage. Damn, what a fine boy! His, not Prescott's and he'd make sure that didn't change.

"No," he said at last in a firm voice. "No, I didn't order anyone after your brother. I already told you, Scott is no threat to me. I don't want trouble with him to come between us, Rory. You're too important to me and to the Bar K."

Rory wavered, with indecision, with pain. His dark eyes were all too intense. And then he said softly, "I wish I could believe you."

Kincaid stood and came around his big desk. With an unprecedented display of affection, he enveloped Rory in a careful embrace. His grandson didn't resist. But neither did he respond.

"You can, son. This ranch is ours. We're partners. I'm not going to jeopardize that by taking potshots at Scott. If I'd wanted him killed, I would have done it

287

long ago. You know there isn't a rancher in this valley who doesn't want to see a preacher reading words over him. So far, they've left him alone out of fear of my name and respect for you. But that could change in a minute, Rory. If you want to keep your brother safe, you talk to him. You tell him to stick to his Indian courts and leave our affairs alone. I don't expect he'll listen but it'll clear your conscience some."

"You didn't order it done?" He restated that faintly, eyes squeezed shut, trying to summon the faith that had sustained him since Scott's return brought so much upheaval. Needing that sense of trust to cling to.

"No, son. I didn't."

The tension swept from him and Garth Kincaid stepped back, once again concerned for his well-being.

"You sure you're all right?"

"Daddy mended everything that could be fixed," he whispered heavily.

The major examined the splinted hand, the taped knee, the bandaged throat. His expression grew quietly thunderous as he promised, "I'll deal with the one responsible, Rory. Count on it." Then his features gentled. He patted the scraped cheek. "You go get some rest. You look dead on your feet. Has someone taken care of your horse?"

Unable to speak, Rory simply nodded. Yes, someone had taken care of Chance.

"Go on upstairs and get some sleep. Tomorrow, we have the Monthaven money. And the Bar K is going to be just fine as long as it has you to run it with me. I want you back up to full steam beside me."

"Yessir, Major," he mumbled.

Kincaid watched him hobble stiffly from the room

288

and mount the stairs. He didn't offer assistance. The boy could make it on his own. He was tough as boot leather and it would take a lot to wear him down. Denby was lounging in the hall and quickly responded to the quirk of his finger. He closed the double doors and waited for his boss to speak.

Garth Kincaid stared out over the Bar K grasslands. The lands he would proudly pass down to his grandson. And when he thought of the boy being plucked from the saddle by a poorly directed bullet and considered how close he'd come to losing his pride, his joy, his heir, a simmering fury took to boil. He thought of the pain in those loyal dark eyes, the agony of mistrust in his heart and he wanted to reach out and harshly crush out the source of that hurt. No one was going to come between him and the future of the Bar K. No one!

Time to deal with the one responsible.

Kincaid turned to Cole Denby with a ruthless void of expression. The slick schemer knew a moment of total terror.

"It was supposed to be the horse, Major. Monthaven wanted to win the race. No one was supposed to get hurt, least of all, your boy. He must have thrown himself right into the line of fire."

Kincaid winced at that image; of his precious grandson throwing his life away to save his brother's heathen soul. Such a sacrifice could not—would not be borne!

"I don't care about that," he said coldly. "He's going to pay for every second of pain he's brought to this house. Denby, I want your boys to teach a lesson and I want it harsh. I don't care how you do it. I want Scott Prescott on his knees!"

289

* * *

Norah paused in the brushing of her hair when she saw Cole's reflection in the glass on her dressing table. He appeared to be studying her with a tolerant amusement and the sight of his smirky grin grated on her. She resumed her brushing until electricity snapped through the glossy strands.

"His lordship tells me you two lovebirds had a bit of a tiff over the Prescott boy."

"Rory's hardly a boy. He's older than I am and to-day I feel positively ancient. Besides, Charles and I are not lovebirds. That was one of your schemes, not reality. Please try not to confuse the two."

"I hope you'll set me straight and we can both enjoy a laugh over the misunderstanding, but Monthaven seems to think you're not going to England with him."

"I'm not laughing, Cole. And I'm *not* going."

Cole moved up behind her, lifting the luxurious weight of her hair in his hands. "You're letting the chance of a lifetime slip through your fingers, you know that don't you?"

"Maybe."

"Oh there's no maybe about it. You'd be living like a queen, Norah. You'd have money and servants and jewels and I'd have a nice profit so I could see to re-placing you. No matter what I might have said in the past, I'm not looking forward to that. You have a sin-gular talent, my dear, a certain coldness of conscience that quite sets you apart from most silly females. You've always known what you wanted and you haven't let anyone or anything stop you from going after it. I have an incredible admiration for you, you know. You've risen above everything in your past to become—a real lady."

She was surprised to find he was sincere. Even

290

though they weren't the kindest of compliments, it touched her oddly to hear such sentiments from the selfish Cole Denby. Perhaps he had a small sliver of a heart after all. Perhaps he would understand.

"For some reason," he continued while playing with her hair, "you seem to have taken a dislike to his lordship. Now, I'm not trying to push you into his arms if you don't want to go but I am curious as to why you've suddenly dug in your heels. What is this virtual paragon lacking?"

"I don't love him, Cole."

The quiet words stunned him for a long moment.

"Love him?" He threw back his head for a tremendous laugh. "Love him? What has that to do with anything? When you have money, you don't need love. Love is for poor people who can't afford anything better. Norah, with Monthaven's fortune, you could have the world at your feet. You could . . ." He stopped. And he looked at her carefully, wondering what was so different. And not wanting to believe what he saw. "It's that *boy*, isn't it? What in God's name is so special about a big, brawny beast of a man who smells like horse and would have you serving up grub to a batch of hungry cowboys at four in the morning and dropping a baby like a spring calf every year?"

Norah's jaw gripped rebelliously, refusing to look at the grim picture he presented.

"I suppose you *love* him."

"Yes."

Cole laughed, even harder this time. "Why Norah, that is the most ridiculous thing I've ever heard tell of! If you want him, bed down with him but then have the decency to take his money and run when the time comes. I can't believe you'd be content standing out in the back breeding alongside the rest of the stock. And don't you think for a minute that old man Kincaid will let you stay once he knows the truth. Men like him don't let scrub animals in with the money-making beef. You think he'd let his grandson mix it up with a woman like you? Do you think a swaggering fool like Rory Prescott is going to slap his brand on spoiled goods?"

"He already knows and he still wants to marry me."

"He knows *everything?* I don't think so or we wouldn't still be here." He took hold of her mulishly set jaw in a compassionate grip. "Norah, be smart or you'll end up with nothing. We'll be gone in a couple of weeks. And when I go, I'm planning to take everything that isn't nailed down. If you stay, you'll be staying with nothing. And he'll hurt you, Norah. He doesn't want you. He wants what he thinks he sees. He doesn't love you, not the real you, and he's going to throw you away. Men like that don't want anybody's woman. They want to spoil their share but they want the women who bear their children to be pure as the driven snow. Do I have to spell it out?"

No. Rory had already done that.

"I'm not going with Monthaven," she said softly.

"Suit yourself, my dear. I've already given you my thoughts on it. Do what you want. Love him." Cole snorted. "What nonsense." Then he smiled, a slow, sly smile. A woman who fancied herself in love was a woman who could be made to do most anything.

And he wondered how much a man like Garth Kincaid would pay to keep the world from knowing his grandson had married a woman of Norah's background.

His smile widened. Any way he looked at it, he was coming out ahead.

* * *

For two days, Rory crawled out of his bed only when absolutely necessary. One of those times was to watch Lord Charles Monthaven leave the Bar K in his luggage-laden buggy. Alone.

His sense of victory dimmed as hours passed. Because Norah stayed away. That first day, he wouldn't have noticed, anyway. He slept hard and long, his minutes of awareness dulled by gray distortion. He'd drag himself up from the fog of weakness at a woman's touch, her name upon his lips, but it was Ruth, his father's housekeeper, not Norah, who sat beside him, drying his fevered brow. So he'd sink in disappointment back into those heavy, healing mists. He wished that thick haze had lingered, for the second day, he woke hurting. And no matter what he did, he couldn't get comfortable. He twisted and thrashed restlessly, searching for relief from the merciless throbbing in his wrist. Only steady doses from the bottle of rye his grandfather brought him gave some degree of ease. Mind clouded to the gnawing pain, he lay in a stupor as the day passed, unable to think, barely able to move. When he opened vague eyes to darkness, he thought Norah was with him. He smelled her tantalizing scent, felt the light brush of her fingertips along his cheek. He thought he felt her lying beside him, palm rubbing his chest in slow, reassuring circles when he tried to say her name and could only moan. He tried to cling to the awareness of her but it faded and in the morning, he couldn't be sure she'd been there at all.

Except he could smell violets.

No more of the bottle, he decided right then. No more staying abed indulging in miseries. He got himself up, got himself dressed — awkwardly with teeth gritted, and got himself downstairs. From the porch swing he watched dawn break over Kincaid land and his heart beat hard and proud in his throat. Soon, the sun was warming his face, soaking up some of his hurt and he basked in it like a basin lizard, with eyes closed and thoughts floating.

" 'Morning."

Scott?

As delighted as he was surprised, Rory greeted his brother with a broad smile and a cheery, "Heya, Scotty. Come on up and sit a spell." As he started to push his stiff leg from the swing seat, Scott shook his head, impassive eyes scanning the front of the house from his neutral stance upon the bottom step.

"I can't stay. Just thought I'd stop over to see how you were getting on."

"I'm doing. How 'bout some coffee or one of Ruth's dang-fine breakfasts?"

"No. Thanks."

Rory frowned, feeling as though he was trying to coax some wary wild thing up onto the porch with offers of tempting bait. It shouldn't be that way and this morning, he had no patience with it. "Well, you seen me, so go on and get back to whatever you was doing."

But Scott lingered, placing care for his brother over his dislike of being on Kincaid property. He came up onto the porch and leaned back against the rail, observing Rory in silence. He could see the evidence of pain etched at the corners of his eyes and the weakness in the shadowed circles beneath them. And he saw in his tormenting mind's eye, his brother sprawled upon the ground, leaking his life's fluids while he rode off without looking back.

"Somethin' else on your mind, Scotty?"

"How you fixing with the funds Monthaven left?"

Bemused by his interest, Rory told him, "Using it to file claim on the land along the waterways. Hell of a thing, paying for ground we been feedin' over for years."

"Filing legal?" Scott couldn't contain the question.

Rory regarded him with careful inscrutability. "We're filing."

Scott smiled tightly. That meant shrewd old Major Kincaid would have every cowboy on his payroll lining up to make a fraudulent bid for land he had no intention of settling. But he hadn't come to argue politics or morals with his brother. Rory was a rancher at heart and that placed an insurmountable difference between them. If he couldn't close that gap, he'd go around it.

"I didn't come by to give you a lecture."

"Good."

"Daddy hated the thought of you being aground so he had me bring Rosebud over."

"Rosebud?" Rory gave him a pained smirk and leaned down to get a look at the horse. And danged if the roan filly wasn't a distinctive pinkish color. Scott hadn't so much as cracked a smile but Rory figured he was laughing himself silly inside. And so would every man-jack on the Bar K. He settled back against the swing. "Tell Daddy thanks for the thought but I ain't riding no pink horse named *Rosebud*."

"Told him you'd say that. Fine by me. Probably be too much of a handful for you right now. I was thinking of breaking her in for Gena."

"You'd put your little wife on a horse I couldn't ride?" Then Rory bit back his indignation to smile cautiously. "Scotty, why you trying to prod me into getting on that there prissy horse? I ain't gonna sit up there an' have the boys sidesplitting over me."

"Like I said, fine by me," he drawled so smoothly his brother grew more suspicious. "Too bad you aren't color blind. The filly's a sweet little goer. I'll take her on back and see if Daddy has something a bit more — sedate and ordinary for you. Something that wouldn't look so God-awful alongside the color of your hair. I was kinda looking forward to having you ride out with me this morning but I guess I could have one of the fellas hitch the buggy —"

"All right," Rory growled. "Enough. Saddle 'er up but be quiet about it."

Scott leaned back over the rail and hollered down to one of the hands at the barn. "Hey, bring Rory's gear on up here and saddle up Rosebud for him."

"Rosebud?" There was a pause then a loud guffaw. "Rosebud!"

Rory ground his teeth. "Thank you for handling that so subtle, Scotty."

" 'Welcome."

"Well, don't jus' sit there grinning. Help me get my boots on. I can't quite manage one-handed."

Scott approached carefully, not sure his brother wasn't just trying to coax him within striking range. But after trying to shove the boot on his injured leg, he could see the truth in the sudden graying of his features. It was only half on when Rory popped a sweat of agony. Scott eased it off his foot.

"Jus' give it a good yank," Rory said through clenched teeth. But Scott had another idea. He went to his saddle pack and drew out a pair of hard-soled moccasins. He tossed them to the frowning cowboy.

"Here. Those'll slip right on."

Rory slid his feet into them and scowled uncertainly. "House slippers and a pink horse. Hell, I ain't never gonna live this down."

But he had to admit, the moccasins cushioned the pain in his knee and the little filly had the prettiest gait and softest mouth he'd ever seen.

"Hey, Rory," one of the hands yelled as the two Prescotts rode in a lope across the yard. "What whore did you steal that horse out from under?"

The men who'd gathered indolently along the corral rail shared a good laugh and Rory grinned at them amiably. "Glad you fellers got nothin' to do this morning. 'Spect all them stalls clean as my mama's tabletop by the time I get back." Then, with the briefest nudge, he set the filly into a showy canter as smooth as a rocking chair to ride. "Wouldn't know good horseflesh if it kicked 'em upside the head," he grumbled to his brother's vast amusement.

For all its ugly color, the filly was sweet. She glided. Rory never felt so much as a jolt to his tender knee. The slightest twitch of his hand telegraphed an instant response. He'd expected that from Chance but not from a mount he wasn't used to. And begrudgingly, he was impressed. A man in the West depended upon his horse and rope even more than his sidearms and he knew in that first ride that Rosebud was the kind of horse a man could trust.

Rosebud? What the heck kind of name was that? He couldn't be calling his horse by any sissy name.

"Atta girl, Bud," he crooned softly, stroking the daintily arched neck. The filly gave an unexpected hop and snorted an objection. He grinned. Just what he needed, two cussedly independent females dogging his days and nights.

It felt good to be in the saddle, out on the free-rolling range. The musty feel of infirmity and the achiness of grief paled in the wash of warm sunlight. His daddy and Scott must have figured it would and he loved them fiercely for it.

"Where we headed, Scotty?"

"To see Two Sparrows."

The name meant nothing to Rory at first until he saw the neat little farm. The Walters's place. Then he remembered the promise he hadn't had time to keep. The spread was quiet. A full line of dried clothes hung in the early morning sunshine. Scott called a greeting in the Sioux tongue and rolled to his feet while Rory dismounted more slowly.

Scott felt it then. The hair at his nape bristled and crawled. His breath shivered lightly.

"Rory . . ."

His brother's hand went instantly to his rifle scabbard. "What is it?"

"I don't know. Something."

Scott moved Indian-quiet, Indian-cautious, around the side of the sod house Two Sparrows and his sons had been rebuilding. Two by three foot slabs of grass and roots were piled in a wheelbarrow waiting to be stacked into a wall. Something was wrong. His nostrils flared, filling with a sweet, sickly smell that he couldn't quite place until he turned the next corner. And was dropped to hands and knees.

"Scotty?"

Rory hobbled as fast as he could, slowing in confusion when he heard the sounds of terrible retching.

"Rory, don't come back here." Scott's voice was thin, shaking.

Too late. He came up to where Scott was on all fours, dry-heaving helplessly. And the smell drove scalding bile up into his own throat.

They must have been hanging there, cooking in the

298

sun, for at least three days. Jason Walters and his two sons. Rory dared a brief glance before gripping his brother by the band of his jeans and dragging him backwards to where the air was fresh. Scott stayed face down in the dirt, wracked by spasms of violent reaction while Rory leaned against the sod house, trying to keep from joining him there.

"Aww, jeez, I ain't never seen nothing like that before," he moaned when he had control of his quaking stomach. He swallowed the acidy taste in his mouth as Scott flopped over to a sitting position at his feet. He was gray and dripping sweat. "I'll get you some water, Scotty. Jus' breathe deep."

However, as Rory limped into the dim soddy, he was driven back by the same pungent smell of death. He grabbed up a towel and the closest pot and backed out in a hurry. With water from the well, he mopped Scott's colorless face with the wet towel, then laid it over the back of his neck.

"The missus is inside," he said softly.

Scott looked up through anguished eyes. "Has she been—"

"No. Shot. Once. Don't look like she had no notion about what went on out back." He dipped his hand in the cool water and splashed his own face, letting the chill revive him. "Lordy, Lord, Scotty, who'd do such a—" He broke off abruptly.

He knew. The killings hadn't been ones of random violence. There had been no theft of stock, no violation of Mrs. Walters. It was a clear and graphic warning.

Numbly, he muttered, "We'd best get to burying 'em."

"No," Scott blurted out, nearly retching again at the thought of getting close to the decaying corpses. "Burn it down and them with it."

They rode back to the Bar K with a smudge of black smoke behind them. Neither spoke. There seemed nothing safe to say as inner tensions built and quivered.

Why didn't I do something?

Why didn't you do something?

Norah was in front of the barn, dressed in her tight, tan britches and about to swing up on a horse. She stood down when she saw them and waited with an oddly expressionless face. As they reined in, she went directly, not to Rory, but to Scott and placed her hand over the bronze one resting on his thigh.

"Scott." Her voice thickened with anxiety over the saying of his name. "Scott, your mother was just here. It seems the horse pulling Gena's buggy came back to the Lone Star in broken traces. There's no sign of the buggy. Or your wife."

Chapter Nineteen

Scott gave a piercing wail and jerked his horse around. Without thinking, Rory snagged the reins with his broken hand, crying out sharply but not letting go.

"Scotty. Scotty, wait." It took him a minute to get control of his voice. "Think first. Where was she going? Where would we find her?"

Gradually, the wildness left his brother's gaze and was replaced by calmer thought. He raked a hand through his black hair, panting slightly. "She was—she was talking about riding out to the Cheyenne reservation. She'd been teaching some of the older children to read. She was going to wait for me. We were going to go together. She was going to wait." His eyes dulled with anguish. "Rory—"

"We'll find her."

"I'm going with you," Norah insisted and when neither man protested, she quickly filled the saddle. "Which way?"

They went cross country, riding hard, riding silent.

They found the buggy on its side, forks broken, wheels long since stilled from their frantic spinning. Empty.

"Gena!" Scott's cry echoed eerily across the wide, unbroken plain.

At Norah's suggestion — she was thinking far better than either of them — they parted to search separate areas. There was no telling how far the buggy had traveled without its driver. Then Rory's strained shout brought them together.

"Scotty. Here."

Scott was off the horse before it stopped, skidding his way down into a shallow gully. Where Gena Prescott lay crumpled and unmoving. Her cheeks were smudged and her dress grass-stained but there were no obvious signs of injury. To her. Scott put an unsteady hand to the curve of her abdomen, waiting, breath suspended. But he could feel none of the vigorous movements he'd so delighted in over the last months.

"We've got to get her to the Lone Star." His voice was surprisingly even. "Rory, can you rig up one of the horses to the buggy?"

"Sure." After a pause, "Scotty, is she all right?"

And his flat reply was, "I don't know."

Rifle shots from the Lone Star called Ethan in from his search of the road into Crowe Creek. By the time he arrived, Gena was stretched out, pale and motionless upon the bed she and Scott shared. His stepson was bent over her, his features stiff and waxen. In one hand, he clutched her still fingers. The other spread wide atop her rounded middle.

"I'm gonna need some room in here and a lot more light. Ora, fetch me some lamps." He stripped off his coat and began to roll his sleeves. "Scotty, you're gonna have to trust me and wait downstairs. Scott?"

Glazed golden eyes lifted. "Daddy, why hasn't she come around yet? Why haven't I felt the baby move?"

302

"I'll take a look see and I'll be able to tell you better," he answered with a quieting calm. "Rory, take your brother downstairs and see he stays there. Norah, you make the boys some coffee and lace it liberal with some of what's in that jug in the cupboard. And see that they don't drink it all. Ora, I'm gonna need you."

The group dispersed silently, Scott yielding his bedside vigil with a gentle assist from his mother. When she'd closed the door behind them, Aurora turned anxiously to her husband.

"Ethan, the truth."

"Don't know yet, Ora. Could be she's in shock. Could be she's bleeding inside."

"The baby—"

"Can't help but be one hell of a fighter."

"Oh, Ethan, if something happens to either one of them, I don't want to think of what that'll do to Scott."

"Then don't think on it. Ora, I delivered Scotty and I plan on bringing our first grandchild into this world. Now bring that lamp over here and pour that whiskey over my hands." He looked down at the fragile woman on the bed. "And you hang on, Gena, hear. There's no way I'm going down there to tell that boy I lost you."

When Norah came out of the kitchen with the strongly doctored cups of coffee, only Rory was in the big room. He stood at the huge stone fireplace staring down into the cold grate.

"Where's your brother?"

He jerked his head toward the door. "Went outside. Wanted to be alone. I want so bad to be able to do something for him."

She put the cups down carefully. "What can I do?"

He turned. She took one look at the tragic cast of his features and went to put her arms around him. He leaned on her, curling his good arm around her waist, pressing his cheek to the top of her sweet-smelling hair.

"Norah, it'll kill him if Gena or the baby dies. There won't be nothin' left inside him that wants to go on."

And remembering how she'd felt when Rory's horse came dragging him into the Prescotts' yard, she had to agree.

Norah rubbed his back reassuringly and walked him over to one of the big, limb-hewn chairs his father made. "Sit down, drink your coffee. I'll take this outside to him then I'll come back in and we'll wait together. All right?"

He smiled weakly. "Thank you."

"For what?"

"For stayin'. I love you so much, Norah."

She stood, quivering inside with fracturing emotions. Outwardly, she just smiled back and touched fingertips to his cheek.

It was so bright outside, she had to blink several times to focus. Scott wasn't on the porch as she expected. She called out to him and walked to the steps. It was then she saw him, kneeling in the yard, his back to her. Praying? Being half-Lakota, did he pray? She thought about withdrawing and leaving him undisturbed but there was something so lonely about him on his knees in the dirt. She approached slowly, heart swelling with sympathy for what he must be suffering. And then she walked around in front of him and saw what it was Scott Prescott was doing.

He was using his big bladed knife to cut chunks of

flesh from the inside of his arm.

Blood ran in rivulets, forming a dark pool in the palm of his hand. What shocked her nearly senseless, was his face. Not a trace of emotion flickered there as he carved his skin as if whittling a stick.

For the first time in her life, resourcefulness failed her. Norah panicked.

"Rory!"

He burst out of the house, running with an awkward, stumbling gait and she met him halfway.

"Do something! He's cutting himself to pieces!"

Rory slowed and held her firmly by the arm, partly to secure her and partly to hold himself up. "It's all right, Norah. It's got something to do with the way the Sioux grieve." He garnered his stomach to face the barbarity of what his brother was inflicting upon himself and limped over to him. "Scotty."

Scott could move like nothing he'd ever seen. One second, he was on his knees and the next, he was balanced on the balls of his feet with the knife blade arcing outward. It sliced an inch short of his vitals.

"Get away from me," he snarled, crouched with steel in hand and dangerous as any wounded wild thing. Molten eyes glittered, clearly beyond the edge of reason.

"Scotty, easy now. I ain't gonna let you hurt yourself. Gena'd never forgive me." He took a step closer and the knife lashed out viciously, again, just missing his shirtfront.

"Leave me alone. Don't interfere in what you don't understand or you'll be the one getting hurt."

"Hell, Scotty, if you wanted my gizzard, you'd had it with the first swing."

While Norah gasped in terror, Rory took two quick forward strides and jerked his brother up in a crushing embrace, pinning him there fearlessly while the knife blade flailed and finally fell. Scott clung to him, fingers grasping, clutching frantically in his despair.

"And I do understand," Rory whispered gruffly toward the ducked dark head. "I love her, too."

"Oh, God. Oh, God, Rory, what am I going to do? What am I going to do if she dies?"

A low, keening wail tore from him, setting goose bumps up along Norah's arms. A moaning, animal-like sound, not human. How had she ever thought Scott devoid of feeling? If anything, he was carving his heart out right before them in a display of unimaginable love for his fragile wife. And she was suddenly, terribly afraid that Scott Prescott had slipped into tortured madness.

An hour later, the three of them sat together by the cold fireplace. Scott had long since given up his frantic behavior and the chilling sobs. He sat still, occasionally blinking but otherwise, almost trance-like. He'd let Norah bind up his arm and he cradled it against his chest, though she doubted if he was in pain. He looked beyond the reach of all feeling. And that was more frightening to behold than the wild man he'd been.

Ethan's step upon the stairs brought them to their feet as one but it was Scott who asked for all of them.

"Daddy?"

"She's asking for you, son."

Still cautious, he wanted to know, "Is she all right?"

"Far as I can tell. We'll keep her down and quiet and a close eye on her for a while."

He wasn't ready to breathe easy. "The baby?"

"Kicking like a mule."

Scott let out a shaky gust and scrambled for the stairs, bolting up them.

"Can we see her, too, Daddy?"

Ethan waved Rory and Norah up but cautioned, "I don't want her tired out. You let Scotty do the talking."

Scott was on one knee at their bedside, Gena's frail hand engulfed between his dark ones. He was kissing her palm, her fingers one by one, murmuring soft, husky things in a language she didn't speak but could understand so well. The language of his heart. Her other hand rose to stroke his black hair then touched upon the fresh wrapping on his arm.

"What happened?" she asked faintly.

Scott met her concerned gaze with one steeped in desperate devotion. "I was calling your soul back to me."

Gena didn't appear shocked or censorious. Nor did she mock the strangeness of his customs. Instead, she smiled at her half-pagan, half-Sioux mate and said softly, "Thank you. Your sacrifice must have pleased your gods well for I am here."

He pressed her knuckles to his lips. "Are you strong enough to tell us what happened? The horse came back. We found the buggy overturned. Did the animal run away with you?"

Gena looked embarrassed and uneasy. "No. I let my fears run away with me, I'm afraid. Scott, I'm so sorry I caused you all such worry."

"You and the baby are well and that is all that matters. What frightened you, *mitawicu?*"

She looked more agitated and Ethan placed a warning hand on his stepson's shoulder. But she answered evenly enough. "Some riders approached me. I didn't know them. They—they began to say ugly things to me." She colored hotly.

"What kind of things, Gena?" Scott insisted tightly.

307

"Things about you and about what having your baby made me. Things that made me angry. I — I hit one of them with the buggy whip but he pulled it from my hand. One of them was holding the horse's head. They started to dismount, saying you needed to be taught a lesson. And that's when I got scared. I don't think they meant to do more than frighten me but all I could see was Morning Song and the men who attacked her. I'm sorry I wasn't braver, Scott. It was my fault the accident happened. I made the horse run. I wanted to get away from them and their nasty talk. I wanted to get home. I wanted you. The buggy hit a rut and I was thrown. I don't remember anything after that. Oh, Scott, I could have killed our child with my foolishness. Please forgive me."

Scott's eyes glittered but his smile was achingly tender. His big hand caressed over her distended belly. "Hush. None of that. The fault wasn't yours. And I am very proud of how brave you are." He kissed her hand again and Gena looked relieved. "These men," Scott asked quietly. "You said you didn't know them. Was there anything about them that you remember?"

"Scott, please —"

"Gena, was there?"

Gena's worried gaze cut over to Rory then she told her husband, "No. Nothing."

He intercepted that look and heard that lie spoken upon the lips of the one he loved. And he knew there were only one or two people in the world she loved enough to protect that way. And one of them was his brother. He smiled down at her then leaned over to lightly kiss her lips. "You rest, Gena."

"Scott?" Her hand clutched at his.

"I'm going to walk for a minute. I need to clear my head. I'll be right back." His hand cupped her cheek

308

while he pressed his own to the other. "I love you more than life," he told her softly.

Gena watched him leave the room. And her eyes began to well up with tears. "Rory?"

"Whatcha need, Sis?" he soothed, sinking down awkwardly beside the bed. Her grip was amazingly powerful on his hand.

"Rory, something's wrong with Scott."

"Oh, now don't you go a-worrying over Scotty. You shook him up pretty good—"

"No. No, listen. It's something awful. I can feel it."

"Gena-honey, Scotty's fine—"

"No." Her tone firmed stubbornly. "Rory, I know him. I know Scott better than anyone. It's like a light just went out inside him. Please, please don't leave him alone."

"Gena—"

"Rory, the men who attacked me were riding Bar K stock. And I think Scott knows it."

She didn't need to explain it any clearer. He kissed her wan cheek quickly and straightened. "I'll look after him, Gena."

But by the time he reached the front porch, all that was left of his brother was a faint whorl of dust. In the direction of the Bar K.

Garth Kincaid examined the figures and projections Cole prepared for him. If even half the investments paid off, they were going to be very, very rich. And the Bar K would prosper in the uncertainty of the twentieth century. That was all important. And worth a toast.

He was turning in his big chair, reaching for the Scotch on his sideboard, when he felt a whisper of

309

movement and heard the quiet shush of drawing steel. And then, a voice straight from hell purring behind him.

"I told you you wouldn't hear me coming."

Scott.

He didn't so much as move a finger in response. And he wasn't truly alarmed, not at first. Scott Prescott was one of the few incorruptibly moral men he knew, so he wasn't afraid. He should have been. Instead, he slowly eased back in his chair and swiveled to confront the shadow at his back. Scott was uncomfortably close. In his hand was a gleaming blade, its edge already dulled by someone's blood. That gave Kincaid a moment of pause.

"To what do I owe the pleasure?"

Scott smiled, a hard flash of white teeth against copper skin. "Oh, this time, the pleasure's mine entirely."

"What do you want?" All pretense fell away. For once, his loathing for his daughter's bastard son was plainly exposed upon his harsh face.

"I've come to see you answer for your sins." The drawling voice was a silky whisper.

Kincaid gave a snort. "Oh, come now. That's stretching a bit even for you. Have you become a redeemer of lost souls as well as a champion of lost causes?"

"I'm not here to redeem your black soul. I'm here to send it to hell."

Then, Garth Kincaid looked into his grandson's eyes. And he knew pure terror. There was no life behind that golden glaze, just an emptiness and an incredible fire. Like looking straight into an inferno of the damned.

"Get out of here." His rumbling command had just

310

the slightest tremor to it. And Scott grinned fiercely. A smile of promise.

"Not until we settle things. Not until you pay for the pain you've caused my people. Not until you make restitution for every inch of ground you've stolen. Not until you ease the hurt of breaking my ribs and my trust. Not until you make amends for Jason Walters, his sons and his wife. Not until you answer for my wife and my child!" That last tore through clenched teeth and the fires in his eyes roared.

Kincaid blinked. "Gena? What's happened?" The sound of genuine concern in his tone set Scott trembling furiously.

"You son of a bitch. You could have staked me to a tree and pulled the flesh off my bones and I wouldn't have come after you. Because of Rory, because of my love for my brother. He was the only thing standing between me and your hair. But you — you touched my wife, you threatened my family. You endangered my child. And you'll die for that."

Garth Kincaid was breathing hard and fast and his mind was just as labored. His wife! Damn Denby. How could he be so stupid? Nothing else would have torn the veil of civility from a man who prided himself on his control. That was it. Reason. Scott would always hear reason even from madness.

"Scott, you don't want to do this. I am your grandfather, your mother's father."

"Since when?" he sneered.

"I made you what you are today."

Scott laughed at that, a low, rippling chuckle as cold as the first running melt of spring. "Yes. Yes, you did."

"They'll hang you!"

"It is a good day to die, old man."

311

Kincaid saw his own murder reflected in that bottomless stare. And he wouldn't just sit by and let this half-breed madman strip him of his hair. His hand shot out, bracing the arm wielding the knife while his other dove inside his desk drawer. His fingers closed around the butt of a primed pistol and he brought it around in a deadly bead upon his grandson's chest. Scott's forearm flew up, knocking the barrel upward so it discharged uselessly into the ornately plastered ceiling. They struggled. Kincaid was a bear of a man, his strength untouched by the years. But Scott was flushed with the killing blood of vengeance, with the violent blood of his father's people. And as Lone Wolf, he'd been taught from childhood how to fight to the death.

The big chair went over, spilling them both, still grappling, onto the tiled floor.

"Ruth!" Kincaid screamed out to the woman at the door. "Ruth, call for help!"

But she stood, still and stunned, seeing the man she'd let into her bed as lover and the babe she'd held in her arms to ease the emptiness of her own life. How could she choose between them?

A sudden chopping blow from the tough old man set Scott's head ringing. He was a strong enemy, a dangerous enemy. Scott ignored the pain of that and another fierce fist to the midsection. He'd been in pain all his life. Blocking it out was instinctive. He didn't see the snarling man writhing beneath him as his mother's father. He didn't see his face at all. He saw Rory's boot soles unmoving in a shadowed barn. He saw masked faces hovering over him as hot, smelly tar scalded his skin. He saw his childhood friend, Morning Song raped of her purity, her dignity, her rights. The poverty of his people. The horror of what was done to Two Sparrows and his family. Gena lying crumpled at the bottom of a ravine. Gena . . .

With a wailing Lakota yell, he jerked back the blade. He could hear Bar K hands crowding the room but he paid them no attention. Nothing could stop the fateful purpose of his blade except—

"Scotty!"

He froze. His brother's voice reached through the haze of fury to snag upon his soul. Rory.

Rory was shocked into a brief second of immobility by the savage sight that greeted him. His grandfather flat on his back. His brother astride the old man's chest, knife blade glittering in his hand. It was the movement of the men beside him that snapped his horrified trance.

"No!" he cried out as pistols raised. "Put 'em down! Put 'em down, damn you!" Panicked breath jerked in his chest, strangling the irregular beat of his heart. Oh, God! What was he going to do?

"Rory?" one of the men questioned, echoing his confusion. "What you want us to do? It's your brother."

"Get out. All of you get out."

The men grumbled, tense and agitated by the pending violence of the situation. But deferring to their young boss.

"Here," one of the hands murmured. A pistol was pressed into Rory's palm. He looked down at it vaguely, then to the two figures across the room. Behind him, the Bar K hands crowded in the hall, silent, expectant.

"Scotty," he called out softly. "Scotty, back off."

"I can't," he panted harshly. "Not this time."

"Gena. Scott, think of Gena, the baby."

The golden gaze sparkled. "I am. I am thinking of

313

them. Of them in danger as long as he lives. As long as I live."

Rory's insides recoiled at that casually spoken claim. He meant it. Scott meant it. There was no doubt in his mind that his brother could calmly take the life of their grandfather. For Gena. He'd seen that cool call for retribution before, when he had Jake Spencer beneath his blade. And Rory had stopped him from using it on the man who shot his wife. That man had escaped justice. Scott's steady stare told him plainly that Garth Kincaid would not. Even if he had to die in the process. And that, Rory wouldn't allow.

"Scotty, please. Don't do this. I can't let you do this."

"Walk away, Rory."

"I can't." It was a tortured whisper. "Oh, God. Scotty, please."

Just then, Kincaid surged up in an attempt to unseat his attacker, yelling out at the same time, "Shoot him, Rory! For crissake, kill him!"

A sharp blow from the back of Scott's hand silenced him but the click of a pistol hammer kept him from doing worse. He looked up to see his brother, gun in hand, its dark bore pointed directly at him and he saw his destiny.

"Scott, let him up."

"No. You know what he is, Rory. You know what he's done. It stops here, now." The blade lifted slowly. Golden eyes locked with brown.

"Rory, shoot him!" Kincaid screamed. "He's going to kill me!"

No one doubted it for a second.

It was a hoarse whisper. "Scott, please. Don't make me do this. Please!"

Scott stared up at him, at his brother. He saw the

314

horrible anguish pooling in his eyes. He saw the unwavering aim of the pistol in his hand. So, this was it. This was the time. He wasn't afraid. He spoke his brother's name softly, lovingly. Then he turned his back with a terrible Sioux war cry to bring the knife plunging down.

The booming report of the gun wasn't loud. The pain smashing through his chest wasn't bad. The impact stunned him. The knife fell from his fingers. It was the awful knowledge that Garth Kincaid lived that tore like agony through his soul. That and Rory's name. Scott pitched forward, feeling the pump of his blood with every heartbeat. Thoughts moved sluggishly. He wouldn't be there for the birth of his child. Oh, Gena . . .

Garth Kincaid heaved the pinning weight off him. The knife blade clattered harmlessly on the tiled floor as Scott Prescott spilled to one side. The old man glared at the still features contemptuously, then turned to his grandson with relief.

"The crazy bastard was going to kill me."

Rory made a soft incoherent sound in the back of his throat. The pistol dropped from slack fingers. Slowly, he hobbled across the room, breath sobbing from him with every painful step. He dropped down, not beside the shaken old man but next to the still figure of his brother.

"Oh, Scotty."

With infinite care, he gathered his brother up, shuddering when the dark head fell loosely against his shoulder, shaking at the slick, warm feel of blood beneath his hand.

Kincaid had scrambled up and was pouring himself a stiff whiskey. He bolted it down before facing the sight of Rory cradling his would-be killer in his arms.

"Get up, Rory," he said with a quiet sternness. "I'll call someone to take care of that." When his grandson didn't move, he said reasonably, "He was going to kill me, son. You had no choice. Let him go. You did the right thing. You saved my life."

"No," Rory muttered thickly into his brother's short black hair. "I saved his."

He got up then, with Scott still clutched to his chest. Bad leg buckling, he swayed but Kincaid made no move to steady him.

"Rory, what the hell are you doing? I'll send for the law to take care of it."

Rory looked at him vaguely as if he didn't understand. Then he said in a voice raw with determination, "I'm taking my brother home."

In that second, Kincaid saw the possible end of everything. If Rory left his house, he might never return. He watched his grandson, his heir, his hope for the future move haltingly to the door, staggering beneath the weight he carried. Scott Prescott's feet and a single arm swayed tauntingly with each stumbling step.

"Stop him."

Ruth reached out to touch her palm to Rory's damp cheek. Her own were streaked with tears. She stepped aside to let him by.

"Stop him!" Kincaid bawled at the men lingering in the hall.

The Bar K hands parted, giving Rory room to walk through their midst.

An empty whiskey glass shattered against the wall. "Dammit!"

Rory wasn't sure how he made it down the steps. His knee was on fire, barely able to support him. His wrist shook with the strain of carrying Scott's legs.

But he managed. And then he did the one thing that had lived in his nightmares for over a year. He draped the body of his brother over his saddle and dragged himself up behind.

Rory was bringing Scott home to their mother.

Chapter Twenty

Norah stood on the Prescotts' front porch, worrying. Upstairs, Gena was finally resting. She'd been frantic after Rory rode out in pursuit of her husband and that wasn't good for either mother or child. Tension gathered and roiled beneath the timber roof, a storm long brewing about to break. The air was thick with its current. Seeking an escape, Norah slipped outside to enjoy the late afternoon colors pooling on the horizon.

Aurora Prescott moved past her without a word. Carriage rigid, she went to the steps and stared out toward her father's ranch. Norah wondered what she was thinking but she wouldn't ask. Aurora hadn't given her leave to be that familiar with her family's private life. Norah stood back, silently, wondering about the woman who'd given birth to two such strong and vastly different sons—of two men worlds apart. Here was a woman of admirable courage, a woman without compromise, a woman who had it all. And Norah mused quietly over how different things might have been if her own mother had had a grain of Aurora Prescott's nerve.

Those steely nerves were fraying. Norah could see the other woman's restlessness as she scanned the horizon. And she knew exactly when she saw them coming. Her body quivered like a divining rod. Norah walked up beside her, not close but near. And the two of them strained to see who was on the single horse that crested the final hill to the Lone Star.

Then Aurora took a shaky breath.

"Ethan," she called in a strange little voice, then louder, "Ethan!" And she was off the porch, running through the Dakota grass, skirts swirling about her legs in a hampering tangle.

Rory drew in the reins and let his mother run to them. His features were stark and stricken. "Mama." The word moaned from him.

But she never looked up at him. Her attention was on her older son. "Scotty? Scotty! Oh, my God. Ethan, he's been shot!"

"Move outta the way, Ora," Ethan said gruffly. He put an unsteady hand to the seeping wound, then to the side of Scott's neck. Without a word, he hauled him off Rory's mare and carried him, limp and bleeding, into the house with Aurora weeping at his heels.

Norah stood clutching the reins of Rory's little mare. Her eyes were frantic with distress. "Rory, what happened? Did your grandfather do that? Was there a fight?"

Rory slid off the back of his horse and kept on sliding. His knee refused to hold him, collapsing, spilling him down on all fours. Where he stayed swaying in time to his sawing breaths. Norah knelt down before him and worriedly touched the thatch of bright hair as his hat dangled unnoticed by its tie strings.

"Rory, what happened?" she repeated softly.

"I lost him. Norah, I lost my brother."

319

Ethan strode into the house, calling curtly, "Clear the table, Ora."

Gripping one end of her linen cloth, Aurora whisked it off, sending Haviland tea cups flying. Ethan put Scott down across it and began stripping off his coat.

"I'll be damned if I'm gonna keep mending these boys if they're in such an all-fired hurry to get tore up again," he grumbled. "Ora, fetch me my—" She was there, with his medical kit in trembling hands. He took it with one of his and her up to his chest with the other, whispering huskily, "Steady now, sweet thing. I'm gonna need you. Don't go falling to pieces, hear?"

"He's alive then?"

Almost in answer to her disbelieving words, Scott moaned and shifted on the table. She was instantly bent over him, stroking his sweat-beaded face as her husband cut open his coat and shirt to bare the wound. It was low, in the meaty part of his shoulder blade. And the bullet was still inside. He mopped around the hole then did some brief prodding. Scott jerked and groaned on his way back to consciousness.

"Easy now, son. It's real clean and neat. Have that ball out of there slick as you please. You understanding me?" The dark head gave a convulsive nod. "Good. Now, I'm gonna do this right now, real quick so you won't go losing no more blood. I'll get you something for the pain and something to bite down on."

Scott shook his head and gritted out, "Just get it done, Daddy."

"All right. I'm gonna roll you over onto your belly. You grab onto the edge of the table. Tight. Your little lady's upstairs sleeping so if you think you're gonna yell out, you clamp something in them jaws. I don't

320

want to deliver a bullet and a baby in the same night."

"Yessir."

Ethan prepared the area of the wound and ordered, "More light."

Aurora held a lamp suspended but the light flickered erratically in her shaking hands. Norah reached up to take it. "Let me do that, Mrs. Prescott," she offered quietly and the other woman relented with a grateful nod.

Scott's fingers groped for the edge of the tabletop and he found them laced firmly through another's grip. He looked up to see Rory's somber features close to his own.

"I got you, Scotty."

He immediately tried to pull back with a raw accusation. "Why didn't you let me finish it, you son of—" The rest was lost as the probe for the bullet began. Scott's fingers clamped tight and twisted, savaging Rory's poorly healed wrist. But neither of them made a sound of complaint.

"Gotcha, you nasty, man-puncturing piece of hell," Ethan declared proudly as he withdrew the slug.

And from the stairs, there came a hoarse cry and a whisper of dread.

"Scott?"

Aurora was quick to catch her as the pregnant woman came hurtling across the room.

"Scott! Oh! Oh, my God!"

"He's all right, Gena," Ethan soothed as he set the misshapen bullet down on the table. "Just took on an unhealthy dose of lead."

"Someone shot him? Who?"

There was silence. No one had thought to ask.

"Scotty?"

Scott didn't answer his father. He was breathing

321

heavy into the pain, his fingers kneading Rory's then pushing away from contact with him.

"Rory?" Ethan's voice was sterner. "Dang it, boy, I'm getting sick of stitching up bullet holes in the two of you. You talk to me. Who did this? Was it Kincaid? If it was, I'm taking down my Sharps and I'm gonna blast a hole in that old bas—"

"No." Rory choked it out then swallowed hard. "I did."

"What?"

The dark eyes lifted and there was no doubting the sincerity of his gaze. "I shot him, Daddy."

An unholy shriek burst from Gena. She pulled free of Aurora and lunged. The fierceness of her slap snapped Rory's head back a good six inches. "How could you?" she screamed at him, while Aurora struggled to hold her still. "He trusted you! I trusted you! You lied to me. You lied. You told me you would keep him safe. You promised me!"

"Gena . . ."

"You promised!"

"Gena, I tried. I did the best I could."

"By putting a bullet in him? How could you do such a thing to your own brother? For that ranch? For a bunch of cows? Are those things worth more than Scott's life?"

"If you'd listen to me—"

"No, I don't want to listen. I want you to leave. I want you to go back where you belong!"

Rory had gone deathly pale. "Gena, I'm sorry." He reached out a hand to the distraught woman but it was his mother who struck it away. He stared at her, incomprehensibly.

"Perhaps you'd better just go home," she told him brittlely.

322

He looked even more confused and blurted, "Mama, I am home." Then he looked from her stiff features to the way fury had distorted Gena's from their gentle, affectionate lines into violent disgust. And he took a stumbling step back. "Aren't I?" He glanced at Scott, who was as white as he was from loss of blood and to his father in desperate search of an answer.

"Go on, son," Ethan told him softly. "This ain't the time for it."

Rory made an awful sound in his throat and wheeled about clumsily in his haste to escape the condemnation of his family. When Norah made a move to follow, Ethan caught her arm.

"Let him go, girl. I need you here. Ora, set Gena down and get her quiet. Let's get this finished up."

Rory was clutching at the porch post for balance, his bowed head a reflection of the fiery setting sun.

"How you holding up, pard?"

"He gonna be all right, Daddy?"

"He'll mend. I reckon you hit what you was aiming for or he'd be cold by now. You want to tell me what the Sam Hill happened over there?"

Rory sucked an anguished breath. "Daddy, I didn't want to do it. He didn't give me no choice. He went after the major with his knife. He was gonna kill him. I had to stop him. Daddy, honest to God, I sooner die than hurt Scotty."

"I know that son." His arm rode easy across the sagging shoulders.

"But Gena and Mama—"

"Will understand better hurt than hung. In time."

Rory closed his eyes tight, trying to squeeze out the way his relationship with his brother had gone from the playful teasing of that morning to bloodshed and damning curses. "Will Scotty?"

Ethan had no answer for that quiet plea. "I don't know, Rory." He patted his son's back encouragingly. "You might as well go on back to the Bar K whilst things here are so stirred up. I'll talk to your mama and Gena and get them to understand—"

"I don't. Daddy, I don't understand. How could things grow so ugly so fast?"

Ethan Prescott scowled toward the Bar K. "Not all that fast, son. Them seeds was planted a long time ago and we're just tasting the poison of their fruit. You just got yourself planted in a bad spot."

"What am I gonna do?"

The simplicity of that request was overwhelming.

"You do what you think is right and I'll back you. You ain't done nothing wrong, nothing to be ashamed of but I know me saying that ain't gonna keep your belly from aching for a good long while. You and me both know you done a man's share of promise keeping." He fingered the bandage covering Aurora's clever stitchery. "Was that Kincaid, too?"

"I don't know. He says it wasn't."

"You believe him?"

"Wish I could, Daddy. Wish I could."

When Garth Kincaid looked up and saw his grandson standing in the doorway, it was an effort not to show the relief he felt. He'd come back! But something in Rory's pinched features kept him from celebrating that fact right away. They looked at one another warily, then Rory's gaze strayed to the hardwood floor where Ruth hadn't been able to scrub up the stain of his brother's blood.

"Come in and sit down, Rory. I was about to pour a drink. I'll make it two."

"I don't want nothin', Major."

"You look like you need it, boy."

Rory limped slowly to one of the big chairs and eased himself down. He took the glass from his grandfather and held it upon his knee, studying the color and quality of the liquor. His expression was grim.

"Scotty's fine," he said suddenly, then gave a small, wry smile. "Jus' in case you was curious."

Kincaid frowned at that news and for once, answered honestly. "I'd hoped you'd killed him."

Rory winced but inside he was too numb to have shown more of a reaction. God, what a fool he'd been to think he could heal the split in his family.

"I trust he'll be in shape to travel when the sheriff gets there with a warrant for his arrest in the morning."

"What?" Rory came out of his somber musings with a jerk.

"The man is clearly dangerous. He came at me with a knife. He would have killed me if you hadn't shot him. He needs to be locked away—"

"No. He needs to be left alone."

"Rory, the man is unstable—"

"Because you almost killed his wife and baby! How the hell did you think he was going to take something like that? And you know, Major, I don't blame him. I'd have done the same thing. No. It stops here. It stops now. You file for your warrant and when the law comes around asking what happened, I'll tell them me and Scotty was indulging in some horseplay and the gun went off accidental. They'll believe me. How many men'd put a bullet in their own brother on purpose?" His features worked bitterly, then firmed. "No.

325

It ends now. I want my family left alone. Any of Denby's killers so much as look at 'em and you're gonna wonder why you thought Scotty was the dangerous one."

Finally, Rory took down the drink of whiskey, needing its burn to cut through the thickness of emotion in his throat. "I want Denby's men off the Bar K range by daybreak. I see any of 'em hanging around after that and I'll shoot 'em where they stand."

Kincaid faced down the rebellion in his grandson's gaze by saying flatly, "You agreed not to interfere."

"I didn't know you was planning to murder whole families and scare pregnant women."

"What did you think I had planned, Rory?" he countered searingly. "You knew what to expect. You agreed to any measures necessary to preserve the Bar K and those orders stand."

He did know and that horrible guilt twisted around the curls of whiskey in his belly. He knew and he'd done nothing. He'd seen Kincaid pay off Jake Spencer and had done nothing. He'd agreed to look the other way and had, by his silence, sanctioned his own brother's shooting. He might as well have shoved Gena out of the wagon himself. The stench of death at the Walters's farm rose up around him and he could once again feel the warmth of his brother's blood upon his hands. He was far from clean. By doing nothing, he'd condoned the actions of the Bar K range protectors. And the weight of their misdeeds crushed down upon his shoulders.

"I'm giving new orders," he said quietly.

"What?" Kincaid came up out of his chair. "Just who do you think you're talking to, boy?"

Rory stared him down somberly. "A man I've respected all my life. A man whose boots I wanted to walk in so bad I was willing to stop watching where I was putting my feet. I wanted to be jus' like you and right now, that scares the hell outta me."

Kincaid's tone gentled. "Rory, I've told you what to expect when running a ranch like this. And I know it's harsh and it's hit you hard because it's struck so close to you. You've got to rise above those things—"

"Rise above my conscience? How do you sleep nights?"

"I sleep just fine," he said calmly and Rory was shocked because he believed him.

"Son, you do what you got to do—"

"No." Rory shook his head. "No. You're not doing it because you have to. Maybe at first when there weren't no law out here, but not now. You're doing it 'cause you want to. 'Cause it's easier and faster and it gets you what you want. And mostly you got away with it 'cause folks was too scared to say no to you. Scotty said no and you tried to run right over him— your own grandson! Well, now I'm saying no. You gonna have your fancy gunmen kick the hell outta me, too?"

"Rory, you're talking crazy."

"No, I'm telling you how it's gonna be if you want me to stay on. Half this ranch is mine. I ain't gonna be no silent partner. This bullying of the farm folk and the Sioux, it's gonna stop. We're cowmen, not gunslingers. This ain't the '70s. It's the start of the twentieth century and it's gonna be run in the legislature not by Judge Lynch out on the range. You want power, you lobby ole Teddy in the White House, you don't run your cows through some dumb farmer's crops. This ain't about pushing people around no more. It's about politicking. You want to live in the past, you're gonna lose everything you built. And I

327

worked too hard to see that happen. That's the way it's gonna be on the Bar K. You think different, you go out and ask any of them fellers in the bunk house whose orders they're set to follow, yours or mine."

Garth Kincaid sat silent while Rory stated his cold, mutinous words. He was seeing something new and strong evolve before him; the man he'd raised his grandson to be. Only he hadn't expected his own creation to rear up and strike out at him. He was furious. And he was at the same time so damned proud. He'd be passing the Bar K into tough, capable hands. But he wasn't ready to let loose the reins yet.

"You know what you're doing, boy?" he challenged gruffly.

"I sure as hell hope so," Rory admitted with a poignant candor. "I don't want to lose my family, Major and I don't want to lose the things we've shared. I'm a rancher. I want to keep what we've built up here on this good green grass. But I want to feel good about how we're doing it. We gonna work on this together or am I gonna walk on outta here?"

There was a long, tense pause. The two men regarded each other with a new awareness, with a tenuous sense of equality. Then Garth Kincaid sighed. "I wouldn't have taken you on as partner if I didn't want that, Rory. You run things the way you want to, boy. Maybe it's time I stood back out of the way." He came around his big desk and put a hand on Rory's shoulder. "I've never been so proud of you as I am right now, son. As of now, you're man enough to sit in that chair."

He left Rory in the study and drew up when he saw Cole and Norah lingering in the hall. He took the Bar K manager aside and said with quiet intensity, "I want you to clear all the guns off the ranch. Set them up some place inconspicuous until we need them. And if Rory asks to see the books, you know what set to show him."

"Yes sir, Major. I sure do."

"And Cole, stay away from the Prescotts. That boy in there is worth more to me than evens. And after this all quiets down, perhaps Scott Prescott will suffer some unfortunate — and fatal, accident."

"Yes sir. Life's full of those unfortunate surprises."

Norah watched the Bar K patriarch mount the stairs, wondering if she'd ever in her entire life felt such fear and loathing for another human being. And the thought of the same cold blood running in Rory Prescott's veins was a frightening one.

"I'll have no part of it, Cole," she said softly.

"Of what, Norah?" he asked, calmly drawing and sampling the scent of a big cigar.

"Of killing Rory's brother. I'll tell him and I'll go to the law if I have to."

Cole bit off the tip of the cigar, then casually reached out for a handful of frothy lace that adorned her bodice. His fingers clenched with threatening strength. "You're not telling anyone anything, Norah dear. Because you're not the only one who can do a share of talking. You want your fine cowboy to get a clear picture, then we'd better tell him everything. About you, about us. You ready to do that? Let's do it now." He started to tow her toward the study. Norah dug her heels into the plush floor runner and twisted in his grasp.

"No, Cole," she cried softly. "Please." She'd seen enough pain in Rory Prescott's eyes for one day.

Cole eased his grasp. "Now you're talking sense. You leave things alone, Norah. Let me handle them. There won't be any killing. You have my word on it.

329

We're not going to be here that long. Let Kincaid see to his own dirty work. All I want is his dirty money. That suit you, my lovely?"

She nodded stiffly and he let her go. And he grinned as she hurried into the study, completely unconcerned with what she might say to Prescott. He knew his Norah, after all and she always thought of herself first.

Rory was still seated in the same spot, staring aimlessly at the big empty chair behind his grandfather's desk. He heard Norah come into the room but he didn't acknowledge her. Not until she sank down beside his chair and rested her head upon his good knee. Then he placed his palm upon those glossy locks and stroked them absently.

"I've wanted to sit in that chair for the best part of my life," he said in an oddly hushed voice. She didn't think he was speaking to her so Norah stayed silent, letting him talk through his misery. "I just never knew how hard it was gonna be. I figured if I could learn all there was to know about ranching, I could fill it fine. 'Cept sitting in that chair ain't got nothin' to do with cows, it has to do with corruption. And I jus' can't look the other way no more."

Norah nestled her cheek against his hard thigh and closed her eyes, aching for the pain in his words. His fingers continued their gentle caress.

"Growing up out here, Scotty was the only friend I had. I'd tag on after him, jus' amazed by him. I was so proud of him, my big brother who knew so much about everything. I was ten when mama sent him off to school in the East. I didn't understand why he had to go, I just knew there was this big emptiness in me that I couldn't get filled back up. Mama, she just moped around like the sun and stars had been snatched outta her life. Daddy, he

330

was busy building up the Lone Star and I was in the way more than anything. I come over here to the Bar K like a lost pup whining for attention and like a stray, I sorta stayed where I was fed. The major, he passed out scraps and hell, I was starving for 'em. He let me follow him around, pestering him with questions and never once laughed at 'em or shooed me away. He made me feel like I was someone important. Went on my first roundup at eleven. The major let me ride nighthawk and I remember thinking whilst I was sitting out there in the dark with all them stars overhead, that my life was perfect. I had everything I could ever want and I would do whatever it took to make my grandfather proud of me to thank him for letting me belong. 'Cept kill my own brother. Ain't nothin' ever gonna be the same after today. Ain't none of 'em gonna forgive me for what I done. And I ain't never gonna forgive myself."

"I wish I could help take the hurt away," Norah said softly.

"Then stay with me tonight, Norah. Jus' be with me."

Wordlessly, she stood and helped him rise up off the chair. With his hand in hers, she wound his arm around her capable shoulders and encouraged him to test her strength. By the time they had gotten halfway up the stairs, he was relying on it. In the still cool darkness of his room, he made no protest when she undressed him, easing his clothing over the heavy wrappings. Then he sat, watching her shed her travel-worn things down to the smooth pearlescence of her skin. Desire felt uncomfortable alongside his moody anguish but she made no demands, simply coming to him, holding him for a long silent moment. And when she kissed him, she didn't seem to mind his lack of response.

331

"I ain't gonna be good for nothin' tonight, Norah," he confessed wearily. "So if you don't want to stay, that's all right."

Norah threaded her fingers back through the luxurious flame of his hair and kissed him again, very gently. "That's not why I'm here, Rory. This isn't about me. It's about you."

He smiled faintly, recalling his impossibly confident words. He didn't feel confident now. But the tender stroke of her palms across the splay of his cheekbones made him feel wonderfully loved.

"Come on, cowboy. Lay yourself down and put yourself in my hands."

"Yessum."

"Roll over on your belly. There. How's that?"

He gave a low moaning rumble of pleasure as her fingers manipulated the tight muscles of his back and shoulders. She worked out the tension gradually, feeling him give and relax an increment at a time. There was no way she could put her hands on him with any degree of detachment. His body was too arousing. She plied the hard swells and taut curves and plains, finding it harder and harder to ignore the way his tanned flesh shifted with a powerful ripple like warm sensuous satin. By the time she reached the toned temptation of his flanks, she was breathless and in need. She slid up over him, rubbing her breasts along the broad expanse of his back, up to where she could nibble at the nape of his neck.

"Rory," she whispered with a throaty passion.

"Ummm."

"Rory?"

He took a heavy sighing breath and was asleep.

She gave a gusty moan and forced the shivers of want to subside. Another time she would see them deliciously met. For now, she'd be content to curl close and savor his presence beside her.

Unable to claim a restful calm, Norah let her attention wander from her slumbering companion to her surroundings. Rory's room. Rory's bed. How many nights had she lain awake down the hall imagining him stretched out where he was now? And how many times had she imagined how it would be to share it with him? For one night. For all her nights. Making love with him, waking up with him. Just holding him the way she was now. How long could she have this slice of heaven before it crumbled down around her? How long could she remain silent when speaking the truth could keep the unspeakable from happening? He would never forgive her if her silence brought his family harm. But neither would he forgive what that truth would reveal about her. Cole was right. Love was folly.

But that didn't stop her from loving.

Chapter Twenty-one

She'd expected — hoped — for several different things from Rory Prescott in the morning. For him to wake her with one of his stunning kisses. For him to touch her body. For him to hug her close and whisper all husky and hot, *I love you*. Yes, she'd wanted a lot of things from him as the sun spread warm over his big bed. But for him to be gone was not one of them.

"Rory?"

Norah sat up, clutching the sheet that covered her to her naked breasts. Feeling ridiculously needy. And disappointed. How could he just walk out and leave her? The idea that he'd slipped out of bed to dress and go while she was there beside him without a stitch on made her grit her teeth in chagrin. He was the one who'd asked her to stay.

But not as his lover.

She was used to men wanting her for her body, for the sheer pleasure they could take from her. But never had she known a man to need her — to just need her for herself. Without sex. Without demands. Without expecting a return. Last night Rory Prescott had wanted her with him because her presence eased his aching heart. He'd asked her to stay because he trusted her enough to seek that unassuming comfort from her. He loved her enough to let her see his vulnerability. She shook with an unexpected tremor. Without demands? Oh, no that wasn't true. He was demanding she respond in kind. Not by pushing himself upon her. Not by taking what she would give. But by waiting. The clever cougar on the limb. How had she forgotten that? He was waiting for her to come to him. And that realization scared her half to death.

Damn him!

In a sort of panic, she pulled on her clothes and fled the room where he'd tucked her beneath his blanket with a familiar care. She took a bath, in water as cold as she could stand it and dressed again with teeth chattering. But all it took was one look, one glimpse of him to flush all the heat right back through her.

He was in the big corral working a calf with his new mare. With pressure from his knees and signals from the twitch of his good hand, he guided the filly in close circles, cutting back and forth to herd the frisky calf. The mare was light of foot and could change up in a hair's breadth of space. At the same time, he was speaking to her, low, steady words of encouragement and praise. Norah leaned against the top rail and watched him with pleasure. Transferring the reins awkwardly to his still fairly useless left hand, he played out a loop with his right and let the rope move in an easy rhythm beside the animal's side. At first, the mare was very aware of it and reacted nervously. Finally, she accepted the humming circle the way she had her rider and responded without hesitation.

"Atta girl, Bud. Good girl. Cozy on up there. That's a girl. Let's do it together, jus' you and me. That's right. Head 'im off. Good. Don't look now but we got us an audience. A danged fine lookin' one, too. Don't you go gettin' jealous now, hear. Carry me in close, Bud. Good girl."

Norah wasn't sure when he caught sight of her. His concentration never seemed to wander from the galloping calf. The lazy rotations of his rope suddenly became all business. It sang out smoothly to hitch up the wiggly calf and Rory tied it off with a not too fast or too neat figure eight.

"Stand, Bud. Stand hard."

The mare planted all fours while the calf twisted like a pan-fish at the end of the rope. But when Rory climbed down and went around to release the loop, she gave and a quick bolt of the lithe young animal entangled him in Manila. The hemp snapped around his legs. Unbalanced by the tender knee, he went down hard on the seat of his Levi's. Norah gave a start of alarm but he was instantly working his way down the rope to set the bucking calf free. Then, muttering a good half and half of profanity, he dropped the rope in the dirt and hobbled away from where the mare stood, trembling and uncertain. When he stopped, his rigid back set to her, Rosebud ambled up behind him and began to nudge for his attention with an insistent nose. He ignored her for a time, then finally gave in and stroked her gently, all the while scolding gruffly.

"You do that well," Norah called out, wryly.

"What's that?"

"Get the ladies to come begging your pardon."

" 'Cause they know I don't hold a grudge and I'm right generous with my rewards." He gave her a sassy grin and began recoiling his rope.

"I seem to remember that."

Looping the coil on his saddle horn, Rory walked over to where she was leaning. He was moving better,

336

with more confidence. And she noticed he was wearing some sort of moccasin on his feet, the way his brother did. From his foot gear, she let her eyes trail with a leisurely appreciation up to where his dark eyes gleamed wickedly.

"You're quite a sweet talker, too," she observed. "You always flatter them so outrageously?"

"When I want a good performance out of 'em. Ladies like to hear that kind of thing." He rested his forearms on the rail, bringing his face close to hers. Their gazes mingled with a playful intensity.

"I would have liked to have heard some of it this morning."

His expression suddenly sobered. "Hey, well, I'm sorry about that."

"Me, too."

He shuffled his feet in a moment of endearing boyishness, then sighed. "The truth of it, Norah, is I had me some thinking to do and it was danged hard to concentrate on anything when I rolled over and got me a face full of soft woman." Lightly, his thumb rubbed over the rounded curve of one breast. The reaction was instant. Norah's breathing altered into a husky cadence. Her back arched, bringing the puckered nipple into impatient contact with his hand. Rory looked a bit surprised, then arrogantly pleased.

"Oh, honey, if I'd knowed things were as bad as all that, I'da waked you up this morning." The innocent touch took on a subtle purpose and Norah moaned his name softly. "Now, Norah-honey, don't you look at me thata way lessen you want me to tug you through them rails and shuck you down right here in front of half my crew."

Her eyes smoldered. "Let them look."

His laugh was sultry and full of promise.

337

There was a not so subtle throat clearing and one of the hands announced, "Ma'am, here's the horse you was wanting."

Norah tore her avid gaze from the hot, dark stare long enough to accept the reins and murmured a vague thank you. When the cowboy turned away, grinning, Rory's fingertips began a tempting study of the underside of her breast.

"Goin' somewheres?"

"Thought I'd ride out and pay a visit to a sick friend. Want me to convey your regards?"

The tantalizing caress stopped. Rory stepped back warily. "I don't know if that'd be such a good idea." The preoccupation was back in his taut expression and Norah reached out to soothe one tanned cheek.

"I'll let you know how he is. I figured you'd be worried and would be too stubborn to go see for yourself."

"You doin' this for me?" He sounded stunned and absurdly gratified all at once. Before she could answer, he trapped her face between his hands and kissed her, long and with longing. A hungry, needy kiss that intensified her already chafing passions to an unbearable degree. Her arms snaked around his neck, pulling him close with unmistakable fervor. And from one of the gawking hands came a whistle and a call of "Attaboy, Rory!"

He broke away then, breathing hard and grinning wide. "Norah-honey, you find yourself with nothin' to do later on this morning, you look me up so's we can finish this here conversation." He glanced around at the number of grinning cowboys who weren't mannerly enough to pretend not to be staring. "Someplace a bit more private."

Norah stroked along his jawline, coaxing him back

338

up close. "I'm sure they haven't the vaguest idea of what we'll be doing."

"Of what they'd like to be doing, maybe, but not of what I mean to do to you."

"And what's that?" she asked with a breathy expectance.

"I'm gonna spend the rest of the day and night workin' you and by the time I'm ready to slip those lovely legs around me, you'll be answerin' to my call. By the time I slide up inside you, I'll have you roped, ridden and gentled and I'll have me the finest filly in the Dakotas."

Norah's imaginings flowed like liquid fire. Still, she couldn't resist challenging his swaggering confidence. "Pretty sure of yourself, cowboy. I don't know if I like being compared to your saddle horse."

"There ain't no comparison, honey," he drawled with a growling certainty. "I put my horse away dry when I'm done. You, I aim to put away wet."

Norah jerked him up and ravaged his mouth. His suggestions scalded her senses and flamed her with urgency. Not caring that they were lip-locked over the corral rail with a goodly number of the Bar K hands enjoying the show, she knocked his Stetson back and drove her fingers deep into his fiery hair. Holding him hard so her tongue could lunge and lick and lap wetly all over his parted lips.

Suddenly, he was prying her away, panting hard but looking beyond her with a sharp interest.

"Rory?" She turned to follow his gaze and saw a buckboard careening in through the Bar K gates.

"Gena," Rory whispered in a taut little voice. "Oh God, something's happened to Scotty."

He vaulted over the fence, landing hard but ignoring the pain that shot up from his knee. And he was running, throwing himself in front of the racing horse, heedless of the danger while wrestling it to a stop. He rushed back to where Gena was clinging to the seat, making harsh gasping sounds.

"Gena?"

She looked up at him through eyes wide and frightened. "Rory. The baby."

He went stone still. "What?"

"The baby's coming. Now!"

It had been a restless night for both of them. A low throb had started in Gena's back, probably from all the day's tension. Every time she managed to doze off, Scott would jerk her up with the panicked cry of his brother's name. Since he never came fully awake from his troubled dreams, it was an easy matter to soothe his brow and murmur softly until he was quiet again. But getting herself settled was another thing altogether.

Her thoughts were of Rory, too. Seeing her husband stretched out on the dining table having a bullet cut out of him had thrown her into shock. She wanted to scream, to strike out in fear and horror at the one who'd caused it. Rory shot him. It had been instinctive, that slap she'd dealt him. Even immediately afterward, when she was still flushed with upset, she couldn't believe she'd done it. She hadn't thought herself capable of such a mindless act of violence. Until she saw the hole in her husband's body and felt the surge of fury for the one who'd put it there. It was all so unbelievable. Like a nightmare. None of it could have happened, should have happened. The men taunting her into nearly losing her babies life. Scott's odd behavior at her side. Rory shooting him. Her slap, the devastation in his eyes. It was all so crazy.

340

Until Ethan put it all in context. By shooting his brother, Rory had very probably saved him from the end of a rope. She owed him thanks, not the fierceness of her condemnation. But it was hard, getting past that first glimpse of Scott bleeding, of the spent slug in Ethan's hand.

Poor Rory. How her heart swelled for him. How awful and alone he must feel, pushed away from the bosom of his family when he needed their understanding so very badly. How could she have ever said such terrible things to him, knowing how much he loved Scott. How it must have torn the soul from him to cause his brother pain, and then to have her compound his guilt with her shrill words of blame. What an unforgivable thing she'd done to her very best friend, to the man she loved like a brother.

Finally, she slept only to be shaken from it by a disturbance in the room. It was early and her first thought was that it was Ethan or Aurora come to check Scott's wound. But as she listened and heard the familiar movements, she realized it wasn't. It was Scott—up and getting dressed.

She hauled herself up on her elbows to demand, "What are you doing?"

He favored her with a brief, distracted glance, not even with his full attention. No answer. And that hurt. It was then that she noticed he was buttoning up the vest of his fine blue serge suit. His fancy Eastern suit. Already he'd pulled on his all business narrow toed shoes. She sat up in alarm.

"Scott? Where are you going?"

He spoke while he dressed, as if in a single-minded hurry. "I'll be back before dark, or try to be."

"Before dark? You shouldn't be out of bed let alone up and around for so long."

341

"I'm fine, Gena," he argued with a touch of annoyance in his voice. Except that had to be a lie. His father had taken a bullet out of him just the day before. He had to be hurting. Most men would still be prostrate and groaning. But her husband wasn't most men. He was Lakota. "I've got some business that can't wait." He picked up some sheets of paper almost hesitantly, then quickly folded and tucked them into his coat. "It's waited far too long already. If I don't do it now, it might not get done."

"What are you talking about?" He was so somber. So intense. He was scaring her. And when he turned and finally met her gaze, she was terrified. His eyes were still glazed by that lack of life, that hollowness that reflected back none of his generous soul.

"I don't have time to explain it to you." Then, he started for the door.

"Scott!" He was frowning slightly when he looked back. "You weren't going to kiss me goodbye?"

Something flickered in his impassive face, a deep, unfailing light of love. Seeing her stark expression, her eyes welling up with tears, her hands clutched over the huge vulnerable belly, shook him from his distant determination. With her name whispering soft on his lips, he crossed to take her up in his good arm, holding her close, kissing her temple, her cheek and finally her mouth with a hard, desperate vigor. When she made a confused sound, that near assault became infinitely gentle with a tenderness she knew how to tap in him.

"Oh, Gena, I'm sorry. I love you. You know I love you and that little baby. Our baby. But I've got to go, now, and it's so hard I don't dare put it off another minute. Please let me go and believe that I love you more than anything in this life. And that there's nothing I would not do for you."

"Scott, please be careful."

"I will. I'm not the one in danger." With that cryptic claim, he kissed her again, with a long, lingering passion. "I'll see you tonight. Now, you promise me you'll take it easy. Your time's getting close and after yesterday, I don't want you taking any chances."

"I'll be good," she vowed, stroking his face, his hair, his neck and shoulders. "And I won't worry." What a lie. She was already. But she'd learned to smile as she let him go. "I love you, Scott. God speed."

After he'd gone, Gena couldn't shake off her feelings of uneasiness. Nor could she dutifully stay in bed. She rolled onto her feet and dressed slowly, rubbing her back between each stretch or bend. The tension there was really quite uncomfortable. If Scott was going to be gone on some mysterious business, she would find some way to distract herself from fretting for the sake of the baby. And she knew just what she'd do.

Ethan wasn't enthusiastic about harnessing the buckboard. But he was in favor of her plan to see Rory. She wheedled and pleaded prettily and made every promise conceivable to go slow and easy. He wanted to ride alongside but knowing he was right in the middle of installing indoor plumbing that Aurora had been begging for and that he'd snatch at any excuse to postpone it, she waved to him cheerfully and headed toward the Bar K. And she completely forgot to tell him about her nagging backache.

A backache which was in reality eight hours of first stage labor.

She was within three miles of the ranch when she realized what was happening. A terrific pain seized

343

her middle and abruptly the floorboards were puddled between her feet. She fought down the first wave of panic. The baby was coming but baby's were slow about it. The Bar K was closer and Ruth would be able to tend her until Ethan arrived. There was no reason to hurry, no reason to give way to fright. Until the second and third and fourth wringing contractions shook her. Minutes apart. Like earthquakes in their severity. Breathing hard, she urged the horse to a quicker gait but the jouncing movement seemed to hasten nature along. She bit her lips and tried to remember all the things Ethan had told her to do. Breathe deep and regular into the pangs. She gritted her teeth. How easy for a man to say when he wasn't about to drop a child in a racing buckboard. Her insides knotted and twisted tight. She clung to the seat and wailed aloud.

"Scott! Scotty!"

And miles away on the road to the state legislature, Scott Prescott reined in abruptly and looked behind him. Finally, he shook off the odd prickle of intuition and nudged the horse onward.

By the time Rory climbed up beside her, Gena was huffing and puffing intently. He took one look at the damp boards and her sweat-dappled face and swallowed hard.

"By 'now', you don't mean right now this minute, do you?"

She nodded frantically, blowing like she was trying to start wet kindling.

"Oh, no, you can't do that."

Her fingers twisted in his shirt, balling it up into tight fists. "Well, I am and I do mean now!" Another time, she might have found his petrified stare vastly amusing. "Get Ruth. She'll know what to do."

"Ruth went into Crowe Creek."

It took a minute of hard breathing for that to settle in. "You mean she's gone?"

" 'Fraid so."

"Then you'll have to do it."

"Me!" He pulled away from her and if she hadn't had such a good hold on his shirt, he looked as though he would have wiggled out of it and gone running. "I ain't doing no such thing!" he yelped. "Norah's a woman. She can help you out."

"Rory, I've never so much as held an infant let alone delivered one!" Norah cried, aghast.

"Somebody do something," Gena wailed, shaking through another tremendous cramp.

Rory and Norah exchanged wide eyed looks of uncertainty, then Norah took a deep breath. "Let's get her up to the house."

"No. Too far," Gena panted. They believed her.

"Rory, what do we do? You must have delivered calves and foals and the like. It can't be that different."

His round gaze dropped to where Gena's knees spread wide to accommodate the drop of her belly. Oh yes it was! He cast a desperate glance to the cowhands and hollered, "Any of you fellers know anything—" Before he finished, they were scattering. "Useless cowards! One of you fetch my daddy and don't spare the saddle leather."

"Rory . . ." Norah urged.

"Rory!" Gena pleaded.

"All right, already, let me think," he shouted at them. "Get her down, get her calm and check for position of the ca—baby." He eased the trembling, grasping arms around his neck. "Hang on for a second, Gena. I'm going to put you down in back. It ain't the best accommodations but it's all we got."

345

She nodded and squeezed tight. Norah ran around and dropped the tail gate, clamoring up into the straw littered wagon bed as Rory gently settled the groaning woman onto the unyielding boards. Gena scooted into a half-seated position, hanging onto Rory's arms with tense fingers.

"Oh, heck, Gena-honey, this ain't no place to be having a baby."

"Have you ever-ever known a Prescott to wait for anything to be convenient?" she panted. "This is fine." She leaned back between the spraddle of Rory's upraised knees and rested her head back on his chest. Her fingers hooked around the backs of his thighs, digging into muscle with all the pinching ferocity of a charley horse.

"Norah, you'd best take a look see," he advised nervously.

Norah eyeballed him with a wish to kill. "You should be doing this. You know what to look for."

"God'd strike me dead if I was to look under them skirts. You'll know what you're looking for when you see it."

Features tight with discomfort, Norah rolled back the other woman's hem and lacy petticoats. Then she stared in obvious shock.

"What?" Rory demanded. "What?"

"I think you'd better have her start pushing," Norah said faintly.

"All right, Gena-honey, you heard the boss lady. I want you to grab on to me as hard as you can and shove for all you're worth. That's it. Attagirl!"

"Scott," she moaned, her head thrashing weakly beneath his chin. "I want Scott!"

"He ain't here, Sis. I gotcha. Sorry to be seconds at such a time."

In a moment of brief respite, Gena fit a hand to his cheek, the one she'd emblazoned with her wrath. "Oh, Rory, I'm the one who's sorry. I didn't mean to hurt you or those things I said to you. I was on my way here to tell you that."

"Well, hell's bells, Gena, you didn't have to go dropping the baby in my lap to prove it."

Her soft chuckle became a groan. Then, she was panting again. "Oh, Rory, you always could make me laugh. What a story we'll have to tell this baby."

"Well, darlin', let's get back to work. Norah there looks about to swoon dead away."

"I am not," she snapped testily. But she hated to admit to the truth of it. Never in her life had she been exposed to this particular side of womanhood and it made her decidedly queasy. If gentle Gena Prescott could bear up under it, so could she. She looked up at the fragile woman and wondered how she'd find the strength to expel the child from her body. She looked done in, her face feverish, her fair hair matted damply about her brow. Wrapped in Rory's arms, she seemed too small to have courage so big. He was encouraging her softly, with tender, soothing words and Norah experienced an odd quiver. In that second, she could imagine him coaxing her through the process of birth, his arms hugging, his voice guiding, his love sustaining.

"Norah, how things looking?"

She shook off the fantasy and got back to the surprisingly bloody reality. She hadn't known new life came heralded by such pain and gore. She looked and gave a sudden cry.

"Oh, Gena, red hair! It's got red hair! If you want to see for yourself, you give a big, long push. Now!"

347

The three of them suspended breaths and strained in tandem to bring that baby into the world.

"A girl! A beautiful little girl," Norah cried in exultation. She lifted the slippery newborn up just as it gave a lusty howl.

"And she's got Scotty's war cry," Rory exclaimed in delight. "And Uncle Rory to beat off her beaus. Good work, Sis." He kissed her cheek soundly and helped ease the baby into her mother's arms. "You, too, Doc."

When an anxious Ethan and Aurora Prescott arrived, the trio were seated comfortably in the wagon bed cooing over the wrinkly, red infant. Shooed out of the way, Norah stood beside Rory in the yard, unaware of exactly when their hands had meshed together, but liking it. She watched Aurora's strong features melt into a helpless wonder at the sight of her first grandchild. An unfamiliar emotion closed her throat up tight. It was the crush of her hand that finally brought Rory's attention from his new niece. And he frowned in concern.

"What's this?" he asked softly, brushing a trace of dampness from her cheek.

Mortified and confused by her loss of control, Norah scrubbed at her face and muttered thickly, "Nothing." But Rory wouldn't be put off and there was no way to explain what was stirring and surging inside her.

"Norah-honey . . ."

"I'm going inside to change. I'm all—messy." With that, she bolted for the house, not stopping when she heard him calling, not slowing when she heard him cursing his infirm knee as he chased her up the steps and the stairs. Finally, outside her room, he caught up to her and jerked her around to face him.

348

"Now would you mind a-tellin' me what the—" He broke off as she cast her arms around his middle, clutching for all she was worth. He held her, puzzling over the shake in her shoulders. But he'd tried asking what was wrong before and she'd run from him. This time, he'd say nothing, waiting to follow her lead.

He didn't have long to wait. Norah reached up with both hands to pull him down to her. Her mouth was hard, aggressive upon his. Almost angry. Considering how much he'd been looking forward to it, he should have been wildly aroused. But he wasn't. Something was wrong with the desperate way she was kissing him. With the way her tongue pushed past his teeth and thrust around inside his mouth as if fishing for a marble in the bottom of a glass. Her fingers twisted in his hair, hurting. Her body arched against him, rubbing, insistent, demanding a response. And he couldn't give one. Because for some reason there was no passion in what she was doing.

Her fingers flew down the front of his shirt to open it, hands darting inside, palms moving over his chest in greedy circles. Then, when those anxious, dexterous fingers worked the front of his Levi Strauss's, she said with a growling urgency, "I want to make love to you, Rory."

"I figured that much but don't you think we'd best get behind a closed door somewheres before you go dropping my drawers around my feet?"

As if it was more annoyance than necessity, Norah opened the door to her room and herded him inside. The minute it closed, she was undressing them both with hurried tugs and anxious yanks, scattering clothes as indiscriminately as she scattered kisses. On his face, on his shoulders, on his chest, his belly. Hungry, avid kisses. Kisses that should have excited but

349

didn't. Because she wasn't excited. She was—what? Rory was confused. He caught her chin in his hand and tipped her face up. Her eyes were wide, bright. But not with desire. She was—scared?

Then she was all over him again, open-mouthed and deliberate in the placement of her hands. He felt like he was back-pedaling fast as he could down a steep hill with a runaway freight threatening to roll right over him. He tried to gentle the kiss but she'd have none of that. He tried to hold her, to slow the rushed caresses so they could take some enjoyment from each other. But Norah wasn't after enjoyment. He wasn't sure what it was she wanted from him. Other than the obvious. And it wasn't like she had to bulldog him to get his cooperation there.

What was wrong?

She was moving against him, her full breasts soft against his chest, her hips grinding over his, her hands stroking, quickening a reaction. And, hell, he was a man and he loved her more than anything. It didn't take much to goad physical need into overcoming mental reluctance. The edge of her bed bumped the backs of his legs. Off balance, he went down with Norah on top of him. While his arms flailed out like a drowning man's trying to haul them farther up on the mattress, she straddled him, rising up and slamming down. She gasped softly at the feel of his impaling fullness but almost immediately began to move, as if to wait, to savor would invite—what? Pleasure? Emotion? Engulfed by the searing, sucking heat of her body, Rory gave up the struggle. He let her ride him hard and fast with her own desperate rhythm that somehow didn't include him at all. He let her savage his mouth and cling to his shoulders with talon-like fingers. And when he felt her release quake around him, he sensed her relief rather than rapture. As soon as the last harsh spasm shook through her, Norah was off him, curling on her side with her back to him. Done with him. Not interested in touching.

Rory stared up at the tester. He was breathing hard, an unsatisfied tension clenched low inside him and a feeling of unspecified alarm holding him helpless. He had no idea what had just happened between them. She said she wanted to make love but there'd been no loving involved. Was this how the upstairs gals of Crowe Creek felt when they picked their two bits up off the night table? Physically frustrated, emotionally untouched? Used for something that had nothing to do with shared pleasure? He didn't like it. Not at all. It made him angry and incomplete. But because he loved Norah Denby, he would try to understand.

She was crying. That surprised him. She resisted when he rolled her toward him, into the circle of his arms but once there, she immediately burrowed close. She said his name once, sounding—in pain. Suddenly scared, he didn't know what else to do except hold her.

Norah gave up. It wasn't an easy surrender. She'd fought with everything she had against the crowding panic in her heart. She'd hoped with a final desperation that reaching a shattering climax would release the tension inside. That sexual fulfillment would be the answer. But it wasn't and never had been. Not with Rory. She was exhausted from waging battle. Her defenses were demolished, her resistance crushed. She felt his palm moving in slow, comforting circles along her spine. She felt his lips easing kisses atop her head and her anguish twisted tighter. Why did he have to be so nice to her? Why did he have to be such a fun-filled companion; provoking, pleasing, promising more and better things to come? Why did he have to know how to combat her every ready objection; with a broad grin, with a husky laugh, with a smoldering look, with a loving touch? How had she let herself like him so much, enjoy him so greatly, love him so completely? He'd beaten her a long time ago, back in a hotel room in Wyoming; she just hadn't been willing to concede defeat. Now, there seemed no hope for it. The truth had struck her along the strangest avenue. Through the birth of a child, through a mother's selfless struggles, through a grandmother's smile. And she couldn't fight it anymore.

Trying to think of a way to ease her weeping, Rory looked for a ready distraction. He hugged her close.

"Wasn't that little baby something? All them tiny fingers and toes. I don't think I've ever seen something so ugly and at the same time, so danged pretty in my whole life. And red hair. That's got to please Mama to no end. And maybe the major, too," he added pensively. "I didn't think something so small could make such a big noise."

"I don't want to talk about that baby," Norah cried almost angrily as she shoved away from him and rolled to her opposite side.

Rory sighed and forced down his impatience with her. He touched her shoulder, feeling it quiver in response, in rejection. He leaned down to kiss her neck, feeling her tense and tremble.

"Then let's talk about something else. Like what's wrong."

He gripped her shoulder and turned her onto her back. When she would struggle, he eased his weight over the top of her, pinning her effectively to the bed. Pinning her gaze with the intensity of his own.

"Norah-honey, please talk to me. I ain't got the slightest idea of what's going on with you. Don't shut me out like this."

She gave in with a shaky sob. The resistance, the arguments, the cold reasonings all fell before the tenderness in his request. So she told him.

"I love you, Rory."

She touched his face with trembling hands.

"I want to give you little red-haired babies."

She heard him draw a rattly breath and hold it.

"I want to marry you, Rory Prescott."

Chapter Twenty-two

For the longest time, Rory just stared. Then, he began to frown. Norah was crying, looking miserable and broken. She noticed his hesitation and sniffed.

"I thought that was what you wanted?"

"It was," he said softly. "Ever since I first laid eyes on you. It still is."

"Well, you don't look very happy about it!"

"Norah, it'd be a lot easier to be happy if you didn't go treating the idea of loving me and being my wife like it was some God-awful disease I infected you with."

But it was. Rory Prescott was a sickness in her blood, forced through her body with every helpless beat of her heart. And her system had finally succumbed. She wasn't sure that was cause for celebration. She was more frightened by the whole thing than overjoyed. And she couldn't pretend otherwise beneath his penetrating stare.

"I didn't want to love you," she told him with despairing candor. "I never wanted to marry or to be any man's wife. I'm sorry, Rory. I just couldn't stop it from happening. I'm not the sort of woman you should love. I'm not the right mother for your children. But I want to be. I want to be. I want to grow old with you. I want to lie in your arms at night. I want your mother to look down on our children with that same smile. I want to make you happy, Rory. I just don't know if I can. I don't know if I ought to even try. I feel like I should run away from you as fast and as far as I can."

"I'll follow."

"I don't want to hurt you." She stroked his cheeks tenderly. Her voice trembled. "And I don't want you to hurt me. You could. You're the first that could for a very long time."

"Norah-honey, I ain't gonna hurt you. I just want to love you. I just want to share my life with you. It ain't much, I know. I ain't no fancy aristocrat and this ain't no palace or no fine Boston townhouse. But it's yours, if you want it. I'm yours, if you want me. Do you want to marry me?"

"Yes." She said that without hesitation. That much had been true for a long time, too. And she stopped denying it. "I want very much to be your wife."

Tell him, Norah. Tell him everything. Now, before it's too late.

He began to smile, a slow, spreading smile of satisfaction. "It's settled then. Mrs. Rory Prescott. Dang that sounds pretty. You try it on for size."

"Mrs. Rory Prescott," she repeated softly. *Tell him.*

His eyes started to close, smoldering with promise. "Rory —"

His lips parted and settled leisurely over hers, shifting, sliding, as if measuring for the best fit. Eventually, he murmured, "What, honey?"

"Rory —"

"Ummmm?" He was kissing her again, dipping inside with his tongue, drenching her with his desire.

"Rory, there are some things you should know—about me."

"There are some things you should know about me, too, but I ain't gonna be the one to tell you."

She turned her head away, flustered by his teasing and his tempting. "Rory, please listen to me."

"I don't want to hear nothin'. I don't want to know nothin'. What's done, is done. It don't make no difference to me how things are right now. Hell, I know I ain't the first man to love you but like I told you, I aim to be the last one. I ain't been no saint either. I can't promise I'll be one after we're married. But I won't ever cheat on you and I won't ever lie to you. And I won't ever—ever stop loving you."

Norah heard his words with tears starting up in her eyes again. She wanted to believe them. She would believe them! For whatever reason, she'd been blessed with the chance to live her every dream through Rory Prescott. It was time to stop doubting and start living.

"I love you, Rory."

And when they made love, there was nothing hurried about it. It was slow. Sweet. Satisfying.

It had been a long, hard day, riding steady each way. His shoulder pained like the very devil, making him wish he'd taken his daddy's suggestion of a sling. Too proud. In too much of a hurry. And now the pain was pulsing all the way down to his fingertips. Tucking his hand between two shirt buttons provided some support but he was looking forward to home too much to rest and give it ease. All day, he'd been edgy and anxious to get back. So he pushed himself and his horse and he ignored the hurt like he ignored its source. He didn't want to think about that any more than he wanted to think about what he'd done. All he wanted was his own bed and his own wife beside him. And a sleep without dreams.

The house was dark and without smoke on the cool night. Scott drew in his horse and sat the saddle for a long minute, testing the sounds and smells of the evening. Cautious. No one was home. There were no signs of anyone being inside. He scanned the shadows with quick, practiced eyes. And then he saw the little roan-colored mare. Rory's horse.

Rory stepped out onto the edge of the porch and the two half brothers exchanged silent stares. Neither one gave anything away.

"Where you been?" Rory asked finally, noting the dapper suit of clothes Scott only wore when doing serious white man's business. The Sioux were more impressed by a man's actions than his wearing apparel so, as their council, he'd put away his pointy-toed shoes long ago. But he was wearing them today, along with the dirt from a long ride. And Rory wondered why. And he wondered why he was suddenly so angry with his brother's remote expression he could have cheerfully knocked him out of the saddle. Where the hell was he when his wife was crying for him? The tension between them roiled, clouding Rory's reasons for waiting on the darkened front porch.

"Had things to do."

"Must have been mighty important things for you to go tearing off with a hole in you and a wife ailing."

Scott bristled at the mildly offered criticism. How like Rory to bluntly throw it up in his face. A face growing tighter by the second. "They were. Gena's not ailing. And I'm—I'll survive. What are you doing here?" His tone implied he shouldn't be. And so did the narrowing of his eyes.

357

"Got as much right to stand on this here porch as you do," Rory drawled out. The pain, the hurt of all those past years had suddenly grown to be more than he could stand with any degree of pride. Damn Scott for his arrogance! Who did he think he was talking to? Time he told it to him straight. Time he planted his feet firm and quit his good-natured giving. And giving. And giving. Enough. "I helped Daddy replace every one of these here boards whilst you was off at your fancy school with your face in a book. Shingled the roof, built the barn, the corral, did the haying, me and Daddy. I was here every night for supper and laid up there night after night a-listening to Mama cry over you. Where were you when she was laid up sick and Daddy was out with the Northers blowing trying to save the stock? You weren't the one sitting up with her, holding her hands, begging her not to die but you was the one she was askin' for. You was the one she wanted there. Where was you when the blizzards and the droughts hit so hard we couldn't afford food on the table 'cause the animals had to be grained? I'll bet you never had an empty plate. Don't you *ever* ask what right I got to be here when you been gone half my life!" His voice broke like a dam worn weak by ten years of holding in raging waters.

Scott sat rigid, stunned by the rush of anger, wrung by guilt at the truth in his brother's words. He spoke with a quiet fierceness. "I would have been here, Rory. There wasn't a day that went by that I didn't wish I was here."

"Where was you, Scotty, when I needed you? You weren't there when I was a boy with the lonelies so bad I could howl at the moon with the coyotes. Where was you, Scotty, when I was bleeding to death after taking your bullet?"

"What?"

"Home, sweet home? Something so important to you that you couldn't wait to get back here to start ruining the love within our family? You been like a tornado dropped right out of the sky ever since you been back, tearing things up, setting folks spinning while you sit safe in the middle and let them that love you take the brunt of it. Always the grand ideas, always the big promises; to me, to Mama and Daddy, to the major, to Gena but where are you when it comes to keepin' 'em? Where are you? So don't think you can just slide in all slick and smooth as you please and shove me aside. I belong here. This is my home. You got a problem with me on this porch, you come on over here and try to move me, big brother."

"Rory, you're talking like a fool."

"What do you expect? Dumb as an ole stump, remember? Maybe I am, but I been here. For all of 'em. Makin' excuses for why you weren't. Even to Gena whilst she was callin' for you."

"What are you talking about, Rory?" He rolled off his horse to the right side, like an Indian, and advanced toward the porch with short, proddy strides. "And where is everybody?"

"You're so goll-dang smart, you figure it out."

"Where's Gena?" That was an impatient growl.

"Don't go frettin' on it, Scotty. I took care of things for you. Like always."

Scott's left arm flashed out. Fingers bunched in Rory's shirtfront and with a hard jerk, he sent his younger, bigger brother flying off the porch. "Where is she?"

Rory spun and hopped to catch his balance. "At the Bar K," he said, punctuating that with a roundhouse punch. Scott reeled back, catching himself on the porch rail. He reached up to touch his mouth and his fingers came away bloody.

Rory took a wide flatfooted stance and beckoned with all eight fingers. "Come on, Scotty. Let's see what you got. I let you beat the hell outta me ten years ago for telling you the truth about your daddy but I ain't pulling punches anymore. And I ain't takin' no more off you." He let go with another haymaker but Scott was ready, feinting back in anticipation. There was a sing of steel and a knife blade glittered in the night. Rory sucked a short breath. There wasn't a man alive he would back down to in a fight and none who'd put a caution into him once his temper was high but the sight of his brother, all cold-eyed and light on the balls of his feet with that shiver of steel waving in front of him, made him hesitate. For a second.

"You forget how to fight like a decent white man, Scotty?"

"I don't want to fight you."

"No?" he taunted softly. "You mean it don't rile you a-tall that I put that hole in you? It don't gall you something fierce that my name's on the Bar K and you got an Indian tipi out in the dirt? Mean to say you got no bones to pick with me a-tall?"

His snarl of an answer was low and animal-like. The knife blade slashed out, burying itself in one of the porch posts. The instant he released the handle, Scott followed through with a hard smack to his brother's jaw. And while Rory stumbled back, he shrugged out of his coat, slinging it aside. And kicked off his tight shoes so he could bounce lightly on his toes.

"Gall me? You being out here drinking in the grass and sky while I was breathing in the stale smells of the city? You don't know anything about being lonely. You had everything, Rory. Everything. You talk about me hurting the family. And what do you do? Throw in with that land-stealing, woman-raping, man-killing son of a—"

The smash of knuckles silenced him. Rory's voice was hard with fury. "You took his money. You let him buy you all those years in the East. Whilst he was back here thinkin' you'd come home and help him with what you learned, you was busy thinkin' on how you was gonna cut his throat."

"And I would have, too, if you hadn't stopped me. If you hadn't shot me!" His fist connected satisfyingly with the rack of Rory's ribs, driving a rattly breath out. They circled each other warily, searching for an opening, seething and panting with untapped, logic-killing anger. "You're just like him. You could have made a difference, Rory, but you're too damned dumb to open your eyes. He's got you eating out of his hand and you don't care how dirty it is. Covering up for their evil. And now you're sleeping with it, too."

Rory froze, his features pinched up with intensity. "Whatcha talkin' about?"

"Denby's daughter. You know what that man is and it hasn't stopped you from shoving up her skirts and—"

"Why you—"

Rory's swing went wide and he gave a grunt of pain as Scott's caught him low to the midsection. He managed to drive an elbow up, clacking Scott's teeth together noisily but before he could align another blow, his knees were knocked out from under him. He gripped Scott's collar and they both fell together in a tangle of flailing arms and legs.

It shouldn't have been much of a fight. Rory was lamed, Scott winded, both hampered by a bad arm. Still, they tried their best to exact a punishment on the other until faces bled and knuckles tore and breath wheezed weakly. Close-range jabs became ineffective, glancing harmlessly off the other as strength and anger ebbed into a pain they couldn't have inflicted with fists alone. When a dying punch knocked Scott back onto the dirt, unmoving, Rory dragged himself away and half-sat, half-slumped against the steps. He sucked air and swallowed tears as he watched his brother stir and finally roll up to wobbly hands and knees.

"G-Goddamn you, Scotty. Why didn't you look back? I dang-near died for you and lost a damn fine horse." He kicked out his sound leg, grazing Scott's rump and sending him sprawling again. Scott's voice came up from the dust, raw, constricted with emotion.

"Why didn't you do something for Two Sparrows? How could you let that h-happen to him and his family? It coulda been Mama and Daddy and you and me a-laying there rotting for all that bastard cares."

"You liar," Rory groaned.

They were both still for a time, breathing harshly, emptied of the senseless rage that had driven them to hurt one another. Rory forced his eyes to open and tried to glare at his fallen foe. Tried to hold to the hatred but it had blown itself out.

"Scotty, you're bleeding all over the place. C'mere and let me plug it up."

Scott kicked at the hand reaching for him. "Go — t'hell."

Rory bent with a gusty moan and snagged the band of his brother's suit pants, hauling back with all his meager strength until Scott was leaning heavily against him. He wadded up his bandana and tucked it under the seeping bandages, pressing hard against the wound to stem the flow. "Mama's gonna wear on me but good for bustin' up your pretty face."

"Yeah, well, you should see yourself." He toppled by slow degrees until resting across Rory's lap like an old battered cat. Rory held him loosely, dropping his head down until his forehead rested atop his brother's shoulder. His words were gutturals.

"I'm sorry. I woulda done something 'bout them folks if I'da had the time. Ain't nobody gonna die like that again. You got my word."

"Your word. The word of a Kincaid isn't worth the ink on a government treaty."

"The word of a Prescott."

"Awright. I'll take that." He was silent for a minute, taking deep, groaning breaths. Then they stilled. "Rory, I didn't know or I'd have come back for you. You put yourself between me an' a bullet? The race? Of course. That explains it. Whatcha do such a damn fool thing for?"

" 'Cause I love you, Scotty," was his simple reply.

"Helluva love tap you got there." He groaned and straightened with his brother's help. They leaned side by side against the porch, looking like hell, feeling worse but beginning to smile.

"And you got a kick worse than them corn squeezin's of Daddy's. 'Member them?"

Scott laughed and clutched at his ribs. "Oh, Mama was gonna skin us for sure."

"Till you started puking so hard she thought you was gonna die. I could outdrink you even then. Never knowed an Injun what could hold his liquor."

They sat in a companionable silence until Scott gave him a sudden look of remembrance. "What's

Gena doing at the Bar K?"

"I plumb forgot." Rory gave a crooked grin. The other side of his mouth was split and swelling. "She come over this morning to make you a daddy."

"A what?"

"Scotty, you got the prettiest little redheaded baby girl you ever want to see, with her mama's big blue eyes."

Scott stared at him, speechless for a long second, then hugged him around the neck with a choking vigor. His chest convulsed hard then he straightened. "Gena?"

"Said something 'bout makin' you wait two years?"

Scott laughed at that and groaned happily. His eyes turned toward the Bar K, to the one place he couldn't go to be with her, and filled up with yearning. "How long before she can come home?"

"Not till tomorrow, Daddy says."

"Tomorrow," Scott echoed miserably.

"C'mon, big brother. Get me on my feet. I come to take you to her."

Garth Kincaid stood in the doorway watching the two Prescott boys approach in a stumbling reel, hanging on to each other for a precarious balance. They were laughing as good-naturedly as two kids after their first big drunk and the sight of that easy familiarity filled the old man with a bitter panic.

He knew exactly when Scott saw him. All the unsteadiness fled. His body went ramrod straight in defiance of any personal discomfort to effect a defensive front. Noticing the difference, Rory looked up, too, then frowned between them.

"You've got my wife," Scott claimed flatly.

364

Kincaid stared at him for a long moment, then opened the door and stepped aside. "I'm not holding her here against her will."

Rory gave his brother a propelling push to get him past their grandfather. The two antagonists were stiff as a pair of hounds marking off territory. Scott angled slightly so he could keep the old man in his sight, sidling toward the stairs as if waiting for a bullet in the back. There was no forgetting the reason for his last visit or mistaking the tone of his welcome.

"She's upstairs," Rory said unnecessarily to break the tension growing thick and palpable in the hall. He crowded Scott up them, feeling the readiness to do battle ebb only after the rancher was out of sight. Then, he started looking eagerly ahead.

Gena was propped up in one of the front bedrooms, letting her new daughter hold court with her admirers. The room full of family; Scott's parents, Ruth, Norah, but she forgot them all in an instant the second she beheld her husband in the door. She didn't register her alarm at his battered appearance, or that of his brother's beside him. Her arms opened and he came into them without hesitation.

"I should have been here," he murmured huskily into the pale twist of her hair. His fingers clutched.

"Your daughter wouldn't wait. Impatient and stubborn, just like her father. Shall I introduce you?"

Scott sat back on his heels and stared at the bundle of blankets his mother held so reverently. Slowly, he stretched out his hands and Aurora came to place his child in them. She touched his cheek gently, then moved on to the door where Rory hung back from the rest of the gathering. She didn't say anything to him. She hugged him. Long and hard, then kissed his bruised face before leaving the room. Rory smiled faintly and looked back to where his brother stared down upon the sleeping infant with an awed tenderness and stroked a wisp of fluffy red hair off her forehead. His hand looked so big and brown in comparison.

"She looks perfect," he whispered. Then looked up to his stepfather for confirmation.

Ethan grinned and nodded. "That she is."

"Thank you, Daddy."

"Don't thank me, son. I got there in time to clean up. Gena, your brother and Norah did the hard part."

Scott blinked in surprise. Then, he turned and eased his daughter into the cradle of his wife's arms. And knelt for a long moment, looking at the two of them together with an expression of naked love. "You make me proud, Gena. You are my heart and my soul and my strength."

As her big eyes brimmed up with jewel-like happiness, he kissed her, softly, adoringly until she sighed his name. He leaned back just far enough for their gazes to mingle and chided quietly, "Two years? I don't think so."

Gena smiled back, thrilled by the husky note of impatient passion in his low tone. "Neither do I."

He kissed her again with incredible promise.

"This calls for a toast," Rory announced enthusiastically. "Scott, Daddy. The major's got this bottle of brandy older than the hills stashed away downstairs. What say we annoy the hell outta him by drinking it down to the last drop?"

At Scott's inquiring glance, Gena nodded and waved him away. He stood somewhat reluctantly, rubbing the chubby cheek of his peaceful daughter with his thumb. "I'll be back in a minute."

"You don't need to hurry," Gena assured him. "I'm

366

going to sleep for a week."

Scott looked up then, seeing Norah at the foot of the bed. He studied her curiously before crossing to where she stood. Her steely eyes flickered in startlement when he fit his palm to one side of her face and lightly kissed the other with a grateful whisper of, "Thank you."

"She's your great granddaughter, you know."

Garth Kincaid turned to regard his only surviving child with an impassive face. "I suppose that's technically true."

"But you have no plan to accept her as such, any more than you looked upon Scott as your grandson."

"I think you know my feelings on that fairly well by now."

"Or rather your lack of them."

He watched his daughter stride to the windows of his study. She was a handsome woman, yet as tough as any Kincaid man. There was a time when she'd been his pride and joy. Before the Sioux. Before Prescott. There were times when he'd sit among his memories in the parlor and think back upon those days; when his sons were alive and his dear frail wife was beside him back in Minnesota and his precocious daughter made his heart light with laughter. But then came the war and the butchering Santee Sioux. He and a young Aurora had come to the Dakotas to spread roots deep in its rich soil. How many things might have been different if her returning stage hadn't been raided by the Lakota. How many times had he wished in his broken soul that she had died that day along with the others. Until Rory.

"You gave me one fine son, Aurora and for that I

have always been grateful."

"I bore two sons and both are mine," she corrected stiffly. She eyeballed him warily, wondering at his direction.

"You keep the dark one. The boy is mine."

"He is my son, mine and Ethan's. Rory does not belong to you."

"Doesn't he? Ask him sometime where he belongs. He might surprise you. His home is here, on the Bar K. You and yours stick to your valley and leave him here where he's needed. And appreciated."

Aurora was silent for a long, gaging moment. "What are you talking about, Major?"

"You turned him out, Orrie, in favor of the other one. A bad bargain, if you ask me, but I'm holding you to it now."

"Turned him out? Rory? I did no such thing! I've never been partial to one of my sons over the other."

"Really?" Garth drawled out with searing disbelief. And Aurora clamped her teeth together because she realized for the first time that he might be right. Why hadn't she noticed a hint of unhappy, needy loneliness behind Rory's wide smile?

"What do you want?" she demanded coldly of the manipulative man.

"Rory. I want you to cut your ties to him. I'll leave the other one to you, safe and sound but I want the boy, here, with me. No pulling back and forth. Think on it, Orrie. Think of what's best for him, being his own man on the Bar K or being in Scott's shadow at the Lone Star."

"Being your man, you mean."

"You don't know your son. He's a Kincaid. He's got his own mind."

"Then let him use it. Don't interfere in my family. I

368

won't sell you my son any more than I'd let you give Scotty away after he was born. Rory is Ethan's son and he's Scott's brother. The Lone Star is his home and he knows it. I won't close those doors to make it convenient for you. You try to shut him off from us and you'll lose him, I guarantee it. He may be part Kincaid but his name is Prescott and he's not ashamed of it. Even if you are. You push a wedge between him and Scott and you'll regret it. I'll see that you do."

"Is that a threat?"

Kincaid faced Kincaid, neither backing down.

"No."

The three Prescott men sighed as one as the first sips of brandy slid down golden in a toast to Scott's fatherhood. Rory was quick to refill their glasses.

"What'll we lift 'em to this time?"

Ethan studied the contents of his glass and the two men he'd raised. Obviously, they'd made their peace, in the most primitive way possible — by beating it into each other. Their features were sore and lumpy, speaking of the terms they'd hammered out between them and apparently it was an acceptable truce. So he'd leave it alone.

"A toast," he called, raising his glass. "To ties that can't be broken. To family."

Rory lifted his somberly. "To family," he echoed.

Scott was slower to respond. Silently, he tipped his glass and as he drank, canted a glance toward his brother over the rim. His conscience burned hotter than the neat swallow of liquor.

Rory topped them off again and hoisted his high. "I got one." He cleared his throat and beamed widely.

"To my last few days of independence and to the woman who's saving me from it. To Norah, for finally saying yes."

Ethan sputtered in surprise but one look at his son's face made the truth plain. He was getting married to Norah Denby. And he loved her. Now that was surely something to celebrate. From out of his father's back snapping embrace, Rory turned to his brother.

"I'm holding you to your promise of standing up with me, Scotty."

Scott said nothing. He set down his untouched glass and strode abruptly from the room.

"Scotty? Damn!"

Rory caught up to him at the far turn of the porch, where the shadow lay deep and quiet as an undisturbed soul. Not so, Scott Prescott's.

"You don't want to be best man at my weddin'?" Rory asked softly, trying not to choke up on his disappointment.

" 'Course I do, Rory."

Rory frowned at that reply. "Then what's wrong? We don't have to marry up here. We can stand before the preacher at the Lone Star, like you and Gena did. Hell, I don't care where we do it. I'da married her in the hotel lobby in Cheyenne if she'd said yes the first time I asked. Or is there more to it?"

"A lot more," Scott confided flatly. "You may not want me there."

"Not want you? Why that's—Scotty, what have you gone and done?"

"I'm not sure." He refused to meet his brother's uneasy gaze. "The right thing, I thought. Now, I'm not so sure."

"Scotty, what did you do?" Rory demanded quietly.

He could feel panic swelling and a helpless anger shaking and he hated those emotions. "Where were you today?"

"Seeing to things I should have done a year ago. And now I'm thinking I should have left them alone." He looked up suddenly and Rory's insides froze beneath the solemn intensity of his stare. "Rory, how much of the Bar K is in your name? How many of its assets do you personally control?"

"The house and the one sixty it's on is mine. My money's tied up in investments an' improvements to the land. Why? Why you askin', Scotty?"

"I don't want to see you left with nothing."

"Nothing? Hell, Scotty, half of everything you can see from horizon to horizon is mine."

"Not for much longer if things take hold. Because the fences are coming down, Rory, and Garth Kincaid is falling with them."

He had no chance to question him further on that upsetting bit of information. Ethan, Aurora, and Garth stepped out onto the porch. Aurora approached them, her footsteps slowing at the sight of their grim expressions. She went to Rory and put her arms around his neck, bending him down so she could kiss his cheek. He grew puzzled when she didn't release him right away.

"Your daddy and I love you, Rory," she told him with a quiet fierceness.

"Well, shucks, Mama, I know that."

"See that you remember it."

When she stepped back, Rory retained her hand. He'd spotted Norah coming out onto the porch and began towing his mother toward her. Aurora followed, bemused by his sudden flush of anticipation. And by his direction. Still claiming her hand, he put his arm

371

around Norah's shoulders to draw her into his side. He kissed her gently, not noticing the way she had stiffened.

"Mama, Major, Norah and me's fixing to get married."

They stared, both too good at concealing their true thoughts to give anything away. Finally, Garth murmured, "Congratulations, son. Kinda sudden, isn't it?"

"Not to me. Feels like years! But I finally got her to say yes."

Norah grew hot under Aurora's pointed scrutiny. Only the safety of numbers — and Rory's protective presence, kept his mother's tongue in check. She could see the question, though, and knew it would be asked eventually. *What do you want with my son?*

Ethan stepped forward to give his son's intended a hearty kiss on the temple. "That's grand news, Norah. It'll be good to have you in the family."

"Yes," Aurora agreed with a cool reserve.

How had Gena managed to win her over, Norah wondered. She would have to ask. It would seem safer to drag a pup out of a she-wolf's lair than to snatch up one of Aurora Prescott's sons.

"We got to get going. Scotty, you coming?" Ethan waited, sympathizing with his stepson's distress as he glanced back toward the house.

"No, Daddy," Rory put in firmly. "Scotty'll be staying on as long as his family's here." He looked at his grandfather calmly, finalizing that offer with a steady stare. "C'mon, Scotty. Let's get us another look at that little critter."

As Aurora swung up on her horse, Ethan lingered on the porch beside Garth Kincaid, smiling amiably.

372

He looked through the door into the house, watching his two boys walk toward the stairs with Norah between them.

"You know, Major, them two is everything to me. Them and their mama. Something happens to them, it affects me, too. If tomorrow, a bolt of lightning was to come down out of the sky and strike Scotty dead, I wouldn't go cursing God. I'd come straight to you. Because that's who I'd blame. You get my meaning?"

"I don't—"

"And you'd better not. 'Cause you see, Major, if anything was to happen to anyone in my family, act of God or not, I'm coming to see you about it. And when I leave, you'll wish Scotty had snatched your hair. I seen my share of folks dying and know all there is to know about killing ugly. 'Evening."

Chapter Twenty-three

With a groaning sigh, Rory dropped down on the edge of his bed. He hurt. He ached. He lacked the simple strength to reach down to take off the stiff-soled moccasins. Not only was he bruised in body but battered in mind, as well.

The fences are coming down and Garth Kincaid with them.

Now just what the blazes had he meant by that?

He knew his brother. He knew Scott wasn't given to dramatics or false doomsaying. If he gave warning, there was reason for worry.

What had he done?

Left with nothing.

That put a purely terrifying pause to his thinking. Could that happen? Could all those glorious acres of Kincaid grass be snatched away from him? No. Not now. Not when the future had taken on a new importance.

"Here. This should make it better."

Cool fingers slipped under his chin to tip his face up. An even cooler cloth blotted gently over his colorful swellings. He let his eyes close, let Norah soothe the surface ails with her light touch. She made a distressed noise. It was the same kind of female fussing he'd heard from his mama and from Gena when they were lovingly chastising their men. He liked the sound. He liked the attention enough not to care if she chose to scold him. And she did.

"Grown men acting like a couple of boys. And with Gena waiting here beside herself with worry. You two should be ashamed of yourselves. What did you hit each other with? Fence posts?" The sight of his smile made her tone sharpen. "Honestly. I don't know how your family puts up with it. If you think I mean to, you've got another thing coming! I've got better things to do than spend my time patching up your face."

"Yes, ma'am," he murmured, unrepentently.

"Pair of fools." Contrarily, her fingertips moved in a tender caress along the lumpy line of his cheekbone. "What were you fighting about?"

"Oh, you might say it was a little discussion on brotherly love."

"You might, but I wouldn't. Not if you could have seen the two of you standing in that doorway looking like somebody ran a train over you. I hope Gena's giving your brother a piece of her mind."

"She won't be. She's a right reasonable woman."

"And I'm not? Are you saying I'm not?"

"I love you, Norah." He said that suddenly, with a surprisingly somber sincerity. And her disagreeable mood was quickly clipped.

"Oh, Rory," was all she could say before lowering down to taste the truth of it on his lips. He winced slightly at the initial pressure but that didn't stop him from an intense response. His arms circled her trim waist, pulling her between the straddle of his legs. At the end of their kiss, he rested his bright head against her middle and hugged her fiercely. He was panting. Not with passion. With panic.

"Don't leave me, Norah."

375

Her fingers lost themselves in the thick flame of his hair. She smiled, thinking he meant for the night and promised, "I wasn't planning to."

Rory's eyes squeezed shut. *Left with nothing.* What the hell had he meant by that! His embrace tightened. His anxiety tripled. What chance would he have of keeping Norah if the Bar K folded? Would she run just as far and as fast as she could? *I want fine things. I want money, lots and lots of money.* Was that all he had to offer her? And if he didn't have it? Would he still have her?

"Would you be a-marrying me if I was jus' a plain ole month-to-month, outta-the-saddle cowboy?"

He heard Norah's soft chuckle and his heart seized up. "That's the man I fell in love with," she said teasingly.

"But would you a-said yes to that man?"

Thinking he was trying to playfully extort pride-inflating assurances from her, she told him, "I gave up a palace for you, Rory Prescott. I gave up living like a queen to rule over an empire of cows with you."

"This ain't exactly no soddy." She hadn't answered his question. Or had she?

"Thank God for that." The weight of his head moved with the magnitude of her sigh. "I'm looking forward to the rest of my life right here with you."

He leaned back, looking up at her with an almost feverish urgency. "Then marry me now. Tonight."

Norah laughed softly and rubbed her palms over the tense angles of his face.

"Norah, I mean it."

Seeing that he did, she smiled and shook her head. "You are the most impatient man. I haven't even told my father yet."

"Then tell him now. We can ride into Crowe Creek and—"

"And what? Rustle the preacher out of his bed in the middle of the night? Gena would kill us both if she wasn't there. She was actually crying when we told her. A couple of days won't change anything. I'm not going to change my mind."

"I just want you so much!"

"I'm not going anywhere."

He wrestled her down onto the bed. It wasn't much of a fight. It wasn't as though she resisted. He was quickly over her, covering her with his weight, with his kisses, with his caresses. As if they hadn't made love that afternoon. As if they wouldn't be every night for the rest of their lives. Hurried hands were at her voluminous skirts, at the uncomfortable snugness of his jeans. A hard thrust joined them for a rough, elemental mating. Norah moaned in abandon beneath him, clutching at his forearms, writhing in a tangle of excess clothing to entwine her legs around his. Reaching, straining for the rapture he would bring her. His big hand moved under her hips, lifting her up to him, opening her more fully to receive him deep inside where the abrupt and powerful pull of her body's release spilled him close to the womb. As he spent himself with a hard, completing shudder, Rory prayed the seed he sowed would cling with the same desperate vigor with which he held to her. That a child might grow to bind them together. Forever.

Love her until she's too weak to talk or walk or think about leaving you.

Norah lay breathless and deliciously mashed, inside and out. Rory hadn't moved off her. Nor had he relaxed in the aftermath of their union. He was taut, trembling like a spring wound too tight. The urgency of his kiss startled her with its forceful demand. And so did the slow, increasingly strong stroking of his maleness within the wet walls of her body. She was far

377

from ready for this renewed and unexpected on-slaught of passion.

"Rory?" Then she gasped at the sudden vigor of his movements. Her hands fluttered up, catching hold of his slick shoulders. And barely recovered from the first wild ride of pleasure, she found herself anticipating the next just as eagerly at the direction of her big, lusty cowboy.

But it wasn't lust or passion that drove Rory Prescott. It wasn't a potent dash of virility that brought him alive so quickly, that had Norah softly keening beneath him while the sheen of satisfaction was still damp upon her. It wasn't the search for exquisite pleasure or even an awareness of it. He was motivated by a deep, consuming terror. And he spoke of it to her as finally his life pumped into her a second time.

"Don't leave me, Norah. Don't ever leave me."

"I won't," she vowed weakly as he collapsed over her. "I'll be here as long as you want me."

And that answer finally relieved him.

"I hear congratulations are in order."

Cole's dry tones were hardly enthused. Norah scowled at him over her cup of breakfast coffee.

"And just where is your Romeo this morning so that I might give him the benefit of my fatherly advice?"

"He rode over to the Lone Star with Scott, Gena and the baby. You stay away from him, Cole."

He reacted to her dire warning with a lift of his brows. "Now wouldn't that seem a little odd? It's not every day a man gives away his only daughter. At least let me wish the boy well. After all, he's going to be like family to me. Just like you, dear Norah."

"I want you out of here, Cole."

"What?"

"You heard me. I want you packed up and out of my life."

"Well, now," he drawled out slowly. "I don't know about that. This here is a mighty good job. I could be living in the lap of it for at least another six months or so."

Her hands clenched around her coffee cup, just as her insides clenched around the terrible fear that he meant to cause trouble. She thought for a second, grasping for the leverage to force him out of her future. Of course, there was only one thing that motivated Cole Denby to do anything. Fondness for her wasn't it. Money. "I don't care what it's going to cost me. Everything I have saved, it's yours. Take it all. Just leave us alone."

She'd guessed right. She could see the rapid calculation of greed possess his stare. Weighing the best possible payoff. She couldn't have the threat of him darkening her hopes.

"I don't want your money, Norah."

She almost sobbed aloud. She wasn't one to beg. She knew better than to throw herself on Cole's nonexistent mercies. Not knowing what else to do, she told him the plain and simple truth.

"Please, Cole. I love him."

He studied her then, seeing the distress in her fine features, seeing the anguish shimmering in the usually clear chill of her gaze. Somewhat amazed, he said, "I do believe you mean that."

She nodded jerkily. Her eyes pleaded.

"Oh, what the hell. It's only money."

He came around the table and embraced her tightly. For a moment, Norah was tense and disbelieving, waiting for him to pull her hope out from under her. It couldn't be this easy. Could it be Cole Denby had a heart after all? He kissed her cheek lightly, with

379

a warm affection. The breath sighed from her in sudden relief.

"He'd better make you happy," he muttered direly. "If he doesn't, you look me up. I'm sure going to miss you."

She leaned back, wiping at her damp cheeks. "If you ever need anything, Cole," she paused to grin, "don't come to me for it."

He laughed and fingered her chin fondly. "I wish you well, Norah."

And she believed he meant it.

"I'll leave tomorrow. That soon enough for you?"

"Fine," she murmured gratefully. "And leave the cash box."

"Oh, Madame, you wound me to the quick. Don't worry. I've feathered my nest quite nicely off the Bar K's generosity so I won't be hurting for quite some time. You have a good life, Norah. God knows, you deserve it."

Rory clomped into the house, enjoying the rattle of his spurs. It felt good to be back in his boots. His knee was strong. He barely limped at all. And his daddy said in a couple more weeks, his hand would be good as new — if he could keep out of fights that long. His body was healing, his heart was full. Now if only his mind could find some ease.

He hadn't had a chance to talk to Scott, not with Gena and the baby, Dawn, rightly occupying his attention. It hadn't seemed fair to distract him from his happiness. There'd be other opportunities to delve into the meaning of his ominous words. Until then, he'd keep his thoughts busy with other things, like . . .

"Rory!"

He turned just in time to catch her as Norah lunged at him. Her arms whipped around his neck. Her mouth took his with a purely ravenous passion. The propelling force of her embrace unbalanced him and when he tried to take a steadying step back, his heels hit the bottom of the staircase. He went down gracelessly on his rump with Norah stretched out on his chest, kissing him so wildly, he was able to overlook both bruising to his backside and the indignity of being sprawled out on the stairs. His arms went around her middle, crushing her close until her fiery greeting eased to a long, tantalizing exchange of mouth to mouth communication. Then she lifted up to smile down at him.

"I love you, Rory Prescott!"

"I never would have figured."

"I wanted to do that this morning but you were in such a hurry, I didn't get the chance."

"Self-preservation, darlin'. If you'd a done that this morning, I'da never been able to drag myself outta bed. After all yesterday's lovin', you're plumb lucky I'm alive! Good thing I'm naturally bowlegged or I wouldn't be walking a-tall."

"Are you complaining?" Her fingertips teased over his generous mouth as it spread for a wide grin.

"No, ma' am. Jus' saying you'd best not be planning on no Saturday night ride tonight or you'll be disappointed. Lessen it's our wedding night." His dark eyes flared hopefully. "Marry me today, Norah-honey! Let me take you to bed as my wife!"

Norah evaded his hot, seeking lips and laughed. "Rory Prescott, you are impossible!"

"That mean no? Aww, Norah. This waitin' is killin' me!"

"Tomorrow."

"What?"

"How's tomorrow sound? Can you wait that long?"

With a window-rattling, "Whooeee!" he gripped her face between his hands and kissed her hard. Then with cherishing tenderness. Abruptly, he sat up, setting her back from him. "I got so much to do! I gotta get me something to wear an' grab up a preacher an' tell my folks."

She delighted in his flustered excitement. "We could wait another day," she suggested.

"No! Heck, no! I ain't waitin' another minute more than I have to. I'll be ready. Iffen I can get you off my lips and outta my lap long enough." His expression went suddenly still and achingly serious. His fingertips charted one soft cheek. "I love you, Norah. We're gonna be so happy."

She smiled. And she finally believed it.

With his new suit of "marryin' an' buryin' clothes" rolled up behind his saddle, Rory reined his little roan mare up in front of his family's front porch. He was all grins when he burst in on them. First, he knelt beside the maple cradle that had rocked both him and his brother to smile down at his new little niece. An incredible feeling of awe swept over him for the tiny person he'd help bring into the world. And knowing that someday he'd be rocking his and Norah's baby in the same cradle twisted that tenderness tighter. A baby. His and Norah's. His own family. He'd never really thought of it as such a responsibility before. Then he glanced up to where Scott and Gena were sitting side by side. His brother's arm was secured about Gena's fragile shoulders and his expression was positively doting. Rory had never seen him look so content, so secure with his place in the world. Family did that to a man. Gave him roots. A place to belong that went beyond a roof and a piece of ground. And Rory wanted that for himself.

"Ain't she gonna look up at me or smile or nothin'? Heya, Dawn-honey, it's your Uncle Rory come a-callin'." Ignoring Scott's frown of warning, Rory prodded the still blankets with his forefinger. "Daddy, you sure she's all right? Seems like all she ever does is sleep."

"Count your blessings," was Ethan's wry reply.

"You ain't gonna name her something all full of them Lakota vowels, are you Scotty? Gena, you ain't gonna have folks calling your little girl some unpronounceable thing that means 'Bird with Two Red Wings' or 'Pretty Thing With Mean-Tempered Daddy' are you?"

She laughed but Scott leaned forward to cuff at his bright head. "How 'bout 'Poor Girl with Stupid Uncle'?" he growled.

"Stop it, you two," Gena warned, "or I'll be naming her 'Lucky Child With No Living Male Relatives'."

The point taken, Scott and Rory grinned at each other and then looked with a proud male protectiveness down upon the sleeping child. All teasing aside, Scott told him, "She'll take on a Lakota name when she's about four. They're given by the mother's mother or by a medicine man to honor something the Great Spirit has created."

Knowing Gena's family in Boston had severed all ties when she'd married his brother, Rory asked, "Who you gonna get to name her?"

"Daddy," Scott said as he looked up at Ethan Prescott through respectful eyes. "*Wasichu Waken.* White Miracle Man."

"Anything but 'Poor Girl with Stupid Uncle', all right, Daddy?" He watched the blankets wiggle and still with an increasing fullness around his heart. "I gotta get me one of these."

"You've had plenty of time to figure out how it's done," his father drawled.

"That was jus' practicing, Daddy, so's I'd get it right when the time come to make something as pretty as this here little darlin'. Jus' waitin' on the right woman." And he'd finally found her. Smiling, he leaned over to press a kiss to Gena's cheek. "How ya feeling, Sis? Like you could get up and around tomorrow?"

"Like I could dance a reel with you," she said agreeably, bemused by his infectious grin. Something was simmering behind his flashing dark eyes.

"I might jus' call you on that. Oh, 'fore I forget." He pulled a bulky letter out of his pocket and handed it to Scott. "This come for you in town. Tole 'em I'd bring it out to you."

Scott looked at it curiously and broke the seal.

Just then, Aurora came in from the kitchen to exclaim, "I declare, he smelled that pie all the way over at the Bar K. I suppose you'll be wanting supper."

"No, ma'am," Rory vowed as he climbed to his feet and went to embrace her boisterously. "Couldn't eat a thing."

Aurora pulled back and put her hand up to his forehead. She was frowning in concern. "Are you all right?" He did look flushed, almost feverish. "You're not coming down with a touch of something, are you?"

"Yeah," he told her with a grin. "Cold feet. I come over to invite you all to a weddin' tomorrow. Figured I'd best let you know, seeing as how I'm having it here. If you don't mind, Mama." His dark eyes beseeched eloquently.

"Norah?"

"Who else? A 'course, Norah. I love her, Mama."

Aurora's voice was tempered with caution and care for her youngest son. "Are you sure she's the one, honey? Are you sure she'll be content so far from the cities and the social life?"

"What're you saying?" His brow began to furrow.

"Have you given it enough thought? You haven't known each other that long. Does she know how lonely life is out here?"

"I'll see she ain't lonely, Mama." He grinned with confidence. "And she'll have Ruth an' Gena an' little Dawn. An' you to take her in an' show her how to get along, the way you did Gena. You will, won't you, Mama?"

Aurora said nothing. She was studying his face. Seeing his youth, his blind devotion, his big heart. His loneliness. Remembering Norah Denby's cool steel gaze and her air of sophistication.

"Mama, I love her."

And she could see that he did. And she knew what obstacles love could overcome. "We'll make her feel welcome, Rory," she promised with a gentle touch to his cheek.

"Thanks, Mama." He squeezed her hard. Then, from over her shoulder, he saw Scott's face.

Scott looked up from the papers clutched in his hands to his brother. For a brief second, his expression was clear as glass. He was disconsolate. A terrible anguish welled up in his eyes, then, with a blink, was gone.

"Rory, I need to talk to you for a minute."

That was said low and soft but all sorts of warnings roared through Rory Prescott. *Not now. Not now, Scott.* He wanted to back away from whatever brought such despair to his brother's golden gaze. Tonight, on the eve of his future, he didn't want to hear what it was.

But Scott was standing, looking grim as a grave-

385

stone. Sensing something was wrong, Gena caught his hand and she was surprised to see the broken heart in his eyes when he bent down to kiss her. Such a sweet, anxious kiss.

"Scott?"

"I'll be right back."

"What?"

His eyes lifted, following the extreme reluctance of the figure moving out onto the porch. His mouth thinned with pressure. "God, I hate this."

"Scott, what's in those papers?" She was truly alarmed now by his distraught mood and by how it would affect Rory's happiness.

"That's up to Rory."

Rory was standing at the edge of the steps. His posture was stiff with tension. He looked as though he was considering bolting from the Prescott house to escape whatever words he was about to hear. That taut line of defensive terror increased when Scott moved up beside him.

"Can it wait, Scotty?" he asked. It was a quiet, almost desperate plea. "Until after tomorrow?"

"No."

"Scotty, don't. Please." He left the rest unspoken. *Please don't ruin everything for me. Let me have just one day, one perfect day. Can't it keep that long?* He flinched under the feel of Scott's hand on his shoulder. Fingers dented flesh, the muscles beneath it. Foretelling disaster and pain. Rory wanted wildly to shrug off that bracing hand. But he couldn't. Any more than he could deny whatever tragedy Scott was about to hand him. All he could do was prepare as best he could.

"Let's get it done," he said at last.

"I'm sorry." Then Scott handed him the stack of folded pages and waited, watching his brother's world crumble.

Never in his most far-flung imaginings, did Rory expect the heart-savaging shock he received upon looking at the first page. He tried to draw a rejecting breath. It strangled noisily in his throat. He might have disbelieved the first sheet, but there on the second, was the same damning truth. And it hurt like hell. Great, consuming waves of hurt, folding his life, his dreams in on top of him, like a building put up on a weak foundation. The papers rattled frantically in his hands as he looked numbly at the next one.

"A mistake." That faint, futile hope moaned from him.

"No. I wish it was," came his brother's emotion-thick words. "I'm sorry, Rory. I didn't want to see you get hurt."

"Aww, gee, thanks a helluva lot," he choked out through the distress clogging his voice. His chest was jerking hard, struggling with the sobs working their way up. His mouth trembled with them, then, resolutely firmed. The shuddering breaths eased into a dazed sort of calm as he stared up blindly at the waking stars. He closed his eyes and that pure, soft light shimmered along the trail of wetness tracking his face.

"Rory? Scott?"

"Just a minute, Mama," Scott called back toward the house and the family inside. Helplessly, he waited for his brother to digest the bitterness of fate, feeling his agony so acutely, his heart ached with it. He laid his hands on the beaten slump of shoulders, giving them a supportive press. "What can I do?" he asked.

A tremendous sigh lifted and dropped his hands. "Go on an' shoot me. I'm dead inside already."

"Rory . . ." His thumbs kneaded. His soul reached out wanting to give some kind of comfort — knowing he couldn't.

"I can't go back in there. You tell 'em for me, Scotty."

"All right."

Rory swallowed. The need to wail out loud rose up, colliding with that downward movement, creating a huge knotty ache. But he wasn't a Lakota like his brother, who could cry his sorrows to the heavens and be cleansed of grief. He was a Prescott and a Kincaid and supposedly, tougher than that. So, slowly, carefully, he refolded the papers in his hands and forced the dry lump of misery down.

"What are you going to do, Rory?"

His shoulders squared. A sleeve scrubbed across his face, erasing the signs of weakness. And in a surprisingly strong voice, he said, "I'm going to get me some answers."

It was a beautiful night; fresh, clear, the beginning of a whole new tomorrow. Tomorrow. When she'd become Mrs. Rory Prescott.

Norah hugged her arms around herself and sighed happily up at that peaceful Dakota sky. Tomorrow she would put the past behind her. All the anger and loneliness chafing her soul would be washed away in a baptism of love. Who would have thought? Rory Prescott, the teasing, sultry-eyed cowboy who'd swept her off her feet was going to give her all the things she'd never dared hope for. An elegant home. A good family. Enough love to live on for a lifetime. Why had she fought against it for so long? Habit. She'd been fighting all her life, not for happiness but just for simple survival. Now she wouldn't have to struggle alone. She'd have Rory for her champion. All wrapped up in his surrounding care, she'd at last found the strength to test the threads of tender emotion. And they held.

Rory Prescott had woven a fabric of devotion about her that would wear forever. And it felt so good, so warm, so snug. She loved the sense of isolation here at the Bar K. It meant she'd be safe and secure to start over. Good things could take root and grow with Rory's passionate nurturing. How had she gotten so lucky to find this one-in-a-million man? No, she wouldn't question it. She'd just accept and be thankful. And she'd make him such a good wife. She had enough examples to follow now. Gena would help her. If the frail Eastern flower could soften the stoic savage in Scott Prescott, she would know how to corral and tame the rowdy cowboy in his brother. If she wanted him tamed. And she wasn't sure she did.

Just then, she heard his approach and smiled. A full gallop. Would she want it any other way? No.

Long minutes passed as she waited on the porch for him to put his horse away and come up to the house. She heard the swaggering jingle of his spurs before she actually saw him emerge from the darkness. By then, her heart was pounding madly, joyfully and she ran to meet him as he mounted the steps. She said his name and he turned to her. His look stopped her dead.

"Rory?" A terrible dread seized her. "What's wrong? Is it Gena? The baby?"

She started to reach for him but before contact was made, he caught her wrist. And with a firm, purposeful control, pushed her away.

She knew.

He knew.

His eyes were flat, black, and scary because there was no light behind them. He looked at her emotionlessly as if he'd never seen her before in his life. And the panic swelled inside her. Frantically, she fought to hold to her composure. *Say something,* her mind screamed out. *Say anything.*

"Rory . . ." It was a croaking whisper.

With that same methodical gravity, he pulled a packet of papers from his shirt and held them out to her. Norah took them in trembling hands. And then he spoke to her in a cold, lifeless voice.

"Which one of them thieving liars is you, Norah?"

Chapter Twenty-four

Wanted by the State of Colorado for fraud. Wanted San Francisco for embezzlement. Wanted by the authorities of Texas for robbery and extortion. Wanted in Chicago for embezzlement and fraud. Wanted by the State of New York for theft and securities fraud.

Cole Dirbin alias Darby, alias Denby, alias Benton, alias Barton and his female accomplice.

Norah looked at each of the dodgers in turn. So many. Lining up her past from state to state, crime to crime. Leading an accusing trail right into the heart of South Dakota. What was the use in denying it?

"He ain't your daddy. What is he? Your lover?"

"Once," she answered numbly. "A long time ago."

Muscles spasmed along his tight jaw. She could hear his knuckles pop where his hands clenched into fists at his side. "Made a fool outta myself with a woman with a reputation longer than Belle Starr's. At least there's some comfort in knowin' I'm in plenty of good company."

He strode toward the house and Norah raced to put herself in front of him. Her hands braced on his chest to stop him. They clutched desperately in the fabric of his shirt. Her voice was a shaky plea.

"Rory, please . . ."

"Take-your-hands-off-me." Each carefully enunciated word was like a consecutive slap.

She let him go but she refused to let him get past her unless he chose to use force. For the moment, he stood, staring down at her through those blank, killing eyes. So she rushed ahead while she had his attention.

"Rory, let me explain."

"I'll bet you can," he drawled fiercely. "I'll bet you're good at explaining. Lady—and I use that term very loosely—I don't want to hear it."

"Yes you will! Damn you, Rory Prescott, you will listen to me! I love you!"

His expression crumpled. "Awww God." He turned away from her and walked to the rail to lean heavily upon its support. "Woman, ain't you got no shame a-tall?"

"No," she cried forlornly. "No, I don't. Not where you're concerned. Please. You've got to believe me."

"Oh, I did. I believed every word you said. Every damn lie, one right after the other."

"I tried to tell you, Rory. You know I did. You told me the past wasn't important. You told me it didn't matter to you. And _I_ believed you."

"Not matter? I thought you was gonna confess the names of the man—or men—you'd been with. I didn't know you was hiding a stack of Wanted posters thicker than my family Bible!"

"So it does matter," she concluded with a quiet desolation.

He said nothing. His rigid posture said it for him. She was losing him. She was losing everything.

No! She wouldn't just give him up. She wouldn't!

"Don't you want to know why?" she asked with a provoking thrust.

His broad shoulders rose and fell. "I guess," he replied dully.

Oh, God, how she must have hurt him! Tears trembled in her eyes. Sobs quivered in her throat. But she denied both. She wouldn't apologize for the past. The facts wouldn't change no matter how she wept and wailed. So she would give them to him, point blank. Then maybe — maybe, he would understand. Then maybe he could forgive her.

"My mother raised me in a dirty little soddy in the middle of a Nebraska plain. We had nothing, Rory. You can't know how that feels. How spirit-breaking, how empty. My father worked along the railroad so we saw him maybe a half dozen times a year when he showed up to see if we were still where he left us. He told her things would get better, that he'd get a regular job and settle down so we could have nice things, pretty things. And she believed him. She believed everything he told her. So did I, for a while. Then the months between his visits got longer and longer. I told my mother we were foolish for waiting, that if we wanted those fine things, we'd have to get them for ourselves. But she wouldn't listen to me. She kept right on believing. Until he didn't come back. Still, we stayed out on that damned dusty prairie with nothing to eat, with no place to go, with no one to look out for us. We would have starved to death if a family hadn't passed by and offered to take us to the closest town. Even then, she didn't want to go but I made her. I was ten years old."

Rory closed his eyes and tried to harden his heart. He didn't want to think of Norah coming from such a wretched existence. Still, he told himself, it was no excuse. No excuse. And he kept repeating that, over and over as she continued.

"The town we went to was one of those shabby

places, like Crowe Creek, with two saloons for every decent building. My mother was an attractive woman, then. A real slick, handsome *gentleman* started paying court to her, buying her presents and after a while, she got to believing everything he told her, too. She believed him when he said it was just a favor to him to make a friend feel welcomed in town. And then it got to be another friend, then two or three a week. Then every night. And my mother believed him when he told her he loved her. Her and every one of his other girls he had working on their backs to make him money. I told my mother what he'd turned her into but she wouldn't listen. She was weak. She needed a man to tell her what to do, even if it was a bad man. She was used to being dependent on a man for her existence, even the worst sort who used her and lied to her and made her old and ugly because she didn't know how to think for herself. But I wasn't going to be like her."

Rory wanted to stop her. He didn't want to hear where this story was leading. He didn't want to know the kind of woman Norah really was. He wanted desperately to keep his memories safe. But that wasn't possible. No more possible than clinging to a dream.

Norah watched him, trying to read something from the tense and flex of his shoulders, trying to guess if she was reaching him. She didn't want his pity. She wanted him to see, to feel how it was for her when she'd had to make her choices. But how could he, having never known anything beyond the warm embrace of family. And that brought a tang of bitterness to bear on what she told him. She would make him feel how horrible and dirty her existence was, even if she had to shock him right down to the soles of his fancy-stitched boots to do it.

"I was going to school, trying not to hear what the

394

other children said about my mother. By the time I was fourteen, the boys started looking at me with something new in their eyes. I should have been going on picnics and on walks and to dances with them but they only wanted one thing from me—because of what my mother was. And I hated every one of them for thinking I was just like her." Her fingers bit into her arms as she hugged them about herself in an insulating gesture, as if even now, she could hear their taunts, could feel the pawing of the adolescent boys who were sure she was playing some game with them. Only it hadn't been a game to her. It was never a game to her.

"About then, Mother's *friend* decided I was old enough and certainly pretty enough to start earning my own way. And so, one night when Mother was busy entertaining, he came into our room and he held me down and he showed me exactly what his customers would be expecting from me."

Fourteen. *God.* Rory squeezed his eyes tighter. His fingers whitened on the porch rail. Barely into long skirts. Just starting to wear her hair up. Taught the facts of life in the most brutal way possible. His mind burned with horrible images, of a young Norah, fighting, frightened, struggling against an unstoppable force bent on tearing her innocence from her. Hearing the agony of remembrance in her tone brought a vivid picture to torment him. It broke through the walls of indifference and anger he'd been trying to erect. He heard her pain and it twisted inside him. And he turned, despite everything, thinking to comfort her in her vulnerable despair.

Except there was nothing vulnerable about the woman he saw. And nothing familiar. She wasn't crying or even close to it. Her features were as hard and unapproachable as a steep canyon wall. There was a

395

glitter to her gaze as she stared out toward a far horizon that reminded him of Scotty's blade streaking toward the vitals. Cold. Deadly. If she was hurting, she contained her pain well and there was no invitation in her stiff stance that would lend to his offer of compassion. This was a Norah he didn't know. The one whose description was printed on the posters. And the sight chilled him.

"When he was through," Norah continued in that same thick voice, "he told me I'd be his number one money-maker. I would have killed him if I'd had the chance. And I made a promise when he left me bleeding on my mother's bed that I would never let a man hurt me again. Ever! No man was going to use me for his pleasure in exchange for a couple of coins. I would never feel that helpless again." She remembered that vow. The circumstances came flooding back; the pain, the degradation, the suffocating panic, the feeling of being worthless. And the anger came surging up through the well-spring tapped that day, a strong, fierce anger and a pride that said *No More. Not Again.*

"That's when I met Cole. He was supposed to have been my first paying customer. He saw that I was green and scared half to death and so he sat down and suggested we just talk. He had different ideas, big ideas of how I could use my brains and my looks to escape the trap my mother was in. Anything was better than that—anything! So I went off with him, right then, that very night. And he taught me how to be clever, how to be independent, how to use those who use others."

"And about loving." Rory added that in a strange flat tone. The shift from father-daughter to man-woman acted queerly upon his senses, part disgust and part jealousy.

"No. He taught me how to make the most out of

396

being with a man. You taught me about loving."

He glanced at her. The cut of disbelief in his dark eyes slashed her heart but she dared him to disagree out loud with the challenge of her returning gaze. Instead, all he would say was, "And is he still teaching you?"

"No. It's always been business first with Cole and me. The other wasn't to our mutual best advantage."

Rory grimaced. How ruthless that sounded. Why hadn't he ever seen it, this cold, mercenary side of her, lurking like a dark, sinister shadow behind the Norah he knew? Feeling sick inside, he asked, "And what kind of business were you in?"

Norah shrugged casually. "Get rich quick schemes mostly. Getting others to invest their money to his benefit. With me playing his daughter, he was less suspect. And I was the pretty bait, leading them by their lusts into Cole's ventures."

"Like you did with me," Rory observed with a dangerous quiet.

"No." Her answer was firm, almost compellingly believable. If one could believe a liar. "I never meant for that to happen, Rory. I paid you back."

Out of conscience, he wondered, or in order to have the greater gain? His expression must have mirrored his doubts, for Norah frowned slightly. She put out her hand to touch his and he jerked back as if she represented something loathsome. Her lips trembled then thinned.

"I tried to warn you away, Rory. You're the one who forced yourself into our lives, not the other way around. Monthaven was the mark, not you. It was never supposed to be you."

"Because you love me," he drawled out with an icy venom.

"Yes."

The corners of his mouth quirked tightly. "And how many of the men you conned out of their fortunes did you bed down with first?"

Eyes swimming with unshed tears, she met his stare pridefully, silently. She refused to answer. Instead, she reminded, "I tried to keep you from getting hurt. I did everything I could to discourage you but you just wouldn't stop. And then, I didn't want you to stop. You know I tried."

"Everything but the truth."

"Rory, I love you!" she cried desperately.

His reply was harsh. "Don't, Norah. How do you expect me to believe anything you say now?"

"Because I believed you! I believed you when you promised you would love me forever!"

"And I will," he told her sadly. "I'll love you until they nail the lid down over me. I'll love you the way a man hankers for a dream he can't ever have."

"But you can." She grabbed his forearms, ignoring his stiff reaction to her touch. "You can. We can. Rory, can't we start over here? Can't we forget about the past. Please, Rory. Please give me a chance, give us a chance?" She embraced him then, hugging hard to his unyielding form, listening to the thunder crash within his chest. But he made no move to hold her.

"I'm gonna have to think on it, Norah," was all he would say. Then, firmly, dispassionately, he pried her away and strode into the house.

Horribly abandoned, Norah sought out her only other avenue of comfort. From a man who may not have been the best of men, the most reliable of men or even the most trustworthy, but a man who had always been there for her. Cole recognized her pain the minute he opened the door to his room. Without one word of question or chiding, he enfolded her in his arms and let her weep.

"How did he find out?"

"I don't know," Norah sobbed. "Does it matter?"

"Only if you want to stay out of jail. Has he sent for the law?" As his hand stroked her hair consolingly, his instincts for self-preservation were flying ahead.

"I don't think he's thought that far ahead yet."

"It's his brother. I knew that one was trouble. Well, he won't be quite so tenderhearted in his mercies. We've got to get out of here. Norah, I want you to go pack your things and be quick and quiet about it."

She pulled away. "No."

"The game's over, sweet. Time to fold. There's no sense in hanging onto a losing hand."

"Cole, I love him! I can't just leave!"

He sighed with a sad and oddly sincere sympathy. "Honey, he and his family aren't going to accept your reasons for doing what you did and you're fooling yourself if you think they ever could. There's no happy endings for folks like you and me. We just have to go on and get over it. You're one tough little lady. You'll forget all about him, you'll see."

She shook her head. No. No, she wouldn't because Rory Prescott was her chance for a happily ever after. He was the only decent man she'd ever known, the only one with whom she allowed herself the luxury of falling in love. And she couldn't give up so easily. If he wanted to think on it, it was up to her to give him plenty to think about.

"You're not going to let it go, are you?"

"No."

"You're a stubborn woman, Norah."

"I want him, Cole and I know he still wants me."

His gaze roved over her in a candid appraisal. "The man would be a fool not to."

And she knew Rory Prescott was no fool.

* * *

He lay stretched out on his big bed staring up as though at the stars. The windows were open to allow the night breeze and the sounds of the Bar K in. The soft lowing of Kincaid cattle. The yip of a distant coyote and the melancholy answer of its mate. Mournful, familiar sounds. Tonight, lonely sounds.

He wasn't going to rest so there was no use going through the motions. To make himself at least passably comfortable on the outside, he'd stripped down to long underwear that had faded to a pink pastel many washings ago. He'd peeled out of them to the middle and lay back bare chested with the splint on his wrist to pillow his head. In no time, it began to throb in protest. That was good. He needed the distraction from other, fresher aches. Though he said he was going to, he refused to think. He just lay still, letting the tension mass and mount. Another time, he would have bolted for a bottle in Crowe Creek and the welcoming arms of Sally Jean. But that wouldn't help matters now. Hell, that was part of the problem. The woman he loved was a woman just like Sally Jean. Even worse. At least, Sally Jean had always been honest with him. The pressure continued to build. He couldn't drink his way out of it. He couldn't cry his way over it. He couldn't fight his way through it. It grew, compressing his chest, tightening about his heart, putting his thoughts into a constrictive vise. Until the gentle scent of violets twisted it one notch beyond the bearable.

"Rory?"

"Leave me alone, Norah," he said heavily.

"I can't. I won't."

He made himself look at her and that was a mistake. Her hair was down in a glossy cloud about her shoulders. Her lush figure was temptingly wrapped in

400

a shimmer of silk. And as he watched, she loosened the belt and let it drop, shrugged the robe off her shoulders and let it drop. She was naked underneath. His mouth went dry. He couldn't look away.

"I know you still want me, Rory and I'm going to make you love me again."

She slid across the bed and across his bare torso, aiming for his mouth but settling for the side of his neck when he jerked his head away. Where his mother's needlework was healing. She rode the rapid rise and fall of his ribs, her hands stroking there as her kisses scorched along the hollow of his shoulder blades. His breathing was shallow, more from panic than passion. Then, abruptly he caught her upper arms and tried to push her away.

"Stop it, Norah! This ain't gonna settle nothin'."

"It will if you want it to. It will if you let it. Rory, you know you can't stop loving me. I've broken your trust and maybe your heart but I haven't lost that love. Tell me I haven't." That last was a demand — a desperate, almost angry demand that he couldn't, wouldn't, answer.

But she was right. Loving her was something he couldn't switch on and off like the electric lights at the Mansard House in Cheyenne. That loving was all mixed up in a confusion of hurt and hate and pain and disappointment but it was still there beating strong beneath the flesh her lips tempted. And that hot, surging temptation was just the release he needed for the pressure steaming inside him.

And as her lips dragged down his chest, desire followed in a rising tide. Wanting her was something he'd never be able to control. There wasn't enough anger, enough despair in the whole world to put a damper on the way she made the fires burn inside. That part of their relationship had always been honest, right from the start. She'd never pretended she didn't crave him every bit as much as he hungered for her. She may have lied about being a lady but she'd never lied about knowing exactly how to drive a man wild with wanting. Crazy mad to the point of blind obsession. Even with his eyes opened, he couldn't deny her physical appeal, nor could he refuse to respond.

After all, there wasn't going to be a wedding night. This was the best it was ever going to be between them. And he couldn't help but take advantage of it.

Norah was startled by his sudden shift from resistor to aggressor. She found herself turned onto her back atop his tangle of covers with his dark, fathomless eyes blazing down on her. His head dropped down, not to kiss her but to bring his mouth to her breast, where he drew its tender peak into an exquisitely sensitive arousal. Her hands dug into the thick thatch of red hair, holding him there while she cried out softly with the ecstasy he sent shivering through her. She moaned his name with a wonderful satisfaction. He did love her. He did. And he'd forgive her in time. She'd help him forget.

Another eager cry escaped her when his sound hand swept down over her belly and between the quickly assessable valley of her thighs. Where rivers of passion ran deep. He explored them thoroughly as if he'd never ventured to this particular spot before, creating a turbulent wake of response. Her rhythmic gasps increased in tempo, into a hoarse sound of willing surrender as fierce consuming pleasure took her. As she drifted on those sweet after ripples of sensation, she was aware of the intensity of his gaze upon her and she wondered what he was thinking.

He was wondering how many men had seen this particular sight; Norah stretched out flushed and replete with her hair streaming over the pillows, with her eyes full of liquid contentment. How many had she allowed to coax her body into this excited sheen of desire. How many she'd told *I love you* until her partner had emptied their pockets. And were stupid enough to still love her. The pain of not knowing knotted up inside him into an ache as inescapable as his need of her. He heard her say his name, the same deep caressing way that had always thrilled him, that had always made him feel as if he was the luckiest man alive. God, what a fool he was to still want to believe that. He would have married her. He would have had a cold calculating whore for a bride, a caricature that was nothing at all like the lovely Norah Denby he'd fallen in love with. She was no lady and knowing that shattered his tender vision of her as someone worth worshipping for a lifetime. She'd lied to him. She'd won his love unfairly. He wouldn't marry her but he still wanted to have her. For tonight. At least for tonight. He'd more than paid for it, after all.

What was he thinking? Norah's confidence faltered. This wasn't the same boisterous Rory Prescott who had taught her the splendor of making love with a man. He was remote, understandably so, but with a frightening difference. There was no sense of sharing, of giving in the experienced way he encouraged her passions, in the way he mounted her with a hard, claiming thrust of his hips. As he drove into her with a steady, purposeful repetition, she knew what it was. He was taking from her instead of showing her love. That was a difference she understood well. He was the one who explained it to her. He hadn't kissed her. He hadn't displayed any of the tender fondness that made him so special within the protected realm of her heart.

He was using her.

With a wounded little cry of realization, Norah

403

tried to push him off but he was already breathing hard and fast into a shuddering release. He didn't say her name. He didn't look at her. For a while, they lay still in an intimate tangle of arms and legs but at the same time, so very separate from one another. As if it was nothing more than a mingling of flesh and fluids. And when Rory finally lifted up, she was very pale beneath him. Dampness seeped from the corners of her tightly shut eyes. Her soft, lush breasts were quivering with the effort of holding back sobs. It was then the full shame of what he'd done struck and struck mercilessly. What had he done?

Wordlessly, he got off her and went to stand at one of the open windows, jerking up his long johns to protect against the sudden chill, against his sudden vulnerability. The fingers he hooked on the edge of the fine milled woodwork were white-knuckled and trembling. He'd taken her like one of the upstairs girls in Crowe Creek; had used her to vent his frustrations and slake his needs. Norah, the woman he loved. The woman he cherished and vowed to protect from pain. He, who had always been so boastful about his respectful treatment of female kind, had selfishly spent himself within the woman of his dreams as if she was a mere vessel for his use. And he hated it. And he hated himself. And her. Because of what she'd done and what he'd become because of it. Both were loathsome in his eyes and he couldn't accept either.

He heard her stirring but he didn't turn. She was waiting for him to say something but his mind was numb and his heart was so sore it had to be breaking all over again. The irony of it made him laugh, a low, tortured sound of bitter justice.

"I been paying whores to love me all my life. Guess I never figured I'd be doing the same with the woman I wanted for a wife."

There was a quiet click of his door shutting and something inside him closed off just as completely. He sagged against the window frame, exhausted in body, restless in spirit. And he knew he couldn't spend another minute in this house; in the room where his pillow would smell like violets, on the stairs where she'd wrestled him down with her hot kisses, on the porch where they'd sent the swing rocking, in the barn where he could still taste the sweetness of her promises. He had to get away before the madness consumed him. And there was only one place he could go to find shelter in this emotional storm.

He'd go home.

Norah paused only for a minute when she saw him ride from the yard, then she continued to fold her things into a neat stack. She tried to make her mind into a necessary void but her heart kept crowding thoughts up into it. How much clearer did he have to spell it? He would never, ever love her the same way. He might make love to her, he might ask her to stay, he might even marry her but he would never forget and he would never forgive. He had too much Prescott pride. Too much Kincaid arrogance. Too much manly honor to ever compromise his soul between the weakness of heart and the hardness of head. She could stay with him, loving him with all her might and it wouldn't be enough. It would never be enough to totally convince him. There would always be that element of doubt, that damning instant of mistrust. Because good men didn't love bad girls. He'd called her a whore. And decent men didn't love whores. They bedded them, they dallied with them, they might even set them up in a comfortable existence. But they didn't share their lives with them. And

Norah couldn't settle for less.

From her open doorway, Cole took in the open suit-case and the tragedy in her expression. Without a single derisive comment, he took her up in his arms and held her tight. She didn't cry this time. That was his Norah.

"Let's go, Cole. Let's get out of this place. Let's go far away."

"All right, my dear. Things will be better. You'll see." He felt a hard tremor tear through her and surprisingly, a fierce rage welled in his heart. Norah was the closest to family he'd ever known. In his own way, he loved her with a protective fury. Rory Prescott had hurt her and that hurt could not go unanswered.

"He said he'd love me forever, Cole. He lied to me. Just like you said. Just like you said."

"Hush now, Norah. I'll see he regrets it. I'll see that he pays for making my darling cry."

Yes, indeed he would.

Gena sat rocking on the front porch, enjoying the cool of the night. She'd answered Dawn's impatient call for attention and finally both baby and husband were sleeping soundly. She was denied that luxury by an aching body and a heavy heart.

Poor Rory.

It was hard to revel in her own happiness when his life had plunged into despair. If anyone deserved to be happy, it was her big-hearted brother-in-law. He'd always been so unfailing in his support of all of them. Now, it seemed there should be something they could do to shore him up when he would sink in misery. She looked up at the sound of slow hoofbeats and realized she would have her chance as Rory came in on his little roan mare. At a walk. She waited in silence for him to dismount and pat the filly's delicately arched

406

neck. Then he regarded her with a sad smile that wrenched her tender heart in two.

"Heya, Sis."

"Oh, Rory."

He scuffled up the steps and sank down into her upraised arms. Bright head pillowed on her lap, he sighed and muttered brokenly, "What am I gonna do, Gena? I love her. I still love her. I hurt so bad."

"There, there," she soothed as if to a fretful child. She brushed the red hair back from his forehead and stroked his cheek. "Is what she did so bad? So unforgivable?"

"She lied to me, Gena. She ain't at all the woman I thought I loved."

"I know."

He shook his head. How could she know? How could sweet, decent Gena Prescott understand a woman like Norah? How could she have any comprehension of the dark side of human kind, she, who had led such a sheltered life? But she surprised him with her quiet insights, she stunned him with her deep knowledge of despair. Had it been hers? He wondered. Was that why Scotty held her so dear and close to his heart? She spoke softly to his bruised emotions as he knelt at her feet. He felt the healing touch of her love and knew why his brother would never, ever leave her. If his father had the talent to mend the body, Gena's was in mending the soul.

"I know that when people are scared and alone, they make up lies to make life bearable," she told him with a quiet compassion. "And when someone they love gets to believing those lies, they have to keep telling them, not because they want to but because they need to protect the one they love from being hurt by the truth."

Rory was silent for a minute then asked, "Are you

talkin' about Scotty?"

"I'm talking about a prideful man who hid the facts of his past because he was afraid I wasn't strong enough to hear it. Because he was afraid I didn't love him enough to accept it."

"But you were. And you did."

"Oh, yes," she said ruefully as she ruffled his hair, "but not at first. I was so angry with him. And I was so hurt to think that he wouldn't trust me. He brought me all the way out here from Boston to meet his family and didn't bother to tell me that half of them were living in tipis. Oh, I didn't think I could ever forgive him for that."

"But you did."

"Yes, I did. Because I love your brother and I finally understood that he did what he did because he thought he was protecting me. Because he was afraid if I knew, he'd lose me. I was a lot stronger than he gave me credit for. I even surprised myself. It scares me to think that I almost let my own pride get in the way. I almost let him go. I almost lost him, Rory. Your brother isn't the easiest man to live with but I know in my heart and soul that there isn't another I'd have in his place."

"Scotty's a lucky man."

"What about you, Rory?" she asked softly as she kneaded the tension from one of his broad shoulders. "Are you strong enough to accept what Norah's been? Do you love her enough to put it behind you and never look back? Never as long as the two of you are together?"

He closed his eyes and whispered truthfully, "I don't know."

"Does she love you? Don't think about it, just answer from your heart."

"Yes." He sat back on his heels with a sigh. His

408

dark eyes were glittering. "Yes, she does. And I hurt her, Gena. Real bad. I just don't know if we can get back what we had, the way we felt about each other. I don't know if I can take her in my arms and love her proper without thinking of them before me and wondering how it was with them."

Gena blushed at the intimate turn of conversation but she mustered the gumption and the purely female affront to chide him. "And you don't think she's going to wonder about your singular lack of chastity over the last few years? You don't think that when you're late getting back from town after having a few beers with the Bar K crew and she gets a whiff of some dance hall floozie on you that she's not going to wonder if you've gone back to your old ways?" She gave an indelicate snort when he had the nerve to look shocked. "Oh, Rory, be fair. Loving someone is hard work. Don't think that it's not. And trusting is the biggest part of that." She took his pensive face between her hands and leaned over to kiss him, very softly, right on the mouth before standing. "Don't think on it too long or I'll have to give you a motivating kick right in the seat of your Prescott pride."

"Yes, ma'am," he mumbled with a weak smile. But it was a smile.

"Sleep on it, Rory, then get your tail back over to the Bar K in the morning and tell Norah that you love her."

He did love her. As he sat on his family's front porch, slowly rocking, he let his thoughts move freely. And he saw the truth of what she'd been telling him. She hadn't tried to lure his attentions toward a deceptive end. He'd gone after her with the single-mindedness of a rut-crazed steer. And except for the illusion of being Denby's daughter, she hadn't pretended with him. She'd tried to discourage him and he hadn't lis-

409

tened. She'd tried to tell him about her past and he hadn't listened. She'd tried to tell him how much she loved him. And he hadn't listened. He was too busy listening to the prideful rumblings of his heart and head. One too full and one way too empty.

What was he going to do? Marry her? As if it didn't matter what she'd done? But look at all the things he'd allowed to happen by looking the other way. Was she any guiltier of doing what she thought she had to to insure her own survival than he was of wanting to hold his family together?

What if she was pregnant? The idea stunned him for a second, but it shouldn't have. They'd certainly been doing their share of sowing not to reap that one reward. He'd marry her. He wouldn't have to. He wanted to. There was no way he'd allow anyone else to raise his little redheaded baby. There was no way he was going to let anyone else crawl up inside Norah Denby to sow their seeds. He'd marry her. And he'd love her. And maybe the trust would come later.

Chapter Twenty-five

A soft kiss brushing against his cheek woke Rory to the new day.

"Norah?"

" 'Morning, honey."

He opened his eyes and stretched the stiffness from his bones. They were cramped from sleeping sitting up in his daddy's rocking chair. " 'Morning, Mama."

"Coffee?"

"Sounds good."

"Sit tight. I'll bring it out to you."

He murmured his thanks and let his eyes drift shut again. That's when the pain came back. It wasn't as severe or as sharp as it had been the night before. It was as if someone had put a splint on his broken heart to give it ease. It ached but he could manage. Today was supposed to be his wedding day. It still could be.

"Here you go. Watch it, it's hot."

"Thanks, Mama."

While he blew into the thin furls of steam rising from the cup, Aurora lingered by the side of the chair. Her fingertips grazed beneath his ear and along the strong line of his jaw, making him look up in question.

"Are you all right, Rory?"

"I surely have been better." He took a deep breath. "I'm still gonna marry her, Mama."

Aurora said nothing. Her hand stilled upon the slope of his shoulder.

"I owe her that chance. Maybe she did what she did because no one else'd give her one. I could give her a good life on the Bar K, I know I could. I could make her happy."

"But will she make you happy?" When he looked quickly down without giving an answer, she pursued it gently. "Rory, why do you have to be the one who saves her from herself?"

He glanced back up with a poignant candor. " 'Cause I love her too much to send her back to what she was."

Aurora knelt down so their eyes were on the same level. Hers were steeped with care. "Oh, honey, we're not talking about nursing a foal with screw worm. We're talking about marrying someone, someone you'll be responsible for for the rest of your life. Someone who'll have your children and keep your house. Someone who'll see you through your good days and your bad. Is she the one you want there beside you twenty years from now?"

"Was Daddy when you met him?"

She smiled softly, remembering. "Oh, yes he was. And I must say, there've been times when I could cheerfully wring that stubborn Texan's neck but there hasn't been a day gone by that I haven't loved waking up next to him in the morning. That's twenty-four years of living with that man and I don't feel any less in love with him than I did the day he delivered Scotty. And you."

"That's what I want, too, Mama."

"Can she give it to you?"

There was a yearning innocence in his face that wrung his mother's heart dry. "I hope so."

"Then I hope so, too."

From inside the house, Dawn's hungry war cry shook to the rafters. Aurora smiled and got to her feet.

"I'd better start breakfast. No one's going to sleep through that. Are you staying?"

"No. I'd best get on back to the Bar K. I got some talking to do and some listening. I'll be by later on."

"With Norah?"

"Hope so."

A strange buggy was tied up outside the Bar K front steps. Rory lashed Rosebud beside it and bounded up onto the porch. As he reached for the door, two men in shiny serge suits came out. They nodded to him coldly and without a word, climbed into their buggy. Curious about these odd visitors, he went straight to the major's study where he found the old man indulging in an unprecedented early morning whiskey.

"Major? Who were them fellers?"

"Where the hell have you been, Rory?"

The blunt attack took him by surprise, setting him back on his heels and shaking him with a sharp thrust of alarm. "I was over at the Lone Star. Why? What's going on?"

"Funny you should ask." Garth Kincaid gave him an odd, hurting glare as he settled into his big chair. He studied the spread of papers before him with a hard ferocity then looked up at his bewildered grandson. "You don't know?"

He shook his head and ventured a guess. "They from the Board of Live Stock Commissioners or something?" That was the only kind of visit he could understand putting such a rile into Major Kincaid. The only kind of provocation that would have him snapping at him.

"No. They're investigators for the Secretary of the Interior."

Rory blinked and let the import of that sink deep and dire. He dropped heavily into a chair. "What do they want with the Bar K?"

"Our butts. They're here looking into illegal fencing of government land. Among other things." His skewering look was full of meaning but Rory caught none of it.

"Well, hell, get Denby out there scratching around like a badger to make sure all our range is filed on proper."

"Denby's gone. Cleared out early this morning."

Rory sucked a hot breath. "Norah?"

"Room's as empty as our cash box."

Rory fell back against the back of the chair, eyes squeezing shut. "Oh God." The Bar K's troubles faded into insignificance. She was gone. He was too late.

Don't ever leave me, Norah. Don't ever leave me.

I won't. I'll be here as long as you want me.

And last night, as far as she knew, he'd stopped wanting her. She was with Denby, running as far and as fast as she could. Not from her misdeeds. From the cruelty of his parting words. He thought of all the promises he'd made her: *I won't ever hurt you . . . trust me . . . I'll make you so happy . . . what's done is done, it don't make no difference . . . I'll never stop loving you.* How miserably he'd failed to keep them. But there was one he meant to see to. *I'll follow.*

"Rory, we're in a hell of a fix here."

The major's grim tones cut through his distracted thoughts. He opened his eyes and gave his grandfather his full attention. In the back of his mind, he was thinking if he rode Rosebud full out, he could catch them before they reached the train. But the Bar K first.

"I say good riddance to the man. He weren't nothing but a crook anyway. At least he got the filing done with Monthaven's money and there'll be no way they can jerk the range out from under us. Let 'em sniff around. There's nothin' they can find." Abruptly, Rory was aware of his grandfather's pinched look. "Is there?" When the old man said nothing, Rory surged to his feet. "Goddammit, what are they gonna find? The truth? For once, tell me the truth!"

Garth Kincaid seemed to shrivel in his big chair. For the first time Rory could remember, he looked like a tired old man instead of a dynamic rancher baron.

"The filing didn't get done."

"What!"

"Denby thought the money best invested. He had a tip on a Colorado mine and — What are you laughing at?"

"You greedy sonuvabitch, the man's a swindler. He ain't investing a cent for the Bar K. You just gave him our last penny. How could you do that? That money was to file land claims. We agreed on it. Why the hell didn't you tell me!"

"It was my decision to make," the old man said brittlely.

"No, it wasn't! The fences are coming down, jus' like Scotty said and after our blooded stock gets a-mixing with the scrub bulls, we ain't gonna have nothing. Nothing! 'Cause of your greedy want to do everything the quick and easy way. Oh God, we're gonna lose it all."

They sat for a long intense moment of silent brainstorming. Finally, Rory ran his fingers distractedly through his hair and looked resentfully at his mentor.

"I don't understand you."

"What's to understand?" Kincaid growled. "I took a gamble and I lost. I've done it before and recovered just fine."

"You had no right to gamble with what was mine. How we gonna get outta this?"

"How should I know? I'm no lawyer."

Rory sat up straight. "Yeah, but I know a damn good one. Gimme that there stuff." He started to scoop up the litter of papers only to have his grandfather grip his wrists.

"What are you doing, Rory?"

"Taking it to Scotty. If anyone can figure a way to save our ass, he can."

"He's probably the one who sicced them on us."

Rory hesitated only a second then finished stacking the official looking documents. "He'll help out. I know he will. Scotty's never let me down."

But when the grim golden gaze rose from the stack of forms, it offered no such hope.

"There's nothing I can do, Rory."

"What do you mean? What's all that stuff saying? I can't follow but half of it."

Scott searched through the mess spread across the Prescott table to find the original statement. "The Bar K's being investigated for illegal use of public domain, for illegal land filings, for fraudulent sales of beef to a government agency and for suspicion in the hanging death of a public surveyor. From what I have here, your accounts are empty, your ledgers are blatantly falsified and you had at least a dozen known killers on your payroll. Want me to go on?"

"Oh, Lordamercy," Rory groaned. "No. Hell, that's more than enough to bury us twice over." He met his brother's impassive stare. "Scotty, I swear I didn't know about half of that."

"I believe you. But then, I'm your brother."

"Am I going to jail, Scotty?"

Scott put a reassuring hand on one slumped shoulder and he allowed a thin smile. Then he was back to all

416

business. "Not if I can help it. Most of this was done before you had any active role in the Bar K ownership. The old man will take the brunt of it. If you want my advice, you'll liquidate everything as fast as you can. It's going to cost a small fortune to keep this from going to court. I'll start filing motions as soon as I can get the forms filled out."

Rory took a raw, shuddering breath. "Sell it? Sell the Bar K?"

"You can't hold on, Rory. You're broke. Bankrupt. Monthaven's loan money is gone and there's no way you're going to meet the terms of repayment. Whatever you manage to salvage he's going to strip from you in the end."

Unsteady hands covering his face, Rory muttered, "Oh, Scotty, what am I gonna do? I can't lose everything I've worked for, everything I love. How'd it happen? Why'd they turn on us so quick like? What kind of evidence was they talking about?"

"Ledger sheets from the Bar K showing delivery of nonexistent beef to the Cheyenne Reservation Sioux for a percentage of the agent's kickback."

Very slowly, his hands came down. Very slowly, he started to breathe again in harsh little gasps. "Scotty, I gave those to you. I gave 'em to you to put away Sal Garrick. The man's been dead for over a year. That was all taken care of. You gave me your word you wouldn't use that against me." With that clear vision, came the rest. "That's where you were that day, when Gena had the baby. You were out delivering up the nails for my coffin."

Scott's features firmed. He didn't look away from the accusing agony in his brother's eyes. Because he was guilty. Because he'd been right to do what he did. Even if it hurt like hell. "Rory, the man had me beaten half to death. He's stolen the lands of my father's people and helped to starve them. He almost had you killed and Gena and the baby. I had to stop him."

"I was takin' care of that."

"No, you weren't. He was just telling you what you wanted to hear. You can't control a man like him. You don't understand him. You've never seen him for what he really is. You don't look at him and see something that needs stepping on."

"And so you're stepping on me, too."

"I didn't want that, Rory."

"Then stop it. Scotty, stop this. Please."

"I can't."

"Or won't?"

"I can't. It's out of my hands. I'm sorry."

"You're sorry. Oh, God, Scotty, what have you done to me? What have you done? I got nothin'. I got nothin'. Is that what you wanted? Did you want him so damned bad that you didn't bother to look out for me? Like you promised?" He shoved back his chair and started raking the papers into a hasty pile.

"I'll handle things for you, Rory," Scott told him quietly.

The dark eyes flashed up, wildly angry and dazed with a lingering disbelief. "I don't know if I could live through any more of your help." When Scott tried to take the papers from him, he hung on tenaciously. "No. Leave it alone, Scotty."

"Rory, I'm all you can afford."

That broke him right there. He released the papers and sank down in the chair, bright head falling atop his arms. "Scotty," he moaned forlornly, "I'm gonna lose it all. Ain't there nothin' I can do?"

A bracing hand squeezed his shoulder hard. "You got the best lawyer in the state of South Dakota. That should count for something."

Rory sat up and sighed wretchedly. He was past

blaming. He knew exactly why Scott had done what he'd done. He wouldn't judge him for it now. It wasn't important. What was important was saving all he could. And his brother was the man who could see it done. "Okay, what do we do first?"

Scott gave a small, sketchy smile. "You've got a lot of faith, Rory."

His brother gave a raspy laugh. "Accordin' to you, that's about all I got left." Then he was serious. "Help me, Scott. Help me keep the house and enough to build on."

"I'll do my best. But first, you tell the old man that I'm calling it and that he'd better stay clear of me. I'm doing this for you. Personally, I hope he burns in hell."

Fateful words, Rory discovered as soon as he stepped out on the porch. Rosebud was prancing nervously at the rail. There was a pungent scent on the incoming breeze. Smoke.

"Oh dear God in heaven!"

The horizon was black, like the approach of a rapid moving and deadly blue norther. Fire.

Scott spoke a quiet oath from beside him as they stared in a moment of time-suspended horror. Then Rory was off the porch, vaulting up onto Rosebud.

"Rory, wait!"

"That's the Bar K," he cried heedlessly as he jerked the mare around and applied his heels. Riding straight toward that prairie hell.

As their carriage whirred steadily toward the noon train in Crowe Creek, Cole was in a remarkably cheerful mood. As he kept the horse at a good clipping pace, he was full of talk about traveling Europe, his favorite topic when his pockets were plump. Had Norah been less distracted, she would have wondered how he'd managed to fill them but it was all she could do to keep her eyes straight ahead and free of tears. She wouldn't look back. That was her primary rule. Walk toward the future. Never mind how empty it might seem. Never mind that it seemed more like she was running from it down a dead end street. What did it matter, after all? One place was pretty much like another and she looked forward to the days ahead with complete indifference. Cole would take care of things. He always did. She would leave their destination in his hands.

"Perhaps when we're in England, we'll look up Lord Monthaven." Cole glanced sideways to see how his companion received that suggestion. Her stiff expression never altered. "I'll bet in no time at all you could be back in line as his next lady."

"I'm not interested in being tied to any man."

Now that curt reply sounded like Norah. Almost. The words were hers but the vitality was lacking. Give her time, he told himself. She'll come around.

"That's up to you, Norah. Personally, I like having you as my partner. Fine company. Always have been. I admire a woman who can always land on her feet, a winner. Yes sir, that's my Norah. A woman who knows the value of her independence."

Norah blinked hard. Her lips became a thin white line. No more tears, she told herself fiercely. No more crying over what wasn't meant to be. No more sobbing over a man who would give his last dollar to a whore carrying an anybody's baby and turn his back on the woman he professed to love. Love. What did she know about it anyway? A big complication that never led to anything but pain.

Seeing the wavery brightness in Norah's gray eyes, Cole frowned. "He wasn't worth it, you know," he stated at last. "You would have been bored to death within a year stuck way out here in the middle of all this nothing. You'll be thanking your lucky stars you were smart enough to walk away when you get a look at the new clothes in Paris."

"Shut up, Cole."

"My, aren't we peevish. You'll get over it as soon as I get to a jeweler's and buy you something pretty."

"I have enough jewelry."

"A woman can never have enough jewelry."

She would have settled for a plain gold band. A plain, unbreakable circle of love binding her to Rory Prescott. As she listened to the woman Cole was describing, she was surprised not to recognize herself. What a shallow, grasping female he spoke about, one who had no idea of what it was to care or to sacrifice for the sake of love. Was that what she had been? Cold, greedy, manipulative? Would she be that way again in a month's time, a week's? How long would it take her to recover from the conscience Rory had planted inside her?

"Forget him, Norah and enjoy spending his money."

"What do you mean?"

Cole was smiling smugly as he nudged the travel case at his feet. "You'd be surprised how much cash these ranchers keep on hand."

"Cole, you promised me you wouldn't take their money."

"I said I would leave it for you. Since you're coming, it's coming, too. I mean you are entitled to some compensation for the way he treated you."

Norah's features puckered slightly then she murmured, "He treated me like a lady."

"And that's why you were washing me away with your tears last night. The man's a fool and he doesn't deserve to have what he can't hold on to. He couldn't keep you and I've seen to it that he won't be keeping anything else of value either. So you see, Norah, there's no use in thinking about going back because there's nothing there. I can't see you rebuilding from the ashes and that's all Rory Prescott is going to have after breaking your heart. Just like I promised. And I do keep my promises."

"Cole, what are you saying?" She was finding it increasingly difficult to breathe through the intuitive raise of dread. What had he done?

"Let him hang onto his arrogance and snub our kind when he's had to do a little suffering of his own. Let him learn what it is to go without while we're living well off Monthaven's funds." He grinned slyly at her look of dismay. "Now, Norah, dear, investing well is what I do best. And when the returns start coming in, they'll fill our pockets nicely for some time to come. So you see, you can have the benefit of the Bar K fortune no matter where we go."

"He'll come after you, Cole." She knew Rory Prescott. He would come. Not for her but for the Bar K. The one faithful mistress that had always served him best. And she tried not to feel the hurt of it.

"We'll be long gone by the time he thinks of it. You see, I was thinking way ahead. While you were crying your silly eyes out, I was busy making sure our tracks were covered. The funny thing about hired guns is that they don't care who they work for as long as the money's there. Gave them a nice bonus to take care of a little something for me after we'd gone."

"Cole, you didn't! Not Rory." She gripped his arm, fingers digging deep with the strength of her horror. She could barely conceive the thought let alone say the words. "You didn't pay them to hurt him!"

"Only where it counts," he smirked with extreme pleasure. "Stopping a man like that with a bullet is the most merciful thing you could do and I told you, I don't do killing. Just a little something to burn the memory of what he did to you deep."

422

Norah followed his expansive gesture and twisted on the seat to look behind them. And gasped. Jets of black smoke plumed skyward all along the horizon.

"I had the men set the fields afire to cover our departure. They'll be too busy to come looking. And if they are very very lucky, they may have a blade of grass or two left over. About enough to raise a prairie dog."

He settled back in his seat, looking justified and satisfied. Norah couldn't tear her eyes away. The Bar K. The Lone Star. Rory's family. Everything he loved. Everything he cherished. No. This wasn't what she'd wanted. She'd hurt him too much all ready to desire this fiery retribution. All she could think of was the endless green acres of Kincaid grass scorched and useless. Barns and outbuildings in cinders. Homes destroyed. Lives . . . lost. Gena and the baby. Scott. Ethan.

Rory.

"No."

Cole tried to look surprised by her protest but somehow, he just wasn't. Where Prescott was concerned, he'd begun to expect the illogical. "Now, Norah . . ."

"Stop."

"Norah —"

"Do it! Stop."

Cole pulled the buggy up and stared at her in exasperation. "You're not going back there. Why? What good can it do?"

Her thoughts were racing as rapidly as her heartbeats, back across the miles to the Bar K Ranch. Back to Rory Prescott. "Maybe I can help."

"Norah, don't be stupid. In a matter of hours, that whole place is going to look like hell with the people moved out of it."

Her eyes brimmed up anxiously but her stubborn jaw firmed. "He might need me."

"He threw you away."

"Then I'll go. But not until I've told him that I had no part in this. I couldn't live with knowing that he hated me that much."

"The train won't wait, Norah and neither will the boat to Europe. Nor will I."

If he hoped that warning would shake her from her foolishness, he was wrong. "I don't expect you to."

Cole sighed. "This is madness, Norah."

"Probably," she agreed.

"I'll leave your bags at the train station and a ticket. I'll wait for you in Boston Harbor for two days, then I'm sailing."

"I understand." And then, realizing that she might never see him again, Norah leaned over and hugged him hard. Cole Denby was a lot of things but he'd always been there for her. He'd been there with his jaded advice, to protect her and provide for her and in a way, he had become that absent father figure so lacking in her childhood. When he drove away, she would be letting go of the past. And that was scary, even to a woman who prided herself on her independence. She would be all alone and if Rory turned her away, she had no idea what she would do. Start a new life or take the train to continue with the old. She could choose. Finally, she felt free to choose. But now, the only direction she wanted to go was back. They had just passed a farm where she remembered seeing several horses grazing. She'd beg, borrow or steal one of them and could be back at the Bar K in less than ten minutes. Or the Lone Star in twenty-five, depending on how fast the windborne flames were moving. Gathering her skirts, she climbed down from the buggy and snatched up a single bag.

"Goodbye, Cole."

"Norah. Where shall I send your dividend checks

424

when our investments come rolling in?"

She didn't have to think. "Send them to Crowe Creek." Then, she started hurrying back along the road on which they'd come.

Cole watched her with a wry smile curving his lips, then he called softly after her, "Good luck, Norah."

Heat rolled across the grassland, rising in waves, shimmering like a desert mirage. From out of that wavery haze, Rory saw a buckboard approaching fast. He reined in beside a chalk-faced Ruth who'd been on her way to Crowe Creek for help.

"How bad?" he asked with fear-driven bluntness.

"It just came out of nowhere and everywhere at once." Her gaze was glazed with the shock of it. Panic in the stalwart Ruth kicked his own into full steam.

"The Bar K?" he forced out of a too-tight throat.

"The barn went up like kindling. The boys were trying to save what stock they could."

"And the major?"

Her stare was wild. "He's at the house. He wouldn't leave with me."

"I'll get him, Ruth. You go on into town and round up whatever help you can." Already, he was kicking back his heels, sending the little mare streaking toward the ranch.

It was an inferno. Flames engulfed the steep roofline, swirling around the turrets in cones of fire. Heat shattered stained glass in the upper story, colorful shards exploding outward in a rainbowlike glitter. For a long second, Rory was stunned into a stop, his mind unable to comprehend the holocaust consuming his dreams. Several of the hands rode up to him. The men's beards, brows and lashes were burnt to blistered skin.

"Rory, it's gone. Ain't nothing we can do to save it. What do you want us to do?"

425

He sat on his horse, reeling, eyes filled up with the sight of the porch swing disappearing into a ball of flames.

"Rory?"

He jerked his thoughts clear of the devastation to order crisply, "Get 'em on over to the Lone Star and start 'em in on working a break. Tell 'em to answer to my daddy until I get there."

There was a whoosh and a searing blast of heat as the front of the house became a sheet of fire. It was so intense they had to back their horses away or lose control of them. With a shirt sleeve up over his eyes to keep them from scorching and steadying the mare with the firm grip of the other, Rory yelled to the other men, "The major? Where is he?" When there was no answer, he brought his arm down and asked again. "Where's the major?"

Their faces screwed tight with emotion until one finally nodded his head toward the blazing pillar. "He's inside, Rory. He never came out."

Inside.

But nothing inside that blazing pyre could still be alive.

And that's when the truth hit him.

"No!"

Rory fell out of the saddle into a stumbling run. The searing heat slapped him back more effectively than the cowhands' tenacious hold on his arms. He struggled against both to no avail and was finally wrestled to his knees.

"Rory. Rory you listen to me," the head wrangler ordered with a harsh sympathy. When his young boss continued to fight, he jerked his elbows high, dropping his face into the parched dirt while another secured his feet as if they were dogging a wild steer. Holding him there helpless and from harm try as he would to buck and twist free. "There ain't nothing you can do for him."

Rory went still, the fight knocked from him. "No." That was a low, moaning wail. The hands that held him gentled their grips but stood at ready should he try anything crazy again. They'd lost one boss. They weren't willing to bury another. They backed off to give him room as he straightened and watched with a mirroring desolation as the Bar K ranch house folded in upon itself in a final burst of flames.

From his study, Garth Kincaid watched the fire devour his precious acres. Already he could hear it eating away at the slate shingles overhead. Soon the smoke would come rolling down the stairway like a graceful lady all garbed in black death. But he wouldn't wait to greet her.

Slowly, he walked across the hall into the parlor and set down his heavy pistol long enough to pour himself a glass of Scotch. Eyes, already tearing from the settling haze, caressed over the mementos of his lifetime, over the faces of his family. A family lost to him, as his empire was lost to him. Choking through him was the terrible knowledge that came that morning. The ledger sheets. Rory had given them to his brother. That was the only explanation. And it burnt clear to the heart and soul of him. He'd lost Rory. He'd lost all hope. The conscienceless ambition had consumed all that he'd built, the life he'd treasured and longed to pass down to first daughter then to grandson. But the price he'd paid was more than they could accept. He saw that now very clearly, just like he saw and forgave the treachery of Rory's deed. Loyalty was a trait he praised above all others and Rory had decided where his belonged.

He didn't look ahead to a future holding nothing for

a man of his pride. A slow tormenting demise at the ruthless hands of Scott Prescott and his self-righteous laws. There was no place in that grim future for a man of his dignity. He wasn't a man who liked apologizing. He wasn't a man to humbly embrace ruin and disgrace. Had he been, he would have welcomed home his daughter and her bastard child all those many years ago. Now he was paying for it. Now he was alone with no dreams to give, with no dreams to hold.

A dire groaning could be heard overhead as destruction raced through bedrooms that had housed four generations of Kincaids. He'd never seen the last one, too proud to look upon the imperfection brought unto the name. A little girl. A little girl who would be taught to respect the name Prescott and the damned heritage of the Sioux but would never understand the honor of being a Kincaid. Like his sons had. Like Rory had. That would be Scott's final sneering affront. All he had fought for, had struggled to hold, would be forgotten. What he built meant nothing if there was no one to carry on the pride.

The smoke was thickening and he knew he couldn't afford to wait too long. He drained his glass and picked up the pistol. If all he loved had to die, there was no point in his survival. And with typical Kincaid arrogance, he chose to pick the time and means of his own death. With a deep sighing breath, he reached out for one last memento to hold close to his heart so he wouldn't be alone when pulling the trigger.

Chapter Twenty-six

Aurora and Gena stood on the front porch of the Lone Star watching the sky darken to an ominous black, streaked with tongues of orange. The horizon glowed like the approach of a fiery dawn and the two women stood close, trying not to show each other their fear. Rory found them there, braced like generations of pioneer women before them, ready to meet any threat that challenged their home. And Lord he was proud of them.

"Where's Daddy and Scott?" he called as he came down off his nervous mare.

"Out running a break with the men you sent over. It's the only chance we have of saving the ranch from that hell coming in on the wind." Aurora glared defiantly toward that flare of orange as if her will alone could hold it at bay. "The Bar K?"

Rory swallowed hard. "It's gone, Mama."

She looked at him sharply, warned by the dragging anguish in his tone. Her heart clutched. But she had to ask.

"The major?"

His jaw trembled before he could lock his teeth tight. Pain filled to overflowing in his dark, smoke-dulled eyes. There was no way he could speak the an-

429

swer without breaking down beneath the heavy grief swelling inside so he let the agony of his expression tell her what she already knew. He heard her hoarse little gasp and swayed as she came to put her arms around him. They clung to each other for a timeless moment of shared loss because both had loved the man inside Garth Kincaid that few others ever saw.

"I've gathered up all the spreads and blankets to soak in—"

Norah stopped in her tracks. She never felt the door bang into her trouser-clad backside. The bundle of quilts slipped one by one to the porch boards until she held the last tight to her bosom. Tight to where her heart banged in hurried jerks of emotion.

Rory.

He stepped back from Aurora to stare at her in a numb sort of surprise. And she waited, breath suspended, for some glimmer of what he was feeling to show in his tense expression. Would it be welcome or rejection? Or worse, indifference. He came toward her slowly, giving nothing away, until by the time he stood before her, she was quivering with an anxious uncertainty. Still, she made herself face him bravely, not with pleading or apology. She wouldn't beg him for a scrap of affection. Even though her heart would have her crumple at his feet and clutch at him for forgiveness. She stood tall and proud, waiting. Praying.

"What are you doing here, Norah?" he asked in a quiet, guarded tone.

"I came to try to save my future. Because everything I love is here."

The wariness melted from his gaze to reveal dark pools of longing so deep and desperate she couldn't help but drown in them. That look bared everything in his soul. The needing, the wanting, the loving.

430

Those things shivered in his voice when he said her name.

"Norah."

Courage failed her when his big hands cradled her face between them. Such a strong, tender touch, it broke down the last of her reserves. Tears welled. Remorse swelled. "Oh, Rory, I'm so sorry about all this. I didn't know. Please believe me. I didn't—"

He silenced her with a kiss.

He tasted like smoke. He tasted of passion. And of an urgency flaming higher and hotter than the surrounding danger. He claimed her breath and her heart with that one searing slant of his mouth. Then he just held her in his arms.

"Rory—"

"Shhh, Norah-honey. I don't have time now. When I get back, I'll listen to whatever you want to tell me. It's enough just knowin' that you're here."

She didn't want to let him go. Especially into the life-sapping strength of the fire when there was a chance he wouldn't be coming back to her. But she forced herself to step back and smile with false courage, like all the Prescott women before her.

"I'll be waiting."

His rough fingers stroked along her cheek in a lingering farewell, the tremor in the tips of them telling of his reluctance to go. Then abruptly, he spun and went to vault up onto his little roan mare.

"Hang on, Mama," he called over his shoulder. "We'll do the best we can to keep you safe."

"Tell your father and brother to be careful!" she shouted after him. "And Rory . . . you, too!"

Desperately, the men sought out any barrier that

might turn the tide of flames from washing over the Lone Star. Kincaid cattle raced ahead of the fire, tails up, bellies low to the ground, their horns clattering as they stampeded in a mad terror into washouts and over banks. While Ethan and Scott and a small crew of men set a backfire to split the roaring inferno, Rory and the others shot several of the scorched Kincaid cows. They were crudely gutted on the spot and the cavities filled with dirt. Then the bodies were dragged across the edge of the flames working them inward to control the spread in the direction of the backfires.

Only the most seasoned, courageous mounts could be turned toward the edge of hell at their rider's hand. Chance would have jumped right into the wall of flames had Rory sent him. Rosebud balked. Terrified by the scent and heat of the fire and frightened by the weight of the carcass lashed behind, she fought Rory's commands and refused to respond. Instead, she sidestepped and trembled, maddened by the sparking embers singeing mane and hide.

"Come on, Bud. Come on, girl. Easy now. Trust me. You gotta trust me now," Rory soothed into the quivering ears. He kept a firm hand on the reins and prodded her damp sides with his knees. "Work with me, girl. Don't let me down. C'mon, Bud. Attagirl. Attagirl."

Slowly, the mare gained confidence under the caress of his voice and guidance of the reins. Rory ran her along the lip of curling grass, holding her in firm, talking all the while, even when his throat grew raw from the cut of smoke. Heat exploded patches of dry grass all around them and more than once he found himself beating at his clothing as it smoldered. Sparks and heat scorched the exposed skin of face, neck and

432

hands. He tried not to think about what lay behind the fire in charred ruin. He had to concentrate on what could be saved, not what had already been lost. And the flames were roaring down toward the Lone Star with the destructive speed of a freight train.

Finally all the worn grass around the ranch was burned away. The riders swarmed into that charmed circle as if defending it against a marauding attack. Sacks and saddle blankets were dredged in troughs and buckets. Horses were secured in the corrals to keep them from bolting into the path of the merciless blaze. It was too late to run, it was upon them. Howling like a tornado, raging like the denizens of hell. Threatening to swallow them whole. And never in her life, had Norah been so afraid.

The first tongue of flame hit the black strip of backfiring. Fire spread out in both directions, racing along the perimeter with an insatiable fury. Smoke rolled overhead, obscuring the light of day as riders ran drag along the edges to hold the line from advancing any farther. They made small bobbing figures against the red sheets of devastation. The cavvy of horses screamed in terror as combustion sent a stack of hay up like a torch. The men were on it with a vengeance, beating it out before it could spread to the barn.

Norah and Aurora ran about the yard, dousing young stripling trees with water and stomping out eager flickers that lit in the grass about their feet. All at once, Norah turned to see the hem of Aurora's dress ignite. Seeing she wasn't aware of it, she threw herself upon the other woman, knocking her to the ground, smothering the young flames with handfuls of dirt. Before Rory's mother could utter thanks, she looked up and gasped in dismay.

"The roof. My God, the roof."

They ran to the edge of the porch in a panic. Under that roof was all the Prescotts owned, all their memories, all their joys. And baby Dawn squalling loudly in her cradle.

"Give me a boost," Norah cried and without argument, Aurora made a cup of her hands. Then, the three women made a bucket brigade; Gena dipping at the trough, Aurora passing it up, Norah drenching down the curling boards that were beginning to smoke in the heat. The sound of the infant's frightened wails kept Gena sobbing but Aurora was curt with her logic. As long as they could hear her, the baby was fine and Gena was needed outside.

From the rooftop, Norah had an overview of the surrounding miles. She could see the fire sweep around the ranch, leaving it an oasis of green in the midst of scorched blackness. She caught occasional glimpses of the cowboys but couldn't identify Ethan Prescott or his sons. The smoke was thick and suffocating. Still, she fought down the searing feel of it in her lungs and the wracking coughs shaking through her to see the last embers extinguished. Only when Aurora shouted up at her did she think to stop and come down. And then it was like falling into a blistering darkness.

She awoke to find herself stretched out on the ground. Aurora was sponging her face and neck with a wet towel. On the porch steps, she could see Gena rocking her fussing child. Her questioning gaze was answered by the older woman to the accompaniment of a grim smile.

"We saved it. Now all we can do is wait to see what's left to build on. And to pray for all the men to come back safe and sound."

Though they'd stopped the path of the fire from engulfing the ranch, their work wasn't over. Throughout the long hours of the night, the trio worked with lanterns held high, searching out smoldering pockets and twists of smoke in the corral dust and the yard. The stink of smoke pervaded. They didn't speak. It would have been too easy to voice their fears and break down the fragile wall of strength surrounding their efforts. At sunup, the first of the Bar K cowhands rode off the blackened plain, their horses kicking up spurts of soot in dark curls. Wordlessly, Aurora and Gena made coffee and breakfast and Norah served the singed and sooty men. They mumbled husky thanks and took their stench of smoke and filtering ash outside to eat in weary silence. Some talked of the millions of acres gone in all directions but mostly they just sagged and rested. Norah knew some of them and they paused when she questioned them about the Prescott men but none of them could reassure her that they were safe. Not everyone had escaped the unpredictable course of the fire. They solemnly told of at least a half-dozen unrecognizable bodies covered up in the barn. So she served in tense apprehension and she looked at each dirty, blackened face that appeared at the door, hoping, always hoping for the sight of the familiar. And finally, that fierce prayer was answered.

"Gena," she called into the kitchen as a filthy figure stepped through the front door. There was a loud clatter as a platterful of biscuits fell from numb fingers.

"Scott!"

Gena filled his arms in an instant and began to wildly kiss his grimy face. Her tears left streaks as white as his smile. Finally, he had to catch her smeared cheeks in his hands to hold her still for the long, steadying attention of his mouth. Then, after he'd satisfied himself with the sight of his sleeping

435

daughter and Gena was tucked beneath his arm, he went to embrace his mother. She clung to him in a moment of weakening relief then asked, "Your father and brother?"

He shook his head. "I haven't seen them since last night, Mama."

And the waiting began again.

He came in so quietly at first they didn't see him. He was a dirty shadow in the door, shoulders drooping, head hanging, heart heavy with the despair of what he'd seen and done. He'd spent the last few hours going through chamber after chamber until his revolvers were hot in his hands, putting Kincaid cattle out of their misery. He found them, burned, wading in gray ash with hoofs charred around the fallen windmills bawling wretchedly for water. He'd ridden over miles of burnt range where the fences Garth Kincaid had spent his lifetime erecting now stood like charred butts in the ground dangling wire that was crisped and worthless. He'd come home when he'd run out of tears and run out of the heart it took to be merciful.

"Rory," Norah whispered in an odd little quiver when she saw him standing there inside the door. Slumped, unmoving, beaten. He looked up at her through eyes so dazed and dulled by pain and smoke, she almost wept out loud. That look spoke tragic volumes. She couldn't move. The sight of his grief paralyzed her.

Then Aurora caught sight of him and rushed to hug him. He hung in her embrace, eyes closing in the blackened face, shoulders moving in a heaving sigh.

"I need to sit down, Mama, but I'm all dirty."

She laughed. The sound had an almost hysterical edge. "Sit," she told him. "I'll be shoving soot out of

436

this house for months to come. A little more won't make any difference."

As he shuffled across the room, he saw Scott and gave a faint grin of greeting. Then he frowned. "Where's Daddy?"

"You haven't seen him either?" Aurora asked softly.

"Now, Mama, I'm sure he's fine. We got strung out for miles just before dark. It could take him a while to get here."

She nodded jerkily but the haunted look in her eyes plainly said she wouldn't be convinced until she saw the big Texan come through the door. And as soon as she turned away, determined to be brave for the sake of her children, she heard the beloved registers of his accented voice.

"Everybody all right?"

"Oh, Ethan!"

He looked a bit surprised but not at all displeased by the intensity of her greeting. And returned it lustily in kind. "Well, now, sweet thing, that's something a man likes to come home to."

She caressed the unevenly singed beard and claimed, "We wouldn't have had a home at all if not for Gena and Norah and the fellows from the Bar K."

Ethan looked sadly at his son. "I heard about the Bar K and the old man and I'm right sorry."

Rory nodded slightly and sank down into one of the cushiony fireside chairs. He was too tired for any more emotion. That is until Norah knelt beside his chair and touched his hand. His fingers surrounded hers possessively. She started to rise up with a frown and his grip tightened.

"Norah?"

"Your hands are burned. I need to put something on them before—"

"I need you to tend to my heart first," he said softly.

But she didn't come back down to him. Instead, her features grew taut and distant with a defensive stiffening. The truth wouldn't wait.

"It was Cole," she said quite clearly. "He had his hired guns set fire to the range to cover his escape. He stole all the Bar K funds, Rory. I didn't know. I don't expect you to believe that but I really didn't know." Then she waited, silently, pridefully for him to accept or reject her words.

"I believe you," he said even softer than before. Then he lifted her trembling captive hand up for a gentle kiss. That tender exchange, even more than her heroics to save the Prescott home, made a place for Norah Denby among them.

There was no time for further talk or reassurances. More men rode in, some in need of Ethan's medical attention, some just needing a meal and a cold drink. The Prescott men were busy tending stock and trying to assess the damage. Ethan's evaluation was grim but he was confident they could rebuild. Rory wasn't as hopeful. At least his family had their house and outbuildings. The Bar K was gone. And so was its dynamic ruler. Mother Nature had saved the government a lot of time and trouble. And left him with an empty future. When he wandered into the house, his mother took one look at him and stood with arms akimbo.

"Rory Prescott, you get out of those filthy things, and I mean right down to the skin, and get in the tub. It's not doing me a lick of good to clean in here if you go tracking an inch of soot and sweat wherever you go."

"Mama—"

"Now! And don't worry. I have every intention of

438

making your brother and father suffer just as much as soon as they come in."

He sighed. Aurora was in no mood for cajolery, sulky looks or sullen complaints so he'd just do what he was told.

"And I'll bring in some ointment for those burns as soon as you've soaked clean enough for me to find them."

"Yessum," he grumbled dispiritedly.

With clean clothes and a jar of soothing cream in hand, Aurora was about to knock on the door to the bathroom when Norah intercepted her.

"I'll do that, Mrs. Prescott."

Aurora's brows shot heavenward. Nothing shy about this one! "My son is in the bath."

Without any change in expression, Norah relieved her of the denims and shirt then balanced the jar of cream on top. She met the other woman's eyes directly and told her with unwavering candor, "I love your son and I plan to take very good care of him from now on."

"Well . . . Don't let me stop you," she drawled out with a chilly reserve.

And Norah surprised her with a grin. "I won't."

Then Aurora returned the surprise by saying, "Good for you."

Rory was all scrunched down inside the big porcelain tub, soaking in his second bath. The first draw of water had a good quarter inch of grime floating on it by the time he was done scrubbing. The second he meant to enjoy. He heard the door open but didn't peer out from under his hat.

"Mama, would you mind knocking afore you come busting in! I ain't no little boy anymore."

"I know that for a fact."

439

He sat up so quick, his Stetson dropped off to float on the surface. He caught at it hastily and gave it a drying shake. Norah pretended not to delight in the sight of him crowded naked into the tub as she arranged his clothes on a chair. He was eyeballing her warily when she turned.

"Let me see your hands."

"What for?"

She displayed the open jar of cream and his nose wrinkled up.

"What is it? Is it gonna sting?"

"Don't be such a baby. Give me one of your hands."

She knelt down on the tiles beside the tub and took the reluctantly proffered hand in hers. The backs were seared and red. When she eased the ointment over them, his mouth tightened and his forehead popped a sweat. It more than stung and she regretted her scolding. He was breathing raspily by the time she finished. Norah was almost in tears. That was too much for Rory. He'd seen and shed too many tears over the last few days, enough for a lifetime. And these, glistening over a little minor discomfort, couldn't be borne.

"Oh, honey, it ain't that bad. Don't go a-blubbering or you'll wash it all off and have to do it again." She leaned her cheek into the palm of his hand when he reached up to touch her face. Her eyes were swimming.

"I'm sorry that I hurt you."

"I'll heal up just fine."

They weren't either one of them talking about his hands.

"I love you, Rory."

He grimaced and looked away.

"You said you believed me," she challenged with

440

more strength than she was feeling inside. *Don't turn away from me now, Rory. Please.*

"I do. It's just that I don't have nothin' to offer you anymore. I ain't got no money. I ain't got no home. No land. No cattle. I'm busted, Norah. I got nothin' but what you see here."

Her cool gray eyes did a slow study of what she could see. And she smiled. "I believe what I've got here is what I've wanted all along."

"But Norah, I ain't rich. I can't buy you the things you deserve. I—"

She put her hand over his mouth to halt the long forthcoming list of what he didn't have. Because of his grandfather's ambition and Cole's greed. "You wait here just a minute."

Rory soaked miserably for a time then looked up when she came back into the room and took the Stetson off his head. She upended it and dropped a one hundred dollar note into it.

"There. Now you can't say I didn't do my part in making you rich."

He just stared.

"I don't want things, Rory. I want you. I want to share in your love. That's all. What we don't have now, we'll build up together. We're already rich in everything that counts. I know it won't be easy."

"Nothin' worth havin' is easy," he remarked quietly.

"Is that another one of your mother's sayings?"

"No, but here's one of my daddy's for you." He was starting to smile. It felt good to smile after all the misery. "Wet them lips, sweet thing, 'cause mine are burning."

And he kissed her hard to prove it. And that felt good, too. He let his kiss deepen, letting it explain things that his awkward words never could. Like how

441

much he needed her right now this minute to ease a monumental hurt. He needed the laughter she could inspire in his battered heart. He needed the warmth she could kindle in his chill soul. He just plain needed her to go on living. His big hands stroked up and down her arms, coaxing her into a sensual daze. So she didn't have time to object when he pulled her over the side of the tub and into the water with him. A huge wave of it sloshed out on the floor as Norah squirmed to right herself. She slipped on the puddled tiles and scowled at him furiously. Her damp clothes clung in all the right places to earn his wide, roguish grin.

"Look at what you did!"

"I'm lookin' and I'm likin' it."

"I'm all wet. What am I going to put on?"

Grin broadening, he held up a washcloth. "How 'bout this?"

"Very funny."

He thought so. Then his smile faded and his eyes grew all smoldery. "Well, you gonna climb on in here with me, or what?"

She cast a shocked glance at the door. "Here?"

He eased on down in the water so his knees stuck up and his chin topped the rim. His smile was perfectly wicked. "Why do you think Mama insisted on havin' such a big tub?" Norah blinked. "Well? You gonna start shuckin' or stand there drippin'?"

She started shucking.

There wasn't a lot of room for two but any more wouldn't have been quite so sinful as they wiggled against each other all sleek and wet. After a long, thoroughly reacquainting kiss, Norah sighed and rolled so that she was laying back on him with her head on his shoulder. His hands began a soapy massage over her damp breasts.

"All that stuff is washing off," she warned. "I'm going to have to put it back on again."

"Be worth it," he rumbled contentedly. Then his arms banded her slippery body and held tight. "You came back." Those three words spoke it all. "Even after I was such a blame fool."

"I should have told you the truth."

"It shouldn't have mattered."

Norah hesitated then asked, "Does it?"

He kissed her temple, her cheek, her jaw and muttered huskily, "No, Norah-honey. It don't matter a-tall."

She twisted around in his embrace. The sliding of skin on skin was delicious. "Rory—"

"Rory!" That was Ethan bellowing on the other side of the door. "Get on outta there. You ain't the only one lookin' to get clean tonight."

With Norah naughtily licking and sucking on his neck, he managed a strained, "Can't you use the creek?"

"The creek! I didn't spend a good week a my life puttin' in indoor plumbing so's I could use the creek. Now you get your lazy—"

The door jerked open nearly as wide as his jaw dropped. For exiting the flooded bathroom floor was his son wearing a pair of hastily donned denims and Norah swathed in his shirt. And nothing else. His eyes dropped to the turn of shapely leg.

" 'Scuse us," Rory grinned cheekily. "Daddy, you best not let Mama catch you a-lookin' at another woman like that."

"Hell, I ain't dead," he grumbled and slammed the door.

"Rory," Aurora called, stepping out of the kitchen.

443

She heard a sound on the stairs and caught sight of her son's bare feet and the sassy flash of his shirt tail around Norah Denby's knees as they hustled around the second floor landing. Her brows were still elevated when she returned to her bread dough.

"What's wrong?" Gena asked, looking up from where she nursed Dawn in the corner rocker.

"Guess I'd better finish taking up the hem in my good dress tonight. Looks like I'll be needing it after all."

They fell down on the bed together, lip-locked and leg-tangled. Rory lifted up when Norah started laughing.

"What?"

"I think your mama saw us."

He grinned down at her, enjoying the sight of her spread next to naked on his bed. "She ain't gonna care. Mama's got a real soft spot for a case of everlastin' love. Long as it's followed real quick like with a proper ring."

Norah went still. Even her breathing stopped.

"Lessen you don't want to get hitched to a stubborn, bowlegged cuss of a cowboy like me." Then he waited, holding his breath.

Instead of yes, she said, "When?"

"Not tonight, 'cause I don't plan on gettin' up off this here bed till mornin'. How 'bout tomorrow? Or do you need an extra day?"

"No! Heck no!" She seized his face between her hands and pulled him down to her.

And neither of them left the bed until morning.

* * *

They were married the next afternoon by the same preacher who read over Garth Kincaid the following day. It took that long for the rubble of the Bar K to cool. Rory found his body in the parlor with the heat-twisted remnant of a picture frame in his hand. The gun he took from the other, wrapped it in his bandana and tucked it out of sight within his pocket. That was something no one else need know about. The photo had curled and crumpled to ash but he remembered it well. It had been one of his favorites; a young Aurora Kincaid posed beneath a frilly hat. He felt an incredible surge of anger toward the old man for losing his will to fight beside him. But then promised softly in his heart to see to the rebuilding.

Norah was there to join him in the ashes of his grandfather's dream, to lift him up and turn him away toward where the others were waiting. Aurora was weeping against Ethan's solid shoulder with a quiet restraint. Her tears were for the memory she'd held as a child. Scott stood stoically with Gena and the baby. The emotion darkening his gaze was for his brother's pain. Ruth stood with the same pride that had served her through all the years when she'd been good enough for a lover but not good enough for a wife. And at a respectful distance stood the hatless crew of the Bar K, adrift and somber.

Rory took a minute to hug Norah. He sagged. She felt the grief, the terrible sense of abandonment shake through him in a weakening wave. His breathing faltered in the wake of that uncertainty. She closed her eyes, willing him her strength.

"Rory?" one of the hands called hesitantly. "Whatcha want us to do about the fences?"

Norah would have held to him longer but the words pulled him away, toward his responsibilities. He straightened and turned to them. "Tear 'em down," he growled out with an authority that snapped them from their inactive slumps. "We got new boundaries to fence and I want 'em up by sundown tomorrow. Well? Whatcha all standing around for? We got a ranch to run."

To a man, they clapped on their hats and scrambled to obey the boss of the Bar K. And Rory and Norah Prescott went, arm in arm, to join their family.